# Scandalous Fictions

# Scandalous Fictions

## The Twentieth-Century Novel in the Public Sphere

Edited by

Jago Morrison

and

Susan Watkins

First published 2006 by
PALGRAVE MACMILLAN
Houndmills, Basingstoke, Hampshire RG21 6XS and
175 Fifth Avenue, New York, N.Y. 10010
Companies and representatives throughout the world

PALGRAVE MACMILLAN is the global academic imprint of the Palgrave
Macmillan division of St. Martin's Press, LLC and of Palgrave Macmillan Ltd.
Macmillan® is a registered trademark in the United States, United Kingdom
and other countries. Palgrave is a registered trademark in the European
Union and other countries.

ISBN-13: 978-1-4039-9584-1 hardback
ISBN-10: 1-4039-9584-2 hardback

This book is printed on paper suitable for recycling and made from fully
managed and sustained forest sources.

A catalogue record for this book is available from the British Library.

A catalog record for this book is available from the Library of Congress.

10   9   8   7   6   5   4   3   2   1
15   14   13   12   11   10   09   08   07   06

Printed and bound in Great Britain by
Antony Rowe Ltd, Chippenham and Eastbourne

*For Lily and Luke*

# Contents

# Acknowledgements

We would like to thank all the contributors to this volume for their enthusiasm and commitment, their timeliness and their patience with queries. Anna Sandeman and Tom Herron were very helpful in the early stages of our thinking about the book, Mary Eagleton encouraged us throughout and Louise Jackson, Sue Chaplin, Michael Bailey and Pieter Bekker provided valuable advice on sources. Jago Morrison would like to thank Sue Morgan and the School of Cultural Studies at the University of Chichester for their financial assistance in producing the index. Susan Watkins would like to thank the School of Cultural Studies at Leeds Metropolitan University for funding a period of research leave in semester 1 of the academic year 2005–06, during which substantial progress was made on the book. We would also like to acknowledge, with thanks, the following: Anthony Stidolph (Stidy) and Yves Vanderhaeghen for giving their permission to reproduce the cartoon in Figure 1, which first appeared in *Weekend Witness*, 4 October, 2003, p. 9 and Tony Grogan and Jovial Rantao for giving their permission to reproduce the cartoon in Figure 2, which first appeared in *The Sunday Independent*, 5 October, 2003, p. 8. Finally, our thanks must go to Alison Morrison and Ian Strange for their support and encouragement always.

JAGO MORRISON
SUSAN WATKINS

# Notes on Contributors

**Fiona Becket** is a Senior Lecturer in English Literature at Leeds University, UK. She is a specialist in Literary Modernism and in particular the work of D.H. Lawrence. Her publications include *D.H. Lawrence: the Thinker as Poet* (1997) and *The Complete Critical Guide to D.H. Lawrence* (2002). She is co-editor, with Scott Brewster, Virginia Crossman and David Alderson of *Ireland in Proximity: History, Gender, Space* (1999) and has also edited special editions of the journals *Études Lawrenciennes*, the *D.H. Lawrence Review* and *Moving Worlds*. She is currently working on two further books, a monograph and an edited collection, each focusing on literature and the environment.

**Kai Easton** is Lecturer in African Literature and Diaspora Studies at SOAS, London. She has also taught at the universities of Sussex and Rhodes and was, until recently, Andrew W. Mellon postdoctoral fellow in English at the University of KwaZulu-Natal, in South African. Her areas of specialization include South African literature, gender and the cultures of travel, and theories of fiction and history. Her book on J.M. Coetzee (Contemporary World Writers) will be published by Manchester University Press.

**R.J. Ellis** is Head of English and American Studies at the University of Birmingham, UK. His interests include Beat Writing and mid-nineteenth-century African-American writing. His publications include *Liar! Liar! Jack Kerouac, Novelist* (1999) and *Harriet Wilson's 'Our Nig'* (2003). He also edited editions of *Our Nig* (1997) and *A Chronicle of Small Beer* (2004) and edited the collection of essays, *Faulkner and Modernism* (2000). He is currently the editor of the journal *Comparative American Studies*.

**Sean Latham** is Associate Professor of English at the University of Tulsa, US, where he serves as editor of the *James Joyce Quarterly* and Director of the Modernist Journals Project. He is a specialist in James Joyce and Modernist Literature. His publications include *'Am I A Snob?' Modernism and the Novel* (2003) and *Joyce's Modernism* (2005). He has also published articles in *New Literary History*, *Modern Fiction Studies*, *Journal of Modern Literature* and elsewhere. Research on his current book-project, *The Art of Scandal: the Open*

*Secrets and Illicit Pleasures of the Modern Novel,* has been supported by grants and fellowships from the National Endowment for the Humanities, the Harry Ransom Humanities Resource Center, and the Oklahoma Humanities Council. He is a past board member of the Modernist Studies Association and a trustee of the International James Joyce Foundation.

**Marilyn Sanders Mobley** is Associate Provost for Educational Programs and Associate Professor of English at George Mason University in Fairfax, Virginia, US, where she also founded and was the first director of the African American Studies Program. A well-established specialist on Toni Morrison, Black women writers, African American literature, critical race theory and postcolonial studies, her publications include the award-winning *Folk Roots and Mythic Wings in Sarah Orne Jewett and Toni Morrison: the Cultural Function of Narrative* (1991), and an edited volume for the Schomburg Series on Black Women Writers, 1910–1940 (series editor, Henry Louis Gates, Jr), as well as articles in *The Southern Review*, the *Women's Review of Books*, the *Colby Library Quarterly*, the *Journal of Negro Education*, *SIGNS*, and selected scholarly publications. She is currently working on a book-length study, provisionally entitled *Spaces for the Reader: Toni Morrison's Narrative Poetics and Cultural Politics* and a volume of essays, *The Strawberry Room: and Other Places Where a Woman Finds Herself.* Marilyn Sanders Mobley is a founding member and former president of the Toni Morrison Society and now serves on its advisory board.

**Jago Morrison** is Head of English at the University of Chichester, UK. He has published widely on twentieth-century anglophone literature and culture, including *Contemporary Fiction* (2003). Articles focusing on postcolonial and postmodernist literatures have appeared in the journals *Critique*, *ARIEL* and elsewhere. Jago Morrison is currently working on a study of English language fiction from 1945–89.

**Shailja Sharma** is Associate Professor of English at DePaul University, Chicago, US, with specialisms in modern and contemporary British culture, postcolonial theory and film studies (notably the work of Stanley Kubrick). She has published on questions of 'race' and ethnicity in contemporary Britain, and on the writings, cultural context and reception of Salman Rushdie in journals including *Twentieth Century Literature* and *Yearbook of Comparative and General Literature*. Shailja Sharma is on the advisory board of *South Asian Popular Culture*. Her edited book on 'New Cosmopolitanisms' was published in 2006.

**James Smethurst** is Associate Professor, W.E.B. Du Bois Department of Afro-American Studies, University of Massachusetts-Amherst, US. He has published widely on African American Literature and Culture, including

*The New Red Negro: the Literary Left and African American Poetry, 1930–1946* (1999) and *The Black Arts Movement: Literary Nationalism in the 1960s and 1970s* (2005), and is co-editor, with Bill Mullen, of *Left of the Color Line: Race, Radicalism and Twentieth-Century Literature of the United States* (2003).

**Sue Vice** is Professor of English Literature at the University of Sheffield, UK. Her most recent publications are *Introducing Bakhtin* (1997), *Holocaust Fiction* (2000) and *Children Writing the Holocaust* (2004), and she is currently working on a study of the playwright Jack Rosenthal.

**Susan Watkins** is Senior Lecturer in English Literature in the School of Cultural Studies at Leeds Metropolitan University, UK. Her interests include twentieth-century women's fiction and feminist theory. She is co-editor, with Graham Atkin and Chris Walsh, of *Studying Literature: a Practical Introduction* (1995) and author of *Twentieth-Century Women Novelists: Feminist Theory into Practice* (2001). She is currently writing a book on Doris Lessing for Manchester University Press's Contemporary World Writers series and has recently edited a special issue of the *Journal of Gender Studies* with Mary Eagleton on the future of fiction and the future of feminism.

# Introduction: the Twentieth-Century Novel in the Public Sphere

*Jago Morrison and Susan Watkins*

*Scandalous Fictions* is an attempt to explore the twentieth-century novel as a public form, bringing a fresh critical gaze to some of its landmark texts. Our approach is to work by example, considering the multifarious development of fiction in this period through the prism of ten texts which, in different ways, have invaded public consciousness through scandal. In an attempt to reflect the cultural and geographical breadth of twentieth-century fiction in English, the book discusses the work of authors writing from five continents and from a variety of social and ideological contexts. Their fictions were accused, variously, of being obscene, blasphemous, libellous, seditious, even racist. Each of these cases is different: rather than attempting to fix some narrow definition of scandal, we are interested in representing the variety of challenges that the twentieth-century novel has offered to its readerships and at the same time, the challenges that readerships have often offered to texts. One of the book's starting points is to consider the ways in which such texts have been pilloried, traduced and appropriated, often disastrously for their writers.

By the beginning of the twentieth century, the novel was already established as a major public form. Even in the mid-Victorian period, writers like Dickens enjoyed circulations of up to 100,000 for serial fiction[1] and the commercial explosion of the yellowback in Britain and the dime novel in the United States in the last decades of the nineteenth century make it reasonable to speak of mass novel readership well before the turn of the century. By 1900, as David Vincent shows, almost 100 per cent of young adults in England could demonstrate a basic level of literacy[2] and by the middle of the century the ability to read and write was near-universal in both Britain and North America. By the century's end, the UNESCO Institute for Statistics was reporting total world literacy rates of over 80 per cent for all adults, rising closer to 90 per cent for those aged 15–24.[3]

How basic literacy rates might relate to a culture of novel reading is obviously a complex question. What is clear, though, is that the powerful upward trend in literacy in the twentieth century is directly reflected in the growth

1

of book consumption. To take the US example, the report of the Public Library Inquiry in 1949 estimated that 25–30 per cent of all adults were book readers.[4] In 1975, the polling organization Gallup found that 56 per cent of Americans had read at least part of one book in the previous month, with as many as 85 per cent having done so in the previous year. Moreover, within this mass book-reading culture in the United States, the novel was found to be a major presence: in the Gallup study at least, 'serious' fiction was found to account for a steady 40 per cent of all book reading by both regular and occasional readers. In other national and regional contexts, it is true, the novel's prominence is much more variable. For example, it is difficult to argue that the novel's popularity in anglophone Africa equals that in Britain and North America. The critic Wendy Griswold has argued that even in the case of a major fiction-producing nation like Nigeria, evidence from both polls of reading habits and from observation of the book trade suggests that the consumption of novels probably accounts for a much smaller proportion of all reading than it does in the UK or USA, with vocational and self-help books much more likely to top the sales lists. At Nigerian book markets, as she says, 'textbooks or books on law and religion occupy the prominent front-of-the-store positions that would be given over to the latest thrillers or best-sellers in an American or European bookstore'.[5] Nevertheless, the mass success of the novel as, initially, a colonial import and later as an important strand of national culture in West Africa should not be under-estimated. As Stephanie Newell's work shows, for several decades prior to independence in the 1960s the market for novels in British Africa figured as a major part of the business of larger international publishers such as Faber & Faber and Heinemann.[6] After independence, the success of African writers like Amos Tutuola and Chinua Achebe signalled a radical extension of this novel-reading culture, in which the literary consumption of both children and adult readers was concertedly encouraged and reshaped.

Nevertheless, if the reading of fiction was a mass phenomenon across many areas of the English-speaking world in the twentieth century, the cultural position occupied by the novel itself has often been a strange and ambivalent one. On one level, as this book will demonstrate, the novel has continually been feared by educationalists and others for its irresponsibility, lack of ethical seriousness and/or tendencies towards sedition. In England in the 1930s, the influential critic Queenie Leavis felt able to liken popular novel reading to an unpleasant 'drug habit';[7] such anxieties are reflected in public discourse on fiction in other countries as well. The Ghanaian school-mistress Marjorie Mensah is far from alone in voicing her concerns about the pernicious effects wrought by novels on her students in 1935, complaining in *Times of West Africa* that 'many of our girls are reading books that can do them no earthly good'.[8] Over the century as a whole, such concerns, especially about the dangers of exposure to the 'wrong' sort of fiction, persist to a remarkable degree, even amongst progressive educationalists such as Richard

Hoggart, whose classic *The Uses of Literacy* (1957) includes censorious discussion of 'railway reading' such as gangster fiction, sold to commuters 'who would not... take this kind of book into the house'.[9]

In the same period, however – and partly through those very qualities of transgressiveness and slippage that render it an object of suspicion – the novel has continued to be acknowledged as an important site for the negotiation of communal mores, social identities and collective memory. Riven as it was by world wars and cold wars, atrocities and genocides, the twentieth century was also an era of sexual, cultural and ideological revolutions, each variously inscribed across the fictions it produced. In recognition of this, a major concern in this book has been that of understanding the ways in which the eruption of scandal around iconic texts is interwoven with vaster shifts and tensions around gender identities, nationalities, ethnicities and sexualities. At the same time, in selecting ten texts whose reception has been transfigured by notoriety, we have sought to build a better understanding of the ways in which scandal itself becomes, in the twentieth century, one of the primary means through which a public space and voice are negotiated for fiction.

## Public/private fictions

As a product of European modernity, one of the fascinating and provocative features of the novel in the course of its development has been its capacity to test the boundaries between ostensibly separate spheres of public and private life. Amongst many early practitioners, certainly, the novel is seen as a form which, in contradistinction to the romance, on the one hand, and journalism on the other, engages concerns of public virtue and probity partly through an attention to the domestic and the quotidian. Even in the case of an early, hybrid text like Aphra Behn's *Oroonoko* (1688), there is a characteristic appeal to eye-witness evidence and journalistic integrity in the narrator's address, 'there being enough of Reality to support it, and to render it diverting, without the addition of invention'.[10] A generation later, such spurious appeals to authenticity are already sufficiently established as part of the pleasure of the text for Defoe to tease the reader of *Moll Flanders* (1722) with an account of the cares he has taken as 'editor' to give 'no lewd ideas, no immodest turns' to his report, even if the transcription of a wicked life 'necessarily requires that the wicked part should be made as wicked as the real history of it will bear, to illustrate and give a beauty to the penitent part'.[11]

In this example, the public/private boundary is exploited in a particular way, with the address to public virtue working partly as a ruse for the titillating exploration of private indecency. In the equally powerful, metonymic tradition in the novel, on the other hand, this equation is often reversed, with the representation of private lives providing the framework for exploring larger social, political and historical concerns. In a text like *Caleb Williams* (1794), for example, if we follow Godwin's own commentary, the use of single personalized narrative is specifically chosen as an accessible way of encoding a larger political analysis.[12] In response to critics, indeed, Godwin defends the novel in quite instrumental terms, as an attempt to make readers of lesser education question the axiomatic status of current social and political structures, 'in a word, to disengage the minds of men from prepossession, and launch them upon the sea of moral and political enquiry'.[13]

For a critic of realist and post-realist conventions in the novel like Elizabeth Ermarth, one of the most important features of the eighteenth and nineteenth-century novel is the way its evolving use of narrative perspective enables the illusion of an intersubjective point of view. That is, a view which partakes of multiple private perspectives in order to generate the sense of an empirically observable, objective world.[14] Clearly, questions about the nature and possibility of such a collective, public vision, and challenges to the complicity between realist authors and readers that it is founded upon, are a major feature of the literary history of the twentieth century, from Modernism to Postmodernism. As the texts examined in this book demonstrate, the century saw extensive experimentation with the formulation of narrative perspective in the novel. In the midst of this long revolution in fiction, however, the novel's basic, straddling stance between private and public seems to have survived comparatively unscathed. In an important way, as we will see, the scandalous intermixture of private and public continues to be what we expect from the novel.

If a text like Joyce's *Ulysses* (1922) is simultaneously hailed as a new cultural landmark and derided as the 'literature of the latrine'[15] in the 1920s, then this is only for doing, albeit in a new way, what the novel has always done: exposing the private to a public scrutiny. On one level, this process of exposure in Joyce's novel involves his use of the novel form as a means of baring the innards of consciousness in a shocking and unprecedented way. At the same time, however, as Sean Latham demonstrates in Chapter 1, an equally important aspect of the 'scandal' of *Ulysses* is the way in which it attempts to subvert the principle of privacy in contemporary public life. Constantly flirting with the law of libel, as Latham shows, Joyce radically extends the tradition of the *roman-à-clef*, inserting dozens of satiric references to Dublin contemporaries and teasing the reader with a host of further puzzles about the sources for other characters. In this sense the scandal of the novel lies not just in its frank depiction of sexuality, but in its refusal to domesticate the novel as a realm of comfortable fictions which need not impinge on private and public lives.

As Latham argues, moreover, one of the consequences of the denouement between law and criticism engendered by the novel is to expose the mutually problematic nature of authorial control and of the construct of libel itself. In this sense, the novel can be seen as offering a fundamental challenge to the orthodox modernistic demarcation between the privatized sphere of aesthetics and the 'public' sphere of the law. If Joyce soon discovered in the course of his court battles that his intentions as author were inadmissible as a defence of his text, the trials of *Ulysses* demonstrated equally clearly the bluntness of defamation and libel as tools to contain the novel's subversive and deconstructive potential. As Latham suggests, one of the unacknowledged legacies of *Ulysses* is therefore the unanswered questions it raises about the nature of the autonomy ascribed to the novel as art, on the one hand, and the ability of the law to circumscribe its representative terrain, on the other.

Towards the other end of the twentieth century, with a text like Morrison's *Beloved* (1988), the novel's licence to trouble the private/public boundary causes storms of a different kind. Resented by some as a cynically constructed 'blackface holocaust novel'[16] and received by many others as a 'new masterpiece' portraying slavery 'with a moving intensity no novelist has even approached before',[17] the reception of *Beloved* and Morrison in the late 1980s seemed to mark a sea change in the global reception of African American fiction. In an important way though, as Marilyn Sanders Mobley argues in this book, it is important to recognize that what *Beloved* offers is not some new historical revelation in the traditional sense, nor the introduction of a topic that had not already been well aired. In an important sense, Morrison's text merely fulfils one of the established tasks of the novel, that of rendering the public past through the prism of individual and private lives. As Mobley shows, nevertheless, what this entails in *Beloved*'s case is a profoundly discomfiting process of translation, in which the contents of 'slavery' are carried out of the safety and abstraction of empirical history and into the 'domestic tranquillity' of the American home. Like an unquiet corpse, the novel reinserts the dead-and-buried of the archive in the most personal and visceral terms, re-inscribing the public past as a scene of innumerable open wounds that refuse easy closure. Arriving at a pivotal moment of the US 'culture wars' in the 1980s, the imaginative imposture of *Beloved* can be seen in this sense as a significant intervention in the debates of its time about the foundations and trajectory of America's democracy.

## The novel as public writing

Since the translation of Habermas's *The Structural Transformation of the Public Sphere* into English in the late 1980s, there has been a vogue for considering earlier manifestations of the novel in relation to the emergence of a bourgeois public sphere during the heyday of European modernity. In this book, however, the notion of fiction as a repository for a certain kind of public, liberal-democratic voice is explored in a context different from that of Habermas's work, that of the emergent public sphere in Nigeria in the years surrounding independence. Looking at *A Man of the People* (1966) in Chapter 6, Jago Morrison explores the ways in which Achebe's writing in the late 1960s seems to be trimmed to an ideal model of the novel as a space of public philosophical and political exchange that bears a detached and critical relationship to state authority. *A Man of the People* is read as, in a sense, a last-ditch attempt by the writer to force imaginative contemplation of the trajectory of political culture in Nigeria, at a time when conflicting ethnic loyalties and the problematic architecture of the independence settlement seemed to be propelling the nation towards civil war.

Taken as an empirical analysis of European modernity, Habermas's own description of the bourgeois public sphere is certainly problematic. As feminist scholars such as Nancy Fraser have shown, in historical terms it is difficult to separate out an eighteenth-century public sphere of coffee houses and gentlemen's periodicals from the wide penumbra of 'subaltern counterpublics' that challenged the character and the cultural geography of the bourgeois 'republic of letters', especially along lines of gender.[18] Similarly, in the Nigerian context, it is possible to see the ways in which a multifarious marketplace literature, often catering to specific ethnic and linguistic communities, both complicates and undercuts the attempt by a writer like Achebe to mount a disinterested national address in his fiction. In the wake of the Biafran war, such difficulties are compounded by the writer's own problematic relationship to the notion of Nigerian nationhood itself.

It is by no means the purpose of this book to defend the historical credentials of Habermas's work, or to extrapolate his analysis, in its historical specificity, to a wider context. What Achebe's example does show, however, is the potential pertinence of Habermas's description of the 'public sphere' as an idealized model of free expression and liberal debate, against which the work of many twentieth-century writers can usefully be considered. In the earlier work of Hannah Arendt in *The Human Condition* (1958), the notion of a public, political sphere is defined importantly in opposition to that of the private and domestic (blurred though this demarcation might have become in recent times).[19] In Habermas's analysis, by contrast, it is useful to note that the key public/private dichotomy is not primarily that of the state versus the home, but rather that of the public versus the courtly. For him, the existence of the public sphere is premised on the notion of (male) individuals meeting to discourse on matters of common interest, in a way that is defined neither by their narrow private interest nor by their relationship to church or state. The importance of the literary in the formation of this idealized public space is seen most importantly in terms of the ways in which critical exchanges in gentlemanly periodicals, salons and coffee houses in the early eighteenth century provided the template for a form of public interchange that was to become much more sharply politicized in later decades. As Nick Crossley and John Michael Roberts suggest:

> These spaces of literary debate effectively constituted the infrastructure of what became political publics . . . as topics of debate shifted from art

and literature to politics and economics. And literary debate played a considerable role in generating the cultural resources necessary for critical and rational political debate. Literary 'jousts' spawned and sharpened tools of argument which would later be set to work on more political materials. They generated the convention of meeting to discuss and also the rhetorical competence, discipline and 'rules of the game' constitutive of public reason.[20]

In this analysis, the discussion of poetry, drama and fiction is seen as, in effect, a 'safe' space of cultural exchange whose primary significance is as a precursor to more weighty and trenchant public debate. However, as this book demonstrates, as far as the novel is concerned the relationship between the production and reception of literary texts and the kind of disinterested rationality of which the bourgeois public sphere purports to be composed is clearly a much more complex one. Moreover, what is equally clear is that, product of modernity though it might be, the novel is far from being as rigorously disconnected from systems of patronage as the Habermasian analysis might tempt us to assume. Though the commercial market for fiction in the twentieth century is clearly a major discipline on its producers, the significance of legislative, political and ideological influences of all kinds also imprints itself on twentieth-century texts in innumerable ways.

Certainly, in the case of a text like Richard Wright's *Native Son* (1940), it is by no means possible to assume that for the twentieth-century novelist, questions of patronage are no longer a concern. As the critic Keneth Kinnamon has shown, the text of Wright's novel was ruthlessly edited and cut following submission of his manuscript to Harpers, at the insistence of the white liberal publisher Edward Aswell and under pressure from the Book of the Month Club. A scene of masturbation in a movie theatre, as Bigger and Jack see Mary Dalton and other white girls in a newsreel, was amongst the first casualties, as was material in the Dalton's car showing Mary and Jan having sex, whilst Bigger conceals his erection. In the published text, the scene in Mary's bedroom which precedes her death was stripped of much of its original eroticism, and Bigger no longer fantasizes that Bessie is Mary when they make love later in the novel, before her murder. Other overtly political sections, including sections of Max's analysis of racism in the contemporary USA, were amongst the cuts exacted from Wright's text, with only cursory consultation, as a condition of publication. It is not difficult to argue that the cumulative effect of such an editing procedure was significantly to blunt the political edge of Wright's text and to dilute its discomfitingly licentious elements, in an effort to render the novel more amenable for a white liberal reading public.

As James Smethurst shows in Chapter 4 of this book, the power of censorship produced by the interplay of patronage and the structure of the book market undoubtedly continued as a condition of writing for Wright and other authors in the mid-twentieth century. This is not to say that with

*Native Son* we confront a wholly sanitized text. As Smethurst demonstrates, if some of his more direct representations of race and desire did not make it to the printed version, Wright makes potent use of the 1930s' horror movie and its implicit racial anxieties in order to address issues of class and national consciousness in a more covert way. The novel borrows contemporary horror movie tropes such as the figuring of the monster as stereotypically 'Negro', the threat of 'miscegenation' and the chase as lynching. These conventions are all deployed, Smethurst argues, to heighten readers' awareness of questions about false consciousness and individual self-determination in a racially segregated, capitalist society. Such questions were already current in radical African American writing of the period. To suggest that Bigger Thomas can be conceptualized as a victim as well as the perpetrator of crime, however, was sufficiently scandalous in itself to require a major imaginative reworking of the fictional conventions available to Wright through the iconography of popular film. For readers, the text's innovative interplay between popular film tropes and fictional conventions generates, Smethurst argues, public dialogue about the moral and political situation of African Americans in this period in a new and arresting way.

With a later text like Jack Kerouac's *On the Road* (1957), we see the tension between commercial pressures and critical patronage play out in a different way. In Chapter 5, R.J. Ellis's discussion of the novel and its background shows the ways in which Kerouac and those around him were able to manipulate the public reception of both author and text. A popular status for *On the Road* as the archetypal cult classic of the Beat generation seems to have been secured in this way, despite the fact that many more provocative fictions were published contemporaneously. In an interesting parallel to the case of *Native Son*, Ellis explores the distance between the cultural moment of *On the Road*'s first drafting in 1951 and the text published in 1957. Tracing the revisions that Kerouac made to the text to modify its treatment of homosexuality, he compares it with three novels published in 1952 that were far more daring in their dealings with sex, drugs and criminality. In this way, Ellis claims that the scandal of the novel derives from Kerouac's explicit self-fashioning of the author as model of a dissident sensibility, the leader of a celebrated coterie that was revolutionizing the canon of American fiction. Such re-workings of cultural capital take place, as Pierre Bourdieu claims, at times of social change and upheaval; Ellis demonstrates that the decade following the end of the Second World War was precisely such an era. It was this unique nexus of conditions that propelled *On the Road* towards celebrity status and allowed it to acquire the 'aura' of cult fiction, helping to define the terms of public debate around notions of personal freedom and social permissiveness which dominated America's process of self-examination and cultural realignment in the postwar period.

If the Habermasian opposition between the public sphere and the orbit of patronage can still shed light on the complex position of the novel in the twentieth century, then, it is likewise useful to consider his particular formulation of the 'public' ethos of that sphere, characterized by both freedom of expression and rationality. In Habermas's work, what guarantees the authenticity of this 'public' ethos is, paradoxically, the status of interlocutors as private citizens, able to speak on their own account (if not to their own profit), rather than being ventriloquized by power. In the wake of such theorists as Michel Foucault and Jacques Derrida, clearly, such an idealized notion of free speech is apt to attract a certain scepticism. In considering the position from which novels have been written in the twentieth century, however, it remains once again a useful ideological coordinate. When we think about the strange hybrid status of fiction in relation to the public sphere, indeed, it is easy to see how, from the outset, the novel frequently invokes, exploits and subverts the notion of a 'public' voice rooted in the authenticity of private conscience.

In the case of celebrated holocaust survivor testimonies such as Binjamin Wilkomirski's *Fragments* (1995) or Helen Demidenko's *The Hand that Signed the Paper* (1994), each of which was revealed after publication to be fabricated, questions about the 'authenticity' of narrative voice in the novel are raised in a particularly acute way. Each of these texts invokes a notion of 'witness', asserting their own importance as acts of memory through an appeal to history as an ethical imperative. If Wilkomirski's text was first lauded as a literary *tour de force* and later decried as a work of synthetic opportunism, then this in itself reveals something about the weight of ethical responsibility we continue to invest in the novel as a repository of collective memory, as well as the weight of public displeasure which can be brought to bear where fiction fails to deliver on its paradoxical promise of 'authenticity'. Demidenko's case, as Sue Vice shows in Chapter 9, was somewhat different from Wilkomirski's. Like *Fragments*, *The Hand that Signed the Paper* was initially treated to a degree of critical euphoria, with the award of three literary prizes, before being subject to a flood of opprobrium when the Ukrainian author and media personality Demidenko was revealed as the invention of a middle-class Australian of British extraction, Helen Darville. Rather than being based on family experience, it emerged that *The Hand* was in fact the combined result of historical research and imaginative conjecture. In the case of *Beloved*, as we saw earlier, such a strategy was widely endorsed as a legitimate novelistic technique. In the case of *The Hand*, however, the text's ontological transition from memoir to historical fiction was treated to no such acceptance. A public which, on the novel's initial publication, seemed willing to invest both ethically and emotionally in the novel's marriage of personal experience and public history found its reading position fundamentally altered in the wake of the scandal. In particular, the novel's problematic, apparently untroubled representations of Ukrainian complicity in the holocaust seem to have read very differently indeed as the imaginative projection of a Pom novelist than they had done as the troubled testimony of an actual Ukrainian émigré. In the light of this profound transition in the reception of Darville/Demidenko and the novel, Vice argues, it is clear that the author function is not as dead, nor as separable from the life of the text, as Roland Barthes claimed in 1968.[21] Using Mikhail Bakhtin's theorization of certain types of fiction as 'polyphonic', Vice suggests that the novel's 'affectless prose' and its complex, but apparently simple structure of intersecting narrative voices actually refuse meaningful dialogue, simultaneously working to establish and to conceal a fundamentally 'fixed and undemocratic agenda'. The multiple questions raised by the novel's disturbing public/private narrative voice, indeed, go some way to explaining the unease that readers have experienced when confronting the novel and the scandal that resulted in the aftermath of its publication.

From a literary historical point of view, part of the irony of such cases as Wilkomirski/Doessekker and Demidenko/Darville lies in the fact that, from the outset, the novel has continually played with ventriloquism. If Defoe posed as the editor of the 'real' Moll Flanders and the established editor and translator Mary Anne Evans felt more comfortable moonlighting as the unknown George Eliot when submitting her fiction to the publishers, eighteenth and nineteenth-century authors also frequently found themselves ventriloquized by others. As Michael McKeon notes in the case of *Pamela* (1740–41) for example, the threat that an 'unauthorized' version by someone else might pre-empt the novel's conclusion cast a serious shadow over the production of Samuel Richardson's third volume. Such unwanted interventions by elements of Richardson's readership played precisely on the author's own affectation as merely an editor or reporter, as McKeon shows, when 'spurious imitators and continuers . . . were audacious enough to claim that they, and not the person responsible for these volumes, were in possession of the authentic documents'.[22]

In such examples, there is a complex play between author and reader with the idea of authentic testimony, which both guarantees and at the same time subverts the public spirit or 'virtue' of the text. In the twentieth century, moreover, it is also useful to consider the ways in which novels have often been ventriloquized in a way that is less than playful, read within a certain 'public' register that the texts themselves do not explicitly invite. When *Disgrace* (1999) was cited by the ANC in its April 2000 statement to the Human Rights Commission hearings on racism in the media as an instance of white racism, Coetzee's novel was read as an explicit invitation to white South Africans to emigrate:

> In the novel, J.M. Coetzee represents as brutally as he can, the white people's perception of the post-apartheid black man. This is Hertzog's savage eight-year-old, without the restraining leash around his neck that the European had been obliged to place, in the interest of both the

native and society. It is suggested that in these circumstances, it might be better that our white compatriots should emigrate because to be in post-apartheid South Africa is to be in 'their territory', as a consequence of which the whites will lose their cards, their weapons, their property, their rights, their dignity. The white women will have to sleep with the barbaric black men. Accordingly, the alleged white 'brain drain' must be reported regularly and given the necessary prominence![23]

If this must be seen, at a minimum, as a substantial extrapolation from Coetzee's text, Kai Easton's discussion in Chapter 10 of this book explores the ways in which *Disgrace* seems, itself, to anticipate its own misreading. For the ANC and others, the novel was seen as a betrayal of the public requirement (that is, towards, reconciliation) of a national literature in a time of crisis. Once again, we see an unspoken assumption of public investment in the novel as a repository of national cultural values. In the conclusion to its statement to the Human Rights Commission, the ANC cites the editor of the *Citizen* in March 2000, to the effect that 'racial stereotyping and insensitivity run counter to the kind of society we believe South Africa should become'.[24] The crime of *Disgrace*, as the prize-winning production of a celebrated author, is that it disappoints the public responsibility conferred upon it, or in other words that in some way it fails to appropriately articulate the kind of 'public spirit' that is expected, miring itself in the discredited discourses of the past rather than shouldering the task of national cultural reconstruction. Easton's discussion examines how the novel's engagement with the public sphere was framed by its *censuring* by the hearings on racism and the media, even if it could no longer be formally *censored* under the new South African Constitution.

The ambivalent status of the novel in relation to the public sphere which we see here is perhaps most usefully encapsulated in the Derridean notion of the literary as a socio-political space which in principle carries the responsibility of 'being able to say everything', but is at the same time always inflected with a certain disappointment or insufficiency, a failure to live up to the licence that is granted it. As Easton shows, with *Disgrace* this dichotomy is graphically dramatized in the overwhelming international endorsement of Coetzee's text and the scandalized, even outraged local reaction it generated. As we can see with several of the texts examined in this book, the novel is simultaneously upheld as the mouthpiece of a collective ethical-political consciousness, and delegitimized by its own failure or refusal to inhabit that public voice. For Derrida, this ambivalence and this refusal are of central importance to the literary as an institution:

In the end, the critico-political function of literature, in the West, remains very ambiguous. The freedom to say everything is a very powerful political weapon, but one which might immediately let itself be neutralised as a fiction. The writer . . . can, I'd even say that he must sometimes demand a certain irresponsibility, at least as regards ideological powers . . . which try to call him back to extremely determinate responsibilities before socio-political or ideological bodies. This duty of irresponsibility, of refusing to reply for one's thought or writing to constituted powers, is perhaps the highest form of responsibility.[25]

## Twentieth-century novels and their readers

In a sense, the kinds of responsibility conferred here on the literary text might be seen as diametrically opposed to those implied by the statement of the ANC cited above. To think about the novel as an unruly or even irresponsible form, however, does not in itself allow us to understand the ways in which, as an object of public consumption, the novel is also a mobile and plastic form. In recent years, Salman Rushdie's *The Satanic Verses* (1988) is the best-known example of a text whose specific narrative engagements were comprehensively submerged amid the swirling political currents of its reception. The sentence of death pronounced on Rushdie by Ayatollah Khomeini in 1989 for the crime of 'defaming Islam' was only the most sensational instance of the many forms of political capital extracted from the novel by politicians who could be considered at most as readers-by-proxy. In Chapter 7 of this book, Shailja Sharma explores the way in which, partly in the wake of *The Satanic Verses'* controversy, Rushdie's writing has sought to explore the role of the writer as a public historian, a raveller and unraveller of national histories, and the ways in which this role is complicated by the writer's changing relationship to the British Asian readership he claims to represent. Ironically, as Sharma shows, opposition to *The Satanic Verses* became, in the late 1980s, a unique banner under which a wide spectrum of Muslim youth in Britain was able to unite and focus politically. Clearly, this was a strange and unlooked-for effect for the fiction of a writer who has so clearly styled himself in terms of secularity.

If the cultural position of Rushdie as a writer was interestingly illuminated by the furore over *The Satanic Verses*, Sharma also considers the subsequent trajectory of his career, and in particular the ways in which he seems to recoil from historical engagement in later texts. In his later work, history becomes a cultural remainder, subject to manipulation by a myriad forces, a discourse bereft of the power to form public meaning. In this way she explores the paradox of a writer whose attempt to 'liberate history for the dreamer in all of us' was destroyed by the overwhelming force of his own appropriation. In comparing the force and energy of *Midnight's Children* (1981) and *The Satanic Verses* to the ambivalence and pessimism of *Fury* (2001), Sharma sees a discomfiting process of degeneration in Rushdie's work, towards a drained, deracinated aesthetic capable of expressing little more than alienation.

As we can see in the case of *The Satanic Verses*, as well as that of other texts considered in these pages – *Ulysses, A Man of the People, The Hand that Signed the Paper* – for many novels in the twentieth century, publication has often meant public appropriation and re-appropriation, against the grain of authorial intentionality. Read by governments and bureaucracies on the one hand, and by coteries and reading groups on the other, it is important to recognize the ways in which the novel is always a tool of use for its readerships, rather than an object of passive consumption or instruction. For many individual 'consumers' of the scandalous fictions considered in this book, the reading of a text invested with personal significance is imbricated with struggles for meaning. These struggles may often be formative for the individual's sense of identity as intimate and private, yet also engaged in fundamental ways with a wider field into which others are making incursions through their own writing and reading. In many instances the novels we consider here are books that have redefined readers' understanding of themselves, provided a manifesto to live by and offered, for perhaps the first time, the sense of a wider community in which such a redefinition can take place.

In this context, the fact that many of these fictional 'manuals for living' focus on sexual behaviour and identity is not incidental. What Foucault describes as 'the link between the obligation to tell the truth and the prohibitions against sexuality'[26] is interestingly focused in scandalous fictions of the twentieth century, in which the 'confessional' mode, with all its illusory privacy and intimacy, collides with notions of probity and publicity. That the novel should increasingly be the forum in which this struggle takes place is consistent with Foucault's sense of the development of a dislocation of verbalization from renunciation from the eighteenth century onwards, at the moment when the novel is establishing itself as a major literary form:

> From the eighteenth century to the present, the techniques of verbalization have been reinserted in a different context by the so called human sciences in order to use them without renunciation of the self but to constitute, positively, a new self. To use these techniques without renouncing oneself constitutes a decisive break.[27]

Books like *The Well of Loneliness* and *On the Road* offer readers a sexual and personal identity that hovers, in ironic fashion, between the social outcast and the significant and articulate minority. Both novels create a voice and an identity that is at odds with the conventions of the day; with that identity goes an entire body-styling incorporating clothes, hair, speech and behaviour. Considering the apparent disparity between these two texts, emerging

from separate social and national histories and different positionings in relation to gender and sexuality, it is worth taking the space here to compare two
passages from the novels:

> She went up to London and chose new clothes at a West End Tailor's;
> the man in Malvern who had made for her father was getting old, she
> would have her suits made in London in future. She ordered herself a rakish
> red car; a long-bodied, sixty horsepower Metallurgique. It was one of the
> fastest cars of its year, and it certainly cost her a great deal of money.
> She bought twelve pairs of gloves, some heavy silk stockings, a square
> sapphire scarf pin and a new umbrella. Nor could she resist the lure of
> pyjamas made of white crepe de Chine which she spotted in Bond Street.
> The pyjamas led to a man's dressing-gown of brocade – an amazingly ornate
> garment. Then she had her nails manicured but not polished, and from that
> shop she carried away toilet water and a box of soap that smelt of carna-
> tions and some cuticle cream for the care of her nails. And last but not
> least, she bought a gold bag with a clasp set in diamonds for Angela.[28]

> Yes, and it wasn't only because I was a writer and needed new experi-
> ences that I wanted to know Dean more, and because my life hanging
> around the campus had reached the completion of its cycle and was stul-
> tified, but because, somehow, in spite of our difference in character, he
> reminded me of some long-lost brother; the sight of his suffering bony
> face with the long sideburns and his straining muscular sweating neck
> made me remember my boyhood in those dye-dumps and swim-holes
> and riversides of Paterson and the Passaic. His dirty workclothes clung to
> him so gracefully, as though you couldn't buy a better fit from a custom
> tailor but only earn it from the Natural Tailor of Natural Joy, as Dean
> had, in his stresses. And in his excited way of speaking I heard again
> the voices of old companions and brothers under the bridge, among the
> motorcycles, along the wash-lined neighbourhood and drowsy doorsteps
> of afternoon where boys played guitars while their older brothers worked
> in the mills.[29]

In both passages, the articulation of an identity through specific markers of
clothing and appearance is immediately striking. As Laura Doan has argued,
the 'style' of monocled, shingled 'female masculinity' was not associated
exclusively with lesbianism until after the publication and trial of *The Well
of Loneliness*.[30] It is Doan's contention that the novel and the public persona
of its author, Radclyffe Hall, effected this redefinition by virtue of their
alignment of a particular way of living with a particular sexual identity and
appearance. Critics and readers since then have debated the image of what
we would now call the butch lesbian that Hall created. As Susan Watkins
discusses in Chapter 2, much ire is generated in many of these arguments.

While some believe that *Well* narrowed and confined the range of experience for woman-identified women by creating the image of the sad, lonely invert tortured by her sexual identity, others argue that the novel enabled the creation of a reverse discourse which was adopted and developed by lesbians in ways Hall did not foresee. Watkins demonstrates that scandal in *The Well of Loneliness* centres on its alignment of a number of apparently contradictory conceptions of inheritance. The heroine of the novel – known as Stephen – inherits her sexual inclination towards other women from her father, along with her social position in the English aristocracy and her literary vocation. Stephen's class position has often caused critical discomfort, appearing to militate against the novel's message of sexual tolerance by limiting it to the most privileged. Moreover many more recent critics have also been disturbed by the rather 'essentialist' theorizing of same-sex love between women as congenital sexual inversion: a term defined by contemporary sexology, with all its limitations. As Watkins suggests, the scandal Hall's novel generated at the time of publication and its continuing subversiveness for readers reside in its suggestion that the ostensibly private matter of inversion is entirely compatible with, indeed intrinsically linked to, public discourses of class privilege and love for one's country. In the wake of the First World War this was a dangerous mixture; what made it more dangerous was Hall's belief that fiction itself had a public duty to contain and transmit this inheritance to a wide, middlebrow readership.

Like *Well*, *On the Road* also became a touchstone in the construction of a specific 'outcast' identity. Its pages define members of the Beat generation as experimental, restless drifters and it establishes the counter-culture to USA Cold War politics and domestic consumerism that would emerge in the 1950s. As in the case of *Well*, the novel's infamy occurred as a consequence of the text's celebrity status and the explicit self-fashioning of the author as model of a dissident sensibility, which allowed it to develop cult status. The passage quoted above makes apparent the extent to which this process is written in the text 'on the body' of Dean Moriarty, which bears the weight of the narrator's nostalgia, homoeroticism and a sense of dislocation from prevailing social norms and values.

To use Judith Butler's formulation, this performance of an identity,[31] for example as invert or beatnik, also takes place partly through the reader's identification with the narrator's or protagonist's aspiration to be an author. In the passage from *On the Road* the narrator's desire for Dean is overlaid with his desire to become a writer and to rewrite himself. It is no coincidence that at the moment when Stephen comes to understand her own sexual identity (albeit in the terms of the day) she is also offered the possibility of becoming a writer: ' "You may write with a curious double insight – write both men and women from a personal knowledge"'(208). Writing the self is akin to writing a novel; in reading a novel one is entering into a creative rewriting or restyling of oneself, an experience that may be revelatory or painful but never humdrum. Even nearly eighty years later, a perusal of individual readers' responses to *The Well* posted in the public forum of the online bookseller Amazon reveals that Hall's novel continues to be treated as a 'minority's conduct book':

> I couldn't put this book down and the empathy which she makes you feel with the characters is incredible. This is the first book which reduced me to tears – I defy anyone not to be moved by it. I advise anyone and everyone to read this book as it truly is a fantastic piece of literature.[32]

> I initially struggled with this book but . . . I was rewarded with a beautifully written, moving account of one woman's experience of being born a lesbian in the late 19th century. Enjoyable for all, but especially for those women who's [sic] hearts ache with the desire to be accepted.[33]

> This will reduce you to tears, I have never been so emotionally drained after finishing a book, but I truthfully believe that regardless of your view on sexuality, this is a love story, showing that love will force you to do anything to protect the one you truly care about and adore.[34]

Readers are responding to this novel with passionate engagement, tears, their own advice and exhortations (to read this book) and their own literary production in the form of a review. They are still 'hooked' by the version of sexual identity that the novel seeks to engage them in creating. 'Customer reviews' of *On the Road* posted on Amazon suggest, similarly, that contemporary readers continue to read Kerouac's novel as a personal manifesto:

> I believe every young person should read this book. We need an all new embracing bohemian culture to engulf this country where the landscape will be filled with backpacking youths with journals in their hands hitchhiking from the sliproads of the M1, M25, M4, M6![35]

> Jack Kerouac is an amazing writer, and it does make you want to get out there and do it yourself. It flows and it is real and gritty.[36]

> Get on the road and open yourself up to the fantastic panoramas of Kerouac's travels across America.[37]

> As a 90s teenager Kerouac single handedly redefined my views on life. The energy he puts across in the form of Dean makes me want to pack in my degree and hit the road, experience it all and take mind-bending narcotics . . . Although in today's society it's nearly impossible to do what Sal does, it got the message across to me that to live the life you want you just have to be brave enough to make the decisions. My first experience of Kerouac and the Beat generation but not the last.[38]

Whether or not readers of the novel go 'on the road' literally, the text, like *Well* and other scandalous fictions of this period, takes them on the road of self-discovery. They 'discover themselves' not in the humanist sense used in the clichés of self-help literature but in the far more complicated sense in which Foucault used 'technologies of the self', to mean those practices which 'permit individuals to effect by their own means or with the help of others a certain number of operations on their own bodies and souls, thoughts, conduct, and way of being, so as to transform themselves in order to attain a certain state of happiness, purity, wisdom, perfection, or immortality'.[39]

## Licence and licentiousness

With this in mind, it is perhaps unsurprising that throughout its career, the popular consumption of the novel, especially outside the education system, has been subject to almost unrelenting suspicion. Historically, it is a form whose development is intimately connected to the reading culture fed by early mass-circulation periodicals and the growth of subscription libraries in the eighteenth and nineteenth centuries, whose exponential growth is by turns extolled for the public literacy it promoted and deplored as a disseminator of inappropriate and morally dubious material to vulnerable minds. In this sense the novel is umbilically tied to an ethos of public information and education, and is at the same time a form whose propriety is constantly in question. In the 1921 Newbolt Report which laid much of the groundwork for the structure of public education in Britain and the empire during the twentieth century, English fiction (as opposed to works in Latin and Greek) is seen as a literary medium likely to interest students, encouraging their skills of analysis and self-expression. On the advice of the Inspectorate of the Board of Education it is stipulated, however, that as a form associated with dubious forms of edification, the novel should be used only sparingly in the school curriculum, and not at all in the education of adults in evening classes:

> If a book is to be studied throughout an evening school session, it should be a book which requires study and deserves it. It is this consideration which, in general, rules out the novel as the basis of the study of English in evening schools.[40]

In the middle decades of the twentieth century in Britain, with the institutionalization of the Leavisite 'Great Tradition', there is certainly an effort by the critical establishment to promote the novel as a serious form. This is however at the expense of a rigorous separation between 'literary' and popular fiction, with the former being identified on the basis of technical sophistication but also, and more importantly, on a notion of an emotional and philosophical discomfiture which only authentically 'literary' texts were seen as capable of generating. Thus in Queenie Leavis's *Fiction and the Reading Public* (1932) the 'highbrow' (exemplified by Joyce and Woolf) is importantly characterized by the way it discourages readers from 'fantasying' '(sic)' and for the way it provokes 'disturbing repercussions in the reader's emotional make-up'.[41] E.M. Forster is singled out for particular mention as a writer whose work is distinguished by its 'unpleasant' feel to the middlebrow reader. At the same time, the consumption of fiction by a mass public as a means of 'mental relaxation' is seen unambiguously as a social evil. With its 'sympathetic' representations and 'absence of the disquieting' such middlebrow material must be treated as no more than an antisocial addiction.

The covert influence of such ideas on critical thinking about the stratification of 'literary' and 'popular' fiction in the twentieth century has certainly been extensive. Even in a book devoted to the study of the popular such as John Sutherland's *Bestsellers* (1981), the bestseller is defined in contradistinction to the 'classic' specifically in terms of the formulaic and ephemeral nature of its appeal: 'Once a bestseller is spent, or its formula is spent, no residue is left. This partly explains why popular fiction has no generic sense of sustained progress or tradition.'[42] As many of the chapters in this book show, of course, it is in practice impossible to draw an equation in the twentieth century between texts marketed by publishers as either 'highbrow' or 'middlebrow' and the nature and degree of the public discomfiture such texts might cause. If, as James Smethurst shows, a text like Wright's *Native Son* showed itself capable of scandalizing a nation, this was partly through its citation and appropriation of unambiguously popular forms like that of the horror talkie. As a bestseller, it would hardly be defensible to suggest with Sutherland that Wright's text 'left no residue' in US literary culture after the initial burst of its popularity.

By the same token, if, as Bruce Arnold reports, the first American printing of Joyce's *Ulysses* was marketed as '933 small, thrill-packed pages, with advertisements at the end for similar exciting publications such as *Four Way Swappers*, *The Whipping Post*, Frank Harris's *My Secret Life*, *Bottoms Up* and *The Bawdy Tales of Firenzuola*',[43] then it is difficult to define the specific kind of readerly discomfiture which might inform the theoretical separation between one scandalous text and another. In the 1933 court proceedings which lifted the US ban on *Ulysses*, Judge Woolsey attempted to make such a distinction in his ruling that Joyce's novel, frank as it might be, did not betray 'the leer of the sensualist'.[44] What the relationship could be between the kind of obscenity that might legitimately be required by the demands of artistic experimentation, and the kind that merely panders to the sensual, was left undefined. As we see in this case, as in that of *Lady Chatterley's Lover* (1928), the most controversial distinction operating in this area during the twentieth century was that between the novelist and the pornographer. In 1959 the Obscene Publications Act was in part an attempt to allow the question of artistic merit to be considered when making judgements about obscenity. Indecency had to be considered in relation to 'the work as a whole'. That the presence of explicit sexual content did not in itself prove that the work concerned was pornographic was a distinction that did not operate before the first decades of the twentieth century. Considering the use of literature in education during the twentieth century, moreover, Allison Pease traces a similar opposition. Her examination of the ways in which pornographic tropes and images made their way into modernist literature leads her to the conclusion that 'by training readers in methods of reading that accommodated the body, modernist criticism not only legitimated the body as part of aesthetic consumption and production, it also promoted a more completely engaged, "interested," way of approaching texts'.[45] Such developments in the conventions of reading fiction reinforced the new orthodoxy, in the latter part of the century, that a novel, like pornography, could be sexually explicit, but that a novel dealt with sex with artistic integrity whereas a pornographic text could not.

With a text like D.H. Lawrence's *Lady Chatterley's Lover*, the embattled opposition between the kind of licence to discomfit which informs contemporary conceptions of the literary and the suspicion of licentiousness to which it is still subject, again overshadows the text's reception to such an extent that a virtual 'scandalous fiction' seems to ends up occupying the place of the original text. As Fiona Becket shows in Chapter 3, between the initial publication of Lawrence's text, its confiscation and the lifting of the publishing ban in Britain in 1960, an alternate phantasmagoric *Lady Chatterley* can be seen as taking shape in British culture, based on impressions of Lawrence's personal philosophy which bore little relation to his actual writings. As Becket argues, this process of mythologization has itself, in a strange return, changed and refreshed Lawrence's novel in a different way, so that for contemporary readers the experience of a close encounter with *Lady Chatterley* may become a new kind of defamiliarizing, even discomfiting experience.

If, as we see with the example of Leavis, we see an institutionalized demand for the literary novel to enact a kind of scandal, to articulate what is not banal, expected or conventional, then this clearly raises questions about the institutionalization and regulation of the novel within the public sphere in the twentieth century, in terms of the ethical and legal licence it is granted, on the one hand, and the periodic suppression and censorship to which it is subject, on the other. Earlier scholarship on the subject of censorship tends to view it (somewhat simply) in terms of state repression of individual freedoms, perpetuating a view of the century as one of increasing liberalization with a few setbacks. According to John Sutherland, for example, 'The road to freedom from censorship over the period 1960–77 is best conceived as a series of rushing advances, encountered by stubborn rearguard and backlash actions.'[46] Here, the military might of the forces of censorship are conceived as ineffectual against the flowing tide of intellectual freedom. Although this may be true in the particular context of prosecutions for obscenity in the UK in the second half of the twentieth century, it certainly is not an accurate picture of the broader juridical response to fiction written in the English language in the twentieth century world-wide, as this collection suggests. In fact, the scandalous fiction attracts formal censorship sporadically throughout the century, despite the focus on the connections between the period of literary modernism (1910–1930) and censorship that a number of critics have attempted to make.[47] While it is certainly the case that there were a significant number of prosecutions for obscenity in the UK in the first decades of the twentieth century, it is more likely, as Chapter 2 suggests, that this was a response to contemporary concerns about the national interest in the wake of the First World War than a reaction to modernism. For its prosecutors, indeed, one of the most disturbing aspects of *The Well of Loneliness* was its suggestion that lesbian women might be uniquely fitted for war-work, such as ambulance driving. The novel's implication that lesbians were just as capable of contributing to the war effort as their heterosexual sisters, with a form of heroism quite different from the mere capacity to restock the nation, troubled normative gender assumptions in a way that Hall's detractors found particularly difficult to navigate.

Clearly, this collection does not focus solely on those fictions that attracted official censorship. Indeed, a more recent critical literature has attempted to re-theorize censorship as one of the inevitable (indeed necessary and definitive) conditions of writing. Influenced by the work of philosophers and critical theorists such as Michel Foucault, Pierre Bourdieu and Herbert Marcuse as well as by Freudian psychoanalysis, this literature once again highlights the limitations of the Habermasian opposition between traditional culture, dominated by state censorship, and modernity, characterized by the rise of the public sphere in the Enlightenment, in which, he argues, a space for critical commentary on the state came into existence.[48] In Freudian psychoanalysis, the notion of censorship as a mere obstacle to the discovery of desire is likewise complicated by a sense of its creative importance in the formation of the dream-work. As Freud argues in *The Interpretation of Dreams*:

> A writer must beware of the censorship, and on its account he must soften and distort the expression of his opinion. According to the strength and sensitiveness of the censorship he finds himself compelled either merely to refrain from certain forms of attack, or to speak in allusions in place of direct references, or he must conceal his objectionable pronouncement beneath some apparently innocent disguise ... The stricter the censorship, the more far-reaching will be the disguise and the more ingenious too may be the means employed for putting the reader on the scent of the true meaning.[49]

The idea that disguise and allusion may require a productive, creative 'ingenuity' suggests that, as Michael G. Levine claims, it may in fact be useful to consider censorship 'as a condition of writing that is at once crippling and enabling'.[50] An important undertaking of this collection, as we have already seen in the case of *Native Son*, is to demonstrate how scandalous fictions often trace a dialogue between repressed material (of whatever unacceptable nature) and productive rewritings of that material. Equally, in the case of *The Well of Loneliness*, the idea of censorship as constitutive of creative ingenuity may explain some of Hall's surprising and unexpected appropriations of biblical allusion and Catholic metaphor in the rather surprising context of a novel about 'female inversion'.

In developing such an analysis, Michel Foucault's now orthodox critique of the repressive hypothesis further complicates our sense of the symbiosis between repression and the proliferation and dispersal of scandalous sexualities and sensibilities. In this context, the prosecution of sexually scandalous fiction may be viewed, not in terms of the efficacy of such efforts at repression, but rather as evidence of their tendency to enhance the public currency of scandalous texts, and to encourage the circulation of the illicit discourses they embody. As we see with *Lady Chatterley*, the proliferating myth of banned texts in particular makes this process of dissemination an extraordinarily strange and ambivalent one, in which the literary text itself may stand as little more than an 'incitement to discourse'.[51] Similarly, the case of *Ulysses* illustrates the ways in which the popular cult of a legally circumscribed text often further manifests itself in the form of an underground, commercial pressure for bootlegs, paratexts and 'alternative' editions. At the same time, as Herbert Marcuse argues in the essay 'Repressive Tolerance' (1965), it is by no means sufficient to think in some simple sense of the market as the antithesis of censorship. Although Marcuse claims that 'censorship of art and literature is regressive under all circumstances'[52] his essay suggests that, in an important way, the market may be the most effective neutralizing mechanism of all: 'The danger of "destructive tolerance" (Baudelaire), of "benevolent neutrality" toward *art* has been recognized: the market...provides a "complacent receptacle, a friendly abyss"...in which the radical impact of art, the protest of art against the established reality is swallowed up.'[53]

Robert C. Post has avoided the dilemma of making a meaningful distinction between 'good' and 'bad' forms of censorship by returning to Foucault's understanding of the radical dispersal of power: 'if censorship is a technique by which discursive practices are maintained, and if social life largely consists of such practices, it follows that censorship is the norm rather than the exception'.[54] This 'constitutive' or what Bourdieu terms 'structural' view of censorship contends that literature, like any specialized language, is 'the product of a *compromise* between an *expressive interest* and a *censorship* constituted by the very structure of the field in which the discourse is produced and circulates'.[55]

Critics working with such a conception of censorship have developed the idea that the very function of the 'expressive author' and indeed, our modern conception of literature, could only emerge as a consequence of censorship.[56] As Foucault has argued of the author function elsewhere, 'It would be pure romanticism to... imagine a culture in which the fictive would operate in an absolutely free state, in which fiction would be put at the disposal of everyone and would develop without passing through something like a necessary or constraining figure'.[57] That the cult of the author associated with the novel in modernity is a historically contingent phenomenon associated with a specific distribution of power relations, moreover, is something that has been well established by critics such as David Saunders and Ian Hunter. Cherished beliefs about authorship – for example, that writers are entitled to privacy and that intellectual work has a privileged status – came into operation in the early modern period and remained in place in the twentieth century. However, as Saunders and Hunter suggest and this collection bears out, it is important to recognize at the same time that the legal process just as often denies the author function the respect we have come to associate with it as it upholds the myth of its authority.[58] In fact, most twentieth-century prosecutions for obscenity were against publishers or printers rather than authors; authorial intention was considered irrelevant in determining obscenity in the Hicklin judgement of 1868,[59] just as it was in the trials of *Ulysses* and *The Well of Loneliness* in the 1930s. Radclyffe Hall attended the trial of her novel but was threatened with removal from the court when she intervened to protest at the presiding magistrate's interpretation of the scene involving lesbian women's war-work discussed above.

The 'scandalous' fiction as it is represented in this book, nevertheless, has not necessarily been the victim of formal censorship.[60] Nor are all the novels we discuss sexually explicit. Nor, however much we might wish this to be the case, has the scandalous fiction necessarily resulted in the creation of a 'dissident' authorial sensibility. Even if a capacity to disturb, defamiliarize and discomfit might be regarded as an integral part of the 'literariness' to which many writers have aspired in the twentieth century, many others were anxious for acceptance in mainstream culture and were horrified by the notoriety that attended publication. It is certainly the case that, as Adam Parkes contends, many authors have exploited the ' "theatre of censorship" – the social space in which texts and authors become subject to public censure and legal action',[61] often thereby raising questions about the institution of censorship itself. At the same time, however, as our discussions of such writers as Joyce, Hall and Lawrence suggest, it is also important not to overestimate the extent to which authors have been able to control interpretation of their texts in the public arena. It is a truism of literary theory that whatever the author intends, readers may read otherwise; this is nowhere more obvious than in the career of many of the scandalous fictions discussed here. For Jonathan Dollimore, the very process of approaching literary texts, with the necessary engagement of fantasy and desire that reading entails, is always a dangerous and open-ended process. As he suggests, 'to take art seriously must be to recognize that its dangerous insights and painful beauty often derive from tendencies both disreputable and deeply anti-social'.[62] In the texts examined in this book, that is certainly very often the case. As we have seen, however, the production of literary scandal is always something that takes place in the space between writers and readers. It is not to texts alone that we must look, if we want to form a more adequate understanding of the twentieth-century's scandalous fictions.

## Notes

1. Raymond Williams, *The Long Revolution* (London: Chatto & Windus, 1961).
2. David Vincent, *Literacy and Popular Culture: England 1750–1914* (Cambridge: Cambridge University Press, 1989).
3. UNESCO Institute for Statistics, *Regional Youth and Adult Literacy Rates and Illiterate Population by Gender for 2000–2004* (Quebec: UNESCO, 2005).
4. Bernard Berelson, *The Library's Public: a Report of the Public Library Inquiry of the Social Science Research Council* (New York: Columbia University Press, 1949). Such findings are corroborated by polls conducted by Gallup between the 1950s and 1970s, published by the Book Industry Study Group as *Reading in America 1978* (Washington: Library of Congress, 1978), which evidenced a continuing upward trend in the proportion of the population who were 'regular readers of books'.
5. Wendy Griswold, *Bearing Witness: Readers, Writers and the Novel in Nigeria* (Princeton: Princeton University Press, 2000), 110.
6. Stephanie Newell, *Literary Culture in Colonial Ghana: 'How to Play the Game of Life'* (Manchester: Manchester University Press, 2002).
7. Queenie Leavis, *Fiction and the Reading Public* (London: Chatto & Windus, 1965), 19.
8. Newell, 92.
9. Richard Hoggart, *The Uses of Literacy* (London: Chatto & Windus, 1957), 210–11.
10. Aphra Behn, *Oroonoko, or The Royal Slave* [1688] (London: Norton, 1973), 1.
11. Daniel Defoe, Preface to *The Fortunes and Misfortunes of the Famous Moll Flanders* [1722] reproduced in George Barnet, ed., *Eighteenth-Century Novelists on the Novel* (New York: Appleton-Century-Crofts, 1968), 30–1.
12. See William Godwin, Preface to *The Adventures of Caleb Williams, or, Things as they Are* [1794] (New York: Rinehart, 1960), xxiiv.
13. *British Critic* 6 (July 1795), cited by Pamela Clemit, *The Godwinian Novel* (Oxford: Clarendon Press, 1993), 94.
14. Elizabeth Deeds Ermarth, *Realism and Consensus in the English Novel: Time, Space and Narrative* (Edinburgh: Edinburgh University Press, 1998), 66.
15. Aramis, 'The Scandal of *Ulysses*', *Sporting Times*, 34 (1 April 1922), 4.
16. Stanley Crouch, 'Aunt Medea', *New Republic*, 3796 (19 October 1987), 38–43; 40.
17. Walter Clemons, 'A Gravestone of Memories', *Newsweek* (28 September 1987) 74–5; 74.
18. Nancy Fraser 'Rethinking the Public Sphere: a Contribution to the Critique of Actually Existing Democracy', in Craig Calhoun, ed., *Habermas and the Public Sphere* (Cambridge, MA: MIT Press, 1992), 109–42.

19. Hannah Arendt, *The Human Condition* (Chicago: University of Chicago Press, 1958).
20. Nick Crossley and John Michael Roberts, eds, *After Habermas: New Perspectives on the Public Sphere* (Oxford: Blackwell, 2004), 3–4.
21. Roland Barthes, 'The Death of the Author', *Image, Music, Text*, ed. and trans. Stephen Heath (New York: Hill and Wang, 1977), 142–8.
22. Michael McKeon, *The Origins of the English Novel* (London: Radius, 1988), 357.
23. *Statement of the ANC at the Human Rights Commission Hearings on Racism in the Media* (Johannesburg: ANC, 5 April 2000): http://www.anc.org.za/ancdocs/misc/2000/sp0405.html.
24. Citation from Tim Du Plessis, *The Citizen*, 31 March 2000, ibid.
25. Jacques Derrida, *Acts of Literature*, ed. Derek Attridge (New York: Routledge, 1992), 38.
26. Michel Foucault, 'Technologies of the Self', in *Technologies of the Self: a Seminar with Michel Foucault*, ed. Luther H. Martin, Huck Gutman and Patrick H. Hutton (London: Tavistock Publications, 1988), 16–49; 17.
27. Foucault, 'Technologies of the Self', 49.
28. Radclyffe Hall, *The Well of Loneliness*, ed. Alison Hennegan (London: Virago, 1982), 187. Further references are to this edition.
29. Jack Kerouac, *On the Road* (Harmondsworth: Penguin, 1991), 9.
30. Laura Doan, 'Passing Fashions: Reading Female Masculinities in the 1920s', in *Fashioning Sapphism: the Origins of a Modern English Lesbian Culture*, Between Men – Between Women: Lesbian and Gay Studies (New York: Columbia University Press, 2001),
31. Judith Butler, *Gender Trouble: Feminism and the Subversion of Identity* (London: Routledge), 1990.
32. A reader from Wales, UK, review dated 12 December 2001: http://www.amazon.co.uk/exec/obidos/ASIN/0860682544/qid=1136394788/sr=1-1/ref=sr_1_18_1/202-3008110-6704620. Further reviews of *The Well of Loneliness* can be found at the same link.
33. gerlinky@yahoo.com, review dated 9 March 2000.
34. lorna_j from East Anglia, review dated 12 April 2005.
35. manic_obsessive_2000 from East Surrey, UK, review dated 14 September 2004: http://www.amazon.co.uk/exec/obidos/tg/stores/detail/-/books/0141182679/customerreviews/qid%3D1136395384/sr%3D1-4/ref%3Dsr%5F1%5F2%5F4/202-3008110-6704620. Further reviews of *On the Road* can be found at the same link.
36. A reader from England, review dated 16 September 2001.
37. sal_paradise37@hotmail.com from Greenock, review dated 9 March 2001.
38. A reader from Devon, England, review dated 7 December 2000.
39. Foucault, 'Technologies of the Self', 18.
40. Newbolt, Henry *The Teaching of English in England* (London: HMSO, 1921), 138.
41. Leavis, *Fiction and the Reading Public*, 60.
42. John Sutherland, *Bestsellers: Popular Fiction of the 1970s* (London: Routledge, 1981), 11.
43. Bruce Arnold, *The Scandal of Ulysses* (London: Sinclair Stevenson, 1991), 198.
44. Arnold, 61.
45. Allison Pease, *Modernism: Mass Culture, and the Aesthetics of Obscenity* (Cambridge: Cambridge University Press, 2000), xiv.
46. John Sutherland, *Offensive Literature: Decensorship in Britain 1960–1982* (London: Junction Books, 1982), 4.

47. Adam Parkes's focus is on modernism more than on censorship when he contends that 'the development of literary modernism was shaped in significant ways by an ongoing dialogue with a culture of censorship' and that 'important aspects of modernism may be appreciated fully only when the extent of its engagement with this culture is recognized'. Adam Parkes, *Modernism and the Theatre of Censorship* (Oxford: Oxford University Press, 1996), viii.

48. See for example Richard Burt, *The Administration of Aesthetics: Censorship, Political Criticism and the Public Sphere* (Minneapolis: University of Minnesota Press, 1994), xix, who claims that 'underlying this [Habermas's] historiography is a series of interlocking conceptual and historiographical oppositions between criticism (or art) and censorship; state censorship externally imposed and self-censorship; public access and privatization (corporate commodification versus fair use); a repressive early modern state censorship and an enlightened modern public sphere (which emerged with the institution of fine arts and literary criticism). The essays here suggest, however, that criticism is not radically opposed to censorship; rather, these practices are on a continuum.'

49. Sigmund Freud, *The Interpretation of Dreams, Vol. IV, The Pelican Freud Library*, trans. James Strachey, ed. James Strachey assist. Alan Tyson, present volume ed. Angela Richards (Harmondsworth: Penguin, 1976), 223–4.

50. Michael G. Levine, *Writing through Repression: Literature, Censorship, Psychoanalysis* (Baltimore: Johns Hopkins University Press, 1994), 2.

51. Michel Foucault, *The History of Sexuality Vol. I: The Will to Knowledge*, trans. Robert Hurley (Harmondsworth: Penguin, 1979; 1998), 7–35.

52. Herbert Marcuse, 'Repressive Tolerance', in *A Critique of Pure Tolerance*, ed. Robert Paul Wolff, Barrington Moore Jr and Herbert Marcuse (Boston, MA: Beacon Press, 1969), 95–137; 89.

53. Marcuse, 88.

54. Robert C. Post, *Censorship and Silencing: Practices of Cultural Regulation* (Los Angeles: The Getty Research Institute for the History of Art and the Humanities, 1998), 2.

55. Pierre Bourdieu, 'Censorship and the Imposition of Form', in *Language and Symbolic Power*. ed. and introd. John B. Thompson, trans. Gino Raymond and Matthew Adamson (Cambridge: Polity Press, 1991), 137–277; 137.

56. Within this critical tradition, particular attention has been paid to the early modern period as an important historical locus for the formation of such ideas. What Annabel Patterson calls the 'hermeneutics of censorship' were then widely agreed and understood. Under the constraints of the Star Chamber and the licensing system, writers used various parodic and satirical devices which relied on the central concept of literary ambiguity in order to cloak their political meanings. Annabel Patterson, *Censorship and Interpretation: the Conditions of Writing and Reading in Early Modern England* (Madison: The University of Wisconsin Press, 1984), 8–9.

57. Michel Foucault, 'What is an Author', in *Modern Criticism and Theory: a Reader*, ed. David Lodge (London: Longman, 1988), 197–210; 209.

58. David Saunders and Ian Hunter, 'Lessons from the "Literatory": How to Historicise Authorship', *Critical Inquiry*, 17 (1991), 479–509.

59. *Regina v. Hicklin*, 3 Queens Bench 360, 362 (1968).

60. There are a number of important, scandalous novels that we do not consider here. Other novels that provoked trials for obscenity in the twentieth century include D.H. Lawrence, *The Rainbow* (1915); Henry Miller, *Tropic of Cancer* (1934);

Hubert Selby, *Last Exit to Brooklyn* (1964); William Burroughs, *Naked Lunch* (1959); Alexander Trocchi, *Cain's Book* (1963).

61. Parkes, xi.
62. Jonathan Dollimore, *Sex, Literature and Censorship* (Cambridge: Polity Press, 2001), xi.

# 1

# The 'nameless shamelessness' of *Ulysses*: Libel and the Law of Literature

*Sean Latham*

In a now famous 1922 photograph, James Joyce appears seated in Sylvia Beach's Shakespeare and Company bookstore at 12 rue de l'Odéon on the bohemian left-bank of the Seine. He is nattily dressed, sporting a bow tie, a neatly trimmed goatee and slicked hair that gives him a distinctly bourgeois air of elegance and sophistication. The large black patch covering his left eye, however, warns us that something is amiss, as does the large poster on the wall behind him – a reproduction of the vibrantly pink *Sporting Times* of 1 April 1922 proclaiming 'The Scandal of "Ulysses"' in large black letters.[1] In the foreground, Joyce and Beach appear to be studiously examining ledger books and order slips for the text, which is denounced in the paper behind them as the production of 'a perverted lunatic who has made a specialty of the literature of the latrine'.[2] The poster hovering behind them becomes an advertisement, attempting to lure cultural tourists as well as the Parisian avant-garde into the store. There they could obtain a very expensive copy of the book that outraged American and British censors were seizing and burning at their borders. In buying a copy of *Ulysses*, early readers also bought a little bit of that titillating scandal that has only just begun to fade. This photograph of Joyce and Beach, in fact, has become so iconic precisely because we have never really stopped proclaiming the scandal of *Ulysses* in the classroom, in literary scholarship, and in the popular press. This was true when Samuel Roth published not one but two pirated editions in the United States and it remained true when the Collectors Publications edition appeared containing 43 pages of advertisements for pornographic books and magazines.[3] Much like *Madame Bovary, Lady Chatterley's Lover* and the other books treated in this volume, Joyce's novel is inextricable from the legal scandal that both preceded and survived its publication.

As a scandalous object, *Ulysses* has been consistently cast as the hero of a modern morality play, tilting at the narrow-minded censors and anti-vice crusaders who dared to suppress this bold portrait of human sexuality. Joyce, Katherine Mullin argues, actually anticipated this role for himself, becoming a subtle 'agent provocateur' who responded to Victorian prudery 'through the creative appropriation of prevailing debates about art, morality, and sexuality'.[4] At the heart of this scandalous encounter, of course, lies the text's blunt treatment of sex, ranging from Leopold Bloom's masturbatory encounter with Gerty McDowell on Sandymount Strand in the 'Nausicaa' episode through the sado-masochistic fantasies of the brothel in 'Circe', to Molly Bloom's night-time thoughts in 'Penelope', the section which Joyce himself described as 'probably more obscene than any preceding episode'.[5] Judge John Woolsey's decision to lift the American ban on *Ulysses* in 1933 further emphasized the importance of sexuality in the book's suppression. According to the legal definitions then in place, he struggled to determine whether *Ulysses* was an obscene text that might 'stir the sex impulses or lead to sexually impure and lustful thoughts'.[6] His famous conclusion that the 'net effect' of the book 'was only that of a somewhat tragic and powerful commentary on the inner lives of men and women', at once freed *Ulysses* from the grip of the censor and transformed it into an icon of free speech and aesthetic integrity. The issues of censorship and scandal adjudicated in this case lodged the text at the interface between the two increasingly autonomous spheres of moral and aesthetic judgement while appearing to confirm their separation. As Max Weber, Jürgen Habermas, and Pierre Bourdieu contend, by the early twentieth century, modernity had become powerfully shaped by the decoupling of moral, aesthetic and scientific judgement, shards of a once more organic totality that were now free to develop under their own rules and procedures.[7] Joyce's book became a scandal because it jumped the gap separating morality and art, temporarily exposing both the contradiction and the distance between these two discourses. Indeed, scandal in this case might best be defined as the precipitate of the encounter between law and literature which falls out when these two otherwise typically independent spheres of thought and judgement enter into sudden and very public conflict.

Reconceived in this way, the scandal of *Ulysses* encompasses far more than its sexual frankness, allowing for a much wider consideration of its continuing ability to cross the boundary between the institutions of morality and art. The scandals which have more recently enfolded the book, in fact, have very little to do with sex, turning not on questions of obscenity but on debates about copyright and textual integrity. This round of scandal was set off by the appearance in 1984 of a critical edition that not only created a new reading text but also provided a complete list of the multiple textual variants then available. Two years later, Random House published the reading text by itself as the 'Gabler edition' of *Ulysses*, shot through with various changes both large and small that set off rounds of furious public debate. With the American copyright on the original edition set shortly to expire, scholars began to prepare their own editions that would compete with this 'corrected' text while creating an array of slightly different editions. With the passage of the Sonny Bono Copyright Term Extension Act in 1998, however, the copyright on *Ulysses* was extended for an additional twenty years and the furore over the accuracy of the Gabler edition gave way to a series of legal arguments that again placed the novel between the competing rationalities of art and the law. The debate now turned on the rights of the Joyce Estate to control the text and its various adaptations as well as the exact legal status of the original 1922 edition.[8]

This scandal may not have the sexual piquancy which accompanied the book's original publication, but it has once again provoked a confrontation between morality and art – in this case between the rights of the Joyce Estate to its intellectual property and the demand from artists and scholars that it be allowed to circulate freely. Legal sanctions defining intellectual property rights as well as obscenity serve both to delimit and define what Bourdieu calls art's 'conquest of autonomy', powerfully shaping the otherwise seemingly autonomous field of cultural production.[9] Just as Mullin cogently reveals the ways in which Joyce anticipated and even exploited his encounter with the censors while crafting *Ulysses*, so too Paul Saint-Amour contends that Joyce actively engaged many of the debates about copyright which have more recently mired his text in scandal.[10] These critics reveal the multiform ways in which Joyce manoeuvered his book into the gap between the aesthetic and legal fields, deliberately staging their creative confrontation in order to map the limits of his own creative freedom. The scandal of *Ulysses* thus continues to lie in its potent ability to provoke this jarring encounter and thereby reverse or at least retard the autonomization of social life within modernity.

The debates about both obscenity and copyright have largely restricted our focus, however, to the limitations of censorship – the ability of the law, that is, to repress or prohibit the circulation of a particular text. Too narrow a focus on the explicit legal mechanisms of censorship, however, not only preserves the liberal image of *Ulysses* as an icon of free expression but also deflects attention from the complex ways in which the text struggles with the far more subtle mechanisms of repression structuring the aesthetic field. In this chapter I want to argue that there remains, in fact, one additional scandal, largely overlooked, which shapes *Ulysses* even more profoundly than either sexuality or intellectual property. It pervades the book from its opening to its closing pages and has troubled generations of critics, who have developed tortuous intellectual arguments in order to evade its most troubling implications. Hugh Kenner alludes to it glancingly, describing Joyce's decision to abandon the convention of the initialled dash when writing about real people and events, a practice that dates back to the very rise of the novel. 'In the year 19—, in the city of D—', Kenner writes, 'that would have been the decorous way to go about it.'[11] As Kenner notes, in fact, the French printers who initially set *Ulysses* cared so little for this particular English nicety that Joyce was able to indulge in 'a very orgy... of naming'. This use of real names and places, in fact, accounts for some of the peculiar pleasures of Joyce's text, encouraging readers not only to track references to real people and places in the 1904 *Thom's Directory* but to follow the fictional paths of Bloom and Stephen minute by minute and step by step as they make their way through Dublin. Joyce famously declared *Ulysses* so accurate that 'if the city one day suddenly disappeared from the earth it could be reconstructed out of my book'.[12] There is a danger, however, in such precision, for this particular orgy – like the one in Bella Cohen's brothel – runs a very real legal risk of suppression, not for obscenity, but for libel. In *Finnegans Wake* Joyce alludes to this directly when his 'Shem the Penman', in writing 'his usylessly unreadable Blue Book of Eccles... scrabbled and scratched and scriobbled and skrevened nameless shamelessness about everybody he ever met'.[13] Just as Joyce deliberately provoked the encounter between law and literature when writing about both obscenity and copyright, so too did he engage the unspoken injunction against mixing fiction and history upon which the novel itself was founded. This particular scandal – which landed *Ulysses* once more in the dock in 1955 – is just as explosive as the trials which first banned the text from the United States. Indeed, its wildly libellous nature has scandalized generations of readers, who have nevertheless failed to grasp its challenge to some of our most basic critical and aesthetic categories. Rather than an autonomous work of art, in fact, a libellous *Ulysses* deliberately and provocatively muddles the boundary between history and the novel, threatening the legal definition of fiction itself.

## Literature at the Bar

Joyce first encountered the complex entanglements of British libel law when he returned to Ireland in 1912 to make an ultimately disastrous attempt to force the publication of *Dubliners*. Six years earlier the book had already been rejected by censorious printers unwilling to take the risk of being caught out by the city's Vigilance Society and after repeated negotiations about possible revisions, Grant Richards had declined to publish it. Having secured a new contract from George Roberts of Maunsel and Company, Joyce faced a bewildering array of objections to his work, this time focused initially on the crude language of the characters in 'Ivy Day in the Committee Room' who refer to Queen Victoria at one point as a 'bloody old bitch'.[14] After moderating this passage somewhat – just as he had done in similar negotiations about obscenity with Richards – Joyce found himself confronted by what seemed an even more quixotic demand: that in the same story he remove all references to King Edward VII. Roberts feared that such passages, which described the deceased monarch as 'fond of his glass of grog and... a bit of a rake'[15] might provoke a charge of libel since, as Joyce's own solicitor advised him, the description 'could be taken as offensive... to the late King'.[16] This is certainly not the kind of legal difficulty we most often associate with Joyce's work and to a modern reader the potential threat of this passage has become essentially illegible. Nevertheless, the menace of libel hung precipitously over *Dubliners* throughout the negotiations with Maunsel, as the firm's solicitors grew ever more concerned about the absence of those decorous dashes Kenner describes. The genuine threat of a libel suit in this case was likely to be quite small and Joyce, in an effort to dispel Roberts's concerns, actually wrote a letter to George V explaining his situation and asking that the monarch 'inform me whether in his view the passage (certain allusions made by a person of the story in the idiom of his social class) should be withheld from publication as offensive to the memory of his father'.[17] Not surprisingly, the king's secretary refused to offer an opinion in the case, leaving Joyce with few options, as a book that once ran foul of obscenity laws now foundered on the threat of a libel suit.

Joyce, of course, was apoplectic and wrote an open letter to the press decrying 'the present condition of authorship in England and Ireland' while citing specifically the passage Roberts wanted to change.[18] As the letter notes, Grant Richards had not raised any objections to the description of the king in 1906 and by publishing the passage itself in the paper, Joyce clearly hoped to allay any concerns about its legal status. *Sinn Féin*, in which the letter appeared, did print the passage, though the *Northern Whig* – a far less nationalist paper – declined to do so, no doubt because its editor too was concerned about his potential liability. Joyce himself probably did not realize that following the passage of the Newspaper Libel and Registration Act in 1881, periodicals had a far greater licence to publish such material, since they were merely reporting news rather than themselves making libellous claims. The situation for Richards, however, was far more delicate since libel law in both Great Britain and Ireland allowed for the possibility of civil suits and even criminal prosecution for author, publisher and printer alike. As Francis Holt's influential 1812 study, *The Law of Libel*, notes, 'The offence of libel and slander is proportionately more criminal as it presumes to reach persons to whom special veneration is due. The diminution of their credit is a public mischief, and the state itself suffers in their becoming the objects of scorn; not only themselves are vilified and degraded, but the great affairs which they conduct are obstructed, and the justice they administer is thereby disparaged.'[19] It seems unlikely that by 1911 the Crown would undertake the prosecution of such a libel case, but Ellmann suggests rather vaguely that some kind of informal pressure may nevertheless have been brought to bear upon the firm by Lady Aberdeen, the Lord Lieutenant's wife.[20] In fact, at a stormy 1912 meeting in Dublin, Roberts demanded that all mentions of the king be deleted from the collection. Joyce immediately consulted a solicitor, George Lidwell, who obligingly wrote to Roberts, carefully reserving judgement on the question of obscenity, while effectively minimizing the threat of a libel prosecution brought by the Crown. 'I have read… "Ivy Day in the Committee Room"', he writes, 'and I think that beyond the questionable taste of the language (which is a matter entirely for the author) in referring to the memory of the last two reigning Sovereigns of these Realms, the vulgar expression put into the mouths of the Characters in the dialogue are not likely to be taken very serious notice of by the Advisors of the Crown.'[21] The letter proved to be of little use, in large part because Roberts was receiving his own legal advice from Maunsel's London offices which proved even more wary than its Dublin agent.

At the same August 1912 meeting in which Roberts demanded changes in 'Ivy Day', he made an even more far-reaching request – one so broad that it would eventually sink the entire project and again leave Joyce without a publisher for his stories. This time his concern lay not with the Crown but with the Dubliners whom Joyce dissects in his stories. He began first by requesting that all of the real public houses mentioned in 'Counterparts' be given fictitious names, then expanded this demand to include the alteration or deletion of every real person and place of business mentioned by name in any of the stories. He was furthermore advised by the London office that Joyce should immediately back the publication by securing large sureties in case a successful suit might be brought against the book. Should this fail, finally, Roberts was advised to sue the author for deliberately breaking his publishing contract by providing a text he knew to be libellous. Thomas Kettle, the solicitor to whom Joyce first turned for help, had already advised him that the book might indeed be brought to court, and as we have seen even Lidwell qualified his own opinion and focused it narrowly only on 'Ivy Day'. On 23 August 1912, Joyce made a frantic attempt to save the book, offering to drive Roberts to the various businesses mentioned in order to secure direct permission to use their names. The sense of desperation in Joyce's letters at this point is palpable, as what initially appeared to be a relatively minor quibble about the direct mention of King Edward VII expands rapidly into a wide-reaching series of demands, not only to change the text, but to indemnify the house upon its publication. Though negotiations with Roberts would continue for another week or so, it had become clear that Maunsel would not publish the book and on 11 September, the printer – according to Joyce's now disputed claim – finally destroyed the sheets for fear that he too might be named in a libel suit.

*Dubliners* would, of course, appear nearly two years later without any such editorial objections. In 1912, however, the 'nicely polished looking-glass' he had hoped to hold up to his native city proved only too accurate in its fidelity, crossing a still hazy but nevertheless dangerous boundary between fact and fiction.[22] Roberts and Maunsel, after all, were correct: by using real names and places of business, the stories did indeed run the very real risk of incurring damaging law suits. Within the common law system, libel is legally defined as the publication in a relatively permanent medium of

material – in the words of an 1840 decision – containing 'that sort of imputa-
tion which is calculated to vilify a man, and bring him...into hatred,
contempt, and ridicule'.[23] Holt, in his history of libel, traces the offence back
to ancient times, locating precedents in Sumerian, Greek, and Roman law
before defining 'an injury...which affects [someone] in character' as the
'next greatest injury' after direct physical harm.[24] Within British jurisprudence, however, this otherwise straightforward conception of defamation
has been considerably complicated by the development of two parallel yet
distinct bodies of law regarding libel: one civil and based on common law,
the other criminal and based on the rules of the Star Chamber. The crime
of libel, which originally emerged as part of the government's effort to erad-
icate bloody and violent duels, generated its own unique sets of rules and
decisions. In a criminal case, for example, the truth of a libel cannot be
employed as a defence, thus leaving the prosecutor the relatively easy task
of proving that a book or article was published intentionally and contains
some content potentially damaging to someone's reputation. This rather
strict limitation on the freedom of speech and publication was somewhat
moderated by the passage of the Reform Act of 1843, which allowed the truth
of a libel to serve as the grounds of an affirmative defence of justification
if the facts revealed were deemed to be in the public interest. Oscar Wilde,
who in 1895 brought a criminal charge of libel against Queensbury, finally
fell foul of the courts not when witnesses emerged confirming the charge
that he was a 'somdomite' (sic), but when it was judged that the publication
of such knowledge constituted a public good. The criminal branch of defamation law therefore explicitly limits speech deemed to be damaging not to
the reputations of particular individuals but to the good order and conduct
of the larger society.

Joyce's bare mention of a few pubs and a railway company in *Dubliners*
certainly did not threaten to provoke a criminal charge, particularly in
the early decades of the twentieth century when additional decisions and
reforms had severely limited such criminal prosecutions. Richards and his
London solicitors, however, were much more concerned with the civil tort
of libel which places particular burdens on defendants. As Brian Dobbs notes
in *The Law of Torts*, in the common law, once a publication was found to be
defamatory then 'the defendant was presumed to have published in malice,
the words were presumed to be false, and the plaintiff was presumed to have
suffered damages'.[25] As a consequence of these far-reaching assumptions,
the person or entity that had been defamed neither had to demonstrate
any special damages arising from the publication or even demonstrate to
a court or a jury that the material was false.[26] The truth of a libel can still
serve as a defence in such a case, but the burden of proving that a defamatory comment is true shifts to the defendant. In practice, the relatively
wide scope of defamation has generally been limited to particular kinds
of publication which bring someone into 'hatred, contempt, and ridicule'

by claiming that he or she committed a major crime or acts in such a way as to be unfit for her profession.[27] When Joyce forgoes the dash and describes 'the ten o'clock slow train from Kingstown' in 'A Painful Case' and 'O'Neill's', 'Davy Byrne's', and 'the Scotch House' in 'Counterparts', he runs the risk of bringing these business into ill repute.[28] In his incredulous letters to Nora, he writes of his attempts to find some kind of compromise and assures Roberts that though 'a railroad co. is mentioned once', it is immediately 'exonerated from all blame by two witnesses, jury and coroner'. In the public houses, he further contends, 'nothing happens. People drink.'[29] In attempting to resolve the risk of libel, in other words, Joyce argues that the text is simply not defamatory but is instead merely an accurate representation of the city of Dublin and some of its well-known businesses. Rather than feeling damaged, he desperately concludes, 'the publicans would be glad of the advertisement'. Joyce, in effect, contends that he does not mean to libel anyone and adduces such intentions as proof against any finding of defamation.

In mounting this particular defence, however, Joyce almost certainly misunderstood one additional aspect of the civil tort of libel, which holds that the interpretation of a text is a matter of fact to be resolved at trial. Long before Wimsatt founded modern literary criticism on the cornerstone of the 'intentional fallacy', the intentions of an author had already been legally ruled irrelevant to the interpretation of a text in all cases of libel.[30] In the words of one 1885 decision, 'the question is not what the defendant, in his own mind, intended by such language, but what was the meaning and inference that would be naturally drawn by reasonable and intelligent persons'.[31] Libel cases therefore most often turn precisely on the question of interpretation, transforming the courtroom into a kind of literary seminar where jurors must listen to arguments about the potential meaning of a text and then determine whether or not it is indeed defamatory. Though Joyce may have believed, for example, that the railway company in 'A Painful Case' had been exonerated by the overt description of events in the story, Maunsel's solicitors nevertheless were concerned that the subtle play of irony and the shifting instability of the story might nevertheless introduce a reasonable interpretation that the company had been negligent in its actions. Similarly, the publicans in 'Counterparts' could contend that far from an advertisement, the story in fact harmed their ability to conduct business by falsely asserting that they allowed the profligate consumption of alcohol. I do not mean, of course, to introduce these readings as particularly convincing, but cautious writers and printers had long sought to avoid the risk and considerable cost of a trial by carefully excising the mention of real people and places either by introducing fictional names or resorting to the conventional Victorian dash.

The eventual publication of *Dubliners* in 1914 might seem to vindicate Joyce's arguments and it does suggest that in a world on the brink of

war little attention was being paid to the publication of potentially libellous short stories. The absence of that secretive dash, in fact, has by now
come to seem an integral part of a distinctly Joycean aesthetic in which
fictional events are deeply and perhaps inextricably embedded in the historical realities of Edwardian Dublin. According to his brother Stanislaus, when
Joyce began work on the novel that would eventually become *A Portrait
of the Artist as a Young Man* (1914), he initiated an even more aggressive
assault on the constraints imposed by the restrictions of libel law: 'Jim
is beginning his novel, as he usually begins things, half in anger... It is
to be almost autobiographical, and naturally as it comes from Jim, satirical. He is putting a large number of his acquaintances into it, and those
Jesuits he has known. I don't think they will like themselves in it.'[32]
*Portrait*, *Ulysses* and *Finnegans Wake* all make use of this same technique
and generations of critics have devoted considerable effort to revealing –
inadvertently perhaps – that Joyce indulged in an essentially unprecedented
campaign of libel. Herbert Gorman in an early biography written under
Joyce's own careful guidance notes the frustrating inability of many readers
'to crack the hard nuts of certain paragraphs containing comments on actual
personalities' and concludes that an intimate knowledge of Dublin 'might
heighten one's enjoyment, for the scandalous aspects of [*Ulysses*] would
then be more greatly emphasized'.[33] The extensive guides and annotations,
which provide maps indicating the precise location of Davy Byrne's and
references to real figures, further reinforce the importance of this kind of
material for the book, revealing just how aggressively Joyce invaded not
only the outhouses and whorehouses of the city, but its historical realities
as well.

In taking the importance of such information for granted, however, we
inadvertently overlook the scandalous libels which pervade Joyce's work and
which amount to an aggressive assault on the legal bar against defamation
which wrecked one of his early attempts to publish *Dubliners*. Certainly, the
risks he initially incurred have now receded. In American jurisprudence the
First Amendment's protection of free speech has significantly constrained
the reach of libel, whilst the civil laws in Britain state that the dead cannot
be libelled. Unlike the potent sexuality which still has the power to rankle
and even shock some readers when they come across it, therefore, the dense
web of names and the multifold acts of revenge which pervade Joyce's works
are no longer the stuff of legal wrangling and public scandal. The first time
*Ulysses* enters a British or Irish court of law, however, the case involves
neither Gerty's thighs nor Molly's memories, but Reuben J. Dodd who files
a suit for libel.[34] In the 'Hades' episode, Martin Cunningham tells a story
about Dodd's apparent attempt to commit suicide by jumping into the Liffey
and his father's miserly offer of a florin to the boatman who saved his son's
life. In 1954 the BBC broadcast a reading of *Ulysses* featuring this episode and
Dodd promptly secured from the High Court of Dublin a summons on the

broadcaster claiming damages for defamation. In his affidavit Dodd spells out his complaint clearly, holding to the legal requirement that the passage could harm his reputation and his business:

> James Joyce, the author, whom I knew as a schoolmate, had a personal dislike for me because of what he alleged my father did to his father. And so, when he wrote his book 'Ulysses,' in or about the year 1904, he made some disparaging references, including moneylending transactions, to a Mr. Reuben J. Dodd . . . The passage complained of is a malicious and deliberate libel upon me and its dissemination by the B.B.C. exposes me to personal humiliation and injury. The whole incident described was a malicious falsehood and, in particular, that I attempted to commit suicide.[35]

Dodd won his case, demonstrating that more than thirty years after its initial publication, Joyce's text continued to generate not only scandal but a very real risk for publishers, printers and broadcasters who might find themselves subject to any number of suits. After all, Dodd is but one of the hundreds of real people mentioned in the text, many of whom might also claim that Joyce deliberately sought to bring them into 'hatred, contempt, and ridicule'. In exploring the troubled boundary between fact and fiction, Joyce's works powerfully reveal the legal limits which not only shaped the trajectory of his own career but restrict the autonomy of the aesthetic sphere. The laws of libel establish a legal and interpretive framework for defining and policing the boundary between fact and fiction, holding the intentions of an author in abeyance while placing the meaning of his work in the hands of a jury. Joyce's own aesthetic transgresses these laws. In *Ulysses* he deliberately expands the scandal of his libellous writings to provoke a collision between a seemingly autonomous aesthetic sphere and the web of legal constraints which structure and guide its development.

## Libellous *Ulysses*

In his encounter with the laws restricting libel, Joyce inadvertently reveals an apparent aesthetic paradox: the limits of novelistic realism are defined not simply by a text's indexical representation of social and psychic life but also by the preservation of a rigid generic boundary between fiction and history. George Levine usefully describes realism as 'a self-conscious effort, usually in the name of some moral enterprise of truth telling and extending the limits of human sympathy, to make literature appear to be describing directly not some other language but reality itself'.[36] Working outward from this formulation, other critics and theorists have stressed the disruptive gaps between reality and its representation so that realism grows to include some understanding of 'the radical otherness of the world . . . [and] the failures of representation'.[37] Far from an innocent reproduction of the world, in other words, the realist aesthetic includes some knowledge of its own failure and its distance from the world it attempts to describe.

Joyce's use of historical names and places throughout his works, however, troubles such a conception of realism by insisting on the ability of his work to succeed in reproducing reality, becoming so accurate that it is no longer a fiction at all but a history or an autobiography. The tort of libel largely exists in order to preserve this basic distinction between history and fiction, so that the licence permitted the latter is obtained at the expense of the former. Joyce's Ulysses, however, scandalously crosses and recrosses this generic boundary, consciously disrupting it in order to reveal both the limits of libel and the power of fiction to elude it. Any attempt, furthermore, to reserve a kind of idealized autonomy for this text – by arguing for example that it must be understood essentially as a fiction – is deeply misguided. The book had and retains a potent ability to reach beyond such generic confines and disorder the lives and histories of the people it names. Richard Best, for example, with whom Stephen discusses his theory of Hamlet in the 'Scylla and Charybdis' episode, was a very real individual – an accomplished scholar who would later serve for sixteen years as the director of the National Library of Ireland. When approached by a reporter who wanted to interview him as part of a segment on Ulysses, he responded with what must have become a practised indignation at the book's unique power over his life: 'I am not a character in fiction; I am a living being.'[38] For the poet, physician, and statesman Oliver St John Gogarty, this sense of displacement was even more pronounced and despite the fact that his obituary in the New York Times revealed his fury at the fact that 'posterity would remember him as Buck Mulligan', the article's sub-head nevertheless reads: 'Author and Wit Was Prototype of Character in Ulysses'.[39] As Claire Culleton argues, this assault on the boundaries and structures of genre is more than just an innovative technique, it is also 'the ultimate revenge, in that it condemns a real person to caricatured fabrication'.[40]

There is little doubt that Joyce himself was aware of what he was doing and that his book was indeed intentionally and thoroughly libellous. Unlike those stories in Dubliners which mention only a few public houses and a railway company, Ulysses invokes a vast array of names ranging from individuals, to businesses, to commercial products. Just as he began Portrait 'half in anger', so too this text contains numerous (if often almost invisible) acts of petty revenge. This malicious use of fiction is not at all uncommon in the early twentieth century, as the novelist Hewet laments in Virginia Woolf's The Voyage Out. 'I want', he says, 'to write a novel about silence', but fears that he will by stymied by a public that reads novels only 'to see what sort of person the writer is, and, if you know him, which of his friends he has put in'.[41] H.G. Wells lashed out viciously at those readers and reviewers who 'pander to that favorite amusement of vulgar, half-educated, curious, but ill-informed people, the search for the "imaginary" originals of every fictitious character'.[42] Rather than haughtily wrapping himself in a cloak of indignation, however, Joyce makes explicit in the early pages of *Ulysses* that this is, in fact, a libellous book out to settle some old scores. Atop the Martello tower, Buck Mulligan mocks the sullen and solipsistic Stephen Dedalus before suddenly declaring 'it's not fair to tease you like that Kinch, is it?' In the ebbs and flows of Stephen's consciousness, however, this jovial apology is read as an act of self-defence: 'Parried again', he thinks, realizing that Mulligan 'fears the lancet of my art as I fear that of his. The cold steel pen.'[43] We read this, of course, just as Joyce himself is spearing Oliver Gogarty with that pen, exacting precisely the revenge that Mulligan may have feared but nevertheless failed to escape. In a review of *Finnegans Wake* in 1939, Gogarty would explicitly acknowledge this, writing that Joyce's 'style has its beginnings in resentment' and that he has effectively 'had his revenge' on the Dublin literary establishment.[44]

Gogarty was by no means the only one to recognize his potentially libellous portrait in the book. According to Ellmann, when the book first appeared 'a tremor went through quite a few of [Joyce's] countrymen, who feared the part he might have assigned to them'.[45] George Bernard Shaw wrote in the 1921 preface to *Immaturity* that 'James Joyce in his *Ulysses* has described, with a fidelity so ruthless that the book is hardly bearable, the life that Dublin offers to its young men', an opinion he simultaneously conveyed to Sylvia Beach when he called the book 'hideously real'.[46] Although the sheets had been printed privately in France, Joyce nevertheless took care to employ some pseudonyms in order to avoid the most serious risk of a defamation suit. Gogarty, therefore, appears as Mulligan; Joyce is partially figured as Stephen; and the Englishman Trench is presented as Haines. There are other such alterations, but these three seem specifically devised to help elude a potential charge of libel by at least partially obscuring both Joyce's own maliciousness and the historical antecedents of some of the work's most villainous characters. To bring a libel suit, after all, Trench or Gogarty would first have to admit that they recognized themselves in the text in order to convince a court that they had been defamed. This, in turn, would not only grant Joyce and his work a certain degree of publicity, but would simultaneously allow him to defend himself by proving the portraits in *Ulysses* to be more or less true.[47]

Despite the possible appeal of such publicity, however, Joyce remained concerned about the risks he had run. In a brief note appended to his 1967 essay, 'James Joyce's Sentimentality', Clive Hart suggests that Joyce had 'a still more cogent reason' for avoiding Dublin after 1922 than the romance of exile – namely, 'the certainty of disastrous libel actions if he returned'.[48] The decision to remain out of the reach of British courts afforded him an important bulwark, though it also appears that he did take some additional steps. A research note Richard Ellmann did not incorporate into his biography describes a conversation with A.J. Leventhal who recalls that as late as 1921 Joyce had been explicitly concerned about the threat of libel and asked if any Blooms still resided in Dublin. Leventhal assured him that they had departed, thus apparently reassuring Joyce that he could use the name of the most clearly fictional character in *Ulysses* without undue risk.[49] Had Bloom, in fact, had some sort of clear historical antecedent, the grounds for a libel case would have been quite strong, particularly since the text delves so deeply into his sexual habits and private thoughts. Both in changing the names of certain key players and even in his careful research into the text, therefore, Joyce took careful account of the laws of libel.

These initial precautions only emphasize the importance of defamation law to *Ulysses* and the novel's critique of the legal constraints that shape and define aesthetic practice. In his own attempt to disrupt the intentional fallacy, William Empson argues that rather than developing techniques (such as David Hayman's 'Arranger') for distancing the author from the text and thus affirming the supremacy of fiction, we should instead realize 'that Joyce is always present in the book – rather oppressively so, like a judge in court'.[50] Empson's metaphor is more literal than he perhaps realizes, however, because *Ulysses* puts its readers too in a strangely legalistic position, becoming precisely those jurors who, according to the tort of libel, are alone empowered to determine whether or not a particular character has a historical antecedent and whether or not he or she has been defamed.[51] This begins, as I have already suggested, when the novel itself begins atop the Martello tower, but continues throughout the text in a myriad of ways. It emerges almost comically, for example, in the conundrum of the famous 'man in the mackintosh', an unnamed character who flits mysteriously in and out of the text. Scholars have struggled for decades to arrive at possible identifications for this character, a quest stymied by a stubborn anonymity that at once embodies and satirizes our search for the historical facts behind this fiction. In his study of gamesmanship in *Ulysses*, Sebastian Knowles argues that the book 'is built on the equals sign', a figure that describes not only the parallel paths taken by Bloom and Stephen but our own attempt to locate equivalences for the characters themselves.[52] Bloom himself thematizes our search for the history behind the fiction when, after masturbating on the beach, he strolls to the edge of the tide and uses a stick to write in the sand 'I . . . AM. A' (U 13.1258, 1264). The sentence remains incomplete and any number of studies have attempted to infer the conclusion of this elliptical phrase. Joyce, however, deliberately provokes our inability to know who Bloom actually is – a mystery he quite legalistically preserved as his conversation with Leventhal indicates. Such uncertainty spirals nearly into madness in the 'Circe' episode, where names and identities shift so rapidly and so fantastically that identification becomes a kind of game or puzzle that cannot be easily resolved. Instead, as hypothetical members of the jury, we are left with a paralysing doubt. This doubt effectively exonerates Joyce, precisely because the boundary between fiction and fact cannot be fixed.

The scandal of libel, however, is more than just a component of the book's interwoven symbolic structures, for it constitutes an explicit part of the plot itself, first atop the Martello tower and later in the day when Bloom runs into Josie Breen complaining of her eccentric husband, Dennis: 'He's a caution to rattlesnakes. He's in there now with his lawbooks finding out the law of libel' (U 8.229–230). Bloom quickly learns that Dennis had received an anonymous postcard reading 'U.P.' or perhaps 'U.p.: up' (8.257, 258).[53] Like the man in the mackintosh, this card too has troubled many readers, who not only have difficulty making sense of it, but struggle to discover content so defamatory as to occasion the suit Breen intends to file 'for ten thousand pounds' in damages (8.263–4). Richard Ellmann argues that the card implies some sort of erectile dysfunction, while others have suggested that it is a reference to Dicken's *Oliver Twist*, in which the letters U.P. are used to indicate an old woman's death. Alternatively, it may simply indicate that the somewhat dotty Breen is mentally ill, the two letters signifying that, like weak whisky, he is 'under proof'.[54] All of these readings seem more or less feasible, which means that any case for libel – even if the person who sent the card could be identified – would probably fail. The case, after all, would turn on the meaning of the card and a jury would be asked to determine a particular meaning that was clearly defamatory. The multiplicity of meanings, however, makes it unlikely that a clear finding of fact could be determined. The instability of the text, in other words, which cannot be legally grounded by intention, serves as an effective defence against any charge of libel. Like much of the rest of *Ulysses*, this card can be multiply interpreted and contested, with definitive meaning held in permanent abeyance. The potentially defamatory scandals of the novel, therefore, can be at least partially deflected by the very difficulty of the text itself, the resistance to interpretation serving simultaneously as a testament to its aesthetic power and as a barrier to its prosecution.

Breen, in pursuing his unlikely suit, seeks out the services of John Henry Menton, a real Dublin solicitor with offices on Bachelor's Walk. Like many characters in the text, he also appears amidst the fantasies and nightmares of 'Circe', where Bloom – accosted by the watch and asked for his name – first identifies himself as 'Dr. Bloom, Leopold, dental surgeon' (15.721). This is the name of a real Dublin figure in 1904 and amounts to a skilful act of deception, as Bloom gives his name yet fails to properly identify himself. He then identifies his solicitors as 'Messrs John Henry Menton, 27 Bachelor's Walk' (15.730). This encounter with the guards is immediately preceded by an imagined conversation with Josie Breen, who expresses her mock horror at finding Bloom in Nighttown. Flirting with her, Bloom grows suddenly alarmed when she mentions his name: 'Not so loud my name. Whatever do you think of me? Don't give me away. Walls have ears' (15.398–399). Anxious about the possibility of being caught in a potentially scandalous position, Bloom attempts to conceal his identity behind layers of confusion and misdirection, adopting precisely the strategy that might be employed in a libel trial. Just as a jury must decide on a defamatory interpretation of a passage, so too they must also agree that the plaintiff in the case is actually the person described in the text. In suits involving non-fictional texts, this is rarely an issue, but it typically constitutes the core of an action involving films, novels or plays. In a potentially libel-lous passage describing Bloom's trip to a bordello, Joyce thus evokes the mechanisms of defamation law, once again introducing the Breens and their solicitor Menton through pseudonyms and borrowed names to elude detec-tion. Joyce already knew from Leventhal that Dr Bloom no longer lived in Dublin in 1922, but for his readers this moment would have effectively summarized one of the text's most pressing questions: Who is the histor-ical antecedent of Leopold Bloom? Were he real, after all, he would be the most defamed character in the text and his identification would no doubt spark a major scandal. We now recognize him as one of the few genu-inely fictional characters in the book, but this moment of confusion and misdirection in 'Circe' both obscures his identity and promises to reveal it, sending us into a web of historical and fictional antecedents that hint at some scandalous revelation while simultaneously resisting our investigative efforts.

Throughout *Ulysses*, Joyce deliberately and provocatively troubles the boundary between fact and fiction, thereby pitting legal and aesthetic modes of interpretation against one another in a scandalous yet creative conflict. The pleasure and the frustration of this practice is nowhere more evident than in the 'Scylla and Charybdis' episode, in which more real names are invoked than anywhere else in the text. As the scene opens in the National Library, we are immediately confronted with the figure of John Eglinton, the editor of *Dana* and a well-known man of letters. His name can be tracked through various guides, revealing details of his real and accomplished life; yet we also learn that he is not John Eglinton, that this is merely a pseud-onym he had adopted (his real name was William McGee). Furthermore, he is asking Stephen Dedalus – itself a pseudonym for James Joyce in 1904[55] – about his plans to write a book comically entitled *The Sorrows of Satan*, the title of a wildly popular novel written by Marie Corelli – also a pseudonym for Mary MacKay, who in turn thought she was the reincarnation of William Shakespeare. As if this dizzying array of displaced names is not confusing enough, the conversation is shared by A.E., the mystically initialled name taken by the writer and spiritualist George Russell. Finally, Dedalus, feeling the 'elder's gall' behind Eglinton's question about this novel, merely smiles and thinks of a fragment from a poem written by Oliver St John Gogarty, from which Buck Mulligan will recite when he later appears. This most learned episode, in which scholarly sources are drawn freely from a vast cultural archive, thus begins amidst a chaos of names and identities that deliberately disrupts any attempt to define the fictional limits of the text. By the end of the episode, this confusion is explicit, as 'MAGEEGLINJOHN' asks Stephen 'What's in a name?' (9.901–2). What indeed? As the text suggests, even Eglinton's own identity is neither fully fixed nor circumscribed by his name and one can only wonder what a jury might do were they asked to consider this text in a libel suit. If Joyce defamed Eglinton, does that mean that he also defamed Magee? Does a pseudonym have the same right to a good name that a real person has? Noting their propensity to change names and to adopt distinct public personae, Stephen calls the writers gathered in the library 'cypherjugglers' (9.411) and reminds himself to 'See this. Remember' (9.294). Stephen is every bit a cipher as well, for while we do not know if he remembers this scene, Joyce appears to have done so and recast it as part of the novel. Even more than the nightmare of 'Circe', this episode muddles any distinction between fact and fiction, preventing us from simply accepting the text as pure invention even while it endlessly insists on its historical veracity.

Amid this misdirection, 'Scylla and Charybdis' features Stephen's long-awaited theory of Shakespeare's plays, itself a kind of defamatory attempt to extract historical fact from otherwise apparently fictional texts. Mixing textual and documentary evidence, Stephen draws all manner of libellous gossip from the plays, prompting A.E. to depart and dismiss such talk as 'prying into the family life of a great man', for information that is 'interesting only to the parish clerk' (9.181, 184). In an episode that already mires us in a complex array of names and pseudonyms, however, we cannot leave with the snobbish poet and are left instead with what appears to be something like Hamlet's instructions to the players – that is, an encoded and ambiguously satirical set of instructions from the author himself about how we might go about reading the text.[56] Just as Stephen instructs his listeners in how to draw fact from fiction, so too we as readers (and perhaps even jurors) are also asked to listen to these instructions, applying them not to Shakespeare's plays, but to *Ulysses* itself.[57] Stephen crucially contends that the Bard himself played the ghost in *Hamlet*, speaking to an incarnation of his own dead son, Hamnet, about the infidelity of Anne Hathaway. Rocked by tragedy, however, he speaks to this other version of himself in an act of painful revelation. 'His beaver is up', Stephen notes of the ghost, suggesting that when Shakespeare walked on the stage his own face was visible to the audience as he related this tale of murder and adultery, making fiction 'consubstantial' with fact just as the ghost is 'the son consubstantial with the father' (9.481). This mixture of truth and invention drives Stephen's theory just as it drives our own attempts to read *Ulysses*, mired as we are in the text's deliberate and provocative refusal to abide by the laws of libel and defamation. Even this reading itself seems open to irony as Stephen concludes his performance by telling Eglinton that while he does not believe his theory, he is nevertheless willing to sell it for a guinea. This mocking conclusion again suggests the way we too should read *Ulysses*: neither as fact nor fiction but as an elaborate edifice of gossip and defamation which – like the book in the iconic photograph – can be bought yet never quite believed. 'You are a delusion', Eglinton finally tells Stephen. It is this which finally constitutes the core of Joyce's assault on the legal limits of fiction (9.1064): Stephen is indeed a delusion – a fantasy like the ghost of Hamlet's father which both appears to speak the truth and yet critically resists validation.

'Scylla and Charybdis' concludes with Buck Mulligan revealing his own satirical rendition of the proceedings in the library, a 'national immorality in three orgasms' which mocks all this theorizing as mere intellectual onanism. He reads it to Stephen, telling him that 'the disguise, I fear, is thin' (9.1178), thus rehearsing in his own little drama the same kind of lightly veiled, deeply libellous attacks that Stephen finds in Shakespeare and that we too find in *Ulysses*. The disguise is indeed thin, after all, for we do know that this is both Buck Mulligan's play and Oliver Gogarty's, just as this is both Stephen's Dublin and Joyce's own. Rather than concealing its engagement with historical reality, as Victorian fiction typically did by decorously avoiding the names of real people, Joyce takes it on directly and in the process destabilizes the autonomy of art and the legal institutions designed to maintain a critical distance between fiction and fact. This dynamic of confusion constitutes one of the most remarkable and original aspects of Joyce's work, though he was by no means alone in employing it. Literary modernism, after all, thrived on this kind of textual reprocessing, in which historical and autobiographical facts are mixed shamelessly and often libellously with fictional inventions. Ernest Hemingway, Oscar Wilde, Gertrude Stein, Virginia Woolf and Aldous Huxley are only a few of the novelists who engaged in such experiments, mixing their lives and their writing in often complicated and indeterminate ways. Unlike Joyce, however, many of these authors found themselves either threatened with lawsuits for defamation or actually dragged into court. D.H. Lawrence's *Women in Love* (1920), for example, barely escaped legal action for its brutal portrait of Lady Ottoline Morrell and texts by Wyndham Lewis and Osbert Sitwell were successfully sued and suppressed. Such law suits – like Joyce's wrangling with Maunsel's and Roberts over the names of a few pubs mentioned in *Dubliners* – may lack the romance of the obscenity trials, but they nevertheless revealed a potent legal constraint on aesthetic autonomy.

Obscenity laws for fiction have become largely antiquated and are treated as relics of an earlier and more intolerant era. The tort of defamation, however, continues to delimit and define the boundary of fiction, and it is precisely at this interface between legal constraint and aesthetic freedom that *Ulysses* was lodged. Joyce scandalously recorded 'nameless shameless-ness about everybody he ever met' and in so doing at once courted libel suits and revealed the fragility of the legal constructs on which they depend. As he learned from Roberts, even his own intention could not constitute a defence, nor could it legally guarantee the meaning of any particular passage. In *Ulysses*, therefore, he creates a work that is both blatantly libellous and yet everywhere capable of eluding that charge, in its welter of misdirected names, its aesthetic difficulty and its deconstructive ironies. As this chapter has argued, this constituted a vital aspect of the book's scandal – announced so boldly on the cover of the *Sporting Times*. Moreover, it continues to do so, though critics and readers have ignored, suppressed or failed to recognize this fact. Like the laws of obscenity and copyright which Joyce incorpor-ated and critiqued in this novel, defamation too plays a vital role in the text's exploration of the limits of fiction and the legality of literature. In a 1909 meeting after their friendship had collapsed, Gogarty told Joyce 'I don't care a damn what you say of me so long as it is literature.'[58] Joyce took him at his word and in the process attempted to undermine the very concept of literature itself, exposing the limits of its imagined autonomy while simultaneously challenging the law's ability to delimit the nature and structure of art. Long after Woolsey's decision and the novel's ascension in the canon, this remains one of the scandals of *Ulysses* that we have yet fully to confront.

## Notes

1. This photograph, in fact, has appeared on the cover of two previous works focusing on Joyce and his scandalous fictions: Bruce Arnold, *The Scandal of Ulysses: the Life and Afterlife of a Twentieth-Century Masterpiece*, revised edition (Dublin: Liffey Press, 2004), and Paul Vanderham, *James Joyce and Censorship: the Trials of Ulysses* (London: Macmillan, 1998).
2. Aramis, 'The Scandal of *Ulysses*', *Sporting Times*, 34 (1 April 1922), 4.
3. James Joyce, *Ulysses* (California: Collectors Publication Edition, nd). This is a pirated edition, printed some time in the late 1960s, which advertises an array of porno-graphic novels and magazines, often with delightfully lurid illustrations.
4. Katherine Mullin, *James Joyce, Sexuality, and Social Purity* (Cambridge: Cambridge University Press, 2003), 3.
5. James Joyce, *Selected Letters of James Joyce* (New York: Viking, 1975), 285.
6. *U.S. v. Ulysses*, 5 F. Supp. 182 (District Court, Southern District of New York, 6 Dec. 1933, sec VI); reprinted as 'Foreword', *Ulysses* (New York: Random House, 1961), xiii.
7. A complete discussion of autonomization and modernity is impossible here, but for a very brief introduction see, for example, Max Weber, 'Politics as a Vocation', in Hans Gerth and C. Wright Mills, eds, *From Max Weber: Essays in Sociology* (Oxford: Oxford University Press, 1958), 77–128; Jürgen Habermas, *Toward a Rational Society: Student Protest, Science and Politics* (Boston: Beacon, 1970); and Pierre Bourdieu, 'The Market for Symbolic Goods', in *The Field of Cultural Production* (New York: Columbia University Press, 1993), 112–41.

8. For a summary of many of the legal issues involving copyright and *Ulysses* see Robert Spoo, 'Injuries, Remedies, Moral Rights, and the Public Domain', *James Joyce Quarterly*, 37 (2000): 333–66. Spoo's argument that the 1922 edition of *Ulysses* may, in fact, not have copyright protection in the United States appears in Spoo, 'Copyright and the Ends of Ownership: the Case for a Public Domain *Ulysses* in America', in *Joyce Studies Annual 1999*, ed. Thomas F. Staley (Austin: University of Texas Press, 1999), 5–62.

9. Pierre Bourdieu, *The Rules of Art: Genesis and Structure of the Literary Field* (Stanford: Stanford University Press, 1996), 47.

10. Paul Saint-Amour, *The Copywrights: Intellectual Property and the Literary Imagination* (Ithaca: Cornell University Press, 2003).

11. Hugh Kenner, 'Joyce and Modernism', in *James Joyce*, ed. Harold Bloom (Philadelphia: Chelsea House, 2003), 101.

12. Cited in Frank Budgen, *James Joyce and the Making of Ulysses* (New York: Harrison Smith and Robert Hass, 1934), 69.

13. James Joyce, *Finnegans Wake* (New York: Penguin, 1939), 179, 182.

14. Cited in Richard Ellmann, *James Joyce* (Oxford: Oxford University Press, 1982), 310. The various manuscript copies of the story contain different versions of this passage, which was continually rewritten in an effort to secure publication. For a full record see *The James Joyce Archive*, ed. Michael Groden et al. (New York: Garland, 1977–1979), 4: 181–269. The final version of the text simply refers to Queen Victoria as Edward VII's 'old mother'. James Joyce, *Dubliners* (New York: Viking, 1967), 132.

15. Joyce, *Dubliners*, 132.

16. Ellmann, 314.

17. Ellmann, 315.

18. James Joyce, *Letters of James Joyce* (New York: Viking, 1966), 2: 291.

19. Francis Holt, *The Law of Libel* (London: W. Reed, 1812), 84.

20. Ellmann, 328.

21. Ellmann, 329–30.

22. *Collected Letters of James Joyce*, 1: 64.

23. *Parmiter v. Coupland*, 151 Eng. Rep. 340 (Exch. Pleas 1840).

24. Holt, *The Law of Libel*, 49. The Constitution of Ireland (*Bunreacht na haÈireann*), adopted in 1937, states in article 40, section 3 that 'The State shall, in particular, by its laws protect as best it may from unjust attack and, in the case of injustice done, vindicate the life, person, good name, and property rights of every citizen', thus explicitly granting its citizens protection from defamation.

25. Dan B. Dobbs, *The Law of Torts* (St Paul, Minn.: West Group, 2000), 1120.

26. This is one of the many ways in which the law governing libel differs from that of slander. Thus, in order to bring a general case for slander (called slander *per quod*), a plaintiff must not only prove that the defendant uttered injurious words, but that this act directly caused some financial or pecuniary loss beyond mere damage to one's reputation. There is a special subset of slanderous speech, however, termed 'slander *per se*', which, like libel, presumes damage without any special proof. This includes speech which charges that the plaintiff has committed a criminal offence, is ill with venereal disease, has committed some sexual offence, or is unsuited for his or her profession (see Dobbs, *The Law of Torts*, 1140–1).

27. Dobbs, *The Law of Torts*, 1128.

28. In the published text of *Dubliners* as well as in the manuscript and typescript drafts preserved in the James Joyce Archive, the name of the railway company in 'A Painful Case' is not directly given. Since Joyce mentions this specific objection

in a letter, however, it is reasonable to assume that some version of the story did name the company specifically. Just as he excised the description of Queen Victoria as a 'bloody old bitch', literally pasting a new version into his notebook, so Joyce may also have deleted this specific reference to the railroad company in an effort to shore up his defence against a libel charge. See *Collected Letters of James Joyce*, 2: 312.

29. Ellmann, 331.
30. William Wimsatt, 'The Intentional Fallacy', *The Verbal Icon: Studies in the Meaning of Poetry* (Lexington: University of Kentucky Press, 1954), 3–20.
31. *Bolton v. O'Brien* (1885) 16 LR Ir 97, 108.
32. Stanislaus Joyce, *The Dublin Diary of Stanislaus Joyce* (London: Faber and Faber, 1962), 12.
33. Herbert Gorman, *James Joyce: His First Forty Years* (New York: B.W. Huebsh, 1944), 119, 134.
34. *Ulysses* was suppressed in Great Britain not at trial but through the actions of the Home Office. For a detailed description of these proceedings, see Carmelo Medina Casado, 'Sifting through Censorship: the British Home Office *Ulysses* Files (1922–1936)', *James Joyce Quarterly*, 37 (2000), 479–508.
35. Cited in *Irish Times*, 9 October 1954.
36. George Levine, *The Realistic Imagination: English Fiction from Frankenstein to Lady Chatterley* (Chicago: University of Chicago Press, 1981), 8.
37. Caroline Levine, *The Serious Pleasures of Suspense: Victorian Realism and Narrative Doubt* (Charlottesville: University of Virginia Press, 2003), 17.
38. Typescript note, untitled, from the Richard Ellmann Collection, McFarlin Library Special Collections, University of Tulsa, series I, folder 89.
39. 'Author and Wit Was Prototype of Character in *Ulysses*', *New York Times* (23 September 1957). Richard J. Finneran, 'Buck Mulligan Revisited', *Papers on Language and Literature*, 16 (1980), 209, contends that Yeats was particularly sympathetic to 'the damage done to Gogarty's reputation' by *Ulysses* and did what he could to advance his career. Gogarty's biographer, Ulick O'Connor, took up the cause as well, serving as a witness for the plaintiff in Dodd's libel suit against the BBC.
40. Claire Culleton, *Names and Naming in Joyce* (Madison: University of Wisconsin Press, 1994), 107.
41. Virginia Woolf, *The Voyage Out* (Oxford: Oxford University Press, 1992), 224.
42. H.G. Wells, Preface to *The World of William Clissold* (New York: George H. Doran and Co., 1926), iv.
43. James Joyce, *Ulysses*, ed. Hans Walter Gaber et al. (New York: Random House, 1986), 11.150–4. All subsequent references to this edition of the text will appear parenthetically, citing episode and line numbers.
44. Oliver St John Gogarty, 'Roots in Resentment: James Joyce's Revenge', *Observer* (7 May 1939).
45. Ellmann, 530.
46. Elmann, 507.
47. There was considerable precedent for such a strategic use of litigation. In 1878, the American painter James Abbott McNeill Whistler brought a libel suit against an elderly John Ruskin who had called *Nocturne in Black and Gold: the Falling Rocket*, 'a pot of paint [flung] in the public's face'. The trial was widely covered by the press and helped cement Whistler's own growing celebrity image, despite the fact that he won the case yet received only a token sum in damages. For an account of the trial see Whistler, *The Gentle Art of Making Enemies* (New York: G.P. Putnam's,

1890) and Linda Merrill, *A Pot of Paint: Aesthetics on Trial in Whistler v. Ruskin* (Washington, DC: Smithsonian Institution Press, 1992). Oscar Wilde's criminal prosecution of Lord Queensbury in 1895 may have been partially inspired by Whistler's success, though it produced disastrous results when it ranged beyond matters of taste and ambiguity to the intractable facts of Wilde's sexual life.

48. Clive Hart, 'James Joyce and Sentimentality', *James Joyce Quarterly*, 41 (2003), 35–36.

49. Typescript page titled 'Ulysses' from the Richard Ellmann Collection, McFarlin Library Special Collections, University of Tulsa, series I, folder 89.

50. William Empson, *Using Biography* (Cambridge: Harvard University Press, 1984), 225. For Hayman's influential theory of the 'Arranger', which is designed to mediate between authorial intention and the intentional fallacy, see David Hayman, *'Ulysses', the Mechanics of Meaning* (Madison: University of Wisconsin Press, 1982).

51. In the common law, the power of interpretation is explicitly reserved to the jury as the triers of fact, but before a suit can proceed a judge must first determine that words can, in fact, bear some defamatory meaning. For a full description of this process see Dobbs, *The Law of Torts*, 1131–4.

52. Sebastian D.G. Knowles, *The Dublin Helix: the Life of Language in 'Ulysses'* (Gainesville: University of Florida Press, 2001), 7.

53. As is so often the case in *Ulysses*, the card itself presents a difficult textual crux. Even its potentially libellous content is unclear, since when Bloom initially reads it he sees only the two letters, yet when Josie Breen recites its contents she says 'u.p: up' (8.258). She may simply be running the letters together, or the card itself may contain the colon and word 'up' as well as the letters. The card later resurfaces in 'Circe' (8.485) where Alf Bergan recites it, but since this is an essentially hallucinatory event, it does not resolve this curious aporia which leaves us not only unsure of the card's meaning, but of its contents as well.

54. Robert Byrnes, ' "U.P.: up" Proofed', *James Joyce Quarterly*, 21 (1984), 175–6.

55. Joyce used the pseudonym 'Stephen Dædelus' to sign the first version of 'The Sisters' in 1904, thus only further compounding the interplay of real and fiction names which complicate this episode.

56. Ellmann, 364 argues that 'according to friends' Joyce took this theory of Shakespeare's plays more seriously than Stephen does, suggesting 'that *Ulysses* divulges more than an impersonal and detached picture of Dublin life', but is instead a *roman-à-clef*.

57. Mark Shechner, *Joyce in Nighttown: a Psychoanalytic Inquiry into* Ulysses (Berkeley: University of California Press, 1974), contends that 'Shakespeare, then, is only the pretext of "Scylla"; James Joyce is the text' (27).

58. Ulick O'Connor, *Oliver St John Gogarty: a Poet and His Times* (London: J. Cape, 1963), 84.

# 2
# 'The aristocracy of intellect': Inversion and Inheritance in Radclyffe Hall's *The Well of Loneliness*

*Susan Watkins*

The successful prosecution of *The Well of Loneliness* for obscenity has become one of the landmark cases in the history of literature and censorship in the UK in the first half of the twentieth century. The novel's subject matter – same-sex love between women – was undoubtedly controversial, but its plea that 'sexual inversion' should be considered as congenital and there-fore morally blameless was particularly scandalous. Radclyffe Hall's deploy-ment of the theories of sexologists in *The Well of Loneliness* has been well documented.[1] Indeed, a central focus of critical attention has been the question of whether the popular dissemination of such ideas as 'congen-ital inversion' (as a result of publicity surrounding the novel's trial) proved positive or negative for the expression and explanation of same-sex love between women. Did the novel create the possibility for a 'reverse discourse', ultimately defining a distinct sexual and personal identity with attendant human rights for women who desired other women, or did it pathologize and demonize what had previously been perceived as innocent romantic friendship?[2]

That inversion could be part of human nature from birth is central to the argument Hall makes in *The Well*, as well as to political appropriations of the text that argued for a more tolerant approach to same-sex love. Dollimore claims that: 'bizarre as it may now seem, many subsequent devel-opments in sexual liberation and radical sexual politics can be traced back to the kind of appropriations made by Hall, even those developments which would have appalled her, for example the idea of sexual deviance as poten-tially revolutionary'.[3] Yet the idea that inversion was innate was certainly also a key factor in the judicial correspondence concerning the text and in the magistrate's judgement that the novel was obscene. Although it is not the narrator's sole explanation and justification of Stephen's identity, the model of congenital inversion dominates the novel.[4] In borrowing this model from the sexological literature she had read Hall also makes use of contemporary pseudo-scientific ideas about the *hereditary* status of congenital inversion. However, she transforms those ideas in a number of important ways to create her own model of the inheritance and transmission of lesbian identity. This chapter argues that Hall's notion of hereditary 'lesbianism' is deliberately aligned with a different kind of inheritance: one belonging to a specifically aristocratic, English tradition. I claim that it was the juxtaposition of these two notions of inheritance that partly engendered the novel's scandal, particularly in the context of postwar anxiety about the future of the nation. Even more scandalous was Hall's vision of the novel itself as a means of propagating and disseminating this inheritance. In this essay I will place the novel in various important contexts. Setting her work against that of a number of sexologists, the chapter will examine how Hall revises contemporary ideas about hereditary congenital inversion. Further, I will consider the biographical and social context of Hall's writing in order to draw out her specific aims in defining Stephen's social status. The chapter will also examine Hall's construction of the notion of literary vocation and the literary text itself as an inheritance that carries with it particular responsibilities and freedoms. In addition, the chapter makes use of papers from the National Archives concerning the trial (some of which have only recently been made publically available to scholars[5]) to analyse the impact of ideas about inversion on those with the power to suppress the novel.

## Sexology, inversion and inheritance

A constituent element in the taxonomies devised by the sexologists to describe women's sexuality was what might now crudely be termed the 'nature versus nurture' question and this clearly influenced Hall greatly. Havelock Ellis (whose work Hall had read and who provided a preface for *The Well*) had previously opined that:

> Sexual inversion, therefore, remains a congenital anomaly, to be classed with other congenital abnormalities which have psychic concomitants. At the very least such congenital abnormality usually exists as a predisposition to inversion. It is probable that many persons go through the world with a congenital predisposition to inversion which always remains latent and unroused; in others the instinct is so strong that it forces its own way in spite of all obstacles; in others, again, the predisposition is weaker, and a powerful exciting cause plays the predominant part.[6]

Richard von Krafft-Ebing also makes a working distinction between 'homosexual feeling as an acquired manifestation in both sexes' and 'homosexual feeling as an abnormal congenital manifestation'.[7] (After her father's death, the heroine of *The Well* discovers Krafft-Ebing's work in a locked bookcase in his study, heavily annotated with references to herself.) Edward Carpenter's *The Intermediate Sex* (1896), which is not explicitly referenced in *The Well* and yet, as Doan suggests,[8] is central to it, also develops an argument about nature's role in determining sexual identity: 'Nature, it might appear, in mixing the elements which go to compose each individual, does not always keep her two groups of ingredients – which represent the two sexes – properly apart, but often throws them crosswise in a somewhat baffling manner, now this way and now that.'[9] The metaphor of nature working 'crosswise' is clearly congruent with Ellis's notion of inversion as a 'turn' of the 'sexual impulse' towards 'individuals of the same sex'.[10] This diagonal or inward movement is clearly opposed to the vertical, outgoing metaphors implicit in ideas of inheritance and heterosexual relationship, the significance of which will be examined later.

If ideas about what is 'congenital' are being invoked to explain sexuality at this time, then it is important to explore exactly what would have been understood by the term. 'Congenital' is defined in the 1933 edition of the OED as 'existing or dating from one's birth, belonging to one from birth, born with one'.[11] The word was admitted into the sixth edition of the Academy's dictionary in 1835. As this definition suggests, the fact that something is present at birth does not necessarily connect with or imply the idea that the congenital element might be inherited. Any number of different factors might have caused the presence rather than absence at birth of the congenital element in question. Ellis considered a number of possible reasons for the manifestation of inversion, including latent organic bisexuality, hormonal or 'germ' imbalance, arrested development and infantilism in the sexual organs,[12] but ultimately placed it alongside colour-blindness, congenital idiocy, congenital genius and 'instinctive criminality' as 'a "sport," or variation, one of those organic aberrations which we see throughout living nature'.[13] He twice uses the organic, biblical (and potentially blasphemous) metaphor of seeds falling on already receptive soil to explain the connection between congenital predisposition and actual manifestation of inversion.[14] That hereditary factors are present as important, perhaps we might even say 'latent', explanations for congenital inversion in both the work of the sexologists and in *The Well of Loneliness* is apparent in a number of ways. Ellis explicitly addresses this question, stating that 'this hereditary character of inversion . . . is a fact of great significance, and, as it occurs in cases with which I am well-acquainted, I can have no doubt concerning the existence of the tendency'.[15] Krafft-Ebing designates congenital homosexuality as 'a functional sign of degeneration, and as a partial manifestation of a neuro-psychopathic state, in most cases hereditary'.[16] The question of whether or not hereditary congenital inversion signifies progressive disease and the implications arising will be considered later. In addition to explicitly commenting on heredity, moreover, both Krafft-Ebing and Ellis make use in their method of reporting case histories, of references to family history and any evidence of inherited disorders therein. These family histories are prominently placed (as is conventional in medical case histories) at the beginning of each history, either in the first person, in the patient's 'own' words or in the third person. The presence of these accounts of hereditary disease at the beginning of each case history affords them an explanatory power as frames for the individual, mostly first-person accounts that follow. Somerville claims that the sexologists' obsession with anthropometry (the taking of extensive measurements of the body) evidences an 'assumption that the body was a legible text, with various keys or languages available for reading its symbolic codes'.[17] The 'key or language' of inheritance (apparent in the family histories) works in the same way as continual measuring of the body to frame and thus explain, interpret, or unlock the account of sexual identity given in the case history.

Hall's insistence on the congenital theory and its attendant implication of hereditary sexual identity can be seen not only in The Well of Loneliness but also in her dismay at the famous Colonel Barker case of 1929 and in her letters to the lover of her later years, Evguenia Souline. The case of Valerie Barker, who lived as a man for six years, pretended to be an officer and married a woman, occupied the press and occasioned the following comment from Hall: 'I would like to see her drawn & quartered... a mad *pervert* of the most undesirable type.'[18] The implied distinction that Hall draws here between inversion (authentic; expressive) versus perversion (inauthentic; performative) suggests her concern to stress the inevitability and lack of choice in her own sexual identity, which is mapped on the body in The Well in terms of congenital difference. Later, in a letter attempting to persuade Souline (not yet her lover) that their feelings are not 'wrong' she writes:

> I have never felt an impulse towards a man in all my life, this because I am a congenital invert. For me to sleep with a man would be 'wrong' because it would be an outrage against nature. Can't you try to understand, to believe that we exist – we people who are not of the so-called normal? Where's your medical knowledge? [Souline was a trained nurse] – we do exist and believe me you must not think us perverted. I am not perverted my very dearest heart, nor am I in any way a devil and evil. I have done my share of good, hard work in life as many another invert is doing – Do try, for my sake and for your own, to look upon inversion as a part of nature.[19]

In The Well of Loneliness Stephen is born with narrow hips and wide shoulders and strongly resembles her father. Not only the inheritance of her masculine appearance, but also her gender identification and sexual orientation appear to come directly from her father, a fact that disturbs and 'queers' her pitch with her mother, Lady Anna: 'She [Anna] would think: I ought to be proud of the likeness, proud and happy and glad when I see it! Then back would come flooding that queer antagonism that amounted almost to anger.'[20] Stephen's likeness to her father becomes more prominent as the text progresses. Here Hall echoes her own experience, as her own resemblance to her father provoked irritation in her mother, who insisted that 'not an ounce of the child's blood...came from her'.[21] Hall's repudiation of any kind of maternal inheritance for Stephen carries, as Backus suggests, racial connotations. In making use of Victorian and Edwardian beliefs about Irishness to represent Lady Anna as 'extralinguistic, sensual, emotional, feminine, and also vindictive and childlike or child*ish*', Hall finds an effectual means of 'masculinizing and Anglicizing her inverted protagonist'.[22]

## Class and inheritance

Stephen's inheritance from her father thus encompasses more than mere physical likeness. As the only child, Stephen is next in line to the family property of a substantial country seat (Morton), an accompanying legacy and a corresponding social position in the community, which requires the typical 'gentleman's education' and leisure pursuits (hunting, fencing). Hall's investment in a particular construction of Stephen's aristocratic background has been discussed by critics, often as an irritating elitism which makes the novel's message about sexual tolerance less valid (because class-bound). Ruehl comments that 'the appeal to moral excellence is made in specifically class terms, feeding into current ideas of lesbianism as an aristocratic aberration'.[23] Halberstam remarks that 'John was a social conservative who did not link the outrage of sexual intolerance to other forms of political intolerance.'[24] Stephen's class position is often read as a straightforward representation of Hall's own social position. Bonnie Kime Scott, for example, asserts that 'the "aristocratic" label...was appropriate to Hall's class, and that of the protagonist of *The Well*'.[25] I want to suggest, however, that Hall's deployment of traditional class-bound notions of inheritance is not just a thoughtless reflection of her own privilege but has important connections with her construction of sexuality as congenital and hereditary.

The novel opens with an idyllic evocation of the aristocratic English pastoral tradition where both the landscape and the country house it contains are gendered feminine. Skinner contends that the house 'traditionally functions as a metaphor for heterosexual order'.[26] The narrator comments: 'the house itself...is indeed like certain lovely women who, now old, belong to a bygone generation – women who in youth were passionate but seemly; difficult to win but when won, all-fulfilling' (7). When pregnant with Stephen, Anna regards the landscape with great complaisance as follows: 'these Malvern hills in their beauty...seemed to hold a new meaning. They were like pregnant women, full-bosomed, courageous, great green-girdled mothers of splendid sons' (8–9). The disquiet when the longed-for son turns out to be a girl is, in effect, ignored. Sir Philip, Stephen's father, recognizes her difference early and determines to treat her like a boy. Stephen is given a boy's name and educated and tutored in the ways of the English gentleman, with a fine seat for hunting and a well-trained, scholarly mind, encouraged by Sir Philip as protection against the future problems she may encounter because of her sexuality. Stephen grows up with a deep love of Morton, a 'queer feeling; it was too big for Stephen . . . the spirit of Morton would be part of her then, and would always remain some-where deep down within her, aloof and untouched by the years that must follow' (32).

This cultural inheritance is matched, after her father's death, by the literal inheritance of money and property. The fly in the ointment of this solid gentleman's upbringing emerges *only* when Stephen becomes involved with a neighbour's wife, Angela Crossby. The Crossbys are positioned as nouveau riche. He is a Birmingham hardware magnate and she was formerly on the stage. The county set is 'naturally' resentful at their arrival in the neighbour-hood and purchase of one of the best local houses. Angela Crossby begins a rather desultory and largely platonic relationship with Stephen, resisting further involvement on the grounds that Stephen is unable to marry her. Lady Anna's discovery of the relationship precipitates a crisis that forces Stephen's rupture with her mother, with Morton and the class position and cultural inheritance it represents. Angela's husband remarks that 'I'll hound her [Stephen] out of the county before I've done' (200). Her mother sees her actions as an insult to her father:

> 'Above all is this thing a sin against the father who bred you, the father whom you dare to resemble. You dare to look like your father, and your face is a living insult to his memory, Stephen. I shall never be able to look at you now without thinking of the deadly insult of your face and your body to the memory of the father who bred you. I can only thank God that your father died before he was asked to endure this great shame.' (203)

Unlike Sir Philip, who attempted to position Stephen's congenital inversion as consistent with her *class* inheritance of property, money and a certain social position, Lady Anna views Stephen's sexuality as entirely incommen-surate with Morton and all that it represents. She encourages her to leave. It would seem that the difference in her parents' responses is not merely a consequence of Sir Philip's familiarity with contemporary scholarship on inversion. Instead, it is an attempt to suggest that in seeing his own likeness in Stephen, Sir Philip recognizes the hereditary nature of her sexual orienta-tion and aligns it with other inheritances he has passed on to her. Stephen attempts to retain this conception of herself, arguing that 'As a man loves a woman, that was how I loved – protectively, like my father . . . if I could have

I'd have married her and brought her home – I wanted to bring her home here to Morton... it was you and my father who made this body' (204). Thus, I would argue that the rupture with Morton is traumatic for Stephen not merely because it involves leaving the family home and a familiar social environment but also because it entails isolation from a social position and culture that is recognizable for Stephen in class terms; one which, through the paternal line, makes her sexuality legible. Not only is Stephen hounded 'out of the county' but also out of the country, eventually settling in Paris, where her sexual identity remains legible, but only as one of a perverse community of sexual exiles.

An examination of Radclyffe Hall's social and financial position makes her intentions regarding Stephen's situation clear. Unlike Stephen, Hall was not quite of the 'top drawer'. Her two most recent biographers, Sally Cline and Diana Souhami, establish that her family was, on the Hall side, upper middle-class, including doctors, lawyers and clergymen. It was her great-grandfather who added the name Radcliffe (at this point spelt with an 'i') and her grandfather who traced the family descent back to Shakespeare and took out armorial bearings. A physician, he was rewarded with a knighthood for his work on chest disease. The family seems to have been much more aspirational gentry than aristocracy. Cline comments:

> Although she expressed scorn for her grandfather's status-seeking, John later admitted: 'There are times when I am glad that he had the foresight to entail our handful of family portraits. For I feel that ancestral matters are now too much ignored, that the world cannot go on existing without roots and above all perhaps without traditions. Am I perhaps a snob?'[27]

Hall's father, Radclyffe Radclyffe Hall (known as 'Rat') was, unlike the scholarly Sir Philip, a somewhat louche and feckless character according to Souhami.[28]

Unlike Stephen, Hall's inheritance of her father's estate and personal fortune was complicated by her parents' divorce and her mother's remarriage. Both Souhami and Cline suggest that Hall's mother resented the fact that her personal allowance (fixed as part of the initial decree for separation) was reduced in the final divorce settlement as a consequence of claiming against the grandfather's will on her daughter's behalf.[29] When Hall's father died his estate was held in trust for Hall until she reached the age of 21. During this time it is alleged that her mother and stepfather mismanaged and exploited the fund to suit themselves, which subsequently provoked many arguments between mother and daughter. Cline concludes that 'throughout her life Radclyffe Hall was highly responsible in her handling of money, but also saw it as a means of acquiring love or running relationships'.[30] Her inability to marry her partners and provide financial stability was a source of much regret, particularly in the case of Evguenia Souline, who was more financially vulnerable than Mabel Batten or Una Troubridge.

In the novel Hall gives Stephen the social position and stable family background that she did not herself possess. This is not merely a matter of personal fantasy, I would suggest, but a strategy which works to position Stephen's sexuality as a stable and legible inheritance, an intrinsic part of her lineage. This is nowhere more obvious than in the scene where she chooses a magnificent pearl ring as a birthday present for Angela Crossby. Although she is unable to marry her beloved, the ring is clearly meant to suggest a symbolic betrothal of sorts. Hugely expensive, it is also an ostentatious display of Stephen's capacity to provide for Angela materially, even if she cannot protect her in law. The proprietor of the jeweller's shop recognizes Stephen's resemblance to her father and explains that he knew her father well and made her mother's engagement ring for him:

'Did *you* make that ring?'
'I did, Miss Gordon. I remember quite well his showing me a miniature of Lady Anna – I remember his words. He said: "She's so pure that only the purest stones are fit to touch her finger." You see, he'd known me ever since he was at Eton, that's why he spoke of your mother to me – I felt deeply honoured. Ah, yes – dear, dear – your father was young then and very much in love...'
She said suddenly: 'Is this pearl as pure as those diamonds?'
And he answered: 'It's without a blemish.' (166)

In a series of symbolic equations, the purity of the diamonds in the engagement ring is aligned with Lady Anna herself, with the love Sir Philip felt for her, and then transposed to Stephen's attachment to Angela. Of course this is ironic, in that the pearl symbolizes grief and it has already been indicated to the reader that Angela is not worthy of Stephen's attentions (partly perhaps because she is of an inferior class). Of more significance is what follows. Stephen takes out her cheque book and asks the jeweller if he will require some kind of reference. The jeweller replies: ' "Your face is your reference, If I may be allowed to say so, Miss Gordon"' (167). Stephen's inherited likeness to her father again figures as evidence of her social respectability, which makes her sexuality an honourable inheritance also. This is marked in the scene by the fact that Stephen has to explain that she is buying a ring for a woman friend and begins to feel 'rather self-conscious' (166). We are told that the jeweller is 'openly staring' (166), with the implication that the stare is provoked by sexual curiosity. However, it is exactly at this point that the jeweller asks about the family resemblance, which neutralizes the threat of 'queer' sexuality and explains it away by subsuming it within family history and heterosexual romance.

Radford contends that the novel's dependence on popular heterosexual romance forms constitutes 'a complex irony';[31] certainly, in attempting to position congenital inversion as part of an honourable aristocratic tradition Hall could be accused of elitism. However, her decision needs to be recognized for its subversiveness in a number of contemporary contexts, particularly in relation to sexological and eugenic views about the class distribution of homosexuality, which are almost inseparable from ideas about its frequency in particular races and nationalities. Havelock Ellis writes that:

> On the whole, the evidence shows that among lower races homosexual practices are regarded with considerable indifference, and the real invert, if he exists among them, as doubtless he does exist, generally passes unperceived or joins some sacred caste which sanctifies his exclusively homosexual inclinations.
>
> Even in Europe today a considerable lack of repugnance to homosexual practices may be found among the lower classes. In this matter, as folklore shows in so many other matters, the uncultured man of civilization is linked to the savage.[32]

The conflation of class and race here is not unusual. Somerville makes it clear that 'in scientific and medical studies from this period, "race" could refer to groupings based variously on geography, religion, class or colour' arguing that 'assumptions about race shaped medical models of sexuality and gender'.[33] It is a paradox that despite Ellis's discussion of homosexuality in relation to lower-class status and savagery, both he and (particularly) Carpenter were also keen to associate sexual inversion with artistic aptitude and moral superiority. Carpenter even spoke of the intermediate sex as 'remarkable and (we think) indispensable types of character in whom there is such a union or balance of the feminine and masculine qualities that these people become to a great extent the interpreters of men and women to each other'.[34] Although there is considerable variety in the sexologists' perspectives on the appearance of inversion in particular classes and races, opinion on this particular matter appears to split along a single faultline. Inversion is viewed either as symptomatic of progressive degeneration or as evidence of evolutionary specialization. Siobhan Somerville contends that:

> One of the most important ways in which the discourses of race and sexuality [and, I would suggest, class] intertwined during this period was through the concept of degeneracy, understood as a kind of reverse evolutionary process, in which the usual progression towards more 'civilized' mental and physical development was replaced with regression instead, resulting in a weakened nervous system and the emergence of 'primitive' physical and mental traits...Darwinian models of evolution also held that, as organisms evolved through a process of natural selection, they

showed greater signs of sexual differentiation. As a result, sexual characteristics became a key site for establishing 'normal' and 'degenerative'
anatomy and a perceived lack of sexual differentiation between male and
female signalled degeneracy.[35]

Krafft-Ebing believed congenital homosexuality to be 'a functional sign of
degeneration'[36] whereas Ellis argued that 'it is now widely recognised that
we gain little by describing inversion as a degeneration'.[37] However, both
were alert to the eugenic implications of inherited congenital inversion. Ellis
commented that 'the tendency to sexual inversion in eccentric and neur-
otic families seems merely to be nature's merciful method of winding up
a concern which, from her point of view, has ceased to be profitable'.[38]
The implication here is that sexual inversion may serve nature and the
economy; preventing the reproduction and transmission of other undesirable hereditary traits (eccentricity; neurosis) by diverting the 'normal' sexual
instinct away from heterosexual reproductive sex. Of course the implications of such a statement are key in much of the later sexological work
on race and eugenics. Burdett suggests that: 'biological heredity made sex
the court at which the future would be decided, a future which would be
one of improvement and progress or one of degeneration and decay'.[39] The
category of the 'feeble-minded' (which no doubt included the invert) should
be discouraged from reproducing. Ellis argues that 'Feeble-mindedness is an
absolute dead-weight on the race. It is an evil that is unmitigated... the
unquestionable fact that in any degree it is highly inheritable renders it a
deteriorating poison to the race.'[40]

## Nationalism and postwar anxiety

The situation in 1928, ten years after the end of the First World War, also
emphasized the necessity to encourage the reproduction of only the 'health-
iest' traits. A cultural milieu developed that focused on the urgent restocking
of the nation with able-bodied (and able-minded) young men to replace
those lost in the war. Andrea Lewis contends:

> during the inter-war years in Britain... lesbianism was particularly
> subversive of national, and even imperial goals... In particular, the British
> nation needed people to replenish its citizenry after the war and occupy
> and administer its colonies. The declining birth rate since the close of
> the nineteenth century helped to undermine the national ideology based
> on the premise that population is power. This call to British nationals to
> serve their country placed a heavy emphasis on the need for reproduction,
> particularly for women.[41]

In this context Hall's achievement in *The Well of Loneliness*, is, as Doan
suggests, to place Stephen's congenital inversion not as an indication of

inherited degeneracy but rather as a sign of evolutionary specialization.[42] Stephen's inversion accompanies her typical aristocratic love for country and nation and this is a consequence of her inheritance of a particular class position. It is this nexus of qualities that makes Stephen particularly suited for war-work:

> As though gaining courage from the terror that is war, many a one who was even as Stephen, had crept out of her hole and come into the daylight and faced her country: 'Well, here I am, will you take me or leave me?' And England had taken her, asking no questions – she was strong and efficient, she could fill a man's place, she could organize too, given scope for her talent. (274)

Indeed the contrast between the heterosexual woman and the woman invert and their rather different capacities in relation to the war effort persists. Hall writes that 'even really nice women with hairpins often found their less orthodox sisters quite useful' (275). After all, inverts can start engines, do accounts and lend jumpers because they don't feel the cold. In effect, the war makes it possible for those women who have been born with particular qualities that tend to accompany inversion to make those qualities and the natures that have produced them visible. Hall's militaristic message is that a 'battalion' (275) of congenital inverts was formed as a result of an evolutionary specialization that was of as crucial significance to the war effort as the more familiar capacity of heterosexual women to reproduce the next generation in the face of mass slaughter.

Hall based Stephen's experiences during the war on those of a friend, Toupie Lowther. Cline suggests that she resented not being able to leave her frail lover Mabel Batten and join up or go to the Front with an ambulance unit. Her 'frustration... told on her nerves and became the impetus for her fictional portrayals of women who had found satisfaction in work at the front'.[43] Hall clearly links Stephen's sexuality to a particularly English kind of national heroism that is only possible for inverted women of a certain class and upbringing. Indeed, the value she placed on possessing a secure national identity can be seen during the 1930s when she became obsessed with getting French naturalization for her lover Evguenia Souline, who was a White Russian émigré living in Paris with Nansen status.[44] As Glasgow explains:

> Nansens were in some ways restricted. Issued by no recognized govern-ment, they were not backed by international treaties – or sanctions – that could be invoked in dealing with criminals, political agitators, or other undesirables. So each country honouring Nansens found it necessary to impose restraints congruent with its circumstances and the number and nature of the activities of its refugees.[45]

Souline was unable to travel freely outside France, which made her growing relationship with Hall, who was still living primarily with Una Troubridge, rather difficult to manage, particularly in the context of 1930s political developments. Some of the more unpleasant aspects of Hall's attachment to traditional ideas of class and nation, such as an interest in fascism and an anti-Semitic streak, have been commented on by both biographers and the editor of her letters to Souline.[46] What was scandalous in *The Well of Loneliness*, however, was precisely its construction of a lesbian sexual identity entirely enmeshed within the most traditional patrilineal aspects of English aristocratic life and culture. How Hall envisages the 'passing on' of that tradition to the next generation is also innovative in its recognition of the importance of culture as something that can be transmitted to others as a literary inheritance.

## Literary vocation and inheritance

As well as recognizing her sexual difference, Stephen early on recognizes her literary vocation. Indeed the latter is often justification for the former and vice versa, as Puddle, Stephen's former governess and fellow invert, suggests: 'You've got work to do – come and do it! Why, just because you are what you are, you may actually find that you've got an advantage. You may write with a curious double insight – write both men and women from a personal knowledge. Nothing's completely misplaced or wasted, I'm sure of that – and we're all part of nature' (208). Stephen's literary calling is another part of her paternal inheritance. Her father did not write but was a cultured man of letters and, as we saw earlier, encouraged her scholarship. The link between her literary abilities and her inversion is also one that the sexologists noted. Ellis discusses many literary figures in a section on the 'history' of homosexuality, although these are all male.[47] Krafft-Ebing notes the link with 'brilliant endowment in art'[48] and Carpenter comments on 'the instinctive artistic nature of the male of this class'.[49] The fact that Stephen's congenital inversion is linked with her artistic ability and her privileged position gives her a unique duty, as Puddle suggests, to write the experience of the woman invert. Initially she resists this imperative. Her first novel, *The Furrow*, which is a great success, is a story of 'quite simple people, humble people sprung from the soil, from the same kind soil that had nurtured Morton' (213). She at first thinks that this novel has nothing to do with her own experience of inversion, but realises that it is actually part of her 'curious craving for the normal' (213). Hall concludes:

> These people had drawn life and strength from their creator. Like infants they had sucked at her breasts of inspiration, and drawn from them blood, waxing wonderfully strong; demanding, compelling thereby recognition. For surely thus only are fine books written, they must somehow partake

of the miracle of blood – the strange and terrible miracle of blood, the giver of life, the purifier, the great final expiation. (214)

In an intensely Christological metaphorical nexus, Stephen's first novel is both her child (the inheritor of her bloodline) and a literal atonement for the 'sin' of inversion. Although the equation of book to child is not an unfamiliar one for a woman writer to make, it might appear to be curious, merely compensatory, for a woman writer who never expected to have children because she would never have heterosexual reproductive sex. However, what is of significance here is Hall's attempt to think her inversion forwards as well as backwards. Hall has positioned Stephen's sexual identity as an inheritance that works in traditional manner along the vertical axis of the patriarchal line (rather than in terms of a turn inward or 'crosswise' as we saw in Carpenter and Ellis earlier). What Hope terms her 'arboreal imagery of patrilinear descent... with its figuration of the invert as noble scion'[50] suggests that she cannot bear to conceive of Stephen as the 'end-point' in the family tree.

Stephen's next novel is less successful and she begins to suffer writer's block because, as she recognizes, at this point there is 'a great chunk of life that I've never known' (217). She has never had a passionate relationship with a woman which might conceive/create the next generation, in literary form. After her relationship with Mary, Stephen is in a different position. She is twice alerted to her calling, which is to write the invert's experience in a context (the novel) where it will be read by and console a wide audience. In Alec's bar in Paris she is told that 'the doctors cannot make the ignorant think, cannot hope to bring home the sufferings of millions; only one of ourselves can someday do that... It will need great courage but it will be done, because all things must work toward ultimate good' (395). Medical treatises, despite their influence on Hall, are here found wanting because of the basic assumption that inversion is 'abnormal'. What is needed is a book that does not see the 'normal invert' as an oxymoron. Valerie Seymour, Stephen's friend and leading light in the Parisian lesbian demimonde, makes the same point. Noting Stephen's oversensitivity (the 'nerves of the abnormal'), she also recognizes Stephen's 'respectable county instincts' and comments: 'But supposing you could bring the two sides of your nature into some sort of friendly amalgamation and compel them to serve you and through you your work' (414). The two sides of her nature are not here the masculine and feminine but the congenital invert and the aristocrat.

In the final paragraphs of the novel, Hall clearly expresses her desire to position Stephen's inversion as something akin to her English aristocratic social position; something that can be passed on to the next generation, if not through bloodline and birthright then instead through a literary inheritance. Stephen is grief-stricken, having engineered the collapse of her relationship with Mary, who she wants to protect from the world's derision. She feels that she is surrounded by the ghosts of a multitude of inverts, a spectral presence consisting of 'the quick, the dead and the yet unborn' (446) clamouring that she intercede with God on their behalf. The 'legion' advances and 'possessed her. Her barren womb became fruitful – it ached with its fearful and sterile burden. It ached with the fierce yet helpless children who would clamour in vain for their right to salvation' (446). In this metaphorical pregnancy or annunciation Stephen becomes the voice for the entire 'sterile' class of the inverted: 'there was only one voice, one demand; her own voice into which these millions had entered' (447). The final words she utters that conclude the novel: 'Acknowledge us, oh God, before the whole world. Give us also the right to our existence' (447) are a plea for a birthright of tolerance, which Stephen, who has now experienced love and loss, is now more than capable of voicing. She alone, because of her unique inheritance, can pass it on, if not literally then metaphorically, in a work of literature that will actually be widely read. As Doan contends, 'Stephen's expulsion from the land of her ancestors, the "decaying landed gentry" inaugurates her transition to the "aristocracy of intellect".'[51] Carolyn Burdett explains that Francis Galton, leading exponent of the new 'science' of eugenics, believed that 'progress and improvement lay neither with a decaying landed gentry, nor with a vulgar and self-interested entrepreneurialism, but with the aristocracy of intellect found in the professional classes. Inheritance, in the modern world, meant the passing on of a healthy physique and a good brain, rather than property and land.'[52] Doan argues that Hall incorporates such eugenic thinking in the novel by allowing Stephen to become a 'progenitive facilitator'. In other words, she 'drives her lover Mary Llewellyn into the arms of Martin Hallam, an old friend of Stephen's; in this way, Hall's protagonist fulfils, albeit indirectly, the dictates of her biological destiny to "produce...the advance guard"'.[53] I would argue that this kind of transmission of lesbian inheritance is of less significance in the novel than what Doan regards as a merely secondary mode of production, Stephen's work as a writer.

Hall perceived her vocation in similar ways to Stephen's. Like her, it was only when Hall felt securely established as an author that it was possible for her to contemplate writing The Well of Loneliness. She had published four novels before The Well and was best known for Adam's Breed, which received both critical and popular acclaim. Her desire to write something that genuinely voiced the experience of a significant minority but would be widely read is apparent in Una's account of the novel's genesis:

> She had long wanted to write a book on sexual inversion, a novel that would be accessible to the general public who did not have access to technical treatises...It was her absolute conviction that such a book could only be written by a sexual invert, who alone could be qualified by personal knowledge and experience to speak on behalf of a misunderstood and misjudged minority.[54]

The two aims of writing for a large readership and voicing the experiences of a voiceless minority are clearly echoed in Stephen's words at the end of *The Well*. They may also explain some of Hall's stylistic choices in the novel, which were not popular with the literati.[55]

## The trial papers, inversion and inheritance

The unique combination of ideas about inheritance in *The Well of Loneliness* was a potent one. Hall aligned ideas about hereditary inversion with a traditional English model of aristocratic inheritance along the paternal line and also envisaged that line as continuing in the form of a widely disseminated cultural inheritance propagated by Stephen's novel and by *The Well* itself. This scandalous insertion of inversion into the heart of English traditions was certainly noticed by reviewers and was of crucial importance in the correspondence surrounding the trial and the magistrate's final judgement. With the exception of James Douglas's notorious review in the *Daily Express*, which, as Doan suggests, has often been taken as typical,[56] the majority of reviews were positive. The claim that inversion is congenital was understood: 'the whole thesis is that there is a particular nature from birth that is, in the inscrutable designs of God, set apart from the recognized divisions of mankind, and that the censures of society are therein unjust'.[57] Some commented on Stephen's class position: 'She is reared exactly as an heir to the estates and the title would have been reared.'[58] Other reviews made the connection with the First World War and its impact on English culture: 'Ever since the war, when women displayed such unexpected ability in doing the work of men at the front, there has been a tendency to recognise and discuss in public and not merely in scientific text-books the painful problem of inversion.'[59]

However, it is in the recently released correspondence surrounding the trial that explicit recognition of the novel's threat to the national reproductive imperative can be most clearly seen. In a letter asking a doctor to testify on behalf of the prosecution, the Director of Public Prosecutions, Sir Archibald Bodkin, writes that 'I am afraid in many cases curiosity may lead to imitation and indulgence in practices which are believed to be somewhat extensive having regard to the very large excess in numbers of women over men.'[60] A number of witness statements for the prosecution also made this point. Lilian Barker, Governor of HM Borstal Institution for Girls, admitted herself to be 'precisely the type of woman depicted as Stephen', although she had early on 'fortunately realised that this sex urge was a creative instinct which must be diverted, and I concentrated on work amongst women'.[61] She supported the book's suppression on the grounds that 'the moment is one of great danger, when there are nearly two million women, with what are purely natural instincts, which cannot be satisfied by reason of the surplus of women over men'.[62]

The link between same-sex love between women, the situation created by the war and the future prospects for the nation is made by several eminent physicians in terms that echo the eugenic thinking of the day. James Latham Birley CBE recognizes the threat to England's future if the book is not successfully prosecuted, commenting that:

(1) Unnatural offences are repugnant to ordinarily constituted men and women who form an overwhelming majority of the community. This repugnance is an essential and indestructible part of our human nature and is a reflection of the fact that the sexes are differentiated for the purposes of reproduction.

(2) The enormous energy derived from the sexual instinct must if the species is to survive flow along its natural channels, and to encourage it to flow in abnormal directions is merely a first step towards racial suicide.[63]

He later argues that a 'civilized community' must control sexual perversity by explicit sanction and argues that if taboos against inversion were removed, 'the practice if indulged in extensively would inevitably strangle the race', particularly in the contemporary situation, where 'as a result of the War there is now an abnormal excess of female over male population'.[64] Sir William Henry Wilcox, Consulting Medical Adviser to the Home Office, also contended that 'lesbianism' was 'a vice which, if widespread, becomes a danger to the well-being of a nation, and where in history it has been prevalent in any nation this has been usually one of the indications of the downfall of that nation', concluding that 'for this reason the book must be regarded as a danger to Society and to the well-being of the Nation'.[65]

Concern with the novel's treatment of the First World War and inversion was also a key part of the Chief Magistrate, Sir Chartres Biron's, judgement against the text. He condemned the novel for suggesting that 'a number of women of position and admirable character, who were engaged in driving ambulances in the course of the war, were addicted to this vice',[66] which occasioned a vocal protest by Hall, who was silenced and threatened with being removed from the Court. Interviewed after the case concluded, Hall commented that:

'I particularly take exception to the magistrate's reference to the war work done by British women, whom he has held up to opprobrium in a public court to-day. Those women were the finest, the most courageous, the most sacrificing, and above all, the purest' (Miss R.H. uttered the word 'purest' with great emphasis) 'members of the British Empire during the Great War.'

'That their fine work should be held up to question is a terrible thing. I defy anybody to read that portion of The Well of Loneliness which deals with the war work done by women and to find in the writing of that portion anything but the highest and most reverent respect for the moral character of those women.'[67]

Biron particularly objected to the novel on the grounds that it claimed that the stresses and strains of war could have been a contributory factor in the increasing prevalence of same-sex relationships between women. This caused Hall such distress because it rebutted (as do the above statements supporting the novel's suppression) her thesis that inversion was congenital and hereditary, in line with the finest elements of English tradition. For Hall, the war only made the congenital invert more visible and more legible and gave her a purpose that was consistent with the defence of the realm. For the novel's opponents, the truth of things remained that same-sex love between women was a perversion freely chosen, which could be encouraged or discouraged by a range of social, political and moral factors, including propagation in literature.

The novel's literary quality was commented on by many of its opponents. The precise danger of the novel was identified in its capacity to be widely read and in its elevated moral tone and style. The Director of Public Prosecutions recognized that 'the writer . . . undoubtedly possessing literary ability, has wrapped up this disgusting subject in language which has the veneer almost of elegance'.[68] He concluded that 'the way to deal with this book is to take off the gloves and go for it tooth and nail, using the plainest and most vulgar crude language about the practices which are alluded to in its pages, to knock out thereby the veneer of literary style'.[69] In his judgement, Biron argued that:

> the mere fact that a book is well written can be no answer to these proceedings, because otherwise we should be in this preposterous position, that because it is well written the most obscene book would be free from such proceedings. It is quite obvious to anybody of intelligence that the better an obscene book is written the greater the public to whom the book is likely to appeal. The more palatable the poison the more insidious.[70]

The now somewhat surprising alignment of literary quality with wide readership and consequent moral duty is an almost exact reflection of Stephen's own feelings that her particular experience, position and literary vocation require her to become the spokesperson for her 'kind'. The only difference is the question of how 'duty' is interpreted: in the case of the novel's opponents theirs is to suppress; in Stephen's case it is to assert. The central function of literature as a crucial means of transmitting particular values remains the same.

This is nowhere more apparent than in the following extract from a speech given by the Home Secretary, William Joynson Hicks, to the Authors'

Club, reported in the *Daily Telegraph* almost a month after the case against *The Well*'s publishers was heard and three days before the appeal was dismissed:

> The overwhelming majority of the authors of this country desire to write and publish books which are uplifting and which make for the welfare of the nation, and are in accordance with the principles of 'safety first.' (Hear, hear.)
>
> Remember what the nation means to the well-being of the people of the Empire, and the civilization of the world. The tone comes from you, the authors of the land. If the tone is pure, the blood will go pulsating through the whole world, carrying with it purity and safety. If the stream of blood is impure, nobody can tell the effect it will have right through our empire. (Cheers.)[71]

Joynson-Hicks conceives of an author's national duty as involving the choice of 'safe' subjects which will be transmitted around the world just as the blood circulates around the (presumably heterosexual) body. The author who chooses an 'unsafe' subject will transmit that literary inheritance throughout the globe as a virus that can pollute the entire body politic.

Despite its abandonment of the principles of 'safety first' and its suppression, *The Well of Loneliness* succeeded in 'pulsating through the whole world'. The scandal that resulted was due, in no small part, to the novel's insertion of hereditary congenital inversion into the very heart of the status quo. The novel aligns sexual inversion with the inheritance of a respectable aristocratic social position and a firm sense of duty to one's country. However, this alone would be insufficient to explain fully the novel's subversiveness. Inter-war novels as different as Virginia Woolf's *Orlando* (1928) and Daphne du Maurier's *Rebecca* (1938) have associated queer sexuality with the aristocratic country house and nostalgia for a vanishing world. As Alison Light suggests: 'sexually progressive views were by no means incompatible with a reactionary class politics: we would need to read both [as this essay has done] as part of that traumatised femininity formed in the wake of the Great War'.[72] Hall does not simply espouse what Light defines as 'Romantic Toryism', however. What is different in the case of her novel and particularly scandalous to the establishment is her commitment to transmitting a serious message about sexual tolerance to a wide and middlebrow readership, without resorting either to the erudite innuendo of modernism or the 'romance with the past'[73] of the period's popular romantic fiction.[74] Hall's belief in 'the aristocracy of intellect' actually implies a more democratic notion of the passing-on of a 'cultural tradition' of (lesbian) identity via literature, literature that despite the ban, made its mark on the twentieth century.

## Notes

1. See for example Melanie Taylor, '"The Masculine Soul Heaving in the Female Bosom": Theories of Inversion and *The Well of Loneliness*', *Journal of Gender Studies*, 7, 3 (1998), 287–96; Heike Bauer, 'Richard von Krafft-Ebing's *Psychopathia Sexualis* as Sexual Sourcebook for Radclyffe Hall's *The Well of Loneliness*', *Critical Survey*, 15, 3 (2003), 23–38; Judith Halberstam, 'A Writer of Misfits: John Radclyffe Hall and the Discourse of Inversion', in *Female Masculinity* (Durham, NC: Duke University Press, 1998), 75–110; Laura Doan, 'Lesbian Writers and Sexual Science: a Passage to Modernity', in *Fashioning Sapphism: the Origins of a Modern English Lesbian Culture, Between Men – Between Women: Lesbian and Gay Studies* (New York: Columbia University Press, 2001), 126–63. See also the articles in the section entitled 'New Sexual Inversions', in *Palatable Poison: Critical Perspectives on 'The Well of Loneliness'*, ed. Laura Doan and Jay Prosser (New York: Columbia University Press, 2001), 129–98.

2. For arguments that see the novel as a negative development for lesbian identity see Catherine R. Stimpson, 'Zero Degree Deviancy: the Lesbian Novel in English', in *Feminisms: an Anthology of Literary Theory and Criticism*, ed. Robyn R. Warhol and Diane Price Herndl (New Brunswick: Rutgers University Press, 1991), 301–15; Lillian Faderman, *Surpassing the Love of Men: Romantic Friendship and Love between Women from the Renaissance to the Present* (London: Women's Press, 1985), 314–31. For arguments in favour of the text's construction of lesbian identity see Esther Newton, 'The Mythic Mannish Lesbian: Radclyffe Hall and the New Woman', *Signs: Journal of Women in Culture and Society*, 9, 4, (1984), 557–75, amended version reprinted in *Hidden from History: Reclaiming the Gay and Lesbian Past*, ed. Martin Bauml Duberman, Martha Vicinus and George Chauncey Jr (Harmondsworth: Penguin, 1991), 281–93. Sonja Ruehl uses Foucault's conception of a 'reverse discourse' in 'Inverts and Experts: Radclyffe Hall and the Lesbian Identity', in *Feminist Criticism and Social Change: Sex, Class and Race in Literature and Culture*, ed. Judith Newton and Deborah Rosenfelt (New York: Methuen, 1985), 165–80.

3. Jonathan Dollimore, *Sexual Dissidence: Augustine to Wilde, Freud to Foucault* (Oxford: Oxford University Press, 1991), 50.

4. Admittedly Hall does not stick unfailingly with this argument throughout the book; there are also suggestions that the heroine's sexual identity could be acquired as the result of infantile relationships with her parents, on the psychoanalytic model. See Teresa de Lauretis, 'The Lure of the Mannish Lesbian: the Fantasy of Castration and the Signification of Desire', in *The Practice of Love: Lesbian Sexuality and Perverse Desire* (Bloomington: Indiana University Press, 1994), 203–53, for an attempt to read the novel in relation to psychoanalytic theory.

5. Additional papers from the Office of the Director of Public Prosecutions were added to the following files: CUST 49/1057, DPP 1/92 on 2 January 2005. See http://www.nationalarchives.gov.uk/releases/2005/january2/default/htm.

6. Havelock Ellis, *Studies in the Psychology of Sex, Vol. I, Part Four, Sexual Inversion* (New York: Random House, 1937), 322.

7. Richard von Krafft-Ebing, *Psychopathia Sexualis*, in *Sexology Uncensored: the Documents of Sexual Science*, ed. Lucy Bland and Laura Doan (Cambridge: Polity Press, 1998), 77–91; 77 and 79.

8. Doan, 146.

9. Edward Carpenter, *The Intermediate Sex*, in *Sexology Uncensored: the Documents of Sexual Science*, ed. Lucy Bland and Laura Doan (Cambridge: Polity Press, 1998), 48–51; 48.

10. Ellis, 4.
11. *The Oxford English Dictionary*, ed. J.A.H. Murray et al. (Oxford: Clarendon Press, 1933).
12. Ellis, 310, 254, 310 and 256 respectively.
13. Ellis, 317.
14. Ellis, 270 and 309–10.
15. Ellis, 265.
16. Richard von Krafft-Ebing, *Psychopathia Sexualis, with Especial Reference to Contrary Sexual Instinct: a Medico-Legal Study*, authorized translation of the seventh and revised German edition by Charles Gilbert Chaddock (Philadelphia: F.A. Davis, 1920), 225.
17. Siobhan Somerville, 'Introduction' to Part VII: 'Race', in Bland and Doan, *Sexology Uncensored*, 201–3; 202.
18. Letter to Audrey Heath, 19 March 1929, in Doan, 95. See also Doan's discussion, 89–90 and Halberstam's, 91–4.
19. Radclyffe Hall, Letter to Evguenia Souline, Sunday 19 August 1934, in *Your John: the Love Letters of Radclyffe Hall*, Cutting Edge: Lesbian Life and Literature, ed. Joanne Glasgow (New York: New York University Press, 1997), 50–1.
20. Radclyffe Hall, *The Well of Loneliness*, ed. Alison Hennegan (London: Virago, 1982), 11. Further references to the novel will be incorporated into the text.
21. Diana Souhami, *The Trials of Radclyffe Hall* (London: Weidenfeld and Nicolson, 1998), 4. See also Sally Cline, *Radclyffe Hall: a Woman Called John* (London: John Murray, 1997), 20.
22. Margot Gayle Backus, 'Sexual Orientation in the (Post)Imperial Nation: Celticism and Inversion Theory in Radclyffe Hall's *The Well of Loneliness*', *Tulsa Studies in Women's Literature*, 15, 2 (1996), 253–66; 255.
23. Ruehl, 173–4.
24. Halberstam, 93. Radclyffe Hall's name was Marguerite, but she preferred to be known as John.
25. Bonnie Kime Scott, *Refiguring Modernism Vol I: The Women of 1928* (Bloomington: Indiana University Press), 248.
26. Shelly Skinner, 'The House in Order: Lesbian Identity and *The Well of Loneliness*', *Women's Studies*, 23 (1994), 19–33.
27. Cline, 13.
28. Souhami, 5.
29. Souhami, 5; Cline, 25.
30. Cline, 25.
31. Jean Radford, 'An Inverted Romance: *The Well of Loneliness* and Sexual Ideology', in *The Progress of Romance: the Politics of Popular Fiction*, ed. Jean Radford, History Workshop (London: Routledge, 1986), 97–111; 110.
32. Ellis, 21.
33. Somerville in Bland and Doan, *Sexology Uncensored*, 201
34. Carpenter in Bland and Doan, *Sexology Uncensored*, 48.
35. Somerville in Bland and Doan, *Sexology Uncensored*, 202.
36. Krafft-Ebing, 225.
37. Ellis, 231.
38. Ellis, 335.
39. Carolyn Burdett, 'The Hidden Romance of Sexual Science: Eugenics, the Nation and the Making of Modern Feminism', in *Sexology in Culture: Labelling Bodies and Desires*, ed. Lucy Bland and Laura Doan (Cambridge: Polity Press, 1998), 44–59; 44.
40. Havelock Ellis, *The Task of Social Hygiene*, in Bland and Doan, 178–80; 178.

41. Andrea Lewis, ' "Glorious pagan that I adore": Resisting the National Imperative in Rosamond Lehmann's *Dusty Answer'*, *Studies in the Novel*, 31 (3) (1999), 357–71; 359.
42. Doan, 162.
43. Cline, 97.
44. Nansen identity documents were issued by the League of Nations in the wake of the Russian Revolution to those supporters of the army fighting against the Bolsheviks who had been exiled from the newly formed USSR after the Revolution.
45. Glasgow, 6.
46. See Cline, 181 and 336 and Souhami, 285, 297, 301 on fascist leanings. See Cline, 359–61 and Souhami 311 and 320 on anti-Semitism. Glasgow also discusses both, 8.
47. Ellis, 47–57.
48. Krafft-Ebing, 225.
49. Carpenter in Bland and Doan, *Sexology Uncensored*, 51.
50. Trevor Hope, 'Of Trees and Politics, Wars and Wounds', in Doan and Prosser, 255–73; 257.
51. Doan, 152.
52. Burdett in Bland and Doan, *Sexology in Culture*, 46.
53. Doan, 155.
54. Cline, 221.
55. For the novel's literary reception and context see Radford (1986), Joan Scanlon, 'Bad Language *vs* Bad Prose?: *Lady Chatterley* and *The Well'*, *Critical Quarterly*, 38, 3 (1996), 3–13; Laura Green, 'Hall of Mirrors: Radclyffe Hall's *The Well of Loneliness* and Modernist Fictions of Identity', *Twentieth-Century Literature*, 49, 3 (2003), 277–97.
56. Doan, 2–5.
57. 'Breaking Silence', *T.P.s and Cassell's Weekly*, 11 August 1928, press cutting, National Archives: Customs 49/1057.
58. 'The White Crow', *Glasgow Herald*, 9 August 1928, press cutting, National Archives: Customs 49/1057.
59. 'The Modern Amazon', *Liverpool Post and Mercury*, 15 August, 1928, press cutting, National Archives: Customs 49/1057.
60. Letter to Dr J.A. Hadfield, 6 December 1928, National Archives DPP1/88.
61. Letter from Lilian Barker, 7 December 1928, National Archives: DPP 1/92.
62. Statement by Lilian Barker, National Archives: DPP 1/92.
63. Statement by James Latham Birley, National Archives: DPP1/88.
64. Birley, National Archives: DPP1/88.
65. Statement by Sir William Henry Wilcox, National Archives: DPP 1/92.
66. Sir Chartres Biron, Chief Magistrate, 'Judgement', Bow Street Police Court, 16 November 1928, in Doan and Prosser, 39–49 (45).
67. 'Novel Ordered to be Destroyed', *Manchester Guardian*, 17 November 1928, press cutting, National Archives: Customs 49/1057.
68. Letter to Sir E. Farquhar Buzzard, 3 December 1928, National Archives: DPP 1/88.
69. Letter to Eustace Fulton, Esq, 25 October 1928, National Archives: DPP 1/88.
70. Biron, in Doan and Prosser, 41.
71. Sir William Joynson-Hicks, Home Secretary, 'Safety First for the Nation', Speech delivered to the Authors' Club, reported in 'Home Secretary on Safety', *Daily Telegraph*, 11 December 1928, press cutting, National Archives: Customs 49/1057.
72. Alison Light, *Forever England: Femininity, Literature and Conservatism between the Wars* (London: Routledge, 1991), 58.

73. Light, 156–207.
74. *The Well of Loneliness* is only mentioned briefly in Nicola Humble's *The Feminine Middlebrow Novel 1920s to 1950s: Class, Domesticity and Bohemianism* (Oxford: Oxford University Press, 2001), although I would argue that it resembles the fiction she considers in its 'significant role in the negotiation of new class and gender identities in the period from the 1920s to the 1950s' (5).

# 3
# The Law and the Profits: the Case of D.H. Lawrence's *Lady Chatterley's Lover*

*Fiona Becket*

In November 1960 a jury comprising nine men and three women decided that the publication of the full text of D.H. Lawrence's *Lady Chatterley's Lover* (1928) was for the public good. The trial of the publisher, Penguin Books, excited a great deal of media interest. '*Lady Chatterley's Lover*, beyond its status as a novel, is the most notorious example of literary censorship in the twentieth century, and the novel's strange and fascinating history still holds many secrets.' This is how one commentator on the book's production history begins his summing up of the significance of D.H. Lawrence's final novel.[1] Philip Larkin, in 'Annus Mirabilis' (1974), acknowledged 'the end of the Chatterley ban' as a milestone, for others if not for him.

A period of some thirty years separates the principal episodes of the book's first publication, confiscation and republication. In 1959 an American judge overruled restrictions on the unexpurgated edition; in 1960 the trial at the Old Bailey in the case brought against Penguin Books Limited for publishing, over three decades after it initially appeared, the first unexpurgated version of Lawrence's novel in England was still sensational enough to excite enduring public interest. In English law, *Lady Chatterley's Lover* was the subject of the first prosecution under the Obscene Publications Act of 1959; whatever it did to stimulate public curiosity, it simultaneously brought about a complete revival of interest in Lawrence and the liberationist philosophy ascribed to him. It also provided the cue for less restrictive publishing practices. The publishing house was of course acquitted, and the novel sold in millions. Film archives of the time show long queues formed around bookshops. Stories of the paperback slipped into the brown paper bag for discretion, or concealed by a 'decoy' book to save the reader's reputation, have become part of the history and the mythology of this novel.

In the course of these events a particular kind of Lawrence was produced within the public sphere, grounded on various popular misreadings of the author's 'metaphysic' or personal philosophy. The many audiences for the book created the version of D.H. Lawrence that best suited their intentions. So it was that Lawrence's focus on regeneration meant that he was appropriated as a freethinking sexual liberationist by advocates of free love; as a political anarchist committed to the destruction of class barriers; indeed, as an anti-establishment figure in the most obvious senses. Within literary criticism, dominated in the immediate postwar years by white middle-class men, those who were his champions argued for Lawrence's visionary status most notably in the area of human relations. He was, in the words of Harry T. Moore, 'the priest of love'.[2] Simone de Beauvoir in *The Second Sex* (1949; 1953) had eloquently interrogated Lawrence's representation of women and male–female relations, but the most influential revision of Lawrence's hieratic value came in 1969 with the publication of Kate Millett's *Sexual Politics*, a book which analysed at length and in detail the misogynist dimension of Lawrence's writing, which the critical establishment had either overlooked or dismissed. The critical legacy was either reductive or energizing depending on one's point of view. John Worthen, Lawrence scholar and biographer, for instance, locates the scandal with the feminists 'who prefer to see [Lawrence] as an archetypal chauvinist'.[3] This is perhaps an overly reductive analysis of a range of positions. It could be argued, though, that despite the astuteness of many of the newly aired interpretations, for many, Lawrence's reputation continued to mask the serious intentions of his work. Often viewed as debased and risible, even beyond parody (so successfully did he inadvertently appear to parody himself), only in the 1990s did criticism seriously reassess some of the most problematic aspects of D.H. Lawrence's treatment of gender, sexuality and language.

This chapter will attempt to outline something of what Lawrence felt about censorship and it will briefly consider Penguin Books' motives for publishing the complete text when it did. It will also draw on related material that is often overlooked in assessments of *Lady Chatterley's Lover* such as *Sketches of Etruscan Places* (1932), a book which was written after the second version of *Lady Chatterley's Lover*, and which takes travel writing in some fascinating and unexpected directions. *Etruscan Places* helps us to understand the extent to which *Lady Chatterley's Lover* represents Lawrence's final expression of his theories about the genealogy of the unconscious – the final expression, indeed, of his long-running and highly critical relationship to Freudian psychoanalysis, and the re-location (in Lawrence's specific and personal language of the body), of unconscious functioning to the blood. For all its flaws *Lady Chatterley's Lover* is Lawrence's last and fullest attempt to express the anti-Cartesianism that underpins his most achieved writing. For that reason alone this novel requires fresh attention and a new audience whose reading is not restricted to the romance of the scandal.

*Lady Chatterley's Lover* was written in three drafts, or versions (the first two novels published posthumously as *The First Lady Chatterley* (1944) and *John Thomas and Lady Jane* (1972) respectively) before Lawrence settled on the text we know (initially called 'Tenderness') as the one he wished to publish. His publisher was only prepared to consider an expurgated version, so Lawrence had it printed privately in Italy, in a limited edition for subscribers. He knew that it would be received with suspicion by the authorities. He had already experienced censorship of the work that mattered most to him, *The Rainbow* having been banned in 1915. A year after the publication of the first complete edition of *Lady Chatterley's Lover*, the poetry collection *Pansies* was confiscated and the police also closed down an exhibition of Lawrence's paintings in London's Warren Gallery. This was in 1929. The limited edition of the novel, needless to say, was relentlessly pirated. Profits were not Lawrence's priority, but he lost money.[4]

In a fascinating description of the 'secret third edition' of *Lady Chatterley's Lover* Craig Munro succinctly outlines the practicalities of getting Lady Chatterley onto the streets:

> In late 1928 and early into the new year, Lawrence was still preoccupied with the distribution and further printing of *Lady Chatterley's Lover*. Although the first Florence edition of a thousand copies had sold out, he was now dispatching copies of the cheap paper-covered issue of two hundred, and planning a larger edition to be printed with paper covers in Paris. He was also furious over pirated editions of his novel which were appearing at a remarkable rate in America. The first of these had been on sale within weeks of the arrival of the genuine copies, and by April 1929 no less than five pirated editions were available in the United States. The Paris edition, with a prefatory essay by Lawrence, appeared in May, but the piracies continued to proliferate.[5]

There were two official editions of the novel: the first limited edition, printed and distributed in Florence by the bookseller Pino Orioli, and the cheaper Paris edition on which Lawrence worked in the early months of 1929. Pirated copies tended to reproduce the text photographically from these volumes. Munro makes the argument for Lawrence having been prepared to sanction a third edition printed in London – under the shadow of the authorities in a context of restrictive publication practices – although he died before publication.

The evidence is also that the authorities routinely interfered with Lawrence's mail, which is how *Pansies* came to the attention of the Home Secretary, Sir William Joynson-Hicks (the 'Jix' of Lawence's letters at this time). Booksellers were also vulnerable because the state could threaten the livelihood and liberty of those who imported for sale unsuitable material.[6]

In July 1929 Martin Secker, Lawrence's publisher in London, brought out a mutilated version of *Pansies*. As Lawrence wrote in the foreword:

> Some of the poems are perforce omitted – about a dozen from the bunch. When Scotland Yard seized the MS. in the post, at the order of the Home Secretary, no doubt there was a rush of detectives, postmen, and Home Office clerks and heads, to pick out the most lurid blossoms... I can only grin once more to think of the nanny-goat, nanny-goat-in-a-white-petticoat silliness of it all.[7]

Lawrence did not live to see what the reception of his next book of poems, called *Nettles* (1930), would bring. In it he works out his spleen at the authorities and also at the public for allowing itself to be patronized, protected, infantilized and consoled. In 'The Man in the Street' (569–70) the speaker, who is 'cut dead' for greeting strangers, is eventually run in by the police, 'to teach me why' (570). In 'Innocent England' the policeman is again depicted as the clumsy tool of repressive law-making, in just one of the direct references to the confiscation of Lawrence's paintings:

> Virginal, pure policemen came
> and hid their faces for very shame,
>
> while they carried the shameless things away
> to gaol, to be hid from the light of day.
>
> (579)

In a poem called 'Give Me A Sponge' 'nasty police-eyes' are 'like snail-tracks smearing/the gentle souls that figure in the paint' (580). Elsewhere in the volume critics are represented as neutered beasts ('Editorial Office'). The government, formerly the nanny-goat state, is 'Auntie', a repressive, watchful, joyless old maid, and in 'Change of Government' Auntie Maud comes to 'keep house' instead of the posher 'Aunt Gwendoline'. Whilst it might be a struggle to extol the poetic virtues of this collection, the deeply felt hostility to Britain (*'A right little, tight little I-----sland!'* (575)) and those who govern her cannot be gainsaid.

In an essay about constructions of sexuality in British postwar society, Jonathan Dollimore identifies the importance of the Chatterley trial in these terms:

> it [the trial] illustrates the contradictions in liberalism; as a major censorship issue it is a glaringly 'material' instance of the intersection of literature, sexuality, politics, ideology and law; and it constitutes a fascinating record of contemporary attitudes – especially authoritarian attitudes – to sexual transgression.[8]

For Dollimore, the Chatterley trial was not unequivocally iconoclastic. Instead, its debates were underpinned by assumptions (about women, sexuality and class) that remained intact and active, even given the defence offered at the time of both the book and the conditions in which it could be read. He argues that postwar debates about sexuality, particularly in the fifties and sixties, reflected specific contrasting trends, notably an authoritarian fear of sexuality in the light of an increasingly popular view that sexuality offered a specific challenge to power, and a liberal faith that sexuality, as apolitical, could reveal the authentic self.[9] Penguin's decision to publish provided a platform, Dollimore suggests, for the expression of these trends, hence the book's cultural significance is thrown into relief apart from questions (except indirectly) of literary value.

So why did Penguin decide to publish an unexpurgated version of *Lady Chatterley's Lover* at this point? The answer lies not in the fact of the 1959 Obscene Publications Act alone but in its detail, in particular a clause relating to the defence of the public good. No conviction could result if the publication of an 'obscene' text could be proved to be for the public good, not least in the interests of literature and learning. Furthermore, the Act (which did not have jurisdiction in Scotland or Northern Ireland) also allowed that the opinion of experts in the relevant field, here literature, could be admitted in any proceedings to establish, or otherwise, the merits of a particular publication – hence the roll call of eminent critics and writers as witnesses for the defence at the Old Bailey. So whilst Penguin Books was arraigned for publishing an obscene book, the defence would actually concentrate on the question of the public good. Although *Lady Chatterley's Lover* might indeed be pronounced a dirty book, could publication nevertheless be justified in the interests of literature and learning? And how many experts would be willing to describe its merits under such conditions? Prior to the 1959 Act the evidence of 'experts' had not been admissible – as Susan Watkins discusses in the present volume, literary experts were not called in the case of Radclyffe Hall's *The Well of Loneliness*, for instance, a book which was published in the same year as *Lady Chatterley's Lover*. However, in the Chatterley trial even the exhibits were literary – among other documents the prosecution was willing to introduce *The First Lady Chatterley* as an altogether less offensive version of the same story, whilst the defence felt able to produce Rebecca West's book on Lawrence, as well as Lawrence's own essay 'Sex, Literature and Censorship', to make the point. On the face of it, in publishing the unexpurgated novel, Penguin Books struck a blow for artistic merit in the face of a philistine establishment, and Penguin was acquiring a track record in raising issues of injustice and censorship.[10] A successful commercial business, Penguin was also able to ensure that 200,000 copies of *Lady Chatterley's Lover* went on sale immediately after the verdict was announced, and sales continued to be healthy in terms of Penguin's balance sheet. How different from 1928, when the author, with his privately printed book, sold as a limited edition to subscribers, lost money as a result of those pirated editions (editions now not without interest to collectors).

Many assessments of the Chatterley trial seem to sidestep the very real issue of commercial advantage in being able to 'test' the new improved Obscene Publications Act. Ideally, the successful publisher, vindicated by an enlightened jury, would have a free hand to sell large numbers of books to a recently enthused reading public, eager to see what the fuss had been about. The media, perhaps in particular the newspapers, undoubtedly helped things along in this regard by covering a range of angles, from the usual synopses of the situation to more focused pieces on why and how certain individuals, for instance the Bishop of Woolwich, might speak up in the novel's defence. And, probably, while the story ran, the whole thing improved the circulation figures of several papers. In 1961 Penguin Books also brought out, quite cannily some might say, an account of the trial edited by C.H. Rolph.[11] Whilst that volume says next to nothing about the profits earned through publishing *Lady Chatterley's Lover* even in the weeks after the trial, it concludes by noting that the costs of the case to Penguin, cited in the book as £13,000, were not awarded by the judge, Mr Justice Byrne, despite the fact that Gerald Gardiner QC (defence) argued that the case 'was opened by the Prosecution *as a test case*'.[12] Indeed, Rolph's volume emphasizes throughout that Penguin's principal motivation was the integrity of the work of literature and the restoration of the reputation of the benighted author. As Gardiner expressed it, with regard to the terms of the new Act:

> Our Clients do not regard the book as obscene, and they do regard its publication as of particular importance, for the public good, to vindicate D.H. Lawrence's integrity and non-pornographic intent in writing it, and to enable his place in English literature as a whole to be properly judged in this country for the first time. (23)

Griffith-Jones QC (for the prosecution) was willing to make some concessions – 'that D.H. Lawrence is a well-recognized and indeed great writer' and that 'some of his books have great literary merit' (18) – but urged the jury to concentrate on a moralistic dimension. He noted that the novel might 'induce lustful thoughts in the minds of those who read it', suggested that it celebrates 'promiscuous and adulterous intercourse', and 'encourages, and indeed even advocates, coarseness and vulgarity of thought and of language'. This was before making some well reported and often repeated comments about wives and servants (17). Regarding Penguin's potential profits, Griffith-Jones seemed concerned principally that thousands of copies for sale at 3s. 6d. simply made the book affordable to the majority and, therefore, available to those in possession of vulnerable minds. The defence made the point that Penguin could have published an expurgated edition of *Lady Chatterley's Lover* at any time in their history but had refrained from doing so: 'whether they could have made money or not, they have never published a mutilated book' (26). Here is the publishing house as self-appointed custodian of high culture.

In many respects the Chatterley trial allows us to reflect on the private act of reading. The 1959 Obscene Publications Act meant that for once the offending text had to be judged as a whole; that is to say, the prosecution would not be within its rights simply to identify offending passages from the text – something that clearly the prosecution wished to do in order to make a strong case (the edition used during the trial is clearly marked where it might be hoped to argue that the content is depraved and has the potential to corrupt). With twelve copies of the novel lodged with the police (in order to mark publication) the jury was directed to read the entire book, and judge it in its totality. Then there is the fact of the defence seeking out literary experts in the hope of calling respected individuals – writers and scholars – as witnesses to argue for the relative merits of the unmutilated book, and in passing to comment on the preoccupations, philosophy and intentions of D.H. Lawrence. Certainly the defence was thorough. Many were contacted and many were called as defence witnesses, although some, most famously F.R. Leavis, who thought *Lady Chatterley's Lover* to be a substandard work, declined the invitation to come forward as advocates for the book.

Graham Hough, author of *The Dark Sun: a Study of D.H. Lawrence* (1956), was the first to be called. He began what some, not without levity, have thought the best-publicized seminar to occur in the Old Bailey, being asked at length to evaluate different aspects of the novel. In asking Hough about Lawrentian repetition, for instance, the prosecution inadvertently revealed a problem that many readers encounter with Lawrence's style and terminology. In an episode of close-reading which sought to turn a blind eye to 'purple passages', Griffith-Jones drew attention to the repetition of the words 'womb' and 'bowels' (in the context of Connie's growing feelings for Mellors) in order to ask whether this constituted good writing (47). In response Hough drew attention to the fact of breakdowns in Lawrence's style more generally. He was then given the opportunity by the defence re-examination to highlight repetition as a 'legitimate literary device' (54), with reference to a less highly-charged vocabulary than the language of the body and the so-called obscene words favoured as points of reference by the prosecution. In the light of questions from Gardiner, Hough was also able to refer to Lawrence's belief in marriage: '[the book] is concerned with a very important situation; it is concerned with the relations of men and women, with their sexual relations, with the nature of marriage, and these are all matters of deep importance to all of us' (42). According to Rolph, Griffith-Jones picked up on this in his cross-examination of the expert witness Joan Bennett and thereafter: 'The gravamen of the charge was now that the book was about adultery [ . . . ] Lady Chatterley was indeed on trial' (63). Certainly, in what appears to be a plot-based line of questioning, the suspicion that the book constituted pornography was in danger of being veiled by the prosecution's energetic interest in her ladyship's 'adulterous intercourses', and with a man who is her social inferior, a theme that was emphasized in the summing up by Justice Byrne (231).

Most commentators agree that the controversy which surrounded *Regina v. Penguin Books Limited* led to *Lady Chatterley's Lover* being appropriated by diverse groups with highly particular interests. It was picked up, perhaps unsurprisingly, without much attention paid to the book's place within Lawrence's personal philosophy, and made to do service for various lobbies. Not much has been published on the kinds of misreading that took root in the reception of Lawrence's ideas after the time of the trial. This is in part down to the difficulties manifested in taking the ideas of *Lady Chatterley's Lover* seriously when many of the book's key philosophical passages actually fail at the level of language. The idea of 'phallic consciousness', for instance, is often said to be the foundation of this novel's vision. Some might have difficulty accepting John Worthen's explanation, based on the exploration that persists in *John Thomas and Lady Jane*, that 'the body, whether male or female, or joined as both, is "phallic" for Lawrence when perceived as a whole entity, conscious and unconscious together', but there might be a consensus, with Worthen that Lawrence 'needs a new language' if this is his theme.[13] It is a pity, then, that Lawrence never saw the need for a substitute for 'phallic' in what is otherwise quite a creative personal lexicon. However, he is often damned by partial readers. In work which precedes *Lady Chatterley's Lover* Lawrence's phrase 'blood-consciousness' offers a case in point. Here the 'consciousness' part of the word-form is frequently overlooked. Instead, the 'blood' element, often taken to signify in the first instance a racial meaning rather than the notion of 'life-blood' – which underpins most of Lawrence's writing on the instinctive life – gets most of the critical attention (although dedicated readers of *The Plumed Serpent* do have an argument in this regard).[14] So, while sex dominates popular and specialist assessments of much of Lawrence's work, in *Lady Chatterley's Lover* the principal preoccupation might also be taken to be language, and some have noted the fatal flaw in that novel, that in seeking to highlight the importance of the instinctive, non-verbal life, it takes refuge too readily, too consciously, in the word.[15]

At the end of *Lady Chatterley's Lover* Mellors, writing to his lady, departs from personal topics to offer a dissertation on Mammon, 'which I think, after all, is only the mass-will of people, wanting money and hating life'.[16] The answer to his complaint lies neither in nationalization of the major industries nor in 'a Soviet'. The men are 'deadened' by their enslavement, writes Mellors, but Lawrence's solution was idiosyncratic and idealistic. His concluding vision is bucolic, folksy and absurd, perhaps 'phallic', built around vigorous young men and their admiring women paying obeisance jointly to Pan – 'that's the only way to solve the industrial problem: train the people to be able to live, and live in handsomeness, without needing to spend' (300). This unexamined position from Lawrence's 'green man' is in part a continuation of an earlier conversation between the 'cronies' (Clifford's friends) which awkwardly links the themes of humanity, the life of the body (Lawrence's enduring preoccupation) and Bolshevism. For Tommy Dukes, Bolshevism and the life of the mind share a dubious foundation in materialism. Charlie May has argued that for the Bolshevists:

> the individual, especially the *personal* man, is bourgeois: so he must be suppressed. You must submerge yourselves in the greater thing, the soviet-social thing. Even an organism is bourgeois: so the ideal must be mechanical . . . Each man a machine-part, and the driving power of the machine, hate: hate of the bourgeois! That, to me is bolshevism. (38)

Dukes adds that this is a definition of the 'industrial ideal', 'the factory-owner's ideal . . . except that he would deny that the driving power was hate. Hate it is, all the same: hate of life itself' (38). And it is interesting to speculate how new readers in the period of the Cold War considered the observation that 'The bolshevists will have the finest army in the world, in a very short time, with the finest mechanical equipment' (38).[17] Quite apart from the issue of censorship which *Lady Chatterley's Lover* embodies, Lawrence's novel identified debates which continued to have meaning after 1928, which is perhaps one of the reasons why Huxley respected Lawrence as a thinker.

A lot of writing took place in Lawrence's life in the time between the final Chatterley novel and the conception and publication of what were once referred to as the 'leadership' novels, that is to say *Aaron's Rod* (1922), *Kangaroo* (1923) and *The Plumed Serpent* (1926), novels in which the connections between manliness and political power are examined. After the completion of the second version of the Chatterley narrative (*John Thomas and Lady Jane*) his trip to Etruscan burial sites gave Lawrence further cause to reflect on his thesis of mighty political machines crushing the life-instinct of spiritual cultures. In the 'Cerveteri' chapter of *Sketches of Etruscan Places*, for instance, Lawrence indulges in a study of Etruscan iconography that would seem to confirm his view of the course of western history. Intrigued by the phallic stones found outside the tombs of men and the stone receptacles (the ark, 'the arx, the womb'[18]) found outside the tombs of women, he first makes a comment about voluntary censorship: 'One can live one's life, and read all the books about India or Etruria, and never read a single word about the thing that impresses one in the very first five minutes, in Benares [Lawrence never visited India] or in an etruscan necropolis: that is, the phallic symbol' (19). Keen to redress the balance, Lawrence proceeds to argue that 'phallic knowledge' (22), evidently possessed by the Etruscans (witness their art and invisibility to the modern consciousness) attracted the ire of the materialist, power-hungry Romans. Here he makes a distinction between a phallic culture (the Etruscans) and the masculinist contours of Roman political power and ambition. The Romans, who were the ultimate oppressors of the Etruscans, 'hated the phallus and the ark, because they wanted empire and dominion and above all, riches: social gain' (20). In anticipation of the suggestion in Mellors' letter at the end of *Lady Chatterley's Lover*, Lawrence concludes that 'You cannot dance gaily to the double flute, and at the same time conquer nations or rake in large sums of money' (20). Critics commonly identify Lawrence's fantasies of a pre-conscious mode of being with myth – a mythic consciousness. In 'Cerveteri', however, he attempts to develop a historical framework within which to situate his thought.

   *Sketches of Etruscan Places* is an important book to read alongside the Chatterley novel. Not only is it written with a consciousness that it is the victors who write history, and that it is the responsibility of the artist to question and overturn orthodoxies (of scholarship and in other spheres), it is also a book which is prepared to comment on censorship and the suppression of ideas. It is commonly acknowledged that when he writes in 'Cerveteri', that 'To the Puritan all things are impure' (10) Lawrence refers to his censors. 'To my detractors', he writes, 'I am a very effigy of vice' (9). His examination of Etruscan culture functions to confirm the centrality to his personal philosophy of Lawrence's dualistic analyses of modern western society and values. In the 'sketches', those whom he imagines to be the descendants of the Etruscans are sensual and vital; the Fascist officials he encounters are products of mental-conscious, materialistic modernity. We are used to reading *A Propos of 'Lady Chatterley's Lover'* (1930), and *Pornography and Obscenity* (1929) as commentaries on the last novel as well as texts which embody Lawrence's final discursive thoughts about his culture. *Sketches of Etruscan Places* is perhaps a more subtle, less angst-ridden commentary for many of the ideas that underpin *Lady Chatterley's Lover*. Lawrence concludes his Etruscan sketches with a dissertation on history and pre-history, emphasizing the division between the pagan and the Christian, and the clues left for us in religious symbols which are the precursors of a more secular art. In the grain of his analysis lie pointers to how his final novel was to be understood, not only in the relationship and dialogues between Connie and Mellors, but in the stagnant intellectual inheritance embodied in Clifford and his cronies. In the chapter of the *Sketches* called 'The Florence Museum' Lawrence writes:

> What we see, in the etruscan remains, is the fag end of the revelation of another form of cosmic consciousness: and also, that salt of the earth, the revelation of the human existence of people who lived and who *were*, in a way somewhat different from our way of living and being. There are two separate things: the artistic or impulsive or culture-expression, and the religious or scientific or civilisation expression of a group of people. The first is based on emotion; the second on concepts. (176–7)

Mellors is perhaps the true 'etruscan'. Crucially, he is neither an artist nor a writer, because in *Lady Chatterley's Lover* these are viewed as not separable from the profit motive and the need for self aggrandizement. Connie wonders at Clifford's attempts at networking with all and sundry, including Michaelis whom he despises, so that he can become known as 'a first-class modern writer' (21). Michaelis, a writer of smart society plays, whose income from America alone is said to be fifty thousand dollars, occupies a curious place in the narrative as Connie's first lover within her marriage. A social climber, he tells Clifford that 'Money is a sort of instinct' (22). His wealth is derived from the popularity of his plays, and he accepts that his work's currency depends on the support of a public that has dropped him by the time Clifford shows any interest. In conversation with the Chatterleys, Michaelis utters the cliché that is expected of any artist who is apparently serious about his art: 'I may be a good writer or I may be a bad one, but a writer, and a writer of plays is what I am, and I've got to be. There's no question of that' (22). 'Culture-expression', in the best sense, is beyond 'Mick' whose emotions are mediated by his consciousness of self. As Tommy Dukes puts it in a later conversation with the cronies, the individuality of modern men is 'overdeveloped', inseparable from a 'craving for self-assertion and success' (32).

Perhaps this observation helps to explain why the most positive statement about art in this novel is about form. The point made in Chapter 9 about the novel form, 'properly handled', is that 'it can inform and lead into new places the flow of our sympathetic consciousness, and it can lead our sympathy away in recoil from things gone dead' (101). As Lawrence concludes *Sketches of Etruscan Places* he draws the reader's attention to the forms of anonymous, essentially public, art in a culture which did not 'die' from within – that is its great virtue. In search of the Etruscans he identifies two clues to help him. 'The first', he writes, 'is the peculiar physical or *bodily*, lively quality of the art. And this, I take it, is Italian, the result of the Italian soil itself' (178).[19] The second clue is in the 'more ideal presence of the symbols. Symbols are at least *half* ideas: and so they are half fixed' (178). As always with Lawrence his terms are difficult to translate, but his conclusion moves beyond the immediate preoccupation with Etruscan religious forms and speaks to the kernel of the developing idea for the novel that preoccupied him at this time: 'So we have the two clues, that of the dominant idea, or half-idea, in the religious symbols; and that of the dominant *feeling*, in the peculiar physical freeness and exuberance and spontaneity. It is the spontaneity of the flesh itself' (178).

Amongst those who championed Lawrence's vision after the trial of Penguin Books in 1960 few made any sound argument for the book's contributions to discussions of form in art (neither did they in 1928). Also after 1960 discussion was concentrated more on prophets than profits, although profits were made, and the reasons for the book's reputation were fixed.

It is difficult to imagine a time now when 'the spontaneity of the flesh' can be taken in the ways Lawrence intended because literature, audiences and questions of censorship have moved on. There is also the issue that for Lawrence's generation the ideas of Freud concerning sexuality and the unconscious were important and influential, and that Lawrence had a great deal invested in dismantling the Cartesian assumptions that underpinned Freudian psychoanalysis. It is one of the many ironies of *Lady Chatterley's Lover* that it resorts to binaries in its treatment of the life of the body and the life of the mind, despite the efforts of the book's language to show them as not separable. The success of the book, however, can be tested in many ways. *Lady Chatterley's Lover* remains one of the most translated of Lawrence's novels, which is double-edged of course. Contemporary readers accept that acts of censorship say more about the preoccupations of the moment than the long-term cultural value of a book. The trial of Penguin Books, as is acknowledged, created more readers for *Lady Chatterley's Lover* than Lawrence might have hoped for, but created too a series of narrowly defined contexts within which the book was actually read. Whether the book ever had revolutionary potential, that moment is gone, and it is difficult to imagine a modern context where that could be reversed. Trial and error, we could say.

## Notes

1. Craig Munro, '*Lady Chatterley* in London: The Secret Third Edition', in *D.H. Lawrence's 'Lady': a New Look At 'Lady Chatterley's Lover'*, ed. Michael Squires and Dennis Jackson (Athens, Georgia: The University of Georgia Press, 1985), 222–35; 232.
2. Harry T. Moore, *The Priest of Love: a Life of D.H. Lawrence*, revised edn (London: Heinemann, 1974).
3. John Worthen, *D.H. Lawrence* (London: Edward Arnold, 1991), 121.
4. Lawrence discusses the pirated editions in *A Propos of 'Lady Chatterley's Lover'* (1930), in *'Lady Chatterley's Lover' and A Propos of 'Lady Chatterley's Lover'*, The Cambridge Edition of the works of D.H. Lawrence, ed. Michael Squires (Cambridge: Cambridge University Press, 2002), 303–36.
5. Munro, 224.
6. We are reminded in C.H. Rolph, ed., *The Trial of Lady Chatterley: Regina v. Penguin Books Limited* (Harmondsworth: Penguin, 1990) that, out of consideration for booksellers who might be prosecuted for selling *Lady Chatterley's Lover*, publication consisted of handing copies over to the police.
7. D.H. Lawrence, *Complete Poems*, ed. and introd. Vivian De Sola Pinto and F. Warren Roberts (Harmondsworth: Penguin, 1977), 423. Further references are to this edition and will appear in the text.
8. Jonathan Dollimore, 'The Challenge of Sexuality', in *Society and Literature 1945–1970*, ed. Alan Sinfield (London: Methuen, 1983), 51–85; 52–3.
9. Dollimore, 74.
10. In 1955 Penguin published Peter Wildeblood's *Against the Law*, which includes an account of his trial for homosexual acts (in the much publicized Montagu Case,

1954) and subsequent imprisonment. Penguin reprinted in 1959. The volume was reissued in 2000 with a new preface by Matthew Parris.

11. Copyright Penguin Books Ltd, 1961.

12. C.H. Rolph, ed., *The Trial of Lady Chatterley: Regina v. Penguin Books Limited.* Reissued with a foreword by Geoffrey Robertson (Harmondsworth: Penguin, 1990), 249. Further references appear in the text. See also Rolph's *Books in the Dock* (London: André Deutsch, 1969) about censorship and publishing in Britain.

13. Worthen, 118.

14. *The Plumed Serpent* belongs to a different place in Lawrence's thought, compared with *Lady Chatterley's Lover*, and Kate in the former novel bears a philosophy very different from that embodied in the Connie–Mellors relationship (although Mellors' reasons for hating women and sex in Chapter 14 of *Lady Chatterley's Lover* are foregrounded in *The Plumed Serpent*).

15. See for instance Michael Bell, *D.H. Lawrence: Language and Being* (Cambridge: Cambridge University Press, 1991), and Linda Ruth Williams, *D.H. Lawrence* (Plymouth: Northcote House, in association with the British Council, 1997).

16. D.H. Lawrence, *Lady Chatterley's Lover* (Harmondsworth: Penguin, 1994), 300. Further references are to this edition and appear in the text.

17. Harold Macmillan visited Moscow in 1959 for talks with Krushchev, and Washington in 1960 to discuss the nature of Britain's independent nuclear deterrent.

18. D.H. Lawrence, *Sketches of Etruscan Places and other Italian Essays* (Harmondsworth: Penguin, 1999), 20. Further references are to this edition and will appear in the text.

19. Let's remember that Lawrence was an accomplished translator of Giovanni Verga.

# 4
# 'You Reckon Folks Really Act Like That?': Horror Films and the Work of Popular Culture in Richard Wright's *Native Son*

*James Smethurst*

The scandalous intersection of race, sex and politics (or perhaps more accurately, interracial sex and politics) has long been extremely powerful in the United States as a tool of social policing (or, less frequently, as a challenge to such policing) and as an engine of popular culture, whether one is talking about the relatively recent revelation that segregationist icon Strom Thurmond had a 'black' daughter, the prosecution of Michael Jackson (and the intervention of the Nation of Islam), or the display of Janet Jackson's breast after a simulated sexual assault by Justin Timberlake during a Super Bowl half-time show. Of course, as the Jackson-Timberlake incident shows, negotiating the boundaries between the sort of scandal that sells and the sort that brings a repression or pressure for self-censorship with a commercial downside is tricky, balancing in Jackson's and Timberlake's case enormous publicity with the risk of suppressive legislation or forced self-censorship restricting a range of potentially scandalous broadcast media practices. In important ways there is a parallel here with the Motion Picture Production Code, a film industry code adopted in 1930, and seriously enforced after 1934. In the writing and production of his 1940 novel, *Native Son*, Richard Wright was highly aware of this treacherous terrain, especially treacherous in the context of the Jim Crow United States. In order to make the novel acceptable to the Book of the Month Club, he was forced to excise passages deemed too sexually graphic, involving masturbation in a movie theatre, or politically controversial, involving Communists.

At the same time, much of the book's sensational charge obviously comes from its approach to interracial sex, particularly in the famous scene that culminates with the death of Mary Dalton at the hands of Bigger Thomas. Immediately before Mary Dalton's death, Thomas finds himself sexually aroused as he tries to get the drunken, semi-conscious young white woman to her bedroom. He begins an intimate contact with Dalton that blurs the boundaries between consensual sex and attempted rape. She seems to respond to him, but can hardly be said to be in a state to give informed consent – in fact, the text describes her as having 'given up'.[1] However, Dalton's blind mother appears like a ghost, preventing any sexual contact beyond a couple of kisses and a touch on the breasts. In a panic to avoid detection, which might provoke a potentially fatal legal (and extra-legal) hysteria, Thomas tries to quiet the drunken Mary Dalton, accidentally smothering her. Ultimately, this more or less accidental death and the presupposition of interracial rape (more than Thomas's actual rape and murder of his black girlfriend, Bessie Mears) does in fact lead to Thomas's death. This scene is, of course, so familiar to students of modern literature that its thrillingly shocking suggestion (and interrupted initiation) of inter-racial sex, straddling the line between rape and consent, might seem a little ho-hum to us now – especially if we are reading the novel in an academic setting. But it certainly was shocking and thrilling then – enough to cause a panel of readers for the Book of the Month Club much anxiety about the book's reception even after Wright accepted their suggested revisions.[2]

However, Wright did not simply utilize scandalous images to sell books, but also interrogated ur-stories of popular culture in his novel. *Native Son* deeply engages the popular culture of the day (film, newsreels, tabloid journalism, pulp fiction, comic books, posters and so on) formally as well as thematically. A major portion of the work Wright attempts to do in *Native Son* is to examine how scandal, especially the scandal of interracial sex displaced onto an impossible and immoral relationship between monster and victim that lies at the heart of the early horror talkie, is used both to sell and to police popular culture – and the social order – through a strange amalgam of fear, desire and sympathy. This policing does not eliminate the thinkability of such behaviour, but instead encourages it as a means of mystifying social relations and class and African American national consciousness. At the same time, Wright depends on the thematic and formal resources of popular culture at least as much as on Dostoevsky, Dreiser and Malraux to structure his cultural critique.

One obvious part of this critique is apparent in the novel's discussion of how popular culture produces and manages scandal, largely determining what is and is not a scandal or a social terror. Early on in the novel the possibility of scandalous miscegenation is raised by a distinction of skin colour between the two 'black boys', Bigger and Buddy Thomas, and their 'brown-skinned' sister, Vera. The potentially shameful, yet titillating nature of this miscegenation is heightened by the proximity of the mention of Vera's skin colour to the scene where Bigger, Buddy, Vera and Mrs Thomas turn their eyes as the others get dressed in their tiny kitchenette apartment. However, this sort of racial crossing does not rise to the level of public outrage in so-called 'mainstream' popular culture – much like the case of Essie Mae Washington-Williams whose parentage was a widely-held secret, yet never emerged as a public scandal until after Thurmond's death.

Of course, in part what Wright is doing here is pointing up the divergence between the African American folk culture of the grapevine and 'mainstream' popular culture. Not only was the figure of the black slave/servant rape victim and white master rapist a prominent part of African American folklore, but so, Wright claims in the novel, was the story of wealthy white women who sought liaisons with black men, again often their servants:

> He remembered hearing somebody tell a story of a Negro chauffeur who had married a rich white girl and the girl's family had shipped the couple out of the country and had supplied them with money. (36)

The white male rapist and the white woman sexually obsessed with black men were also familiar figures of African American literature. The sexually rapacious slave master was a central topos of such antebellum narratives by black authors as Frederick Douglass's *Narrative of the Life of Frederick Douglass* (1845) and Harriet Jacobs's *Incidents in the Life of a Slave Girl* (1861). The wealthy white woman fascinated with the alleged hypersexuality of the black male was a later literary convention, a product largely of the early Jim Crow era (and the heyday of first wave feminism and its anxieties), but one that still dated back at least to James Weldon Johnson's 1912 novel, *Autobiography of an Ex-Colored Man*. However, this figure did not generally circulate in 'mainstream' popular culture in the same manner or to anywhere near the same degree that the black rapist did in so-called 'mainstream' popular literature and the mass circulation press.

Of course, Bigger Thomas and his black peers are in many respects far more connected to 'mainstream' popular culture, especially the movies (both feature films and newsreels) and pulp magazines, than to southern African American folk culture. Despite his birth in the South, the religion and folk-ways of his mother are nearly as alien and incomprehensible to him as his life, fears and desires are to Mrs Thomas. Even his interpretation of the sexuality of rich white women is informed at least as much by the movies as by the grapevine. Thomas does not have any apparent interest in or knowledge of 'high' literature, whether by black or white authors. Still, as Vincent Perez notes, long before Frederick Jameson made his observations about reification and utopia in popular film, Wright shows Thomas and his gang to have a complicated relationship with the films they watch.[3] When Thomas and fellow gang member Gus 'play white', they act out scenarios assembled largely from a pastiche of film and newsreel clichés:

> 'Send your men over the river at dawn and attack the enemy's left flank,' Bigger ordered.
> 'Yessuh.'

'Send the Fifth, Sixth, and Seventh Regiments,' Bigger said, frowning, 'And attack with tanks, gas, planes, and infantry.'

'Yessuh!' Gus said again, saluting and clicking his heels.

For a moment they were silent, facing each other, their shoulders thrown back, their lips compressed to hold down the mounting impulse to laugh. Then they guffawed, partly at themselves and partly at the vast white world that sprawled and towered in the sun before them.

'Say, what's a "left flank"?' Gus asked.

'I don't know,' said Bigger. 'I heard it in the movies.' (21)

The movies, then, become a fantasy of power, freedom and a cool competence. The young men 'play white' in ways that both mock and reinforce their place in the racial imaginary of US popular culture. While, anticipating Louis Althusser, Wright argues that mass culture interpellates or fixes Thomas as a second-class citizen/subject (and mystifies that interpellation), he also claims that Thomas and the new generation of urban working-class African Americans are not simply passive receptacles of mass culture, but to a certain extent fashion their own meaning from it. In this sense he adapts the notion of African Americans as 'nation' in the South and a 'national minority' in the urban North, also known as the 'Black Belt Thesis', that was the official doctrine of the Communist Party of the United States of America (CPUSA) and the Comintern from the late 1920s until the 1950s. Wright suggests how a subjugated nation or national minority might exist without a distinct folk culture or language – or would continue to exist as members of the oppressed nation found themselves in the urban world of consumer capitalism (or 'Black Metropolis' to use the title of the classic 1945 study of black Chicago by Horace Cayton and St Clair Drake for which Wright wrote the introduction).

Perhaps the two dominant characteristics of mass-culture scandal according to Wright are desire (or hunger) and terror, which inhibit true self-consciousness and an ability to understand the larger system. While the base that generates these characteristics, to use the terminology of CPUSA-style Marxism of that era, is economic, this desire and terror is largely displaced onto and mystified by a nexus of sex and race. Even when a bomb-throwing Communist appears in the movie, *The Gay Woman*, Thomas and his fellow gang member Jack imagine Communists 'as a race of folks who live in Russia' (35). The appearance of the Communist terrorist in a film that has to that point been devoted to the scandalous activities of a rich woman and her lover provokes the woman to return to her industrialist husband out of a sort of class solidarity. Again, Thomas and Jack are both strangely sceptical of and taken in by the film:

'She's going back to her old man,' Bigger said.

'Oh yeah,' Jack said. 'They got to kiss in the end.'

Bigger saw the rich young woman rush home to her millionaire husband. There were long embraces and kisses as the rich woman and the rich man vowed never to leave each other and to forgive each other.

'You reckon folks really act like that?' Bigger asked, full of a life he had never seen.

'Sure, man. They rich,' said Jack. (35)

As Michel Fabré and Margaret Walker record, Richard Wright was from his childhood a fanatic moviegoer, seeing as many as three films a day. A number of commentators have also attempted to demonstrate the ways in which this fascination with popular film, generally the crime melodrama, inflects *Native Son*.[4] Of course, as noted above, various movies and the act of moviegoing do much to set the stage of the novel. However, at least as important as the films of gangsters, molls, Reds, fallen women, femmes fatales, and the savages of colonial Africa that actually appear in the novel is the genre of the early Hollywood horror talkie. Perhaps more than in any other genre one finds scandalous sexual relationships openly structured by terror and desire. In a time when interracial sexual relationships were far too explosive to represent on the screen (and actually prohibited by the Motion Picture Production Code), horror films frequently depicted a white (and sometimes virginal) woman as the sexual or sexualized prey of a monstrous man who can be seen as standing in for a racialized alien. In the 1931 version of *Dr Jekyll and Mr Hyde*, Mr Hyde stands over the blonde prostitute/chorus girl Ivy Pearson (whom he eventually murders) on a bed, shouting 'I'll show you what horror means.' Hyde's appearance, often described as 'Neanderthal' (including by the film's director Rouben Mamoulian), resembles popular cartoons of Africans and African Americans as a combination of human and ape with hair kinkier, skin darker, and nose flatter, in short more stereotypically 'Negro', than the 'Anglo-Saxon' Dr Jekyll, with apish incisors and considerably more body hair.[5] Of course, one of the anxieties attending this sexual or sexualized assault inherited from gothic horror literature is that it is also a sort of seduction, featuring a raging female desire or immorality that makes the woman susceptible to the monster, as seen in Count Dracula's transformation of Lucy Westenra into a bloodthirsty siren in the 1931 *Dracula*. Yet, strangely, another recurrent theme of these horror films is the monster as social victim or at least as an object of sympathy trapped in a nightmare he or she cannot escape except through death. Even Dracula, perhaps the least sympathetic of the 1930s' film monsters, is allowed to speak the famous line of Stoker's novel: 'To be dead, to be truly dead, that would be wonderful.'[6]

One of the films with the most obvious intertextual relationship to *Native Son* is the 1931 *Frankenstein*.[7] Unlike the super-intelligent and hyper-articulate creation of Victor Frankenstein in Mary Shelley's 1818 novel, the filmic creature played by Boris Karloff is an overgrown, hideous infant, a near-animal capable of only the most rudimentary speech, resembling descriptions of Bigger Thomas in the popular press after he has been captured by the police:

> His shoulders are huge, muscular, and he keeps them hunched, as if about to spring upon you at any moment. He looks at the world with a strange, sullen, fixed-from-under stare, as though defying all efforts of compassion.
>
> All in all, he seems a beast utterly untouched by the softening influences of modern civilization. In speech and manner he lacks the charm of the average, harmless, genial, grinning southern darky so beloved by the American people. (260)

Though the creature of the film and that of Shelley's novel share a huge stature and features that make them seem of a different race from their creator, the social nature of their identification as monstrous is emphasized far more in the film than in the novel. The monster of the novel almost instantly emerges from its unnatural birth into an existential rage and an Oedipal love/hate relationship with Frankenstein, where the creature of the film has no such self-consciousness, but has monstrousness thrust upon it through the reactions of the humans it meets. Unlike Shelley's monster, the creature of the film lacks any real self-consciousness; instead it is, by the end, motivated by desire and fear and the rage (and guilt) that these generate. As Boris Max, the defence lawyer, points out at Bigger Thomas's trial, Thomas, too, had been a monster whose 'thwarted life expresses itself in fear and hate and crime' without any genuine self-knowledge or self-consciousness (359). However, Thomas's monstrousness is socially created, in large part as a product of mass culture, to an even larger extent than that of the creature of *Frankenstein* (the film). Unlike the huge and hideous creature of the film, Thomas is only of average or slightly more than average height and physically unprepossessing. As James A Miller notes, Thomas is the leader of his gang as much for his ability to verbalize their common feelings as from any physical quality.[8] Nonetheless, the newspaper article presents a sort of reading of Thomas, especially his blackness, that converts him into a combination of Frankenstein's monster, King Kong and Mr Hyde *à la* Frederic March's stereotypically Negro 'Neanderthal' (a connection that the article draws, describing Thomas as being 'like an earlier missing link in the human species' [260]). For example, the article claims 'though the Negro killer's body does not seem compactly built, he gives the impression of possessing abnormal physical strength' (260). It also gives the impression that Thomas, like Frankenstein's creature in the film, is barely able to speak.

Of course, as was the case with most of the early horror talkies, there is a subtext of 'miscegenation' (and an accompanying notion of the obsessive sexual attraction of non-'white' men to 'white' women) underlying the film that resonates with Wright's novel. The shocking accidental death of a small girl, Maria, at the hands of the creature, though like the mirroring death of Mary Dalton unintentional, invokes the psycho-sexual landscape of lynch violence (not, perhaps, unlike the mob violence that killed Thomas's father in the South before his family's migration to Chicago). The sexual subtext of the encounter between the creature and Maria is so obvious as to be almost humorous. 'I'm Maria. Will you play with me?' announces the girl in middle-American tones at odds with the ersatz Central European landscape of the film. 'Would you like one of my flowers?' she asks the creature. The girl and the creature toss flowers into a lake. When he runs out of flowers he throws her into the lake and she drowns. The discovery of her body by her father sets off a frenzied hunt for the murderer. The torch-carrying villagers (led by the police, the mayor and Victor Frankenstein) chase the monster across the weird landscape of mountains and ruins near Castle Frankenstein, again mirrored in Wright's novel in the scene where the police officers with flashlights pursue Bigger Thomas across the weird ruined landscape of the South Side.

While a mob of villagers with torches and dogs in pursuit of a monster became such a familiar (and parodied) convention of the B-horror talkie that it soon entered the realm of camp, it is worth recalling that within the context of the early twentieth-century United States such a pursuit was more familiar as a staple of the representation of lynching in literature and popular culture. The horror film, then, not only became and continued to be a way of talking about 'miscegenation' in popular culture, it also became a medium through which the related subject of lynching could be raised in a way that, as Elizabeth Young points out about *The Bride of Frankenstein*, made the object of mob violence both a monstrous threat to society and a victim.[9] Though the precise nature of the death of Thomas's father in a 'riot' down South is unclear, the familiar horror (and gothic literary) move of nightmare repetition, in which Thomas essentially becomes his father, is hard to miss as Wright attempts to give readers a sense of the terrible weight of history in the present (to paraphrase Marx) through a structure of feeling already present in the horror film and gothic literature.

As in the film version of *Frankenstein*, the obvious question arises in *Native Son* of who is the real monster, the clearly monstrous Thomas, who is a small-time thug, thief, mugger, bully, coward, and ultimately, murderer and rapist, or the system that produced him (and, for that matter, the philanthropist Dalton who donates ping-pong tables to a recreation centre on the South Side paid for by a minute portion of rent money he receives from the black tenants of slum housing that he owns). This notion is expressed in the film most clearly in the scene near the end where Victor Frankenstein is fighting in the tower with his creation. One of the villagers sees them and shouts: 'There's the murderer, now', leaving open the question of who the real culprit might be. The film *Frankenstein* and its sequel the 1935 *Bride of Frankenstein* portray the creature as both victim and monster, an unnatural not-quite-man unable to live. In one of the crucial differences from Shelley's novel, in both the original film and, strangely, its sequel, Victor Frankenstein and his wife Elizabeth survive while the creature must die, again as both victim and monster. One might say that a sort of liberal-humanist critique is expressed here in which a general human intolerance and cruelty is denounced – and yet, another end is unimaginable.

The other classic horror film of the 1930s most heavily invoked in *Native Son* is the 1933 *King Kong*, drawing on the widely circulated racist figuration of Africans and African Americans as 'gorillas' and 'apes' (and with ancient human ancestors, particularly 'Neanderthals', which were popularly associated with apes in pseudo-Darwinian rhetoric).[10] Quite a few commentators have recognized in King Kong's obsession with Ann Darrow an engagement with heightened anxieties about 'miscegenation' in the post-World War I United States.[11] Both the racist figuration of black people as 'apes' and its monstrous connection to Thomas arise on several occasions in *Native Son*. While watching the rich and adulterous woman dancing with her lover at a fashionable nightclub in *The Gay Woman*, Thomas fantasizes about being 'invited to a place like that just to find out what it feels like'. Jack responds by rewriting *The Gay Woman* as a horror film with Thomas as the monstrous lead:

> 'Man, if them folks saw you they'd run,' Jack said. 'They'd think that a gorilla broke loose from the zoo and put on a tuxedo.' (33)

Though both Thomas and Jack break into laughter over Jack's comment, demonstrating its complex nature as both a sort of reification of social control and as a rebellion against that control, it is hard to read this passage without thinking of King Kong loose in New York, 'out of place in a white man's civilization' (260), as the newspaper describes Thomas at the inquest. Thomas is also characterized as a 'black ape' (373) and a 'maddened ape' (376) (as well as a 'black lizard' [373], a 'mad dog' [374] and a 'rapacious beast' [374]) by States Attorney Buckley. If the pursuit of Thomas by the police recalls the mob's chase of Frankenstein's creature, then the moment when Thomas is cornered on the water tank echoes the famous scene of Kong on the Empire State Building. Thomas is slowly dislodged from his hold on the water tank by a high pressure hose and falls much as Kong does from the Empire State Building – a connection that is made more explicit as someone shouts: 'Kill that black ape' (253).

One of the crucial aspects of *King Kong* is the way essentially economic relations are mystified by scandalous popular narratives of desire and terror. The famous post-mortem on Kong offered by the colonial-era adventurer, showman, film-maker, entrepreneur, Denham ('Oh no, it wasn't the airplanes. It was beauty killed the beast') was an outrageous self-justification and distortion of the sequence of events that killed Kong, a sequence that, as in *Frankenstein*, produces sympathy and a sense of just inevitability. It was Denham, after all, who knocked out Kong with state of the art gas bombs, brought him to New York on a ship in chains of chromed steel (summoning an image of the middle passage), and sold tickets at $20 a piece to see 'the eighth wonder of the world'. The capture, enslavement, and transportation of Kong also raise one of the distinctive aspects of the film. *King Kong* is the only major horror talkie of the 1930s and early 1940s that is set significantly in the United States rather than England, Wales, Germany, Transylvania, Egypt or some generic Middle-European or tropical setting. Thus, when Wright speaks of African Americans as part of an American tradition of true horror at the end of the 1940 essay 'How Bigger was Born', which came to serve as an introduction to *Native Son*, Kong, an American monster created through American 'free enterprise' and 'American ingenuity' (and apparently motivated by an American fascination with miscegenation), acquires a particular resonance. Denham's comment is also exactly the sort of tabloid tagline that purports to encapsulate the meaning of an event, but instead is a merchandising come-on that prevents any real understanding of what produced it, much like 'NEGRO RAPIST FAINTS AT INQUEST', a headline that is not precisely a lie, but along with the accompanying article (in which Thomas is again compared to an ape) suggests that his fainting was solely the result of being confronted by the sight of his accusers without noting the obvious signs of starvation, dehydration, lack of sleep and physical abuse (including the tearing off of two of Thomas's fingernails) that might also explain his collapse.

When citing literary ancestors, critics still associate *Native Son* most often with Dreiser's *An American Tragedy* (1925) and Dostoevsky's *Crime and Punishment* (1866). As Barbara Foley notes, though the framings of *Native Son* and *An American Tragedy* differ, there is a sort of parallelism in their stories. However, in general, as she suggests, one of the hallmarks of the naturalist tradition in the United States is a tension set up between the protagonist's belief in the individualistic notions of self-reliance, self-fashioning and free will that are seen as the ideological cornerstones of American society and the implacable forces of nature and society, especially social class, that actually drive the protagonist to his or her appointed end.[12] For example, Clyde Griffiths in *An American Tragedy* delusionally believes in his ability to refashion himself so as to rise above the poverty of his youth. His murder of his pregnant girlfriend, Roberta Alden, is a desperate and foolish attempt to maintain that ability. As Foley points out, much of the power of the novel derives from a social critique that allows the reader to understand that his delusions (not to mention the murder of the working-class Alden) are products of a social system in a way that Griffiths himself never grasps.[13] Even Raskolnikov in *Crime and Punishment*, an obsessive, bitter, self-loathing man crushed by poverty, believes that he can fundamentally alter the terms of his life through the robbery and murder of the pawnbroker Alyona Ivanova.[14]

Conversely, though clearly driven by unconscious or semi-conscious fears and desires largely induced by mass culture and the prohibitions of Jim Crow, Bigger Thomas has little belief in his genuine ability to refashion his life, which he finds blocked by white people at every turn – at least not in the sense that Griffiths or even Raskolnikov thinks of such refashioning. He senses (and everyone around him, including his mother, predicts) that he is going to come to a terrible end. He cannot accept the trap that he finds himself within. He thinks about it constantly. He fantasizes about what it might be like to be outside the trap, but he never really believes that he could get outside. Unlike Raskolnikov, Thomas and his gang cannot bring themselves to rob the storekeeper Blum, largely because their fear tells them that such an act would redefine their relationship to the system so that they would not be allowed to live. Even the deaths of Mary Dalton and Bessie Mears, each in their way the result of his hunger and terror, are attempts to maintain himself within the trap. He cannot even bring himself to leave the South Side to escape the police. It is true that after he has killed, dismembered and burnt Mary Dalton he feels he has embarked on a new life of action. But this life, like that of Rinehart in Ralph Ellison's *Invisible Man* (1952), depends on a knowledge of white blindness that would allow him to operate within the cracks and contradictions of race and class identity in the United States. Thus, one might say that Thomas has an incipient class and racial consciousness that Clyde Griffiths (and Raskolnikov) lack, even if he has only the vaguest sense of what a 'Red' might be and is indifferent or even hostile to the idea of labour unions (with their considerable history of racial discrimination in the United States). If he does not fully comprehend the system, or himself for that matter, he does understand that there is a system that works against him and other poor black people. While he more or less accepts the mass-culture vocabulary of what success might constitute because he has no other way of speaking about it, again, he and his friends do not accept these terms uncritically, but often with bitter laughter that mocks the system as well as themselves.

The monsters of the classic American horror film are similarly trapped. Whether their monstrousness is the result of some supernatural cause (such as a curse or the bite of a vampire or werewolf) or weird science, they find themselves in a sort of existential wheel with no escape but true death and with no real control over their actions and fate. Again, unlike the many protagonists of the naturalist novel, they do not believe they can have any real control – hence Dracula's longing to be 'truly dead'. They are all outsiders or aliens that invoke racist and nativist anxieties while engaging the related fear that the alien is as likely to emerge from within as from Transylvania, the Lower East Side or the South Side – a fear emphasized by the fact that the vampire, mummy, invisible man, brute, was once a human (often an 'Anglo-Saxon', highly educated human). In many instances, even true death is not really the end in the horror movie. More than any other genre of film in the 1930s and the 1940s, the horror film produced sequels featuring monsters that had apparently been destroyed in a previous movie. The very supernatural or quasi-supernatural nature of the monster, accompanied by the nightmare logic that structured the gothic narrative out of which the horror film significantly emerged, made such a reappearance plausible. Even if the monster did not literally reappear, often it is able to reproduce itself through a vampire's or werewolf's bite, a formula or scientific apparatus rediscovered, and so on, suggesting that the monster/beast, the mad scientist, solicitor, or foolish explorer who unleashes a curse, the female prey/obsession/partner/beauty, and so on, are not, despite often intense and agonizing introspection, individuals, but interchangeable examples of types. Again, this has an obvious resonance with *Native Son* in which both States Attorney Buckley and Boris Max present Bigger Thomas as a type, even if their readings differ. Like the horror film, as Max argues, there will be many sequels in which the apparently dead Thomas will return to life – and more Mary Daltons will die; more Mr Daltons will be baffled by crimes as inexplicable to them as the supernatural killings of a vampire or resurrected mummy; more mobs with torches will chase monsters across ruined landscapes; and so on. In fact, in his courtroom plea to spare Bigger Thomas's life, Max draws upon the familiar language, tropes and imagery of the horror film, including displaced fears of miscegenation, in a compound of *Dracula, Frankenstein, Dr Jekyll and Mr Hyde* and *The Mummy*:

> 'But the corpse returns and raids our homes! We find our daughters murdered and burnt! And we say "Kill! Kill!"'
> 'But, Your Honor, I say: "Stop! Let us look at what we are doing!" for the corpse is not dead! It still lives! It has made a home in the wild forest of our great cities, amid the rank and choking vegetation of slums! It has forgotten our language! In order to live it has sharpened its claws! It has developed a capacity for hate and fury that we cannot understand! Its movements are unpredictable! By night it creeps from its lair and steals toward the settlements of civilization!' (362)

The structure of Max's speech mirrors that of Wright's novel in some important respects. Again, both set up their argument by drawing on the horror film with its engagement of racist and nativist fears about the outsider (and the outsider within us) that have at their base an economic motive, but that are often figured as a horrifying and fascinating miscegenation that blurs the line between rape and depraved consensual sex. Both draw, too, on the horror film's strange sympathy for the monstrous alien, a sympathy often engendered by a sense that the monster has been produced, trapped into monstrousness, by forces not entirely of its own making: it does not have any real control over its actions. As noted above, both the novel and Max's speech do not simply, to use Barbara Foley's notion in a different context, parallel the classic horror talkie of the 1930s and 1940s, but display the themes, tropes and language of the horror film in ways that can hardly be missed. However, both the speech and the novel have at least one significant difference from the horror genre: a self-reflexive notion that the system can be understood, and that the individual and the collective people can take responsibility for their acts – though perhaps that is a lesson that Thomas learns more completely than Max. While the individual might have little control over his or her destiny, collectively it might be possible to break out of the wheel of fate and fear. Max's speech so transparently renders Thomas's life and Thomas's crimes (and, indeed, the way race structures and is structured by the society of the United States) in terms of a horror film that it brings attention to what we might now call the constructed nature of race, and of narratives of hierarchy and power that manufacture and regulate race. At the same time, Max, like Wright, uses the horror genre to try to draw the fear, pity, desire, and ultimately the sympathy of the audience.

In other words, if Bigger Thomas had fallen to his death after being knocked off the water tank by the spray of the fire hose (or had been killed by a mob like his father may have been), perhaps an insincere or self-deluded commentator would have made the sort of philosophical epitaph that Denham made about the end of Kong, mixing sympathy with relief, but occluding the real meaning of Kong's monstrousness and demise. In short, it would have been in many respects a typical horror story. However, Thomas survives long enough to be tried. Though both Buckley and Max cast Bigger as monstrous lead in a horror film, something else happens that changes the genre of *Native Son* and also provides a sort of interpretive guide to the book and its relation to popular culture, to the way that popular culture shapes the various discourses of the United States, including literary, scientific and legal discourses.

Max does not simply write a script of the horror movie of Thomas's life, and the life of 'the resentful millions' of African Americans, but he is a sort of critic who in his summation to the court and in his private conversations with Thomas interprets the meaning of that film, attempting to lay bare its devices and the material base of the terror, desire, rage and sympathy mystified in statements like Denham's 'It wasn't the airplanes. It was beauty killed the beast' or Buckley's 'It is a sad day for American civilization when a white man will try to stay the hand of justice from a bestial monstrosity who has ravished and struck down one of the finest and most delicate flowers of our womanhood' (373). Max also suggests the nature of the duality of popular culture, how someone like Thomas could find the idea of monstrousness both imprisoning and empowering, how the idea of being a great ape, or a sort of Hyde free to act out all his desires without fear or conscience, might give him a sense of freedom – a sense that a white audience might strangely and perhaps shamefacedly feel. He even suggests, as does Wright at the end of 'How Bigger was Born', that this horror is produced by people even as it produces them, and that class and racial domination structure this horror that is, as Marx famously suggested, part of the scaffolding that helps maintain such domination. Max, like Wright, claims that it is 'the belief in the hearts of men' that holds up the skyscrapers of 'steel and stone' (389), and yet brings into being its own gravedigger (another familiar icon of the horror film as well as Marxism), generating unrest and anger that is cast as monstrous. One possibility that Max raises is that workers and oppressed nationalities can understand the horror, can understand their rage, and then perhaps find in collective understanding the agency that is denied to the individual to change the fate that seems to be predestined.

Of course, another possibility that the book raises, anticipated in Marx's notion that barbarism was the other plausible destination of human society besides socialism, is that segments of the working class, mesmerized by various mass-culture narratives of fear and desire, will opt for fascism (an option that holds an appeal for Thomas who at one point imagines with approval a black Hitler or Mussolini). Hence the political need for inter-pretation, for going beyond horror narrative and popular culture generally through such interpretation, even if it is necessary to use popular genres that not only imprison the working class and the various oppressed groups as they were understood by the CPUSA in the 1930s, but also allow them an avenue for the figuration of their own interests and desires, however distorted. In this, *Native Son* can be seen as a companion to 'Blueprint for Negro Writing' (1937) where Wright posited folklore as the cultural base of African Amer-ican nationalism and proclaimed the need for black authors to 'accept the concept of nationalism because, in order to transcend it, they must *possess* and *understand* it' (48).[15] In *Native Son*, Wright considers the complicated relationship of the children of the 'Black Metropolis' to the popular culture that, though less simply theirs than the folk culture of their parents and grandparents, does not simply interpellate them, but provides them with an avenue for their own dreaming of national, class and individual agency. Again, the question is not whether to ignore or destroy popular culture, but to '*possess* and *understand* it' – and, to transpose Marx once more, to change it.

Of course that is not easy. Strangely, in the end, Max seems more confused than Bigger. He at least professes to believe that there is still hope for Thomas to survive, for the governor to intervene, when Thomas, in keeping with a sort of racial and class sense that he possessed from the start, knows that it is over. In the ambiguous ending of the novel Thomas seems to take Max's lesson to heart in many respects and accepts the responsibility for his actions in ways that scare Max, his 'eyes full of terror' (392). 'What I killed for I *am!'* shouts Thomas to Max. 'What I killed for must've been good!' he adds (391–2). Yet despite the note of terror in these words, that might be, in the spirit of Max's earlier explication, a recognition of a class and Negro national spirit lying beneath Thomas's violence, or of something more truly monstrous (as monstrous as the killing and dismemberment or disfiguration of two women actually were), these are not Thomas's last words before saying good-bye to Max. He also tells Max to 'Tell Jan hello' (392). While it is not clear that for all his sympathy and analytical abilities Max learns anything from Thomas that he can accept, Mary Dalton's boyfriend Jan Erlone has been enlightened about the 'national question', which Wright suggests in 'How Bigger was Born' is the gothic 'shadow athwart' the national life of the United States (*Native Son*, xxxiv). Even though Thomas tried to frame Erlone, an earnest Communist who was initially nearly as naive and patronizing as Mary, Erlone is able to see the question more clearly through his contact with Thomas during the inquest and trial, and is able to see beyond the monstrous shadow. If there is hope that someone as unsympathetically thuggish, even pathological, as Thomas, and as patronizing and clueless as Erlone, can get beyond that shadow, then there is some larger possibility of getting beyond the cultural wheel in which the 'utopia and reification' inherent in mass culture, to use Frederick Jameson's famous formulation, are in uneasy balance.[16]

*Native Son* is one of many works of what might be thought of as the extended Popular Front period of cultural production that remained fairly consistent from the mid-1930s until the early 1950s, whatever the political zigs and zags of the CPUSA and the international Communist movement during those years. As was also particularly the case in the work of such Left African American writers of the period as Langston Hughes, Lloyd Brown, Frank Marshall Davis, Owen Dodson, Ann Petry, Gwendolyn Brooks and Margaret Walker, the engagement with and analysis of the work of popular culture of *Native Son* is complex and fundamental to its project, anticipating in many respects the work of various sorts of critics broadly associated with cultural studies and Marxism, who, especially in the English-speaking world unfortunately, often take the notion of a 'vulgar' Marxist approach to culture in the 1930s as a given. Popular Front approaches to mass culture have often been seen as naively and sentimentally sunny as well as effacing of ethnic and national difference. *Native Son*, however, with its simultaneous invocation and critique of popular culture, especially the horror film, in dialogue with works that self-reflexively draw on and investigate the cost of these usages, such as Davis's 'Snapshots of the Cotton South' (1937), Hughes's 'Note on Commercial Theatre' (1940), Brooks's *A Street in Bronzeville* (1945), Petry's *The Street* (1946), Brown's *Iron City* (1951), and, as Barbara Foley has shown, early versions of Ralph Ellison's *Invisible Man*, is squarely within the discussions and debates about contestation and control in popular culture that characterized Popular Front literature and art.[17] The novel also serves as a reminder that the similar discussions and debates of the Black Arts era of the 1960s and 1970s and, later, of cultural studies as situated in the United States had a considerable foreground in radical African American literature.

## Notes

1. Richard Wright, *Native Son*, 1940 (New York: Perennial, 2001), 83. All page citations of *Native Son* refer to this edition of the abridged 1940 text. As Hazel Rowley notes, Dalton more clearly responds to Thomas sexually in the earlier, unabridged version of this moment in a scene that was excised at the behest of the Book of the Month Club along with other passages that highlight Dalton as an enthusiastic libidinal actor – though the notion of interracial sex, even consensual interracial sex, was not as taboo in American fiction as Rowley suggests, but had been a staple of African American literature since the mid-nineteenth century – not to mention in such now canonical modernist works as William Faulkner's *Light in August* (1932). It might also be worth pointing out that while Rowley may be correct in claiming that these changes weakened the book in certain respects, they actually are more consonant with Wright's use of the horror film outlined in this chapter. In other words, Wright may have accepted the cuts for artistic reasons rather than simply acquiescing to a timid and arguably racist panel of judges for reasons of convenience. Hazel Rowley, *Richard Wright: the Life and Times* (New York: Henry Holt, 2001), 182–3.
2. Rowley, 183–4.
3. Vincent Perez. 'Movies, Marxism, and Jim Crow: Richard Wright's Cultural Criticism', *Texas Studies in Literature and Language*, 43, 2 (2001), 156. Perez's essay is an extremely useful general overview of the ambivalent nature of Wright's use of popular culture in his early work – and of the limitations of the Frankfurt School model of mass culture for analysing the complex work that popular culture does in Wright's early fiction. For another valuable take on the contradictory nature of Bigger Thomas's viewership of Hollywood films, see Jacqueline Stewart, *Migrating to the Movies: Cinema and Black Urban Modernity* (Berkeley: University of California Press, 2005), 98–107.
4. Michel Fabré, *The Unfinished Quest of Richard Wright* (New York, 1973), 200; Margaret Walker, *Richard Wright, Daemonic Genius* (New York: Morrow, 1988), 220–4; Ross Pudaloff, 'Bigger Thomas as a Product of Mass Culture', in *Readings on Native Son*, edited by Hayley R. Mitchell (San Diego: Greenhaven Press, 2000), 98–106; Charles Scruggs, *Sweet Home: Invisible Cities in the Afro-American Novel* (Baltimore: Johns Hopkins University Press, 1993), 95–7.
5. Rouben Mamoulian (director), *Dr Jekyll and Mr Hyde*, Paramount Pictures, 1931. If one watches the initial transformation of Jekyll into Hyde in slow motion or frame by frame, its racial character is particularly striking. It is significant that this physical devolution of the actor Frederic March with the use of much make-up in the 1931 film differs quite a bit from the 1920 silent version in which John Barrymore creates his Hyde almost entirely through facial expression and only a minimal amount of make-up, as well as from Robert Louis Stevenson's original account of Hyde as being pale and dwarfish, if more physically vigorous than Jekyll. The 1931 film's connection of Hyde to racially overdetermined popular American portraits of the so-called 'Neanderthal Man' and apes closely resembles the newspaper description of Bigger Thomas in *Native Son*. (Interestingly, the

*New York Times* review of the film also comments on the apelike character of Hyde.) Of course, Stevenson's novel, too, describes Hyde as 'troglodytic'. However, there the pale, dwarfish appearance and 'murderous mixture of timidity and boldness' of Hyde have more to do with displaced British anxieties about class and notions that the factory system was producing two nations or two races of the English people (with Hyde taking on stereotypical features of urban slumdwellers) seen in much nineteenth-century industrial literature, finding perhaps its most extreme expression in the Eloi and Morlocks of H.G. Wells's *The Time Machine* (1895), than the common American association of 'Negroes' with Neanderthal Man and apes. Robert Louis Stevenson, *The Strange Case of Dr Jekyll and Mr Hyde*, 1886 (London: Penguin Books, 1979), 40; Mordaunt Hall, 'Frederic March in a Spendidly Produced Pictorial Version of "Dr Jekyll and Mr Hyde"', review of *Dr Jekyll and Mr Hyde* (Paramount Pictures movie), *New York Times*, 2 January 1932, 14.

6. Tod Browning (director), *Dracula*, Universal Studios, 1931.

7. James Whale (director), *Frankenstein*, Universal Studios, 1931.

8. James A. Miller, 'Bigger Thomas's Quest for Voice and Audience in Richard Wright's *Native Son*', *Callaloo*, 9 (summer 1986), 502–3.

9. Elizabeth Young. 'Here Comes the Bride: Wedding Gender and Race in "Bride of Frankenstein"', *Feminist Studies*, 17, 3 (autumn 1991), 422–9.

10. Merian C. Cooper and Ernest B. Schoedsack, *King Kong*, RKO Radio Pictures, 1933.

11. For the most extended treatment of *King Kong* and race, see James A. Snead, *White Screens, Black Images* (New York: Routledge, 1994), 1–36.

12. Barbara Foley, 'The Politics of Poetics: Ideology and Narrative Form in *An American Tragedy* and *Native Son*', in James Phelan, ed., *Narrative Poetics: Innovations, Limits, Challenges* (Columbus: Center for Comparative Studies in the Humanities, 1987), 192.

13. Foley, 'Politics of Poetics', 193.

14. One might add that the classic crime melodrama is also characterized by a sort of self-willed demonic Romantic hero who is brought low at the end not only by police bullets, but also by a realization of how he has been deluded by his self-image. Charles Scruggs perceptively distinguishes the final emotional collapse of the typical gangster hero from the lack of such a collapse on Thomas's part (95–7). While Scruggs associates this concluding deflation of the gangster hero with the strictures of the Motion Picture Production Code, it is worth noting that it had also been characteristic of some of the most seminal gangster films from the period before the code was seriously enforced, notably *The Public Enemy* (1931) and *Scarface* (1932).

15. Richard Wright. 'Blueprint for Negro Writing', in Winston Napier, ed., *African American Literary Theory* (New York: New York University Press, 2000), 45–53.

16. Frederic Jameson, 'Reification and Utopia in Mass Culture', *Social Text*, 1 (winter 1979), 130–48.

17. Barbara Foley, 'From Communism to Brotherhood: the Drafts of *Invisible Man*', in Bill V. Mullen and James Smethurst, eds, *Left of the Color Line: Race, Radicalism and Twentieth-Century Literature of the United States* (Chapel Hill: University of North Carolina Press, 2003), 163–82.

# 5
# Scandalous for being Scandalous: 'monstrous huge fuck[s]' and 'slambanging big sodomies' in Jack Kerouac's *On the Road*

*R.J. Ellis*

*On the Road* is by reputation a scandalous fiction: 'Jack Kerouac's *On the Road*... proved explosive. Under its influence, kids hit the drugs and booze, and ditched home and college for the drifter's life... it was written in three weeks... Sal Paradise and Dean Moriarty... zig-zag the continent in search of sex, drugs, and thrills [as] barely disguised versions of Kerouac and [Neal] Cassady.' It's difficult to know quite where to start scraping away at the accretions of myth and miscomprehension contained in this sketch by Christina Patterson of what she defined in 2005 as a 'Cult Classic'.[1] The novel that was published by Viking in 1957 was not written in three weeks. Though, famously, an early version of it, the so-called 'scroll' version, was indeed rapidly composed on several long sheets of paper in (more or less) a three-week period in April 1951, the novel that was published in 1957 was the product of a long series of retypings, revisions and adjustments to that text.[2] These revisions were then complicated by Kerouac's return to the scroll version just before he typed out the novel yet again, probably in late 1956. This retype did bring *On the Road*'s final version back to a form that was quite close to the scroll version. But important differences remained – including the incorporation of material from letters to Kerouac (mostly from Neal Cassady) and Kerouac's own journal entries.[3] *Road*'s final retyping was then subjected to a sustained editorial process, as Kerouac negotiated with his editors (primarily Malcolm Cowley).[4] Nor does the book depict Sal and Dean zigzagging across America that frequently. Though their several trips together are described, the majority of *On the Road* deals with Sal travelling alone (in the long first section in particular) or with events in New York, San Francisco and, to a lesser degree, Denver. Patterson's suggestion that Sal and Dean search for drugs is in turn largely misleading; this may be somewhat

99

true of the final trip the two take to Mexico, but it is not true of much of the rest of the book. Sal more often comes across drugs than searches for them, and for the first hundred-plus pages his narrative is largely free of any mention of such recreations.

It is true that all of these points have to be made in the teeth of the book's reputation, to which Patterson is in turn contributing. Patterson's use of the characterization, 'sex, drugs and thrills' – deliberately echoing established formulaic sensationalizations ('sex, drugs and rock'n'roll'), also deceives in this fashion: as its readers have repeatedly observed to me, *On the Road* contains disconcertingly few thrills and little sex. As one teenage daughter of a friend commented in 2005, the novel proved a disappointing and uneventful read, measured against its reputation: Sal came across as 'boring', Dean as more exciting, but someone you would not want to be around for too long. Patterson's thumbnail sketch of Kerouac's novel is, however, right in claiming that the book is heavily autobiographical: it is – though, again, the differences between Kerouac's life and the novel are important.[5] By now the question which arises must be: why is this book scandalous?

The answer seems to reside in the one way in which Patterson is wholly right about *On the Road*: it did prove explosive. Quite why is one central question I want to address in this chapter, not least because in important respects there was no obvious reason why it should have been. There were, simply put, far more explosive texts around by the time *On the Road* appeared, and in many ways more sensational texts had been published well before the scroll version was written. Henry Miller's *Tropic of Capricorn* and *Tropic of Cancer* spring to mind in the latter respect,[6] though in this chapter I want to focus upon a few books written more or less at the same time as Kerouac's benzedrine-fuelled typing-out of *On the Road's* famous scroll in 1951. A complex process of reputation-construction is occurring, and this chapter will consider the question of how 'scandal' (be[com]ing scandalized) is constructed around this book, turning it into a scandal (be[com]ing scandalous). In this sense I will be de-essentializing 'scandal' – suggesting that there is no necessary alignment between the amount of sex, drugs and thrills in a book on the one hand and the 'scandal' it stirs up on the other. *On the Road* by 1957 had a scandalous reputation despite being quite tame, not only by twenty-first century standards, but even by those of the 1950s – whether thinking of the standards of 1951/2 or of 1957. In so far as I am using *On the Road* as a species of case study, then, I must caution that, as an example, it is far from typical, though I must immediately add that, when constructing scandal, there are no usual models. What might be loosely described as an ethnomethodological approach is needed, defining the local, moment by moment determination of literary scandal in all its contexts, when exploring the construction of the scandalous.[7]

With respect to *On the Road*, a cultural reading is first called for, taking as its departure point the long delay between the book's inception and first 'completion', on the one hand, and its final publication on the other. There are important differences between 1948–51 and 1956–57, in terms of the dominant constructions of how US society should work. A starting point must be to note that the late forties constitute a very different period to the mid-to-late fifties. The latter period is a largely prosperous time, when the discourses of the Cold War are well established: a time when the Iron Curtain has long descended across Europe (Churchill declared its descent in 1946); when the Korean War has unfolded (between 1950 and 1953); when the Russians have tested an atom bomb (in 1949) and a hydrogen bomb (in 1953). Following anti-Communist initiatives like the Alien Registration Act of 1940 and the House Committee on Un-American Activities (founded in 1937 and directed at Communism from 1947), McCarthyism had in 1950 gained a hold on public opinion, aided by revelations concerning Stalin's excesses and show trials, helping cement in place an enduring anti-Communism before losing sway in 1954 (after McCarthy turned on government institutions). Also, service personnel had returned from combat zones, triggering a gathering remobilization of the patriarchal concept of the domestic. Weakened during the war, when women had entered the military and the labour force in significant numbers, its nostrums were re-energized: one product was a baby boom in the 1950s that reached its climax in 1957.[8]

By contrast 1947–49, the period in which *On the Road* is set, is distinctly different: in each instance where the cast of the mid-fifties is anticipated – the Iron Curtain, the Cold War, the nuclear arms race, increasing anti-Communism, the resuscitation of patriarchal domesticity – the precise cast of these formative influences was yet to be discursively elaborated. In the immediate postwar atmosphere they are more nascent and inchoate, in a transitional economy. The Communist coup in Czechoslovakia and the Berlin airlift of 1948 proved to be precipitants in this respect, dramatizing a changed set of international relations and unleashing uncertainty and anxiety. But other compelling influences existed, to do with loosely defined but very real tensions and articulations, revolving around the immediate consequences of the return of servicemen and women to the USA – a large group of people, mostly young, exposed to international travel to non-US cultures in a way which none but the bourgeoisie and a small cultural elite had experienced previously. But it was an exposure of a particular and stressful kind: not an insulated grand tour with safe conduct, but often a messy immersion involving hostility, danger, death and a fair measure of the involuntary and arbitrary. These exposures, furthermore, were based within a particular kind of institution, the military, frequently homosocial in cast, and involving its young recruits in far from traditional exposures to sex and sexuality. Many of these young people were the children – quite literally – of the Depression, brought up (though not born) during the 1930s. The return of this large population witnessed an initial period of impecunity for many (with one-third of Americans below the poverty line in 1950).[9] Some made hasty embraces of 'normality' – marriages rose sharply.[10] Indeed, one reviewer of *On the Road*, noting that Dean Moriarty had 'three wives', dryly observes, 'This, after all, is the marrying generation.'[11] But divorce rose sharply, too, and women's numbers in the workforce remained buoyant,[12] whilst some ex-service personnel remained liminal figures in US urban society, joining an already-existing underground, dispersed into the towns and cities of the USA – especially the larger cities (a process well recorded in the closing pages of Kerouac's first novel, *The Town and the City*, 1950).[13] There their presence proved disruptive. Urban America's more or less cosmopolitan liminal contact zone, where for many decades the bohemian *flâneur* had encountered poverty and its human penumbra, became complicated by the arrival of women and (mostly) men, discharged from the services and clutching onto both their veterans' payments and their memories of alien encounters that had often been of an unpredictable, edgy and exotic kind. The effect was disruptive. Sal Paradise, *On the Road*'s narrator, noteworthily, is one of these liminals. Or, more accurately, he is not quite, but nearly one of these, if we accept *On the Road*'s autobiographical underpinnings, since Kerouac was not a veteran of the European or Pacific campaigns, but had been discharged in 1942 on the grounds of 'indifferent character'.[14] Yet I must here make the point that this is not something the novel specifies: the precise engagement of Sal with active service is left undefined: all we know is that he is in receipt of a veteran's payments.

In other words, *On the Road*, by the time it was published in 1957, had become something of a historical novel. It treats a period of US history, the late 1940s, during which the disruptive presence of a population of male and female war veterans was interacting tensely with all levels of USAmerican society.[15] But it was published at a time when the resulting disruption had substantially moderated, the 'marrying generation' had often married and reproduced, and instead Cold War USA's characteristic, often paranoid concerns had come to dominate the agenda – the legacy not only of Berlin, Hiroshima and Belsen, but also of McCarthy, Korea and rising tensions over China and Vietnam. It is perhaps worth recalling that Kerouac had sought to get *On the Road* published, wholly unrevised, as soon as he completed it in 1951.[16] The cultural matrix that *On the Road* could have been enmeshed in had it been published in 1952 – the earliest date it could have been released – would have been quite different from the one into which it was launched in 1957.

It needs to be noted as well that the text of *On the Road* would also have been considerably different if it had been published in 1952. The novel that appeared in 1957 deviates repeatedly from the text of the scroll. Where the scroll (henceforth also referred to as *Road* 51) does not deploy pseudonyms consistently, but names such protagonists as Neal Cassady and Allen Ginsberg, the 1957 published version (henceforth *Road* 57) uses pseudonyms.

Whilst a safe assumption is that editorial anonymizing would have occurred in 1951 as it did in 1957, the other differences, though minor, are important. I want particularly to pick out in this respect the reduced emphasis that *Road* 57 places on Dean Moriarty's homosexual propensities. These are distinctly downplayed – as has long been apparent to critics. One of the numerous partial rewrites of *On the Road*, a rewrite discarded sometime during the period 1951–57, eventually appeared in the final section of *Visions of Cody* (1972). In this passage, Moriarty/Cody is revealed as having vigorous sex with the driver of the 'fag' Plymouth on his and Sal's penultimate shuttle across America. *Visions* is explicit: 'Cody thrashed him on rugs in the dark, monstrous huge fuck... slambanging big sodomies that made me sick... I sat in the castrated toilet listening and peeking, at one point Cody had him thrown over legs in the air like a dead hen' (*V* 358–9). By contrast, *On the Road* is obliquely evasive: 'Dean asked him how much money [the driver] had. I was in the bathroom. The fag became extremely sullen and I think suspicious of Dean's final motives, turned over no money, and made vague promises for Denver... Dean threw up his hands... "You see.... Offer them what they secretly want and they of course immediately become panic-stricken"' (*R* 209). Equally significantly, as Ann Charters notes in her 'Introduction' to her 1991 edition of *On the Road*, Allen Ginsberg's homosexual propensities are considerably diluted. Thus, *Road* 57 omits the following passage from *Road* 51: 'Allen was queer in those days, experimenting with himself to the hilt, and Neal saw this... [as] a former boyhood hustler in the Denver night... with a great amorous soul such as only a conman can have. I was in the same room. I heard them across the darkness and I mused and said to myself "... I don't want anything to do with it".'[17]

This change deserves dwelling on, because in itself it marks the way that the disruptive presence of returned male and female veterans had precipitated a heightened visibility for homosexual and lesbian sexual practices in urban city culture (in New York/Chicago/San Francisco in particular). This in turn had precipitated controversy around the Kinsey Report (famously during his research Kinsey interviewed Allen Ginsberg, William Burroughs and, possibly, Jack Kerouac and Herbert Huncke). Its suggestion that no one was wholly heterosexual or wholly homosexual generated debates about latency which were often connected to service peoples' discovery of homosexual or lesbian inclinations during their army service.[18] By the mid-1950s the underlying hegemonic processes pressing towards conformity, allied to McCarthy-inspired conflations of paranoia over Communism and homosexuality, had heightened homophobic responses to these developments. It had become far less easy to consider publishing frank portraits of homosexuality. (The fate of William Burroughs's *Queer* is instructive in this respect, for where *Junkie* was published by Ace Books in 1953, *Queer*, written just afterwards, in 1952, was never brought out by Ace, despite initial interest, and remained unpublished until 1985.[19]) Homophobia and paranoia about 'latency' had taken a concerted cultural grip by the mid-1950s. In other words, by introducing the changes between *Road* 51 and *Road* 57, one 'scandalous' aspect of *On the Road* had been substantially toned down. It is even less explicitly about 1950s' norm-transgressing 'sex' than it might have been.

I inserted the words 'even less' very carefully in the preceding sentence, for – to return to my main argument – an inspection of the kinds of novels treating with the postwar interface between bohemia, inner city poverty and returning servicemen and women published in the early 1950s shows them to be considerably more transgressive than *Road* 57, or, even, *Road* 51. I want to focus on just three of these novels at this point, Chandler Brossard's *Who Walk in Darkness*, George Mandel's *Flee the Angry Strangers* and John Clellon Holmes's *Go*, all published in 1952, the year when, plausibly, *Road* 51 could have been released. Arguably, the content of all of these novels could have led them to be selected as being at least as 'scandalous' as any version of *Road*. I will, then, consider the cultural processes by which *Road* 57 was elected to this 'scandalous' status enduringly, where the other novels were not.

*Who Walk in Darkness* centres itself around three protagonists, Henry Porter, who enjoys the reputation of being able 'to pick up almost any woman he saw' (*W* 9), his girlfriend, Grace, and his friend, the book's narrator, Blake. Porter has served in the army – though probably this draft is the continuing postwar draft (this is left unclear, though he was drafted after 'quit[ting] Berkeley'). He has subsequently married and then broken up with his wife. The parallels with Sal's position at the start of *Road* 57 are suggestive, for Sal, recently discharged from the army, has also just been through a 'miserably weary split-up' with his wife and has dropped out of college (*R* 3). And, like Sal, Blake, 'Regular, loyal, traditional' (*W* 132) is in a buddy relationship – with the more volatile, unpredictable and excessive Porter. The parallels between Porter and Dean are limited, however. Porter (not Blake) is the writer in the book, and a moderately successful one (somewhat further down the road than Sal in this respect). Close disruptive male relationships under strain constitute the common ground between the respective pairings in the two novels, and arguably are the product of a homosocial carry-over from military experiences. Within *Walk*'s 'underground' (*W* 65), furthermore, sex and drugs and – arguably – 'thrills' figure prominently – almost as prominently, indeed, as in *On the Road*. In *Walk*, one central character is the drug-pusher, Cap, concerned to provide his clients with high-grade marijuana:

> 'Did you get?' Max asked...
> Cap nodded his head. 'Listen, man,' he said. 'This is really great charge. The best. I know. But it will cost you.'
> 'How much?' Max asked.
> 'An ace for two sticks.'

> Cap talked thick and strange. He was really high.
> 'That's steep, man,' Max said. (*W* 12)

Alcohol is also consumed regularly in large quantities, and drunken and drug-infested dance parties are attended, where bebop is played:

> The music was fast. If you did not listen to it carefully it did not make any sense to you. Each player seemed to be playing something personal on his own that had nothing to do with what the others were playing, and the whole composition they were playing did not seem to have any pattern. But actually it did. If you listened carefully you heard each player play a variation on what another player had just finished playing, and then he would add something of his own and another player would pick it up from there. (*W* 90)

Brossard's Blake does not quite provide the 'jazzy ride' of Kerouac's first-person narrator, Sal. Rather, a pervasive Hemingwayesque plangency is struck up by Blake's clipped narration. (Symptomatically, boxing provides an important backstory to *Walk*'s main plot-lines.) But drugs, drink and casual sex populate the pages of Brossard's novel just about as thickly as those of *Road*, whilst an important plot turning-point is provided by an abortion. Though I am arguing that scandal cannot be solely generated by content but is rather the product of a complex matrix of cultural factors, were I temporarily to allow 'scandal' to be solely measured by 'scandalous content', then whether Brossard or Kerouac is the more scandalous in this limited (essentialist) sense is unclear.

When it comes to George Mandel's *Flee the Angry Strangers*, however, *On the Road* is clearly the less scandalous, if content alone is again allowed to be the essential consideration. *Flee* is a complexly plotted novel, without a main narrator, and centring itself around the life of an attractive waif-like teenager, Diane. An escapee from a species of reformatory (to which her mother committed her), Diane holds deep allure for a number of men: Carter, married to her dying sister, Edna (who commits suicide); Joe, a Southerner just out of uniform, having fought in World War Two and subsequently as an international mercenary; Stoney, a lecherous, aging, failed painter; Dincher, a besuited young teenage hood who tries to protect her; and Buster, who trusses her up and rapes her (*F* 321–2). If this last sensational detail seems to be in another class to the sort of episode encountered in *Road*, then it immediately has to be added that this is only a small part of the potential the book has for being more sensational. Carter's wife, Edna has been a prostitute; Diane also becomes one during the course of the novel, having previously slept with so many men she has lost track: 'I've been in more guy's pants than you can count' (*F* 216); Diane also becomes a heroin addict and cannot kick her habit despite twice undergoing (vividly described) cold turkey; she helps a team roll drunks on Broadway to make a living; and she participates in sadomasochistic sessions which involve her whipping a homosexual, Timmy, with a leather belt until he bleeds (*F* 306–7). The back-stories are just as startling, such as Stoney's rape of the would-be poet and fringe-of-society, Louella (*F* 99). The book, much more than *Walk*, is packed with 'petty-thiev[ing] . . . dope-pass[ing] "characters"' (*F* 7) and ends depressingly, with an intimation that Diane's downward spiral cannot be reversed.

John Clellon Holmes's *Go*, set besides *Flee the Angry Strangers*, is modest fare, though it has its share of drunkenness and drug-usage, infidelities, violence and homosexuality. Though the latter two are in conspicuously short supply in *Road* 57, *Go* is overall not much more sensational in terms of its content, though towards its end its pace picks up. The arrival of a criminal couple and an addict in the apartment of one of the central characters, Stofsky, where they take heroin and conduct their criminal business (including stealing cars and black-jacking marks), is paralleled with a wretchedly drunken party ending in disaster just as news of Stofsky's arrest comes though. *Go* also deserves mention because of its sharing with *On the Road* of common, drawn-from-life, characters and incidents. It is well known that Kerouac resented *Go*'s publication, feeling that Holmes had pre-empted his own book somewhat and that Holmes had stolen from him, in an act of literary plagiarism, his idea of the emergence of a 'Beat generation' in the immediate postwar period.[20] These accusations are poorly grounded. Holmes widely acknowledged Kerouac's parentage of the term 'Beat generation' (and made this clear in his 1952 essay, 'This is the Beat Generation'; indeed, one 1957 *New York Times* reviewer knew perfectly well that Kerouac had coined the phrase).[21] Kerouac anyway could hardly claim copyright on depicting the lives of his New York associates. Holmes did, however, pre-empt Kerouac (and knew full well what the subject of Kerouac's next novel was going to be). Symptomatic of this trumping was how Nelson Algren, in a review of *On the Road*, described it as treating with the ' "Go" generation'.[22] The 'row' that blew up between Kerouac and Holmes was one (albeit minor) contributory factor in cooking up the 'scandal' that was coming to invest *On the Road* between 1952 and 1957.

However, *Go* is even more interesting for my immediate purposes because of Holmes's decision to give Ginsberg and Kerouac the pseudonyms Stofsky and Pasternak respectively, in a clear reference to the two Russian writers Fydor Dostoevsky and Boris Pasternak. Holmes's motives in making these allusions are not clear cut, though certainly the Beats were great admirers of Russian writing, as Holmes, a peripheral figure within the Beat coterie, knew well. Kerouac, in particular, was deeply influenced by Dostoevsky. Kerouac is probably called Pasternak instead because of Pasternak's engagement in *Dr Zhivago* with detailed representations of Great War, post-Great War and post-revolutionary Russia, in a socially-specific way comparatively distinct from Dostoevsky's intense focus on internal psychology. But such observations do not quite seem to be the full story. Rather, I think that Holmes had a double-edged motive in introducing these pseudonyms.

Holmes was well-educated and cultured, and would have known about F.O. Mathiessen's attempts in his 1941 book, *The American Renaissance*,[23] to establish within nineteenth-century USAmerican literature a major, classic canon of writings. This can be identified as part of a more general process of national cultural-capital building taking place in American Studies, one aspect of a much larger endeavour to establish American soft powers world-wide in the period following World War Two, accompanying the Marshall Plan to counter incipient anti-Americanism and secure the 'West' against Communist infiltration.[24] In part, Holmes's aggrandizing of Ginsberg and Kerouac by giving them the pseudonyms of prominent Russian writers was an attempt to stake a claim for the Beats as mid-twentieth-century writers deserving of attention in the processes of canon-formation taking place in the USAmerican academy. My claim here is substantiated by the way that Holmes, in his second novel, *The Horn* (1958), deliberately relates his (jazz-musician) characters to 'the writers of the great American Renaissance of the nineteenth century... The epigraphs to each chapter... are clues to who is who.'[25]

Yet this is not the whole story, since there seems to be a degree of irony in this choice of *Go*'s pseudonyms as well. They hyperbolize: Ginsberg was scarcely published in 1952; Kerouac's *The Town and the City* had appeared to mixed reviews only in 1950. Holmes would certainly have been aware of this, and his careful choice of the pseudonym 'Pasternak' for Kerouac (and not, say, 'Tolstoy') seems to be setting up a quiet satire on the pretensions of the Beats. Yet, even though the pseudonyms do, I think, cut both ways, by aggrandizing yet debunking Beat aspirations, Holmes's *Go* unavoidably (and deliberately) also contributes to the reputation-building that the Beat coterie was undertaking. Holmes's prominent positioning at the start of *Go* of the emphatic disclaimer: 'The characters and events depicted in this novel are imaginary and any resemblance to persons, living or dead, past or present, is purely accidental' (*G* iv), would have simply fuelled speculation. *Go* attracted a fair degree of attention when it came out in 1952, and its repeated building-up of Pasternak/Kerouac, the writer of 'an annoyingly good novel' (*G* 3), as well as its accompanying criticism of him for his exploitative conduct in his sexual relationships with women, would have heightened a prurient awareness of the Beats.

I say 'heightened' because the impact of *Go* would have complemented the well-documented efforts of Allen Ginsberg (and others in the Beat coterie) to undertake a (self-) promotion of the Beats, always endeavouring to raise their profile through a number of interrelated strategies: contriving to obtain introductions to established literary figures; effecting publication for the Beats' writing, for example by aiding Kerouac in submitting segments of sections from drafts of *On the Road* to literary reviews;[26] organizing events at which the Beats could gather to display themselves and their writing; and stressing their rule-breaking, unconventionality and daring experimentation in a general swathe of publicity work. (Perhaps influenced by such efforts as much as by his own involvement as a publisher's agent, Malcolm Cowley had in 1955 referred enthusiastically to Kerouac's *On the Road* as the authoritative chronicle of the Beat generation in the second edition of his book, *The Literary Situation*.[27]) *Go*'s pseudonyms surely allude to this proselytization.

Making these points begins to answer the question of why *On the Road* emerged as a scandalous fiction in the way that it did, despite the apparently competing claims of Brossard's *Walk*, Holmes's *Go* or (especially) Mandel's *Flee*. It can be seen that 'scandal' in Kerouac's 1957 *Road* is contingently constructed by the particular conjunctions that I am mapping. These in turn shaped the reformation of literary celebrity in USAmerica, in a period post-Scott Fitzgerald (he died in 1940) and in the twilight of Hemingway's monumental career, that affected the way literary scandal interfaced with literary celebrity at this time. The construction of USAmerican literary celebrity was being contemporaneously and unstably transformed. The ideas of Pierre Bourdieu will be particularly useful to me at this point in defining this process. Bourdieu observes how re-delineations of cultural formations are intimately bound up with contestations for power and authority that become particularly acute at times of disruptive social transformation – just as might be reasonably be held to be the case following the end of the Second World War. At such times the struggle for 'cultural legitimacy', as Bourdieu calls it, becomes particularly intense. The issue is for Bourdieu one of 'cultural value' acquisition. Acquiring cultural value is not simply reflexively tied to economic measurements. Rather it is a matter of complex negotiations, in which the individual cultural agent (writer, poet, painter, playwright, actor and so on) strives for an investment with 'charismatic illusion' in order to generate cultural capital (and, of course, eventually, in the last analysis, sales). It seems to me that the post-World War Two period in USAmerica was a time when this theorization holds particular validity (it is worth noting, surely, that Bourdieu first formulated this theory in the late 1960s/early 1970s).[28] To provide a relevant example, Ginsberg's promotions and Holmes's fictionalizations of Kerouac and the Beats were precisely negotiating with the production of 'charismatic illusion' – a quality directly interacting with how the Beats were, through process of publicity and self-publicity, becoming, in Daniel Boorstin's phrase, 'well-known for their well knownness' – unconnected to any actual publication record they might have (or not have), in a process independent of more traditional measurements, founded upon considering 'traditional forms of achievement'.[29] To a significant degree, then, the Beats anticipate the full emergence of egregious 'celebrity' culture capitalization in the postwar phase of late capitalist consumerization. This in turn impacts upon the scandalous construction of *On the Road*.

This occurs culturally through the 'aura' increasingly investing *Road*. This auratic investment (the pun is deliberate) is part of a process intimately bound up with the long delay over the novel's publication. The reference here is to Walter Benjamin, though the 'aura' in question with respect to Kerouac's work is not one depending upon the absence of any reproduction of the artwork (here, *On the Road*), but the novel's increasingly famous failure to reach publication: I will call this an *ersatz aura* surrounding Kerouac's work. Throughout the period 1951 to 1957 there had been a more or less steady build-up of expectation, as *On the Road* acquired the sort of cultural capital reserved for cult works – for example those subject to censorship. As Benjamin puts it, 'cult value would seem to demand that the work of art remain hidden'.[30] *Road*'s publication unleashed and exhausted this *ersatz auratic* build-up of capital, but the wave of interest was of sufficient intensity to generate a continuing, self-validating cultural momentum. The primary channel for this intensification was, of course, *Road*'s contemporary reviews. To legitimate the ersatz auratic reputation of the novel – its unpublished and unread cult status (as if censored) – reviewers construed *Road* in a way congruent with its cult reputation as well as responsive to the changed social context within which the book was being read. Their expectation that the novel would be deviant, as its accrued aura promised it should be, shaped their scandalized response. A mutually reinforcing cascade of reviews results. *Road* is read, in a context within which its engagement with a dislocated and fragmentary culture is indeed controversial, as *scandalous* – and so as more controversial than it comparatively deserves. Consequently the 1957 and 1958 reviewers' focus insistently falls upon the book's depictions of sexual acts and drug consumption, even though these are not particularly frequent and comparatively restrained when set besides other fictionalizations.

A signal of these scandalized expectations is the sheer scale of attention this second novel by a young novelist attracted from reviewers following its publication in late August 1957. Kerouac's first novel, *The Town and the City* had not been particularly well received, though its twenty or so reviews had been mixed.[31] Yet despite *The Town and the City*'s lukewarm reception, *On the Road* received almost fifty notices.[32] Robert Milewski notes that *On the Road*'s publication represented an unmatched high point in press interest in Kerouac – itself an indication of the build-up of auratic charisma surrounding the text and its composition.[33] A signal of this constructive process must be the inclusion by the *New York Times*, just prior to its review of *On the Road*, of Kerouac in a list of nine 'Tellers of New Tales' (in an anticipation of the sort of literary celebrity-ramping that was to become a regular feature of newspapers in later decades). Perhaps a signal of this process was the juxtaposition of a photograph of Kerouac in an open-neck check shirt with a large crucifix around his neck and his write-up as a 'roving author... track[ing] riotous

members of the "beat generation" across the country'. As Kerouac was later
to note dryly, all other reproductions of this photograph cropped out the
crucifix on his chest.[34] Even the photograph's reproduction in the *New York
Times* accompanying the novel's full review a few days later did this; the
juxtaposition was, presumably, held to be just too contentious.

The *New York Times*'s review of *Road*, by Gilbert Millstein, is perhaps the
best known of these early reviews, precisely because it was enthusiastic from
first to last, ending as it does with the dramatic sentence: 'This is a major
novel.'[35] But embedded in it are indications of the sources of the intense
attention to be bestowed upon *Road*: Millstein identifies it as 'the testament'
of the 'Beat Generation' in the way that *The Sun Also Rises* served as the testament of the 'Lost Generation'. This, Millstein indicates, is because *Road* can
be linked to the furore surrounding the 'San Francisco Renaissance' (though
Millstein correctly notes that identifying the novel with San Francisco over-
localizes it). Millstein also links Kerouac's novel to Holmes's *Go*, thus associ-
ating *On the Road* with the emphasis on sex and drugs already identified as
a hallmark of *Go*. Such celebrity framing is accompanied by a focus near the
start of Millstein's review upon the book's sensational content: 'the frenzied
pursuit of every possible sensory impression, an extreme exacerbation of
the nerves, a constant outraging of the body. (One gets "kicks"; one "digs"
everything, whether it be drink, drugs, sexual promiscuity, driving at high
speeds...)'. Such an emphasis was to become constitutive in important
ways, though it was preceded by the tone of a review appearing in the *San
Francisco Chronicle* of 1 September 1957.

Written by Kenneth Rexroth, a well-established San Francisco anarchistic
poet reluctant to become identified with the 'hullabaloo' of the San Francisco
Renaissance, with which Kerouac had become over-easily associated, this
review, too, framed itself by first identifying how *On the Road*'s reputation
had preceded its publication: 'this is pretty sure to be the most "remarkable" novel of 1957'.[36] However, Rexroth's review was otherwise unusual –
and insightful – in important ways. It identifies *On the Road* as a historical novel, observing, if slightly hyperbolically, how the novel treats with
'the hysterical backwash of the most horrifying ten years in human history'
and describes Dean Moriarty as 'rapid[ly] falling apart', having 'broken
some essential spring'. Rexroth largely avoids sensationalizing *On the Road*'s
content, though the book is described as 'pretty frightening'. Rexroth's
approach, however, was soon to become the exception, as Millstein's framing
and emphases carried the day. Carlos Baker's 7 September review for the
*Saturday Review* echoes Millstein (though with hostile intent). Baker's review
largely consists of a summary of the plot, until his space runs out. The
later portions of the book are consequently barely described, whilst his plot-
summary focuses on sex and promiscuity, drug consumption and nudity,
and attaches its distortions to the strap-line, 'an experimental novel about
a generation of thrill-seeking hitchhikers'. In fairness to Baker, it must

be noted that he does pick out the sense of desolation investing the thrills. But, more symptomatically, he ends by suggesting that Kerouac's achievement in his novel is little more than 'to gobble a few verbal goofballs' – so ending his review with a stress on drug consumption.[37] Independent of Baker, though perhaps indebted to Millstein, David Dempsey's review in the *New York Times Book Review* the very next day (8 September) follows a comparable path. Informing the reader that *On the Road* belongs to 'the new Bohemianism in America', Dempsey characterizes the novel as treating with 'depravity' and the 'pathological' Dean, 'given to aimless travel, women, car stealing, reefers, bop jazz, liquor'.[38]

Dempsey's review is relatively restrained in its sensationalism. Instead Carlos Baker's emphasis prevails, aided and abetted by a flock of reviews appearing on 8 September. In the *Washington Post*, Ray B. Browne describes Kerouac as 'the leader of the San Francisco school of writers' and the novel as a catalogue of excess, its characters 'liv[ing] licentiously', in a 'Bacchanalian celebration' of USAmerica as a 'big woman they yearn to crush close, to caress, to rape – and to abandon'.[39] The reviews, if read in quick succession, become repetitive. David Boroff sees Kerouac, like Hemingway, as his generation's spokesman (a comparison prompted by the book's dusjacket), immediately mentions 'hoodlumism' and marijuana, and stresses the presence of 'sex, jazz, liquor, benzedrine' in the novel, as 'characters tumble in and out of bed with aplomb'.[40] Nelson Algren in the *Chicago Sun-Times* praises Kerouac for 'the best account of the "Go" generation', albeit in a generally unfavourable review (which at least did not seek to sensationalize the book along the usual sex-and-drugs line), whilst one day later an anonymous reviewer in *Newsweek* – again invoking the 'Lost Generation' as a point of comparison (so also lazily drawing on the dustjacket) – identifies Dean as 'an animal-like delinquent' driven by his sexual appetites between 'three women stationed in New York, San Francisco and Denver'.[41]

Such emphases prove constitutive in constructing *On the Road* as scandalous. In some ways the strap-line of the *Newsweek* review was symptomatic: 'Crazy, man, crazy'. The die is now cast. Gene Baro follows in line by describing *Road*'s characters as: 'Sexually promiscuous, drink-and-drug riddled, thieving, lying, betraying, they belong to volatility, to movement.'[42] For Baro, *On the Road* is a scandalous fiction indeed, 'a romantic treatment of delinquency'. On September 18 *The Village Voice*'s Arthur Oesterreicher begins his review by first noting 'the public emergence of Jack Kerouac from the hipster underground'. This quickly establishes Kerouac's ersatz auratic charisma, before the review declares him to be 'a *voice*'[43] (though Oesterreicher mostly avoids sensationalization, in an enthusiastic and perceptive review, noting the book's 'hilarity' as well as its 'horror'). The *Saturday Review* of 28 September took the next landmark step, by importing into the mass media the first details of the scroll myth: 'Kerouac got art paper, which comes in twenty-foot rolls and pasted it together. Then he'd start it in the typewriter and begin writing. He could write 18,000 words without changing paper.'[44] The arousal of public interest is the clear aim. Meanwhile the dominant, sensationalizing formula constantly reappeared, as in the October *Harper's* ('they are a bad lot – a bunch of average juvenile delinquents who steal, take drugs, sleep around') and the October *Atlantic Monthly* ('a determined pursuit of euphoria. Dope, liquor, girls, jazz').[45]

So, by 17 October 1957 the formula could be parodied, in a piece by George R. Clay in *The Reporter*, 'A Sleepless Night with the Beat Generation': 'In the apartment Belinda sat drinking aspirin and Coca-Cola . . . Hairbreadth Harry was in the bathroom taking his midnight fix . . . jabbing with the needle into his woesome arm; Popeye was sprawled out with his girl on a stolen bed.'[46] This sort of parody, somewhat off the mark in terms of its explicitness, is yet a reasonable response to the kind of summary that reviewers so often offered. The November 1957 *Playboy* ('There is much drink, all kinds of dope . . . whores and plenty of sex') and the August 1958 *Encounter* ('Mr. Kerouac's hero . . . lives mainly for . . . sex, food, drink, drugs and fast cars') both read like unintentional parodies of this reviewing mode.[47] Having said this, there are, it must be noted, exceptions to this chorus, such as the *Hudson Review*'s magisterial dismissal, which does not deign to summarize the book, Clancy Sigal's essay in the *Universities and Left Review*, disturbingly mixing its distaste for *Road* with what amounts to a racist characterization of African Americans, and *Time*'s review, which sees Moriarty as suffering from a species of 'prison psychosis', a syndrome whose sufferers 'are not really mad – they only seem to be' – an astute critical point.[48]

In this reviewing process, *On the Road*'s characters have persistently, if not quite always, been wrenched from their historical context, placed into the alien cultural context of late 1950s' America, subjected to greater or lesser hyperbolic deformation, made over as scandalous and nearly always undifferentiatedly equated with an exaggerated version of Dean Moriarty, despite the many and clear differences between him and the others. The actual narrative structure of the novel, centring as it does upon an unreliable first-person narrator, is passed by. That Sal's anxious and uneasy exploration of his doubts and inadequacies, placed alongside his recognition of the flawed allure of Dean Moriarty, contains a structure of feeling coloured by the Second World War and its disturbing immediate aftermath is almost always neglected. The reviewers persistently sweep past the way *On the Road* deconstructs the myth of the West, rendered so insularly dangerous and destructive in the face of the globalizing legacies of Pearl Harbor, Hiroshima and Nagasaki, the Holocaust, the creation of Israel, US and Russian nuclear testing, the Truman doctrine of 1947, the Berlin airlift and the formation of NATO in 1949. Three of Sal's four trips are intended to take him *outside* America – on to trans-Pacific voyages (Book One), Italy (Book Three) and, climactically, in Book Four, Mexico, which he does in fact reach, only to discover the power of the dollar, the wealth of America, and the degradation of the developing world in the twilight of the Cold War. *Road*'s description of Mexican Native Americans makes most apparent this sort of contemporary engagement: 'All had their hands outstretched. They had come down from the back mountains . . . to hold forth their hands for something they thought civilization could offer . . . they never dreamed . . . the poor broken delusion of it. They didn't know a bomb had come that could crack all our bridges and roads and reduce them to jumbles, and we would be as poor as they someday' (*R* 299). Just below the novel's frantic surface, a deep-flowing pessimism pounds along, which can be related to the contemporary late 1940s/early 1950s' journals Kerouac kept that provide an account of his disturbed, even suicidal exploration of the postwar writer's artistic dilemmas.[49] *On the Road* is best read as an exploratory performative rehearsal of resulting contemporary identity crises by its two central protagonists. Each brings different degrees of conviction to these rehearsals, in a context where such (self-)discovery is being fiercely impeded by processes of postwar recovery, in an unappetizing imposition of asymmetric socio-cultural norms and expectations. The result is certainly performative excess, but with an accompanying sense of how this excess is self-reflexively a deconstruction of itself (the actor as self-audience). To adapt Richard Schechner, *On the Road* is 'not not itself' in its scandalousness.[50]

What my examination of *On the Road* reveals, I believe, is how the novel's 'scandalousness' is constructed by the 'scandalized': decided not only by its obvious referents, the prevailing socio-cultural 'moral' climates, but also by a complex, shifting interplay – between Jack Kerouac, his coterie, celebrity, the reviewers and the audience – that in itself stands as what might be described as a re-performative matrix, which makes over the finally-published text's representations into an as-anticipated set of cultural role-plays. So when the 15 September 1957 verdict of *Bestsellers* represents *Road* 57 as 'a farrago of dope addiction, fornication, adultery, drunken brawls, thievery and psychotic sweats',[51] this momentary tableau dramatizes how the scandalous construction of the novel has come to dominate. It is the product of its scandalized coding processes. In their immediate context, the versions of the novel constructed by coterie, reviewers, celebrity and other novels together *reconstitute* the novel, whether this resides in a contemporary *Bestsellers* review or in Christina Patterson's 2005 thumbnail sketch. It must and does re-perform as scandalous. In the process, one might say, *On the Road* becomes scandalous for being scandalous.

## Notes

The page references of texts regularly cited in this chapter appear in the text, preceded by an identifying letter, as follows: Jack Kerouac, *On the Road* (New York: Viking, 1957): references are preceded by the letter *R*; Jack Kerouac, *Visions of Cody* (New York: McGraw Hill, 1972): the letter *V*; Chandler Brossard, *Who Walk in Darkness* (New York: New Directions, 1952): the letter *W*; George Mandel, *Flee the Angry*

*Strangers* (New York: Bobs Merrill), 1952: the letter *F*; John Clellon Holmes, *Go* (New York: Charles Scribner's Sons, 1952): the letter *G*.

1. Christina Patterson, 'Cult Classics 2: *On the Road'*, *Independent*, 22 April 2005, Arts and Book Review section, 23.
2. See: Gerald Nicosia, *Memory Babe: a Critical Biography of Jack Kerouac* (1983; rpt. Harmondsworth: Penguin, 1986), 343; Tim Hunt, *Kerouac's Crooked Road: the Development of a Fiction* (Hamden: Archon Books, 1981); Ellis Amburn, *Subterranean Kerouac: the Hidden Life of Jack Kerouac* (New York: St Martin's Press, 1998), 164.
3. See Nicosia and Hunt; see also Dave Moore, '*On the Road*: the Scroll Revealed', *The Kerouac Connection*, no. 10 (April 1986), 3–7; Dave Moore, 'Introduction', to Neal Cassady, *Collected Letters, 1944–1967* (New York: Penguin, 2004); see also Moore, 188; 'Examples of Jack Kerouac's "Borrowings" from the Letters of Neal Cassady', attachment to email correspondence with R.J. Ellis, 15 April 1999; Dave Moore, email correspondence with R.J. Ellis, 13 July 2005.
4. See Amburn, 164; Nicosia, 453; Barry Miles, *Jack Kerouac: King of the Beats – a Portrait* (London: Virgin, 1998), 231.
5. See Nicosia; Amburn; Miles.
6. Henry Miller, *Tropic of Cancer* (Paris: Obelisk Press, 1936); Henry Miller, *Tropic of Capricorn* (Paris: Obelisk Press, 1938). Subjected to censorship in the States, the *Tropics* were not published in the USA until Grove Press brought out *Tropic of Cancer* in 1961 and fought off censorship attempts in 1962. See Charles Rembar, *The End of Obscenity* (London: André Deutsch, 1969), 168.
7. A substantial adaptation of Harold Garfinkel's theory is called for here. I am arguing that scandal is built up from the way that people (coterie, reviewers, audience) actually relate to texts and confront the issues they perceive the text as raising. Consequently an ethnomethodological variant becomes necessary when delineating scandal, to understand how this matrix works. See Garfinkel, *Studies in Ethnomethodology* (Englewood Cliffs: Prentice Hall, 1967). See also John Heritage, *Garfinkel and Ethnomethodology* (Cambridge: Polity Press, 1984), 2.
8. See Helen Laville, *Cold War Women: the International Activities of American Women's Organizations* (Manchester: Manchester University Press, 2002), 1–5; Peter J. Kuznick and James Gilbert, 'U.S. Culture and the Cold War', in Peter J. Kuznick and James Gilbert, eds, *Rethinking Cold War Cultures* (Washington: Smithsonian Institute Press, 2001), 1–13.
9. Susan M. Hartmann, *The Home Front* (Boston: Twayne, 1982), 4.
10. Elaine Tyler May, 'Explosive Issues: Sex, Women and the Bomb', in Lary May, ed., *Recasting America: Culture and Politics in the Age of Cold War* (Chicago: University of Chicago Press, 1989), 154–70.
11. David Boroff, 'The Roughnecks', *New York Post*, 8 September 1957, sec. M, 11.
12. Laville, 2–3; Neil Wynn, *The Afro-American and the Second World War* (London: Paul Elek, 1976), 16.
13. Jack Kerouac, *The Town and the City* (New York: Harcourt Brace, 1950).
14. Nicosia, 106.
15. I take the conflation USAmerica[n], from Malim Johar Schueller, believing with him, that 'American' as an adjective and 'America' as a noun should only be deployed in hemispheric usages. See Malim Johar Schueller, *U.S. Orientalism: Race, Nation and Gender in Literature* (Ann Arbor, MI: University of Michigan Press), 1998.
16. Nicosia, 324.

17. Jack Kerouac, typescript of *On the Road* [the 'scroll version'], 1951, unpublished, printed in Ann Charters, 'Introduction', to Kerouac, *On the Road* (Harmondsworth: Penguin, 1991), xxiv.

18. Miles, 98; Kerouac, 131; Alfred C. Kinsey et al., *Sexual Behavior in the Human Male* (Philadelphia: W.B. Saunders, 1948). Kinsey's *Sexual Behavior in the Human Female* was brought out by the same publisher in 1953.

19. William Burroughs, *Junkie* (New York: Ace Books, 1953); William Burroughs, *Queer* (New York: Viking, 1985). See Barry Miles, *William Burroughs, El Hombre Invisible: a Portrait* (New York: Hyperion, 1993); Oliver Harris, *William Burroughs and the Secret of Fascination* (Carbondale: Southern Illinois University Press, 2003).

20. Nicosia, 342, 370; James Campbell, *This is the Beat Generation* (London: Secker and Warburg, 1999), 123–4.

21. John Clellon Holmes, 'This is the Beat Generation', *New York Times* 1952, rpt. in *Nothing More to Declare* (London: André Deutsch, 1968), 109–15; Gilbert Millstein, 'Books of the Times', *New York Times*, 5 September 1957, 27. Kerouac set the record straight in 'The Origins of the Beat Generation', *Playboy*, 6, 6 (June 1959), 31–2, 42, 79.

22. See Nelson Algren, 'Kerouac Deftly Etches the "Go" Generation', *Chicago Sun-Times*, 8 September 1957, sec. 3, 4. This would have annoyed Kerouac, who had written a story called 'Go, Go, Go' (never published, and probably based on Kerouac's visit to a San Francisco jazz club in August 1949), which may have provided the inspiration for Holmes' title, *Go*; Kerouac anyway had to dissuade Holmes from entitling *Go* 'The Beat Generation'. See Nicosia, 370; Campbell, 123–4; Jack Kerouac, *Selected Letters, 1940–1956*, ed. Ann Charters (New York: Viking Penguin, 1995), 345. The San Francisco jazz club story was probably extracted from, or at least ended up in Kerouac, *On the Road*, (1957), 196.

23. F.O. Mathiessen, *The American Renaissance* (Oxford: Oxford University Press), 1941.

24. See Liam Kennedy and Scott Lucas, 'Enduring Freedom: Public Diplomacy and US Foreign Policy', *American Quarterly*, 51, 2 (June 2005), 309–33. Joseph Nye popularized the term 'soft powers', albeit from a neo-conservative perspective. See Joseph S. Nye Jr, *Soft Powers: the Means to Success in World Politics* (New York: Public Affairs, 2004).

25. John Clellon Holmes, *The Horn* (New York: Random House, 1958); John Clellon Holmes, 'Preface', in Holmes, *The Horn*, 1958; rpt. New York: Random House, 1976.

26. See Nicosia; see also Arthur Oesterreicher, 'On the Road', *Village Voice* 18 September 1957, p. 5.

27. Malcolm Cowley, *The Literary Situation*, Second Printing (New York: Viking, 1955).

28. Pierre Bourdieu, 'Intellectual Field and Creative Project', in Michael Young, ed., *Knowledge and Control: New Directions in the Sociology of Education* (London: Collier Macmillan, 1971), 163; Pierre Bourdieu, *The Rules of Art: Genesis and Structure of the Literary Field*, trans. S. Emanuel (Cambridge: Polity Press, 1996), 319. See also Joe Moran, *Star Authors: Literary Celebrity in America* (London: Pluto Press), 2001.

29. Daniel Boorstin, *The Image: a Guide to Pseudo-Events in America* (New York: Vintage), 57–8.

30. The allusion to 'aura' and the quotation are taken from Walter Benjamin, 'The Work of Art in an Age of Mechanical Reproduction', 1936, rpt. in *Illuminations*, trans. Harry Zohn (London: Jonathan Cape: 1970), 219–53. My contention, in brief, is that a censored literary work in a sense only exists as an original (the unpublished manuscript/typescript), that gives it an 'aura' akin to 'cult value'. See

also R.J. Ellis, 'Grove Press and the End[s] of Obscenity', in Gary Day and Clive Bloom, eds, *Perspectives on Pornography: Sexuality in Film and Literature* (London: Macmillan, 1988), 26–43.

31. See, for example, Charles Poore. 'Books of the Times', *New York Times*, 2 March 1950, 25; John Brooks, 'Of Growth and Decay', *New York Times Book Review*, 5 March 1950, 6; Richard H. Rovere, 'Fever Charts for Novelists', *Harper's Magazine*, May 1950, 115–23.

32. See Milewski for a good listing of the reviews that Kerouac's novels received. Robert J. Milewski, *Jack Kerouac: an Annotated Bibliography of Secondary Sources, 1944–1979* (Metuchen: Scarecrow Press, 1981), 19–56.

33. Milewski, 'Introduction', *Jack Kerouac*, 7.

34. See Kerouac, 'Origins', 31–2.

35. Gilbert Millstein, 'Books of the Times', *New York Times*, 5 September 1957, 27.

36. Kenneth Rexroth, ' "It's an Anywhere Road for Anybody, Anyhow"', *San Francisco Chronicle*, 1 September 1957, 18.

37. Carlos Baker, 'Itching Feet', *Saturday Review*, 7 September 1957, 19, 32–3.

38. David Dempsey, 'In Pursuit of Kicks', *New York Times Book Review*, 8 September 1957, 4.

39. Ray B. Browne, 'Vocal, the Frantic Fringe', *Washington Post*, 8 September 1957, sec. E, 7.

40. David Boroff, 'The Roughnecks', *New York Post*, 8 September 1957, sec. M, 11. Holmes had anticipated the dustjacket's comparison of *On the Road*'s Beat Generation with the Lost Generation in his 1952 *New York Times* article.

41. Algren, 4; Anon., 'Flings of the Frantic', *Newsweek*, 9 September 1957, 115.

42. Gene Baro, 'Reckless Rebels in Search of – What?', *New York Herald Tribune Book Review*, 15 September 1957, 4.

43. Oesterreicher, 5.

44. Jerome Beatty, Jr, 'Trade Winds', *Saturday Review*, 28 September 1957, 6.

45. Paul Pickrel, 'On the Road', *Harper's*, October 1957, 89; Phoebe Adams, 'Ladder to Nirvana', *Atlantic Monthly*, October 1957, 178.

46. George R. Clay, 'A Sleepless Night with the Beat Generation', *The Reporter*, 17 October 1957, 44.

47. Anon., 'On the Road', *Playboy*, November 1957, 17; K.W. Grandsen, 'Adolescence and Maturity', *Encounter*, August 1958, 86.

48. Clancy Sigal, 'Nihilism's Organization Man', *Universities and Left Review*, 4 (1958), 59–65; Anon., 'The Ganser Syndrome', *Time*, 16 September 1957, 105.

49. Some of this does show up in Douglas Brinkley's selection from Kerouac's journals, *Windblown World: the Journals of Jack Kerouac, 1947–1954* (New York: Viking Penguin, 2004). However, I agree with Nicosia and Moore that this is a poor, jumbled edition, inexplicably omitting Kerouac's *'On the Road'* journal housed in the Humanities Research Center, the University of Austin, Texas. See Nicosia, 'Real Kerouac: the Beat Writer's Journals Reveal a Man Apart from his Persona', 17 October 2004, www.sfgate.com/cgi-bin/article.cgi?file=/c/a/2004/10/17/RVGU695CdDD1; Dave Moore, email communication to R.J. Ellis, 26 October 2004.

50. See Richard Schechner, *Theatre and Anthropology* (Philadelphia: University of Philadelphia Press, 1985); Schechner, *Performance Theory* (New York: Routledge, 1988).

51. Anon., 'On the Road', *Bestsellers*, 15 September 1957, 186.

# 6
# Chinua Achebe's *A Man of the People*: the Novel and the Public Sphere

*Jago Morrison*

As Chinua Achebe's most contemporary and most sharply political novel, *A Man of the People*[1] was a scandal from the outset. With its scathing appraisal of Nigerian public life, and apparent call for a military takeover, the text became notorious in January 1966 for predicting the army coup which took place only hours after the novel's launch. This violent anti-corruption purge, carried out by a group of nationalist army officers, marked the beginning of a major power struggle in the region which culminated in the Biafran war.

Achebe's narrative traces the struggles of Odili, a young schoolteacher, to unseat and disgrace a corrupt government minister, in an African state whose contours mirror those of post-independence Nigeria. In this context it explores the growing disillusion, amongst younger and educated Africans, with the new political order that followed independence. Within the framework of the novel, the ruling establishment in Nigeria is represented by Chief Nanga, a self-made man and political manipulator who has climbed the greasy pole to become – with obvious irony – Minister of Culture. For a short while he is Odili's mentor and benefactor, before the young man experiences a change of heart and becomes a socialist activist, campaigning on behalf of the disenfranchised 'ordinary people'. As the plot thickens, Odili attempts to expose Nanga's corruption and resolves to contest his parliamentary seat, before being beaten by the minister's henchmen and knocked out of the race. In the final scenes of the novel, just as all seems lost, the army 'obligingly' stage a coup and Nanga is arrested along with other defrauders of the state. Odili is exonerated and goes on to marry the minister's young and beautiful former girlfriend, on whom he's had his eye for some time.

Both the novel's vivid sense of contemporaneity and the fearlessness of its portrayal of civil and political stagnation mark *A Man of the People* as a departure from the recuperative, historical concerns of Achebe's earlier texts. Importantly, it is also the first of his novels to push beyond the ethnic and

117

regional orbit of Ibo culture, towards an aesthetic whose ambitions are clearly national in scope. That these were conscious departures for Achebe is evident from his commentary at the time. In an interview with the Nairobi *Sunday Nation* in 1967, he characterizes the text as a new development in his writing, focusing and politicizing its address to the problems of postcoloniality:

> Right now my interest is in politics, or rather my interest in the novel is politics. *A Man of the People* wasn't a flash in the pan. This is the beginning of a phase for me, in which I intend to take a hard look at what we in Africa are making of our independence – but using Nigeria, which I know best.[2]

At its launch in 1966, Achebe's effective status as the new Nigeria's poet laureate, together with his powerful media position as director of external broadcasting for the Nigerian Broadcasting Corporation, had created a climate of high expectation and excitement around the novel. Less than eight years after the publication of *Things Fall Apart*,[3] his texts had already become an important presence in the Nigerian high-school curriculum. At home, as contemporary reviews of his work show, Achebe enjoyed a level of cultural authority in the mid-1960s which was only matched by his growing importance as a promoter of African writing abroad. It is fair to say that by 1966 Achebe was, himself, a significant cultural institution in Nigeria. For twenty-first century readers of the novel, it is easy to miss the significance of this context, when considering the novel's unpalatable representation of Nigerian society, and in particular its problematic, ironically utopian 'happy ending':

> The army obliged us by staging a coup at that point and locking up every member of the Government. The rampaging bands of election thugs had caused so much unrest and dislocation that our young Army officers seized the opportunity to take over ... Overnight everyone began to shake their heads at the excesses of the last regime, at its graft, oppression and corrupt government: newspapers, the radio, the hitherto silent intellectuals and civil servants – everybody said what a terrible lot: and it became public opinion the next morning. (pp. 147–8)

The aim of this chapter is to explore *A Man of the People* as a public intervention in contemporary Nigeria, relating it to Achebe's wider experiment with the novel as a political form in the 1950s and 1960s. Before looking more closely at the writer's developing critical stance in the period and turning to the text itself, it is worth understanding the immediate context of *A Man of the People*'s reception. As Achebe admits in the 1967 interview cited above, he had anticipated that some of the novel's controversial content might bring unwelcome consequences, and perhaps even the loss of his job at the NBC. What he could not have anticipated, however, was that a military coup would be executed, exactly as portrayed in his text, on the very night of the novel's launch. On Friday 14 January 1966 a special evening of the Society of Nigerian Authors was arranged to celebrate the novel's publication. The next morning, however, Achebe describes arriving at work to discover a radically changed situation: 'I found the place surrounded by soldiers. I had no idea what was going on. They looked at my pass and saw that I worked there...J.P. Clark who was by this time teaching in Lagos University, dashed over to come to tell me that there had been a coup. When he got to the gate he was nearly shot by these soldiers because he had no business there.'[4]

For a few months, as Ezenwa-Ohaeto's biography shows,[5] the writer attempted to proceed as normal, against the background of a rapidly changing political climate. By May 1966, however, the situation for Ibo professionals in general was becoming increasingly difficult, as a wave of revenge attacks, ostensibly in response to Ibo involvement in the January coup, left thousands dead. For Achebe and his family, a counter-coup in July made things even more dangerous. It emerged that in the mounting climate of suspicion, the army had come to regard Achebe's prescience in describing the January coup as *prima-facie* evidence that the author himself must have been one of the conspirators. As soldiers hunted for Achebe and his family, they were forced to split up, leaving everything, and flee back towards their native East. The following year, when the Ibo leader Emeke Ojukwu announced the Eastern region's secession from the Nigerian Federation and the creation of Biafra as a sovereign state, Achebe decided to throw in his lot with the new rebel republic.

Understandably, the apparent 'clairvoyance' of *A Man of the People* in relation to January 1966 has provided an important focus of critical attention, both for contemporaries and more recent critics, fuelling speculation as to whether Achebe, an important media figure, might indeed have been privy to plans for the first coup. In fact there is little evidence to support this view. In a discussion of the text's 'prophetic' reputation, Bernth Lindfors[6] points out that the novel was actually completed a year before its launch, at a moment in which the possibility of military intervention, as a means of forcing a change of political culture in Nigeria, was being entertained by a variety of writers and intellectuals. Although Achebe's narrative is undeniably polemical in its contents and suggestions, in other words, it also reflects an important stream of political opinion in the mid-1960s.

In his account of the background against which *A Man of the People* was completed, moreover, Ezenwa-Ohaeto shows Lagos as a city in virtual meltdown, with elections to the regional government thrown into chaos by blatant political interference and widespread eruptions of violence:

Contestants were beaten and detained, and ballot papers destroyed... In Ibadan and Lagos many people were subjected to violence; houses were burnt and thousands of people fled their homes. That state of anarchy continued into the new year of 1966 with barricades erected by opposing factions and many commuters killed or spared according to the answers they gave to the roving political thugs.[7]

Set against this context in the Lagos of 1965, then, I would suggest that it is reasonable to link the novel's portrayal of democratic breakdown directly to contemporary conditions in the capital, in which the virtual collapse of the electoral system and the presence of rampaging political gangs had already created the conditions of possibility for military intervention. In his position at the heart of the broadcasting establishment, Achebe would clearly have been far from unaware of calls for radical action in the contemporary media. As Lindfors argues, indeed, the apparently extreme resort of marshal intervention 'was regarded by a number of intelligent observers as one of the few options left for a nation on the brink of anarchy'.[8]

In this context it is worthwhile noting that, if Achebe's protagonist Odili is shown as welcoming the army's intervention at the end of the novel, this also seems to reflect Achebe's own view at the time. Interviewed in early 1967, certainly, Achebe is far from condemnatory of the January coup. At least for the moment, in the interregnum before the descent to civil war, it appears that the coup's undesirable effects – including the curtailment of individual freedoms and suspension of democratic rights – is a price he feels is worth paying, if it promises a clean-up of Nigerian public life:

It is always unfortunate when things have got to a state where military intervention has to take place – but military takeovers are not always bad in themselves. You see, the Nigerian situation left no political solution. The political machine had become so abused that whatever measures were taken, it could only produce the same results. We had got to a point where some other force had to come in . . . I don't think one can say a military takeover is never worth it.[9]

As we have already seen, Achebe remained at this stage unshaken in the pursuit of his literary project, characterizing *A Man of the People* as the 'beginning of a phase' of engaged, political fiction. With the benefit of hindsight, however, it is possible to see that this optimism was far from well-placed. As the same interview indicates, in 1967 he was already working on a fifth novel, intended to pursue and extend the concerns explored in *A Man of the People*. A year later, however, speaking to *Transition* after the outbreak of the civil war, it was already clear that this work had stalled, as Achebe comments anxiously 'I hope I have not retired completely.'[10] Seven years later, in 1975, he had yet to overcome the block, telling the writer Osmond Enekwe 'I'd like to complete the novel I'm working on . . . And so I've been thinking, I've been working out things in my mind, and part of it is the Nigerian crisis. I have to ask myself "What happened to Nigeria? What happened to my relationship to Nigeria?"[11] Essays and interviews throughout this period make intermittent reference to work on the new text, but in fact Achebe was not to produce another novel for twenty years.

In the wealth of subsequent critical assessments of Achebe and his work, almost no attention has been given to the implications of this crisis in his career as a novelist. The question implied here, however – why the work of such a well-established and prolific writer might have stalled in this way – is I would suggest potentially of great interest, because of the retrospective light it casts on the strategies of *A Man of the People*, as well as on the broader nature of Achebe's fictional project.

Clearly, it is important not to underestimate the impact of the civil war experience itself on Achebe. Writing extended imaginative prose against the background of constant bombardments with British-made artillery shells and aerial bombings from Soviet-supplied planes between 1967 and 1970 must necessarily have been difficult. In an interview for *Transition* in 1968, he vividly describes the conditions of life for Biafrans in this period:

> From morning about 7 a.m. to about 6 p.m. there is this tenseness. At any moment they might come. It does not take long – a few seconds – and 120 people are charred to ashes, charred black, and perhaps 20 buildings wrecked, and this is a very real thing. I only realised how nervous I had become when I got out to London about three weeks ago. The first sound of an aeroplane I heard and my first reaction was to take cover. This has become a way of life for everyone, children too. This is the atmosphere in which you live and you try to make life approach such normality as you can.[12]

The early death of the poet Christopher Okigbo, in particular, echoes through Achebe's critical and editorial work for a number of years after the Biafran struggle. Nevertheless, the argument I want to advance here is that the abrupt halt in Achebe's career as a novelist after 1966 reflects more than a reaction to the difficulties of the war. Rather, it needs to be understood in terms of the specific position and function Achebe's earlier work had sought to establish for the novel in post-independence Nigeria, and the ways in which that entire cultural project was thrown into crisis by the events of the period.

Since his emergence as a pioneer of the anglophone African novel, an important focus of 'Achebe studies' has been the ways in which his writing is inflected by a notion of 'commitment'. Without wanting to rehearse well-established arguments here, it is worth acknowledging the writer's own stress on the responsibilities entailed by writing, inasmuch as it helps to illuminate the relationship between his fiction and the public sphere. Asked in 1969 whether he regarded literature as a suitable medium for social or political concerns, for example, he responds characteristically with reference to his own early work:

> Yes, I believe it's impossible to write anything in Africa without some kind of commitment, some kind of message, some kind of protest. Even those early novels that look like gentle recreations of the past – what they were saying, in effect, was that we had a past. That was protest, because there were people who thought we didn't have a past. What we were doing was to say politely that we *did* – here it is. So commitment is nothing new. Commitment runs right through our work.[13]

From the early 1960s onwards, Achebe's essays repeatedly critique what he sees as the contemporary European model of the writer as an iconoclastic outsider, contrasting it with an African idea of writing as public pedagogy and activism. Instead of sitting, revolting, on the margins, where society cannot put them 'in charge of anything',[14] he insists that writers should be expected to lend their powers to the cause of national regeneration. As the quotation above reflects, moreover, the recuperative and archaeological concerns of Achebe's work cannot be separated from this ethical 'commitment'. In a much-quoted article for the *New Statesman* in 1965, he describes his early novels as attempts to help Africans regain a sense of self-belief, putting behind them 'the years of denigration and self-abasement'.[15]

Notwithstanding its more contemporary setting, *A Man of the People* can be seen in one sense as coextensive with these texts in that, whilst it is primarily concerned with present conditions, it still has historical ambitions – that is, to the discovery and public narrativization of Nigeria's historical development. On the other hand, however, it is more difficult to see how the text's presentation of civil corruption and degeneration might contribute to the 'self-belief' of Nigerians, or help to engender a culture of national pride. If in Achebe's earlier fiction there is a clearly discernable project of national reclamation, teaching his readers that Nigeria's past was not 'one long night of savagery from which the first Europeans acting on God's behalf delivered them',[16] *A Man of the People* seems to sit rather awkwardly with this project, in its address to the contemporary national scene.

As the critic Simon Gikandi argues, the pedagogic and recuperative project which we see in Achebe's early texts is inseparable from his concern with post-colonial nation-building. Quoting from Frantz Fanon's influential 1961 study *The Wretched of the Earth*,[17] he argues that:

> in Achebe's writings, there is a fundamental link between the idea of the nation, the concept of national culture, and the quest for an African narrative. Fanon's famous dictum that the liberation of the nation is 'that material keystone which makes the building of a culture possible' finds its parallel in Achebe's desire to liberate the African mind from the colonial complex.[18]

In the early works, for Gikandi, this process proceeds unproblematically, as Achebe traces the seeds of national consciousness in the space between colonial culture and the indigenous traditions of the Ibo. With *A Man of the People*, however, this 'nationalist desire'[19] runs into difficulties, as the writer is forced to confront the ways in which the political underpinnings of the nation have crumbled and decayed. For Gikandi, this process of terminal breakdown has left Achebe 'confused about the nature and function of his art... Clearly, independence had forced the writer to confront a question which he might have taken for granted in the colonial period – what is the necessity of the text in the reconstruction or invention of the new nation?'[20]

This is an interesting argument, I would suggest, but one which does not account adequately for Achebe's own commentary in the period. Indeed, if we put any significant weight on his critical writings of the time, it seems clear that we do need to read *A Man of the People* in relation to Achebe's continuing belief in the Nigerian project and the institution of its national literature. In a 1965 essay, published just as he was completing the novel, for example, he unambiguously identifies this as the continuing cultural priority for writers:

> A national literature is one that takes the whole nation for its province, and has a realised or potential audience throughout its territory. In other words, a literature that is written in the *national* language... After the elimination of white rule shall have been completed, the single most important fact in Africa in the second half of the twentieth century will appear to be the rise of individual nation states. I believe that African literature will follow the same pattern.[21]

As we can see here, moreover, Achebe's (much questioned) choice to work in English directly reflects this commitment to the building of a national literary tradition. Given Nigeria's cultural and linguistic diversity and the historical context of colonialism, he argues, English has become the indispensable medium of communication if writers and intellectuals are to be heard beyond their own regional communities, and to enjoy nationwide networks of exchange. Furthermore, he negates the claims of literature in all indigenous African languages with surprising force: 'These languages will just have to develop as tributaries to feed the one central language enjoying nation-wide currency.'[22]

Clearly, the underside to this strategy is that the choice of English for his fiction also has the effect of denying access to those – including a majority of Ibos – who were not literate in that language. In terms of his much-publicized commitment to cultural regeneration, I would suggest, this is by no means inconsequential. The fact that Achebe is willing to sacrifice this audience in his own home region by writing in the colonial tongue serves to underline, not only the hybrid nature of his fiction as a by-product of British imperialism, but also its umbilical tie to the project of a national literature.

Given *A Man of the People*'s bleak portrayal of the Nigerian polity, in which the suspension of democracy itself appears to be offered as the only hope for the future, nevertheless, it is difficult to view Achebe's aesthetic here as 'nationalist' in any simple sense. Indeed, an examination of Achebe's fictional oeuvre as a whole reveals an absence of the typical strategies of nationalist discourse, as identified by theorists such as Eric Hobsbawm[23] and Benedict Anderson.[24] There seems to be, for example, no obvious effort in his fiction to conjure a sense of national cultural homogeneity which might bolster the fragile 'Nigeria idea'. Arguably, his early focus on Ibo culture could much more easily be seen as privileging regional, ethnic or 'tribal' heritage against the tide of 'national' aspirations. The novels do not generally seek, either, to invent mythical lines of differentiation between 'Nigerians' and 'foreigners'. In the earlier texts especially, a concern with Ibo identity and its metamorphoses in the contexts of colonialism and independence dominates decisively over questions of nationhood. It could be argued, perhaps, that in both *No Longer at Ease* and *A Man of the People*, Achebe does reproduce the (for Anderson) canonical association between national idealism and youth, but I would suggest that this is wrapped up in his texts with a complex – and far from crudely ideological – exploration of colonial education and its shaping effects on the emergent middle class. Finally, Achebe evidently decides against framing his narratives around iconic founding fathers (such as perhaps, Nnamdi Azikiwe) but instead turns his pen to a series of flawed, unlovely protagonists, and to narratives which raise as many political problems and questions as they answer.

Rather than trying to read Achebe's texts as nationalist tracts, then, I would argue that it is more useful to consider his work in terms of the specific role he envisages for the novel within the Nigerian project, as a space of national cultural–political exchange. In this sense Achebe can be seen as positioning his texts, neither as expressions of nationalist consciousness, nor as apologias for Nigeria's development, but rather as a series of provocations to liberal democratic debate about the past and future of the nation. In other words, he seeks to institute the novel as a privileged medium of dialogue within a 'public sphere' of the kind theorized in the period by Jürgen Habermas.

Although Habermas's canonical *Strukturwandel der Öffentlichkeit* is directly contemporary with Achebe's early fiction, the twenty-seven year hiatus before its translation into English as *The Structural Transformation of the Public Sphere*[25] is apt to make the texts feel, from an anglophone perspective, as if they emerge from different eras. Setting Habermas's 1962 study against Achebe's fourth novel, however, illuminates the latter in interesting ways. Whilst Achebe writes from Nigeria in the context of independence and Habermas from that of a West Germany emerging from the shadow of World

War Two, each presents a clear sense of writing in the aftermath of tyranny, and a belief in the importance of free intellectual, cultural and political exchange as one of the central conditions of possibility for the liberal democratic state.

The concern of Habermas's study is to trace the emergence of a bourgeois 'public sphere' in Britain, France and Germany, during the eighteenth and early nineteenth centuries. He theorizes this as a cultural space which exists in contradistinction to modernity's 'depersonalised state authority',[26] an arena of rational expression and debate populated by scientists, writers, artists and literate members of the commercial bourgeoisie. Whilst in a previous era, the very principles of public information and free opinion had had to be fought for 'against the arcane policies of monarchies',[27] he describes the public sphere as a mediator between society and the ruling establishment, guaranteeing public 'supervision'[28] of state activity. In his historical account, Habermas identifies the primary institutions of this new public sphere as the coffee houses and salons which thrived in the urban centres of the European Enlightenment, together with the new organs of literary journalism, such as the *Gentleman's Magazine* in Britain, in which reportage of court news and other information was being supplanted by opinionated commentary, intellectual argument and literary debate. As is suggested in the introduction to this book, considered purely as a historical account of emergent modernity in Europe, Habermas's description of the bourgeois public sphere is far from unproblematic. The argument of *Structural Transformation* is, however, at least as importantly a theoretical as an empirical one. At the same time as he points to specific cultural locations, indeed, Habermas stresses that it is important to understand the public sphere as an ideal space, existing everywhere and nowhere. Likewise, the rational, unfettered and public-minded discourse engendered by the public sphere can be seen as much as a projected ideal as an actually existing space of exchange. In one sense the public sphere is banally ubiquitous; in another, it is almost a chimera:

> A portion of the public sphere comes into being in every conversation in which private individuals assemble to form a public body. They then behave neither like business or professional people transacting private affairs, nor like members of a constitutional order subject to the legal constraints of a bureaucracy. Citizens behave as a public body when they confer in a unrestricted fashion – that is, with the guarantee of freedom of assembly and association and the freedom to express and publish their opinions – about matters of general interest.[29]

As is implicit here, and as Habermas makes clear elsewhere in the 1962 study, whilst he sees the ideal of the public sphere as central to the health of liberal democracy, then, he also recognizes that it is by no means fully or adequately developed in the circumstances of every historical moment and political setting. In the context of the West in the twentieth century, in particular, he regards the public sphere as being under constant threat from a state authority which is increasingly isolated from everyday life, and from the ubiquitous power and pressure of commercial interests.

Setting Habermas's text alongside Achebe's, then, it is possible to see that one of the ways we can read the latter's work, from *Things Fall Apart* onwards, is in terms of the aspiration towards a modernistic 'public sphere' in Nigeria, in parallel with the colonial and post-colonial processes of nation-building. In the more historical novels, certainly, a huge amount of Achebe's narrative effort is invested in establishing the dialogic character of Ibo culture, as well as its strong republican credentials. In *No Longer at Ease*, meanwhile, as critics like Umelo Ojinmah[30] and Benedict Njoku[31] have suggested, Achebe is specifically concerned with the rise of an educated middle class in the run-up to independence, exploring its difficult task of negotiating between an Enlightenment model of public probity and civic responsibility, on the one hand, and traditional regional and kinship obligations on the other. In that novel, I would suggest, the fact that his protagonist Obi Okonkwo ultimately succumbs to the culture of 'dash' and preferment around him is rendered understandable, and at the same time represented as a fall, a betrayal of historic responsibilities.

With *A Man of the People*, set a few years later, Achebe returns to the same concerns. Through the figures of Odili Samalu and Chief Nanga, I would argue, it seeks metonymically to dramatize the struggle in the mid-1960s between the two key social strata: on the one hand, an older caste of Nigerians who had inherited their positions of privilege and power from the departing British, and on the other hand, a newly emergent class of liberal, literate, university educated young professionals. In this sense, the novel can be seen as a microcosmic playing-out of the post-colonial situation of Nigeria in the mid-1960s, together with a hypothetical representation of its future development.

In the novel as a whole, we are encouraged to recognize the complex relationship between these emergent class divisions in the new nation, and the residual culture of ethnic and regional affiliations associated with 'tradition'. If Nanga, as a member of the ruling establishment, is shown as consistently nepotistic and corrupt, for example, the novel encourages us to understand these tendencies as co-extensive with his appeal to tribalism. Nanga's claims to be an authentic 'man of the people' are, moreover, schematically linked to anti-intellectualism. Near the beginning of the text, when we see him in parliament, this antipathy is presented as a key plank in his political platform:

'From today we must watch and guard our hard-won freedom jealously. Never again must we entrust our destiny and the destiny of Africa to the hybrid class of Western-educated and snobbish intellectuals who will not hesitate to sell their mothers for a mess of pottage...'

Mr Nanga pronounced the death sentence at least twice more but this was not recorded, no doubt because his voice was lost in the general commotion. (p. 6)

On the other side of the equation, Odili's high-cultural aspirations and liberal university education situate him, in an important way, aloof from Nanga's world, and this is reflected throughout his narrative by the juxtaposition of Odili's standard English with the idiomatic and pidgin forms given to Nanga and others. At the same time, recalling Habermas's formulation of the relationship between the bourgeois public sphere and the establishment, Achebe contrives to place him in a position of supervision over the minister, installing him as a guest at Nanga's residence in the capital. Later, his mediating position between populace and establishment is formalized through his role as self-appointed people's representative and anti-corruption campaigner.

In Simon Gikandi's reading, Odili is a witness who attempts to represent the difficulties of his time in all their unlovely complexity. As a narrator, Gikandi argues, 'Odili can only content himself with the belief that by acknowledging, and even reproducing, the fragmentary and occulted nature of experience, he has avoided disguise and duplicity.'[32] This approach to Achebe's protagonist broadly accords with that of most critics of *A Man of the People*. However, I want to propose here that an alternative reading of Odili is possible, which leads to a quite different assessment of Achebe's novel as a whole. I suggested above that, as a representative of the new educated bourgeoisie, Achebe positions his protagonist in a supervisory relationship to the minister. At the same time, however, it is also worth noting the extent to which, throughout the text, Odili's role is complicated by his parasitic relation to Nanga. Almost from the beginning, he is placed at the subordinate end of a relationship of patronage, and later, as Nanga's political opponent, he remains essentially reactive to, and locked in personal competition with, the minister. Within the narrative, the effects of this are played out on a political and a sexual-political level simultaneously. As the story develops, Odili becomes more and more personally competitive with his rival, and less and less incisive in his ethical and political vision. Here, for example, Achebe shows him meditating on his reasons for seeking to expose Nanga: 'How important was my political activity in its own right? It was difficult to say; things seemed so mixed up; my revenge, my new political ambition and the girl' (p. 108). This is certainly an interesting narrative choice. In a contemporary review of the novel, indeed, Ngugi wa Thiongo[33] is concerned to note how close to the establishment Achebe places Odili, in a position where he lacks the critical distance to see any chance of meaningful change. Certainly, whilst Achebe uses Max and the other socialists to suggest the possibility of a more developed political critique of the status quo, Odili's gaze never rests seriously on such questions.

In the characterization of his protagonist, Achebe makes Odili profoundly unreflective on many levels. In the narrative, the key sources of his distraction from issues of principle are sexual ambition and jealousy, but even on this level, Achebe chooses to colour his gaze with a pervasive misogyny. Thus whilst Odili confidently equates professional, educated women like Jean with prostitutes, he is intoxicated with desire at the spectacle of Edna as a pleading, terrified child when he visits the Anata Mission Hospital, by her 'convent girl' (p. 137) appearance at Nanga's campaign meeting, and Eunice's 'nervous schoolgirl' (p. 127) image at the Common People's Convention rally. Given that Achebe structures the novel so strongly around the adversarial battle between Odili and Nanga, and through them the struggle between the petty-tribalist establishment and the new educated middle class, then, Odili's emergence as such a weak and objectionable representative of the latter certainly raises some questions, in so far as we approach the novel as a contribution to debate around the future of the post-colonial nation.

These questions are interestingly sharpened, moreover, by the self-conscious likeness Achebe draws between Odili's position and his own. Odili is the same age as the author, and like him, one of the nation's first university graduates. He has a similarly ambivalent cultural background, in relation to colonialism. Odili's father is a one-time 'district interpreter', a conduit between local people and the white colonial administration – a position entailing a certain amount of power but also a level of cultural exclusion. Achebe's father was amongst the first Christian converts in the South East, making the author himself, as he well recognizes, a direct product of the educational and economic preferment that such a position brought under colonialism. In parallel with the socially marginal position of Odili's father in the text, the missionary community of which Achebe's father was a founding member consisted of the people who in *Things Fall Apart* are viewed with disgust as 'empty men'.[34] In these ways Achebe gives Odili a social and cultural background which in important ways mirrors his own: in a further playful reference we also learn that Odili 'had ambitions to write a novel about the coming of the first white men to my district' (p. 58).

I do not suggest here that *A Man of the People*'s protagonist 'is' Achebe, any more than the novel's setting 'is' Nigeria: discrepancies are placed here and there in the text to disallow such a literal reading. Rather, the relationship in each case is closer to the formulation used by Salman Rushdie in *Shame* (1983), whose setting is 'not quite' Pakistan and whose characters are 'not quite' General Zia and Zulfiquar Ali Bhutto.[35] Given the clear points of identification I have cited, however, it is very interesting to see how uncompromising Achebe's novel is in the drawing of its protagonist. Certainly, the text seems at least as concerned to flagellate Odili for his failings as it is to punish Chief Nanga. The latter is shown as corrupt, yes, but this is directly linked in the novel to the structures of clannish loyalty associated with traditional culture. To borrow the language of the text, Nanga is 'eating', but his extended family and the people of his district are also 'eating'. In the minds of his electorate, Nanga is in a position to ensure that Anata gets its share of the 'national cake', and if he is taking a portion for himself, then this is both reasonable and natural: 'Tell them that this man had used his position to enrich himself and they would ask you – as my father did – if you thought a sensible man would spit out the juicy morsel that good fortune had placed in his mouth' (p. 2). In other words, I would suggest that the effect of Achebe's text is to present Nanga's corruption as an organic extension of traditional mores into modern national culture. If Nanga is shown as a retrograde figure whose weddedness to the past stifles both political and economic development, however, Odili is shown as an equally poor progenitor of change. Vain, pompous, misogynistic and elitist, even as a candidate for the Common People's Convention he remains disdainful of the 'silly ignorant villagers' (p. 2) and the city's 'contemptible' masses (p. 138). A far greater proportion of Odili's narrative is taken up with his dubious seductions of women than with any kind of political or social reflection, and he is ultimately revealed as a figure who is as impotent as he is self-regarding.

In Achebe's novel we certainly do get a sense of the appalling social inequalities of contemporary Nigeria, but we see this very much over Odili's shoulder, whilst his attention is focused elsewhere:

> As dawn came my head began to clear a little and I saw Bori stirring. I met a night-soil man carrying his bucket of ordure on top of a battered felt hat drawn down to hood his upper face while his nose and mouth were masked with a piece of black cloth like a gangster. I saw beggars sleeping under the eaves of luxurious department stores and a lunatic sitting wide awake by the basket of garbage he called his possession . . . It was perhaps strange that a man who had so much on his mind should pay attention to these small, inconsequential things. (p. 71)

'So much on his mind' in this passage does not of course refer to political campaigning, but rather to the fact that Nanga has just slept with his girlfriend. Achebe reinforces the irony in the following scene, when Odili confronts Chief Nanga: ' "What a country!" I said. "You call yourself minister of culture. God help us." And I spat' (p. 72). As the narrative underlines, it is sexual competitiveness, and not ideological commitment, which again laces his words.

In the narrative as a whole, I would suggest then, Achebe chooses to offer us a protagonist who is able to show us neither a concerted political critique of the current regime, nor a redemptive vision that might point beyond it. Clearly, this sits interestingly alongside his call in the mid-1960s for a new kind of pedagogically focused, politically engaged literature. If the narrative structure of *A Man of the People* sets up Odili and Chief Nanga as two alternate 'men of the people', representing status quo and educated middle class respectively, it is apparently in order to show them as mutually inadequate, equally compromised by greed, egotism and ambition. On a political level, moreover, the novel declines to offer a redemptive third figure. There are some moderately idealistic, moderately corrupt, moderately inept friends, but no clear representation of the kind of campaigning, ethical and political intellectualism which Achebe calls for in his essays. In the course of the narrative, we certainly do pass through a range of potential contexts for ethical and political exchange – the public meeting, the university, the vanguard party, the literary society – but these are seen as little more than the weak seedlings of a public sphere which is comprehensively overshadowed by the power of the establishment and of neo-colonial vested interests. Against the tidal flow of corruption and graft, the novel leaves military intervention as the only straw for us to clutch at.

In his reading of *A Man of the People* against Wole Soyinka's *The Interpreters* (1967) the critic Joe Obi identifies Achebe's text as one of a raft of 'disillusionment novels' of the mid-1960s, in which writers abandon their erstwhile nationalism and turn to a more questioning analysis of the post-colonial state. The problem with these novels, he contends, is that whilst they might accurately reflect a range of problematic symptoms in contemporary African society, they ultimately fail to 'constitute a radical critique of ongoing reality'.[36] Achebe's novel is, he believes, hard on politicians and the ordinary people, but soft on writers and intellectuals. The author's choice to end with a military coup, moreover, leaves 'an uncomfortable anticlimactic void'[37] where a more developed social analysis should be.

Where this reading of Achebe's text falls short, I would argue, is in its overdetermined focus on an ideological panacea which *A Man of the People* very deliberately refuses to offer. This is not, as I have suggested, a novel of political solutions, and neither is it easy on the new middle class. Rather, I would argue that the concern of *A Man of the People* is to represent the failure of the educated bourgeoisie to constitute a functioning 'public sphere' in post-independence Nigeria, which might have checked and supervised the political establishment more effectively. The story of Odili as a representative of this class is a story of ethical and political inadequacy. As a character, he enacts precisely Frantz Fanon's warning of the backsliding of the new bourgeoisie in contemporary ex-colonial states:

> In an under-developed country an authentic national middle class ought to...put itself to school with the people: in other words to put at the people's disposal the intellectual and technical capital that it has snatched when going through the colonial universities. But unhappily we shall

see that very often the national middle class does not follow this heroic, positive, fruitful and just path; rather, it disappears with its soul set at peace into the shocking ways – shocking because anti-national – of a traditional bourgeoisie, of a bourgeoisie which is stupidly, contemptibly, cynically bourgeois.[38]

In a 1967 essay written not long before his own arrest and imprisonment by the Nigerian military regime, Wole Soyinka bears witness to a growing sense of desperation at the suppression of literary and intellectual debate in Nigeria. In a position where the public sphere is so far excluded that the writer can no longer operate as the 'conscience' of his society, Soyinka concludes, he has little choice but to retreat to the role of 'post-mortem surgeon'.[39] Like Achebe, however, Soyinka by no means absolves intellectuals of all blame. If the writer finds himself now in an impossible situation, he suggests, this cannot be separated from 'failure on his part, in his own right'.[40] Two years later, setting *A Man of the People* in a fuller historical context, Achebe himself is concerned to relate Nigeria's transformation into what he calls a 'cesspool of corruption and misrule'[41] directly to the circumstances of independence. Writing from the Biafran republic, he argues that the chances of establishing a healthy political dynamic in Nigeria were fatally undermined in 1960 by the self-serving manipulation of its constitution by the departing British.

In this essay, his continuing concern with the relationship of writers to the nation and to the public sphere is evident. One of the notable and interesting things about Achebe's stance here, moreover, is his determination to present Biafra – in opposition to Nigeria – as a project with which writers can identify. Indeed, the essay's concluding paragraph consists primarily of a list of literary 'names' who are signed up to the cause. If in *A Man of the People* he charts the failure and dissolution of the Nigerian public sphere in the mid-1960s, in other words, there is a clear desire in Achebe's subsequent writing to represent Biafra as a second chance, both for the writer and the nation. Speaking to *Transition* in 1968, he is keen to stress the same point. Even in the immediate context of civil war, he describes the development of a literary, political and intellectual public sphere in Biafra, very much in the Habermasian mould, whose role is to exercise a shaping, moderating and supervisory function over the developing nation:

A number of thinkers feel that in this new society we must make sure that certain evil practices and abuses about which we complained so much in Nigerian society are not allowed to take root, so we have got to start talking about them now: How do you organise this kind of society? I am, in fact, involved with a group which is preparing papers and documents on the society we would like to see: Just putting down what it is we want and what we want to avoid – as a basis for discussion when the war is over.[42]

Biafra was to suffer a crushing defeat in 1970 at the hands of the Nigerian Federation with its British and Soviet backers, and Achebe's own career as a novelist was to remain suspended for a further seventeen years. Far from signalling the beginning of a new phase in Achebe's writing, indeed, it seems clear that *A Man of the People* should be read as the last expression of his early literary career. As we have already seen, the crisis in Achebe's relationship to the nation engendered by the events of the mid-1960s was accompanied by a directly parallel crisis in his work with the novel. In 1968, he refers to the shock of discovering that:

> one had been operating on a false – but perhaps naive – basis all along. The problems of the Nigerian Federation were always well known, but one somehow felt that perhaps this was part of growing up and given time all this would be over and we would solve our problems . . . Suddenly you realise that the only valid basis for existence is one that gives security to you and your people.[43]

At the beginning of the 1970s, Achebe does publish a volume of poems[44] and a collection of short stories,[45] but in the wake of the crisis in his relationship to Nigeria, it seems clear that despite continuing creative efforts, the novel as a form remains closed to him, and he is forced to move to other modes of expression.

Although it is not until the late 1980s that Achebe overcomes his block with the novel and publishes *Anthills of the Savannah*,[46] it is also important to recognize the ways in which his ongoing commitment to the ideal of a Habermasian public sphere is reflected in other strands of his work. In his establishment of the literary journal *Okike* in 1971 as a forum for new writing, in his redoubled output of critical and political commentary,[47] and not least in his work as a promoter of new African novelists, we can see a broad-based commitment to develop the infrastructure of African literary and intellectual exchange. Writing for the *Times Literary Supplement* in 1972, he castigates African intellectuals for the shallowness of their literary reading, whilst stressing the importance of developing school and public libraries.[48] In a 1973 essay for *Transition*, he launches a full-frontal assault on the doctrine of 'art for art's sake', which he characterizes startlingly as *'just another piece of deodorized dog-shit'*.[49] Novelists and poets are again urged to turn away from the aesthetic traditions of Europe, and especially from the existentialist sensibility of the contemporary Western metropolis. The African writer, he argues, needs to turn his mind and pen to the public sphere: 'For him there is still the inescapable grammar of values to straighten out, the confused vocabulary of fledgling polities.'[50]

Nine years after the civil war, when military dictatorship was coming to an end, and the establishment once again recognized Achebe with the Nigerian National Merit Award, his commentary in the Lagos *Daily Times* showed a continuing ambivalence about the direction of the nation: 'I think I am on safe ground if I say that Nigerian writers are not planning to send a delegation to President Shehu Shagari to pledge their unflinching support. Flinching support is more in their line of business.'[51] On a superficial level, this might be read as the expression of a weakened, defeated commitment, reinforcing the bleak prognosis offered by *A Man of the People*. As I have argued in relation to the novel, however, it is inappropriate to equate the cultural nationalism of Achebe's work with a requirement to uncritically glorify and support the Nigerian state.

Returning to the text, then, I would suggest that we need to read *A Man of the People* – through all its appearance of pessimism – as a reflection of Achebe's commitment to dispassionate engagement and analysis, however challenging to the status quo. If *A Man of the People* was read as evidence of conspiracy by the Nigerian military government in 1966, the novel's portrait, through Odili, of a self-regarding and impotent middle class must have made equally discomfiting reading for much of its liberal audience. Even as it describes the dissolution of the Nigerian public sphere, and predicts the end of liberal democracy itself, it is a novel which demands a response, challenges a different ending. In and through its very scandalousness, in other words, its effect is to assert the novel's survival as a space of public debate.

## Notes

1. Chinua Achebe, *A Man of the People* (London: Heinemann, 1966).
2. Tony Hall, interview with Chinua Achebe, 'I Had to Write on the Chaos I Foresaw', *Sunday Nation* (Nairobi), 15 January 1967, 15–16, reprinted in Bernth Lindfors, *Conversations with Chinua Achebe* (Jackson, MI: University Press of Mississippi, 1997), 23.
3. Chinua Achebe, *Things Fall Apart* (London: Heinemann, 1958).
4. Robert Wren, *Those Magical Years* (Washington DC: Three Continents Press, 1991), 65–6, reprinted in Ezenwa-Ohaeto, *Chinua Achebe: a Biography* (Oxford: James Currey, 1997), 109.
5. Ezenwa-Ohaeto (1997) cited above.
6. Bernth Lindfors, 'Achebe's African Parable', in C.L. Innes and Bernth Lindfors, eds, *Critical Perspectives on Chinua Achebe* (London: Heinemann, 1979), 248–54.
7. Ezenwa-Ohaeto, 108.
8. Lindfors, 253.
9. 'Interview with Tony Hall', in Lindfors (1997), 22–3.
10. 'Chinua Achebe on Biafra', *Transition*, 36 (1968), 31–8; 36.
11. Ossie Enekwe, 'Interview with Chinua Achebe', *Okike*, 30 (1990), 129–31, quoted in Ezenwa-Ohaeto, 196.
12. 'Chinua Achebe on Biafra', *Transition*, 36 (1968), 31–8; 31.
13. Bernth Lindfors, Ian Munro, Richard Priebe and Reinhard Sander, 'Interview with Chinua Achebe', *Palaver: Interviews with Five African Writers in Texas* (Austin: African and Afro-American Research Institute, University of Texas at Austin, 1972), reprinted in Lindfors (1997), 27–34; 29.

14. Chinua Achebe, 'The Novelist as Teacher', *New Statesman* (London), 29 January 1965, reprinted in Chinua Achebe, *Hopes and Impediments: Selected Essays* (New York: Anchor Books, 1990), 40–1.

15. Ibid., 44.

16. Chinua Achebe, 'The Novelist as Teacher', 45.

17. Frantz Fanon, *The Wretched of the Earth*, trans. Constance Farrington (New York: Grove, 1968).

18. Simon Gikandi, *Reading Chinua Achebe: Language and Ideology in Fiction* (London: James Currey, 1991), 7.

19. Ibid., 105.

20. Ibid., 104–5.

21. Chinua Achebe, 'English and the African Writer', *Transition*, 4, 18, (1965), 27.

22. Ibid., 28.

23. Eric Hobsbawm, *Nations and Nationalism since 1780: Programme, Myth, Reality* (Cambridge: Cambridge University Press, 1990).

24. Benedict Anderson, *Imagined Communities: Reflections on the Origin and Spread of Nationalism*, revised edition (London: Verso, 1991).

25. Jürgen Habermas (1962), *The Structural Transformation of the Public Sphere: an Inquiry into a Category of Bourgeois Society*, trans. Thomas Burger with the assistance of Frederick Lawrence (Cambridge: Polity, 1989).

26. Ibid., 19.

27. Jürgen Habermas, 'The Public Sphere', *New German Critique*, 3 (Fall 1974), 50.

28. Ibid., 52.

29. Ibid., 49.

30. Umelo Ojinmah, *Chinua Achebe: New Perspectives* (Ibadan: Spectrum, 1991).

31. Benedict Njoku, *The Four Novels of Chinua Achebe: a Critical Study* (New York: Peter Lang, 1984).

32. Gikandi, 110.

33. Ngugi wa Thiongo, 'Chinua Achebe: *A Man of the People*', in *Homecoming: Essays on African and Caribbean Literature, Culture and Politics* (London: Heinemann, 1972), 51–4.

34. Chinua Achebe, *Things Fall Apart* (London: Heinemann, 1958), 119.

35. Salman Rushdie, *Shame* (London: Jonathan Cape, 1983).

36. Joe E. Obi, Jr, 'A Critical Reading of the Disillusionment Novel', *Journal of Black Studies*, 20, 4 (June 1990), 399–413; 404.

37. Ibid., 408.

38. Frantz Fanon, *The Wretched of the Earth*, trans. Constance Farrington (London: Penguin, 1967), 120–1.

39. Wole Soyinka, 'The Writer in an African State', *Transition*, 31 (June/July 1967), 11–13; 13.

40. Ibid., 11.

41. Chinua Achebe, 'The African Writer and the Biafran Cause' (1969), in *Morning Yet on Creation Day* (London: Heinemann, 1975), 78–84; 82.

42. 'Chinua Achebe on Biafra', 37.

43. Ibid., 31.

44. Chinua Achebe (1971), *Beware, Soul Brother* (London: Heinemann, 1972).

45. Chinua Achebe, *Girls at War* (London: Heinemann, 1972).

46. Chinua Achebe, *Anthills of the Savannah* (London: Heinemann, 1987).

47. See, for example, Chinua Achebe, *The Trouble with Nigeria* (Enugu: Fourth Dimension, 1983).

48. Chinua Achebe, 'What Do African Intellectuals Read?' *TLS*, 12 May 1972, 547, reprinted in *Morning Yet on Creation Day* (London: Heinemann, 1975), 38–41.
49. Chinua Achebe, 'Africa and her Writers', *Massachusetts Review*, 14 (1973), 617–29; 617.
50. Ibid., 628.
51. Quoted in *West Africa*, editorial, 19 November 1979, 2123.

# 7

## 'Precious Gift/Piece of Shit': Salman Rushdie's *The Satanic Verses* and the Revenge of History

*Shailja Sharma*

### Introduction: betrayed by history

Salman Rushdie's work has been formed by his obsession with history and the way its elusive quality constantly betrays those certainties we die to believe. Taking as his target the slippery nature of ontological histories: nationalist, ethnic, regional and religious, his novels show us that these histories have proved less than stalwart; betraying his characters, forcing them to recognize that all that seems solid is in fact air, entrapping them in their claims to truth, permanency and belonging, he delivers them only when they accept their rootlessness as the true human condition. Curious then, that this prophet of transformation and rebirth has himself been witness to the irrevocability of history and the claims of religion and national myths. Curiouser still, he has since found his latest incarnation as a celebrity writer in the country where the erasure of history, of immigrants and others, is a rite of passage. Now he finds himself as a polemicist without an object to hate. Paradoxically, it is since moving to the United States that his novels, both rooted in and rooting against history, have found nothing to attack, and so have been solipsistically about himself, trapped airily without the anchor of history. This cosmopolitan writer, in a fascinating return of the repressed, finds himself without the form of history to sustain his scorn.

During the thirty-two years that Salman Rushdie lived in Britain, his writing consistently used polemic, analysis, and vitriol, as well as the opportunities open to him as a published writer, to speak, sometimes controversially, about broadly left causes both in Britain and elsewhere. His non-fiction book about the war in Nicaragua, *The Jaguar Smile* (1987) was seen in the United States as an apologia for the Sandinistas. His essays for British newspapers, later collected as *Imaginary Homelands* (1991), cover a range of topics, from literary criticism and autobiography to South Asian politics and British attitudes towards Asians in Britain. One particular essay, 'Handsworth Songs', urges a more inclusive history of Britain:

> It's important, I believe, to tell these stories; to say, this is England. Look at the bright illuminations and fireworks during the Hindu Festival of Lights, Divali. Listen to the Muslim call for prayer, 'Allahu Akbar', wafting down from the minaret of a Birmingham mosque. Visit the Ethiopian World federation, which helps Handsworth Rastas 'return' to the land of Ras Tafari. These are English scenes now, English songs.[1]

It's hard to imagine, but in 1987, when this essay was first published, most people found the claim that Britain was a multicultural state hard to accept, including politicians and bureaucrats. The term 'British minority' lay in the future. Britain was in the throes of Thatcherism and immigration was, famously, the 'wedge' issue used to divide the electorate.[2] However, even as Rushdie was calling for a celebration of multicultural Britain *avant la lettre*, as it were, he remained a somewhat privileged intellectual, having little in common with working-class Asian migrants to Britain. In the same essay, he admits: 'I don't know Handsworth very well' (116). Doctrinaire critics might see that as a failure, but it is obvious that Rushdie positions himself, in 'Handsworth Songs' as well as in other essays like 'Outside the Whale' and 'The New Empire Within Britain', as part of this community, among others.

His class position, however, has always complicated the attempt to read him as 'representative' or as 'a voice for' Asian migrants. To do him justice, Rushdie has also avoided any such inflated claims. In fact, in a later essay, he spurns the idea that any writer can speak on behalf of anyone else: 'Beware the writer who sets himself or herself up as the voice of a nation. This includes nations of race, gender, sexual orientation, elective affinity. This is the New Behalfism. Beware behalfies!'[3] It wasn't until the controversy over *The Satanic Verses* in Britain in 1989–90 that the issue of Rushdie's politics and his relationship with the majority of Asians in Britain took on a more charged tone. When mobs in Bradford burned his book they were repudiating Rushdie's claims that his novel was, in fact, about people like them. In the ensuing years, the question of where Rushdie's loyalties lay, or, more precisely, who was loyal to Rushdie's cause, became a complex one. He himself has written at length in 'The Plague Years' about the years during which he had to be provided with government security and hide in safe houses as he feared for his life and the lives of those associated with his book.[4] More pertinently, the controversy surrounding the reception of *The Satanic Verses*, or as it is popularly known, 'the Rushdie affair', has become a landmark in any discussion of multicultural politics in Britain, immigrant and Muslim politics, and the limits of free speech in the contemporary world.

Comparable to 'l'affaire foulard' in France but certainly with a much more international reach, the 'Rushdie affair' complicated traditional Left-Right divisions and became a focal point for writers, intellectuals and readers. In terms of British politics, it brought Muslim clerics from London, Birmingham and Bradford into the public eye and gave them an issue around which to rally their supporters. Historians and sociologists like Akbar S. Ahmed in Cambridge and Dilip Hero in London became 'experts' on race relations, multiculturalism and Islam. Literature and the literary in Rushdie's work became secondary to the sacred hermeneutic of the Koran. It has been sixteen years since the 'Rushdie affair' began. It would be fair to say that, in retrospect, it also provided a justification for the political radicalization of certain factions of Muslim youth in post-industrial British cities. Not that it caused the radicalization, which had causes like poverty, unemployment, and alienation enough, but opposition to Rushdie's novel became a banner under which that alienation could find a voice. As I write, in the aftermath of the 7 July 2005 Underground bombings in London, when commentators, columnists and policy wonks are trying to analyse what went wrong, it seems appropriate to look back at the divisions around the 'Rushdie affair' to see the beginnings of a trend.

If one of Rushdie's aims in writing has been to interrogate the histories of nations and shatter the false unanimity of a national voice and literature, he has succeeded at great cost to himself. His idea that 'writers are the poets of discord', can be found in a number of writings on the *'Satanic Verses* affair'.[5] Historically however, one of the paradoxical outcomes of the discord that *The Satanic Verses* generated was to provide a national voice for South Asian Muslims in Britain, or more properly, British Muslims. This is a somewhat regrettable result for a writer who proudly has called himself a secular man. This phenomenon is also important because it shattered the assumption of solidarity behind appellations like 'black British', 'British Asian' or 'Indian' and 'Pakistani'. Writers and race relations experts on the Left had, optimistically perhaps, largely neglected the place of religion and its centrality to new British identities. As in traditional Marxist thinking, religion had either been relegated to the private sphere, or read as a form of false consciousness. More importantly, since immigration from the Indian sub-continent had traditionally been from the working class, union and worker-oriented organizations like the IWA (Indian Workers Association) had been dominant. The publication of *The Satanic Verses* came at a time when second-generation British Asians not firmly ensconced in working-class politics (or those with more complex identity politics than their parents) found a ready focus for their concerns within religious organizations. It was at once a political and generational cleavage from earlier forms of collectivization.

Paradoxically, in the wake of this controversy, Rushdie's fiction writing has moved away from a direct assessment of those years, though he has dealt with the period in columns and short essays, towards a more introspective analysis of fame, isolation and anger. *The Moor's Last Sigh* (1995), *The Ground Beneath Her Feet* (1999) and *Fury* (2001) have disappointed readers who expected more trenchant analysis. Sara Maitland, an enthusiastic fan of Rushdie and co-editor of *The Rushdie File* (1990), chronicling the history of *The Satanic Verses* in the public maelstrom, called the latter a 'self-indulgent text'.[6] One way to approach the changes in Rushdie's writing since *The Satanic Verses* may be to look at the heightened and exaggerated engagement between his writing and history in the wake of that novel. The years of the fatwa and its aftermath have stripped away any academic sense of history and its power for Rushdie and his readers. For Rushdie, who had always written as an alternative historian, pickling and revealing the post-independence dance of corruption in India and Pakistan, history had perhaps got too close for comfort.

Slavoj Žižek is a careful reader of culture's imbrication within history and the ways in which popular culture, especially film, occupies a space between the production of ideological texts and our consumption of them. In his essay, 'The Undergrowth of Enjoyment' (1999), he uses the Lacanian term, *sinthome*, as that irreducible part of the signifier which resists interpretation and ideological analysis. Post-fatwa, the power of mobs, riots, edicts, religion and belief in its ugliest form, confronted the powerlessness of words, argument and narrative. In experiencing the irreducibility of history to literary discourse, Rushdie must instead portray it as meaningless, entirely subject to commercial manipulation in *Fury*. Encountering the *sinthome*, according to Žižek, we cannot revert to deconstruction. Instead, he says:

> What we must do... is, on the contrary, to isolate the *sinthome* from the context by virtue of which it exerts its power of fascination, to force us to see it in its utter stupidity, as a meaningless fragment of the Real. In other words, we must (as Lacan puts it in *Seminar XI*) 'change the precious gift into a piece of shit'; we must make it possible to experience the mesmerizing voice as a disgusting piece of sticky excrement.[7]

Having experienced the utter fascination and meaninglessness of history through his experience in the wake of the fatwa, Rushdie chooses, in *Fury*, to render it as a 'piece of shit'; random, unimportant, prey to the grossest of consumerist manipulation. In *Midnight's Children* (1981), Saleem's dreams become history, as fiction is spun into history in his head. By contrast, in *Fury*, Solanka ignores history except to turn it into a story for money-spinning. And in the case of Akasz Kronos, his story (history) is available for all to spin out on the internet. It is only by distanciating history 'as a disgusting piece of sticky excrement', that Rushdie can isolate 'the pathological "tic" structuring the real kernel of our enjoyment'.[8] No doubt, in his future writing, Rushdie will rebuild the fiction of context and ideology, subject the world to analysis and critique. But in *Fury*, he rejects the role of fiction as the interpreter of history and instead serves it up as a *sinthome*. It can be experienced only in itself, without making any larger sense.

## Three novels

Any attempt to understand the complex interconnections between Rushdie the writer, his writings as a public intellectual and as a novelist, his *agon* throughout his career with accepted versions of history, his characters as parables and victims of history, would fall under the weight of its ambition. It may be possible, however, to be ruthlessly economical with detail and touch only on three points in Rushdie's career in order to read them as a shorthand to his life and work. Doing so lays no claim to completeness, only an attempt to wrest order out of a human chaos and an oeuvre that is still being written.

The starting point is the Rushdie of *Midnight's Children*. In this, his second novel, Rushdie is the historian of people's voices raised in fierce, personal witness against the elitist histories of the Gandhi clan and the bureaucratic/military/intellectual complex of a country whose history has stubbornly resisted subaltern voices. The deaths of Aadam Sinai, the Hummingbird, and Wee Willie Winkie in the older generation and the lives of Shiva and Saleem and Ganesh in the post-Independence generation, are testimonials to the stubbornness of personal experience and its truths. Here Rushdie grants his characters the power to wrest and re-form history in their own images, determine the fates of sub-continents with table cutlery and use magic to resist power and slip secret powers into the stream of national perpetuity. While Rushdie lived and wrote in London, he painted an India which was chaotic and fecund, powerful in its people and in its stories. He also wrote about his political disappointments with the Emergency (1975–77) and India's betrayal of its founding magic. It was a novel that sprang as much from love as from anger. Rushdie's insider/outsider position, like Saleem's, ended in tragedy. *Midnight's Children* was attacked for its libellous portrait of Mrs Gandhi and banned for a while from publication in India. Questioning history, the novel made history and upended modern Indian literature in English. In England, Rushdie's position as the native-informant intellectual was cemented by *Shame* (1983), and he became the much-fêted writer who put South Asian literature on the map and brought 'magical realism' out of South America and Germany into English, all confirmed by the 'Booker of Bookers' in 1993.

The second phase in Rushdie's career began with *The Satanic Verses* (1988). In this novel, he charts the passage from the sub-continent to Britain, from the Third World to the First and back again. For Rushdie, this novel was as much about coming home as leaving home. After making India and Pakistan's histories the subjects of his two previous works, he was bringing it all back to Britain, his home. In the novel, Chamcha leaves India and then finds a way to return home after suffering his travails/travels. Rushdie wrote this novel as a form of bearing witness to the multiply situated presence (across generations) of South Asians in Britain and their everyday struggles to call Britain home. Later, in the ensuing controversy over the book, when Rushdie insisted that *The Satanic Verses* was in fact a novel about migration, his claims were greeted with scepticism. Yet it is not a false or spurious claim.[9] It is in fact a misreading to read the novel as being overwhelmingly about religion, not about doubt, belief and the mutability of immigrant identities.

Both the characters of Chamcha and Gibreel suffer the shock of arrival as they fall earthwards over England. Rushdie describes their arrival with pity and glee as they outwit the 'authorities' policing the xenophobic nation. Rushdie uses their characters to answer the charges of ignoring cultural and racial difference which had been a hallmark of British governmental discourse from Wilson to Thatcher (via Tebbit), and depicts the monstrous and lovely composite forms that are created by migration. The Manticore, clearly, is created by the British immigration authorities: 'They describe us. That's all. They have the power of description and we succumb to the pictures they construct.'[10] Instead of a story of weepy victimization, however, his characters are also paragons of making do, of telling their own stories and creating new identities. Examples include the characters of Mishal and Jumpy Joshi, Alleluia Cone and the Sufyans, which are also British stories; they hold out as much promise as the Manticore negates. The fire in Club Hot Wax which destroys the establishment monsters also creates the opening for the resolution of the novel. In the two other parts of the novel, the story of Mahound, and the story of Ayesha, the emphasis remains on the conflict between blind faith and imaginative truth, and more specifically on multiple and partial forms of truth. In all these stories, Rushdie depicts the battle between natives and outsiders/immigrants, old forms of corrupt belief and new ways of questioning truth. The authorial weight of the novel is quite clearly, as it was in his earlier writing, oriented towards questioning, scepticism, provocation, and irreverence. It is fitting that the novel, more than his earlier work, deals in the fantastic, the fairy and the monstrous, because what Rushdie lauds here is the power of imagination.

Much like *Midnight's Children*, the *power* to dream, and to create, had become a writer's creed and a political article of faith for Rushdie. The *freedom* to create however, was for Rushdie, less easy to sustain. *The Satanic Verses* became, as is well known, a sort of trial case in Britain and the world, pitting, most crudely, the twin freedoms of creative expression/free speech against the (politically managed) sensibilities of the country's Muslim population. It also marked the political emergence of the South Asian Muslim minority in Britain and its continued battle for political and cultural rights. Battles for recognition and respect, which had earlier been fought in local councils and schools, were now on the national stage, but in a strange and fantastic paradox, they were voiced as a rejection of Rushdie. There were three important insights provided by the 'Rushdie affair': firstly, how strong and entrenched anti-immigrant attitudes were in the British political establishment; secondly, the hold that a reductive political correctness had among British intellectuals and writers; and thirdly, the ways in which class loyalty trumps race and ethnicity in Britain. Wrong became right, Right became Left and demands for cultural recognition became fundamentalism.

The first political objections to the novel were made by the Imam of Delhi's Jama Masjid and by Indian MP Syed Shahabuddin, which led the Indian government, headed by Rajiv Gandhi, who wanted to keep the Muslim vote with his Congress party, to ban the novel. In Britain, the mosques in London and Bradford used the incident to swing members away from the IWA (Indian Workers Association).[11] Rushdie himself lists the positions taken by British politicians on the Left and the Right, and in each case, what swung the balance was political self-interest. Most politicians on the Right sided with Rushdie's right to publish a book, as they saw it, critical of Islam, which was already becoming a favourite bogeyman of politicians. On the Left, many writers and politicians were instead critical of Rushdie, seeing him as culpable of betrayal or deliberate incitement. Two of the best-known instances of such views are Fay Weldon's and John Le Carré's, who claimed that Rushdie had deliberately written the novel knowing it would be provocative.[12] In the case of liberal positions, which saw themselves as also being pro-Muslim, the fallacy of course was to take the category of 'Muslim' as singular and of uniform mind. The most vocal of Muslim groups were also always political groups, so the blind acceptance of them as speaking for the entire Muslim community was as wrong-headed as accepting Rushdie's novel as being only about Islam. But it wasn't simply a Left-Right divide. Within the Tory Party people like Emma Nicholson and Sir Edward Heath denounced Rushdie and the protections offered to him by the government. Within the Labour Party, MPs like Keith Vaz, a British Asian, first supported, then denounced him.[13] What is clear is that the Rushdie 'affair' has served many political ends, but in all cases, neither Muslims in Britain nor Rushdie have been well served by the controversy.

No doubt many believers were upset by the book's portrayal of Islam, but in most cases, listed as well as anecdotal, they hadn't read the book. Instead, being told what the book was about, often by community and religious leaders, they acquiesced in calls for book-burning and for the book to be pulled. Calls for a novel's censorship are not unusual, as this collection suggests, but to demand the author's head consistently over a number of years and to consent in the death of translators, bookstore owners and publishers is surely excessive. The reaction to the threats by those who took them as proof that Muslim immigrants were unassimilable, uncivilized and intolerant was also excessive. In another of those ironies that abounds in this controversy, the novel which told the stories of Britain's immigrants was proof that they could never become British. Rushdie had to choose between defending his community and defending his novel, and more importantly, his life. Ultimately he chose to defend his freedom to write and tell stories:

> It is true that in many Western quarters there is a knee-jerk reflex that leads to anti-Islamic rushes to judgment, so that British Muslims' sense of injury is often justified . . . *For the point is to defend people but not their ideas.* It is absolutely right that Muslims – that everyone – should enjoy freedom of religious belief in any free society . . . It is also absolutely wrong of them to demand that their belief system – that any system of belief or thought – should be immunized against criticism, irreverence, satire, even scornful disparagement. This distinction between the individual and his creed is a foundation truth of democracy.[14]

One organization that stood by Rushdie's right to self-expression was PEN (both the British and American branches – Rushdie is now president of the American chapter) as well as writers across the world. This was seen, in many quarters, as an elitist and class-inflected position: the working-class Muslim masses of Britain on the one hand, the English-speaking, upper middle-class elite of different countries (including India, Egypt, France, the United States) on the other. Is this charge too simplistic?

To answer that, one would have to look at the rather polarized views on Islam held by and about Muslims living in Europe and the ways in which Islam has transcended its position as a private system of belief to become a badge of (dis-affected) identity and one that is inseparable from a political coming of age. Tariq Modood, a Muslim scholar from Britain, has this to say:

> Discourse that sees Muslims as a problem or a threat is not confined to an extreme fringe, nor to popular prejudice, but is prominent in certain elite discourses. Nor are these discourses confined to the right wing. Just as in central Europe progressive politics can use, consciously or unconsciously, a negative 'otherness' in order to project itself, so similarly an anti-Muslim bias can be implicit or explicit in progressive discourse. For example, at the height of *The Satanic Verses* controversy in Britain, one of the most emotive polemics against multiculturalism in general and Muslims in particular came from a prominent liberal feminist.[15]

On the other hand, of course, the subject(s) of Rushdie's novel, the immigrants, the café owners, the illegals, the travellers, the dreamers, turned against him. *The Satanic Verses* is very much a novel about the importance of dreaming the right dreams, or the right to dream differently. However in the novel, the Imam's dream of a pure homeland becomes the counterpoint to Gibreel's dream of changing London itself. His dream is to turn London into a tropical city, which in its turn will achieve a number of other effects:

> increased moral definition, institution of a national siesta, development of vivid and expansive patterns of behavior among the populace, higher quality popular music, new birds in the trees, new trees under the birds... Emergence of new social values, friends to commence dropping in on one another without making appointments, closure of old folks' homes, emphasis on extended family. Spicier food; the use of water as well as paper in English toilets; the joy of running fully dressed through the first rains of the monsoon... Standing upon the horizon, spreading his arms to fill the sky, Gibreel cried: 'Let it be'. (354)

In the world, however, this transmogrification, this re-writing of the West by the rest, did not happen. Rushdie wrote and the Imam unwrote. Khomeini's fatwa put the kibosh on Rushdie's freedom to dream. For the next nine years, Rushdie could not live or dream without the nightmare of death hanging over him.

As Agha Shahid Ali says in 'Farewell': 'My memory is again in the way of your history.'[16] The clash of dreams and history, the negation of dreams by the 'symbolic order', in Lacanian terms, by words and creeds that insisted on the right to 'one' meaning, were in stark contrast to what Rushdie himself had been trying to do all his life: free history from the unitary meaning, the one voice. If one reads Rushdie's writing as an attempt to liberate history for the dreamers in all of us, to argue for the power of personal pleasure to shape our narrative, then its counterweight is the force of official history, one that is both imposed, and in Gramscian terms, that we consent to as a form of ideological seduction. The saddest part in the aftermath of the fatwa was watching Salman Rushdie use words in a failed attempt to placate his enemies.

Rushdie seesawed in his attempts to reach a compromise with these official versions of truth. He was a Muslim, then he was not. He was British, yet critical of British government, and still dependent on it for his protection. He was a writer, not an apostate. The debate about what he was and what he wrote, carried out publicly in newspaper op-ed pieces and declarations of intent, mirrored a nightmare world of Secret Service guardians, hidden locations, close shaves with assassins, and betrayal by community and government. What was private (religion, belief, love, doubt) became public and what was public (the writer, the novel, the publishers, the book) became private and hidden. The symbolic won a victory over the realm of private pleasure, the imaginary. History came down like a huge monster and squashed Rushdie's intellectual loyalties flat. A man who was both Indian and British had to publicly censure the Conservative government for questioning his rights as a British citizen. An intellectual who had been a kind of native informant was disowned by all except by the community of writers. One could argue that these nine years changed Rushdie's relationship to place, nation and history. In his quest for survival, the only people who supported him were his literary community. All historical allegiances gave way to loyalties of class and profession.

*Fury* saw Rushdie's literary move to the United States. Publicly he defended his actual relocation as a fresh start and as an attempt to leave the nine years of forcible and controversial incarceration behind. He also, more controversially, announced that Britain's literary world was too small for him. *Fury* was his first novel after moving to New York, and his first major novel (excepting *The Ground Beneath Her Feet*, 1999) after his emergence from the fatwa. Unlike his previous novel, *Fury* was a self-conscious attempt to reinvent both Rushdie and the Rushdie novel. *Fury* began as a short novella written for the Netherlands Book Week, where Rushdie was the chief guest. In its final form, it expanded but never grew to the size of any of his other novels. True to its theme of reinvention, the novel cedes the ruling narrative logic of his other novels, which all rest firstly, on historical allegory and secondly, on the interpenetration of public and private worlds. Instead, like its protagonist, the middle-aged Professor Malik Solanka, it retreats into interiority. Like Solanka, who spends his days in his Manhattan sublet and speaks incessantly of the fury within him, his lack of human relationships, the novel makes brief and unsatisfying cursory forays into the wider world of New York City. Like Solanka, the novel is isolated from its surroundings and cut off from its literary and social history. What gestures Rushdie makes towards the New World he has migrated into, are less a considered intervention or analysis of an empire flush with wealth and more in the nature of a laundry list: 'New restaurants opened every hour. Stores, dealerships, galleries struggled to satisfy the skyrocketing demand for ever more recherché produce: limited edition olive oils, three-hundred-dollar corkscrews, customized Humvees, the latest anti-virus software.'[17] And later, when Solanka thinks a little more deeply: 'Questions of power preyed on his mind. While the overheated citizenry was eating these many varieties of lotus, who knows what the city's rulers were getting away with . . . the high ones who were always there, forever feeding their insatiable desires, seeking out newness, devouring beauty, and always, always wanting more?'(7). The contrast between this gestural history and the intimacy of lived history in either *Midnight's Children* or *The Satanic Verses* is clear. Rushdie has no real way of situating himself or his protagonist within what he can see very clearly is an alien culture.

One could argue that *Fury* is, in fact, a novel about alienation, and in particular alienation from one's own history. There are a few touches of what we think of as Rushdie's favourite themes: migration, exile, the solaces of fiction and creation. There are the stereotyped loud-mouthed Punjabi workers and taxi-cab drivers, the East European exiles severed from their histories like Milosevic, Mila's father, who tries to escape his fatal name but can't escape his history. Even Neela Mahendra, the beautiful Indo-Lilly who saves Solanka, has a home and a history with claims on her. Lilliput-Blefescu, presumably a thinly veiled allusion to Fiji, and its civil war, becomes a way for Solanka to connect with the politics of *a* homeland, but not *his* homeland. Rushdie wants us to read Solanka as a character who is not only exiled but has exiled himself from all his homelands and cannot find a new one. Solanka's sympathy for the reluctant Cuban celebrity, Elian Gonzalez, 'Elianismo', is equalled by his contempt for the event's hijacking by religious nuts. In denying his homeland lies freedom. But this freedom damages the novel, turning it into a middle-aged travelogue or a publicly enacted attempt to come to terms with the fatwa's aftermath.

In *Fury*, the narrator is conscious of his ambivalence towards the New World, towards New York. Rushdie chooses to make Solanka, like Saleem Sinai in *Midnight's Children*, an authorial double. Like Rushdie, Solanka is in his fifties, with a soft, round face, fair-skinned (with his author's 'cupid's bow mouth' which seems to be a favourite phrase, repeated in the case of Kronos) and has been educated and employed in the UK. He has been married many times, and like Rushdie, driven out of England by the effects of his own creativity. Little Brain, the doll over which Solanka loses control, is easily read as *The Satanic Verses* and its subsequent history, which made Rushdie a celebrity but simultaneously cost him his independence and one could argue, his life, for over nine years. The novel has two metafictional subplots: one is the story of Little Brain, the doll that also symbolizes perfect intellectual freedom (the repeated insistence on Galileo and his resistance to church authorities), but who gets caught up in an Americanized celebrity culture and becomes just another doll; and the story of Akasz Kronos, another fictional counterpart to Rushdie, who creates an entire universe of cyborgs, only to have them attack him. One can see in both these figures Rushdie's attempt to explain the autonomy of fictional creation, as well as their takeover by forces that are organized and more powerful than fiction. In the case of Little Brain, these are the forces of capitalism, and in the case of Kronos, the forces of the Baburians or Mogols (echoes both of Babur, the first Mughal emperor of India, as Rushdie explains, but also of 'barbarians', the generic Greek appellation for people speaking an incomprehensible language). Solanka most overtly becomes Rushdie's mouthpiece in the following passage:

> Ever since Little Brain's censored remarks to Galileo Galilei, questions of knowledge and power, surrender and defiance, ends and means, had gnawed at Solanka. 'Galileo moments,' those dramatic occasions when life asked the living whether they would dangerously stand by the truth or prudently recant it, increasingly seemed to him to lie close to the heart of what it was to be human. (188)

The danger of truth and the prudence of the diplomatic lie, are both clearly echoes of the choices that Rushdie himself made in the wake of Ayatollah Khomeini's fatwa. In 1990, he published a column in the op-ed pages of the New York Times entitled 'Why I Have Embraced Islam', in which he attempted to square his outing as a Muslim with an appeal to the moderate universal principles of Islam.[18] This was followed two years later by a recanting of that position and an embrace of an intellectual's freedom to analyse, criticize, and create. This was in fact a reprise of a position he had taken many times earlier, including in the essay, 'In Good Faith', in which he squares a writer's responsibility with his freedom: 'The Satanic Verses, is in part, a secular man's reckoning with the religious spirit . . . What does the novel dissent from? Certainly not from people's right to faith, though I have none. It dissents most clearly from imposed orthodoxies of all types, from the view that the world is quite clearly This and not That.'[19] In the same essay, he declares that he is not a Muslim even though one of the influences on him has been that of Islam. This seesaw between recanting and insisting on autonomy reveals the multiple pressures of the Rushdie 'affair' on him, as he had to balance the safety of people associated with the novel and his own safety with his beliefs.

The novel Fury, then, can be seen as a continuation of that public and internal debate in Rushdie's work between the forces of faith and scepticism, orthodoxy and heterodoxy. Thus Kronos creates his cyborgs and gives them choice, but being a tyrant, he limits it by his Supreme Directive. And yet, when captured by the Mogols, he, unlike Rushdie, recants, and thus ensures the death of his cyborgs. But by giving in, he also ensures his own demise. As for Kronos himself: 'his fate was obscure. Perhaps the Mogols killed him, even after his abject surrender; or perhaps he was blinded like Tiresias and permitted, by way of further humiliation, to wander the world, begging bowl in hand, "speaking the truth that no man would believe"' (189). Solanka occupies a Tiresian position in Fury; having given up Little Brain, he is doomed to loneliness and sterility in the New World, depending first on Mila and then on Neela to bring him life and creativity. Failing, at the end, to square his creativity with his freedom, he is reduced to shadowing Asmaan and presumably, self-destructing. Like Kronos, his fate remains obscure: 'What were the limits of tolerance? How far, in the pursuit of right, could we go before we crossed a line, arrived at the antipodes of ourselves, and became wrong?' (188). For Solanka, as for Rushdie, these are not just questions for himself but for the zealous world of religious belief as well, the kind of belief that kills from a position of absolute truth.

'Stepping across a line' was also the metaphor that Rushdie used later to deliver the Tanner lectures on Human Values at Yale in 2002. He used the allegory of the Persian myth of Simurgh to insist that line or frontier crossing is the definitive human condition. He expands the definition of frontier to mean boundaries of different kinds: 'the frontier is an elusive line, visible and invisible, physical and metaphorical, amoral and moral'. Furthermore, to cross frontiers is also to question power: 'Alice the migrant sees through the charade of power, is no longer impressed, calls Wonderland's bluff, and by unmasking it finds herself again. She wakes up.'[20] Finding oneself, or having the courage to reject given selves, may be what *Fury* works towards.

## Conclusion: to be born again, you first have to die

Between the fates of Chamcha and Gibreel in his multi-episodic grappling with the ghosts of history, Rushdie remains a writer in progress, developing with each text. In his new novel (at time of writing), *Shalimar the Clown* (2005), by most accounts, he returns to an attempt to write untold histories, complete with context, ideologies and interpretation. This chapter has touched instead on Rushdie's confrontation with, and a turn away from, history. One could argue that in a career spanning three decades, some twists and turns are bound to happen. But for the reader trying to understand Rushdie's *agon* with history, the question remains: which Rushdie shall we read?

> Should we even say that these are two fundamentally different *types* of self? Might we not agree that Gibreel, for all his stage-name and performances; and in spite of born-again slogans, new beginnings, metamorphoses; – has wished to remain, to a large degree, *continuous* – that is, joined to and arising from his past; . . . so that his is still a self which, for our present purposes, we may describe as 'true' . . . whereas Saladin Chamcha is a creature of *selected* discontinuities, a *willing* re-invention; his *preferred* revolt against history being what makes him, in our chosen idiom, 'false'? (427; original italics)

True or false? Continuity or departure from self? This passage, from *The Satanic Verses*, refers to one of the dominant tropes in the novel, that of continuity and authenticity. Though the author seems to suggest that authenticity and continuity are misleading questions, the end of the novel rewards Chamcha for his return 'home' and thus reclaiming continuity, even as Gibreel's efforts at remaining true to his chosen and unchosen roles are doomed to death. The questions about Chamcha and Gibreel hold a certain relevance for our understanding of Rushdie as well. Can history be sloughed off and used as convenient or is it an integral part of Salman Rushdie's work? Precious gift or piece of shit? Can we say that despite the changes in his writing, Rushdie continues to write a kind of history in absentia? Or can we say, we don't know yet?

# Notes

1. Salman Rushdie, 'Handsworth Songs', in *Imaginary Homelands* (New York: Viking Press, 1991), 117.
2. Paul Gilroy, *There Ain't No Black in the Union Jack* (Chicago: University of Chicago Press, 1987).
3. Salman Rushdie, *Step Across This Line: Collected Nonfiction 1999–2002* (New York: Random House, 2002), 60.
4. 'The Plague Years', in *Step Across This Line*,
5. Rushdie, *Imaginary Homelands*, 376–429.
6. Sara Maitland, 'The Author Is Too Much with Us', *Commonweal*, CXXIII, 3 (1996), 22–3.
7. Slavoj Žižek, 'The Undergrowth of Enjoyment', in Edmond Wright and Elizabeth Wright, eds, *The Žižek Reader* (Oxford: Blackwell, 1999), 17.
8. Žižek, 'The Undergrowth of Enjoyment', 33.
9. Shailja Sharma, 'Salman Rushdie: the Ambivalence of Migrancy', *Twentieth-Century Literature*, 47, 4 (2001), 596–618.
10. Salman Rushdie, *The Satanic Verses* (New York: Viking, 1989), 168. Further references will appear as page numbers in the text.
11. Rushdie, *Imaginary Homelands*, 410.
12. Fay Weldon, *Sacred Cows* (London: Chatto and Windus, 1990). The reference to Le Carré is provided by Rushdie in his essay, 'In Good Faith', in *Imaginary Homelands*, 407.
13. Rushdie, *Step Across This Line*, 233.
14. Rushdie, *Step Across This Line*, 287–8.
15. Modood's reference here is to Fay Weldon, 'Introduction', in Tariq Modood and Pnina Werbner, eds, *The Politics of Multi-Culturalism in the New Europe* (London and New York: Zed Books), 3.
16. Agha Shahid Ali, *The Country without a Post Office: Poems* (New York: Norton, 1997).
17. Salman Rushdie, *Fury* (London: Vintage, 2002), 1. Further references appear as page numbers in the text.
18. Rushdie, *Imaginary Homelands*, 430.
19. Salman Rushdie, 'In Good Faith', 396.
20. Rushdie, *Step Across This Line*, 253 and 353.

# 8
# Toni Morrison's *Beloved*: the Scandal that Disturbed Domestic Tranquillity

*Marilyn Sanders Mobley*

> The document, then, is no longer for history an inert material through which it tries to reconstitute what men have done or said, the events of which only the trace remains; history is now trying to define within the documentary material itself unities, totalities, series, relations. History must be detached from the image that satisfied it for so long... The document is not the fortunate tool of history that is primarily and fundamentally *memory*; history is one way in which a society recognizes and develops a mass of documentation with which it is inextricably linked.
>
> Michel Foucault, *Archaeology of Knowledge*

> The borderline work of culture demands an encounter with 'newness' that is not part of the continuum of past and present. It creates a sense of the new as an insurgent act of cultural translation. Such art... renews the past, refiguring it as a contingent 'in-between' space, that innovates and interrupts the performance of the present.
>
> Homi Bhabha, *The Location of Culture*

> Whatever the risks of confronting the reader with what must be immediately incomprehensible... the risk of unsettling him or her, I determined to take.
>
> Toni Morrison, 'Unspeakable Things Unspoken'

In her essay 'The Site of Memory', Toni Morrison discusses the difference between fact and fiction and reminds her reader that her task in *Beloved* is 'to fill in the blanks that the slave narratives left'.[1] Recognizing that the work of fiction requires that she navigate her way through memory 'from the image to the text', she describes the imaginative process that partly accounts for the cultural work of *Beloved*. On one hand, the novel engages readers with the facts of history, sometimes translating those facts for new readers. On the other hand, it is these very acts of translation that confront readers with the intricate network of untold stories. This chapter attempts to argue that Morrison's *Beloved* is a powerful example of scandalous fiction not only because it disturbed the peace when it was published, but also because it exposes in new ways how slavery, by its very nature, disturbed the domestic tranquillity that the nation attempted to establish with its founding. Thus, the novel scandalizes and unsettles the reader with the very substance that fills in blanks, through fiction that neither the slave narratives nor any historical documentation of slavery could ever fill.

With the premiere of her libretto *Margaret Garner* (2005), Nobel Laureate Toni Morrison contributed to yet a third iteration of her Pulitzer Prize-winning novel, *Beloved*. It is doubtful when *Beloved* was published in 1987 that Morrison could ever have envisioned that her fictional resurrection of the Margaret Garner story of an enslaved mother's act of infanticide would later become an Oprah Winfrey/Jonathan Demme film or that it would even later become the subject of a libretto that she would write herself. Indeed, it is likely to be more and more difficult over time to engage in dialogue about the novel, without invoking the other two texts that emerged from it. All three texts reveal the rich historical landscape into which Morrison ventured through her fictional telling of this story of human tragedy and extraordinary love. Although there is a great deal of scholarship on the ways in which Morrison's work participates in the revisionist history that characterized much of the fiction of African American authors at the end of the twentieth century, few scholars have discussed the ways in which Morrison's fiction also intervenes in and signifies on the lived lives of African American people in the present.[2] Examining the three iterations of the Margaret Garner story – primarily the novel, but also the film and the libretto – as well as some of the responses to all three, reveals the ways in which Morrison's fiction has both enabled some of the most difficult dialogues about American slavery and has, by extension, made space for public reflection on how the aftermath of the enslavement of African people on American soil is still shaping the current historical moment and public discourse about American history, race, and identity. The novel signifies, in the broadest sense of the word, on the promise inscribed in the United States Constitution that it would 'insure domestic Tranquility', for 'the people', by unsettling the reader with a history that is anything but tranquil. Morrison's narrative poetics and cultural politics provide 'spaces so that the reader can participate' and suggest that 'the best art . . . is unquestionably political and irrevocably beautiful at the same time'. She has intentionally sought to disrupt this tranquillity by writing about the 'unspeakable things [that have been] unspoken,' and she has sought to do so without succumbing to 'harangue passing off as art'.[3]

The propensity both to return to and remember the past and to comment on the present by turning to the most difficult unspoken dimensions of that past and present are the very features of Morrison's work that have made her one of the world's greatest and most controversial writers. Whether criticism has come from some general readers who claim her style of writing is too difficult, or from scholars and critics who disagree over the connection between art and politics, Morrison's work has continuously garnered praise for its politics, even as she has tried to maintain a distance from the fray. While she has not overtly courted controversy, it could be argued that her texts speak back nonetheless to the cultural, historical and political realities of the moment in which they were published, and thereby render her protestations less significant than reader reception. In fact, given the racialized cultural context from which her characters come, it was inevitable, despite the reluctance of some of her critics to acknowledge it, that Morrison's *Beloved* would stir up the very critical responses and debates about the nation's history with which Americans had not yet come to terms.[4] Thus, *Beloved* is an example of scandalous fiction, not only because of Morrison's expressed narrative intentions about what her fiction does and does not do, but also because of how the novel has operated in culture and in the public sphere as a catalyst for dialogue about race, gender, and identity. In this sense, the novel has taken on a life of its own, simultaneously fetishized for its narrative innovations and excoriated for its unrelenting transgression of historical protocols of race and gender.[5]

# I

The most pronounced and recent manifestation of the controversy that Morrison's fiction has engendered is the response to the libretto, which was co-commissioned for the Michigan Opera Theatre, the Cincinnati Opera, and the Opera Company of Philadelphia. Based on a collaboration between Morrison and award-winning composer Richard Danielpour, the libretto reignited public discord over the facts of the Margaret Garner case, the interpretation of those facts, and what was at stake for the citizens of Cincinnati, Ohio in particular, when it premiered there in July of 2005.[6] An editorial in one of Cincinnati's local newspapers, *The Enquirer*, nearly understates the case by arguing that Margaret Garner's story 'is not an easy story. It is horrific and tragic. It is indeed part of the underbelly of our community's history.' The most telling dimension of the public stir that the opera created, however, was the debate over the reason Margaret Garner fled the Archibald Gaines plantation in the first place. The editorial clarifies the controversy by stating:

> Amazingly, as the Enquirer [sic] reported ... stories are still told in Boone County that Garner's decision to flee the plantation was because of a

moral conflict she had about a presumed adulterous relationship she had with the plantation owner, Archibald Gaines – rather than a desire to flee slavery. Such a notion ignores the reality of slavery. Enslaved women like Garner were the property of their masters and didn't have the power to say 'no.' They were rape victims.[7]

This editorial is just one of several that attempt to articulate the complex layered narrative embedded in the text of the libretto and in the Margaret Garner story itself. The same editorial states: 'Cast members of the opera [which included internationally renowned mezzo-soprano Denyce Graves], during a visit to Maplewood... passionately disagreed with slave owners' descendants about Garner's motive.'[8] On one hand, we must recognize that the libretto is itself a form of fiction. It makes no pretence of a one-to-one correspondence with the facts of the case. On the other hand, however, just as Morrison attempts in the novel to get to the truth of the interior lives of enslaved people rather than focusing on the institution of slavery, per se, she attempts in the opera, to 'expand and deepen the story'.[9] In other words, like the novel, the libretto dips into the reservoir of history and fact, and thereby exposes the emotional residue that had been just beneath the surface all along. A huge element of this emotional residue was indeed among the people of Kentucky and Cincinnati whose early and recent past were frought with racial trouble.[10] Though the opera as a cultural form may have brought positive attention to the area, the substance of the libretto was obviously painful and difficult for many of the citizens to confront in such a public way. Attempts to contain and police the telling of the story only heightened interest in its scandalous content.

From that rich emotional residue, combined with Morrison's fertile imagination and exquisite gift for language, has come a cultural master-piece that is at once beautiful and politically charged in ways which by no means merely recapitulate the achievement of the novel. At the end of Act I, when Denyce Graves, in the title role of Margaret Garner, sings the words 'Only unharnessed hearts/Can survive a locked-down life', we have a palpable example of the text bearing witness to how a people survived at the same time that it comments on the oppression that tested their humanity and their will to survive. Like the novel, the libretto reveals that Morrison's artistic project does not focus on the familiar representations of enslaved people solely as victims of racial domination, but it also invokes a meditation on what resources sustained them and helped them survive in a time of trouble. To a twenty-first-century audience composed of survivors of slavery – both the descendants of perpetrators and of the enslaved – the opera speaks to contemporary private desires for domestic tranquillity, even as the outside public reality and historical protocols of race continue to betray such desires.

The irony is that the opening of the libretto, obviously a high cultural moment in the arts, could not mask the clear hostilities and contradictions over two different claims about Margaret Garner's motivations for fleeing the plantation where she had been enslaved. The opera publicly exposed the continuing influence of racist attitudes about enslaved women, and thus put black women's bodies and the ways in which they attempted to exercise agency over their bodies at the centre of the dialogue. Of course, to argue that Margaret Garner left the plantation over moral torment related to adultery would itself be an indictment against her slave master, Archibald Gaines, notwithstanding racist and sexist attitudes to the contrary. But to acknowledge that her decision to flee was motivated by the understandable and logical desire of enslaved people to liberate themselves from oppression, to own their own bodies, and to enjoy the rights and privileges of freedom, would be to indict, not only the slave master, but also the institution of slavery itself, an institution that is embedded in the history of both Boone County, Kentucky and Cincinnati, Ohio. The opening of Morrison's opera in Cincinnati, therefore, inspired reflection on the public scandal of Margaret Garner's nineteenth-century trial at the same time that it created a new twenty-first-century scandal in the public sphere that was played out on the contested terrain of print media, the internet, and the opera hall itself.

The cast party held at the Cincinnati National Underground Railroad Freedom Center, following the 14 July 2005 premiere, cast yet another shadow of irony on the opera, for it was a reminder that Toni Morrison's native state of Ohio, in general, and the Underground Railroad, in particular, were both sites of freedom for the enslaved. So it was fitting that the cast of black and white actors, along with Toni Morrison Society Biennial Conference participants of scholars and readers from around the world, would all converge at this site, which both memorialized the tragic history of slavery and celebrated the freedom of its descendants. The theme of the July 2005 TMS conference was 'Toni Morrison and Sites of Memory', a theme taken from Morrison's essay by the same name in which she explains her artistic propensity to:

> rip the veil drawn over 'proceedings too terrible to relate'. The exercise is also critical for any person who is black, or who belongs to any marginalized category, for historically, we were seldom invited to participate in the discourse even when we were its topic.[11]

Morrison goes on to explain her artistic process as a fiction writer as 'a kind of literary archeololgy [sic]: [whereby] on the basis of some information and a little bit of guesswork you journey to a site to see what remains were left behind and to reconstruct the world that these remains imply'.[12] While it has become commonplace to argue that Morrison's forays into history are opportunities for remembering and healing for some, the opening of the libretto in the historically charged region of the country where the facts originally played out also meant the reopening of a wound that some were not ready to acknowledge, let alone heal. While it can be healing to remember, the community discord that emerged from the convergence of a major literary/cultural event with the public debate over the content of that event revealed that some would just as soon forget the realities of America's racial history. Clearly, in addition to being a site of risk for the writer, the site of memory for some readers is a site of wilful forgetting for others.

Nevertheless, by the time of the Cincinnati performance of the libretto, many Morrison scholars had already become familiar with the historical, political, and geographical complexities of Margaret Garner's story. Some were aware that Morrison first encountered this story when she was still an editor at Random House in 1974, the year she had editorial oversight for the publication of *The Black Book*.[13] Despite the positive attention that *The Black Book* received as the over 300-year expansive collection of black memorabilia that it was, it would be more than a decade later before Morrison would have the emotional fortitude to return to Margaret Garner's story for the purposes of transforming it into a novel. It would be over another decade before she would attempt the libretto. In between the novel and the libretto, she sold the rights of *Beloved* to Oprah Winfrey, who, along with Jonathan Demme, would transform the novel into the script of the movie by the same name. In an epigraph for the book about the making of the film, Oprah Winfrey says:

> My original intention in making *BELOVED* was the same as Toni Morrison's intention in writing the book: I wanted people to be able to feel deeply on a very personal level what it meant to be a slave, what slavery did to a people, and also to be liberated by that knowledge.[14]

While there is debate as to whether Winfrey's celebrity overtook the film (as Demme was concerned that it indeed might) and whether or not the film could ever capture on the screen what many readers had already experienced in reading the novel, if nothing else, the film, with its reworking of the plot and its cinematic reinterpretations of the novel, engaged viewers and readers in dialogue both with texts and with one another. In that regard, it could be argued that the film both contributed to and extended the controversies that had already emerged from discourse on the novel.

In returning to the story of Margaret Garner to write *Beloved*, Morrison's goal was not to explore the historical details as facts per se, but to reconfigure the collective memory artistically through fiction to arrive at the truths of the interior lives of the enslaved. Or as she says, 'the crucial distinction . . . is not the difference between fact and fiction, but the distinction between fact and truth'.[15] Despite Frederick Douglass's references to Margaret Garner's story in a public speech in 1857 and Frances Ellen Watkins Harper's allusion to Margaret Garner in her 1892 novel, *Iola Leroy*, it would be Morrison's fictional rendering that would create the greatest and most visceral response among readers and scholars alike.[16] The very language Morrison employs to describe her narrative intentions – that is, words such as 'risk', 'confronting the reader', 'unsettling' the reader, and 'rip the veil', to name a few – suggests both the aesthetic intentions and cultural politics that explain the stir *Beloved* created. Although she was focused on 'truth' rather than 'facts', her brief period of research into the institution of slavery took her to historical data found in the notes and diaries of overseers, slave masters, and ships' captains that informed her fictional representation of enslavement. For example, in her research, she discovered a reference to a 'bit' – the metal mouthpiece used to bridle horses – and learned that it was part of the apparatus of slavery. In silencing the unpaid labourers who made up the enslaved populations on their plantations, slave masters who used this device created, in Morrison's words, 'a perfect workforce'.[17] By incorporating this historical example of the apparatus of slavery into the narrative of *Beloved*, Morrison suggests the economic benefits of such an inhumane device for the enslavers, at the same time that she suggests its emotional and psychological consequences for the enslaved.

One scholar, Steven Weisenberger, got so intrigued with the history behind the novel *Beloved* that he undertook the painstaking task of researching the documents of the court trial, the history of the Gaines and Garner families, and the interconnections between the communities that were the origins of this uniquely American story. Weisenberger's book, *Modern Medea: a Family Story of Slavery and Child-Murder from the Old South*, takes its title from the 1867 lithograph of the same name to illustrate the connection between this artistic rendering of the horrific event and his reading of Margaret Garner's act of infanticide.[18] Like the painting by Thomas Satterwhite Noble, the premise of Weisenberger's book is that Margaret Garner's response to the 1850 Fugitive Slave Law is caught up in a web of the interrelated themes of 'miscegenation, sexual bondage, and the black woman as alluring and dangerous Other, themes nineteenth-century Americans typically spoke about in code'.[19] While these themes clearly inform the myth of Medea and Noble's artistic rendering of Margaret Garner, they are not the focus of the cultural work Morrison wanted her fictional account to do, nor do they reflect Morrison's reading of Margaret Garner's situation. Noble's reading of this celebrated case, while it had an anti-slavery sentiment, nevertheless reinforced the focus on the external circumstances of Margaret Garner's life and that of her community. The horror and accusatory stares on the faces of the four white men in the painting, the dead child and the defiant glare of Margaret all rivet the viewer's attention to the white response to the infanticide. Likewise, Weisenberger's book, acknowledging that it is possible to learn more about the white people of the case than it is to know about Margaret Garner and what became of her, offers a more detailed account of the white communities in Ohio and Kentucky, the attorneys who argued the case, and the response to the case in the media and public sphere than had previously existed. In the almost century-long gap of silence, where Morrison's *Beloved* would fill the space imaginatively with the interior lives that could not be known, Weisenberger's research would turn the locus of the story on the white people who enslaved her.

Trying to explain the silence between the nineteenth-century public preoccupation with Margaret Garner and the appearance of the novel in the late twentieth century, Weisenberger asks questions about the long repressed historical subject.[20] It could be argued, however, that though Weisenberger's book fills in the spaces left by time and ignorance with quantifiable facts, details and data previously hidden and unknown, as a historical account, the cultural work it does is quite different from that of Morrison's text.[21] While Weisenberger claims on the last page of his book that it offers a 'common-place approach to the Garner case and slave infanticide in general' in order to read them as 'an offering of profound mother love', Morrison's novel seeks to disrupt the very notion that such mother love is 'commonplace'.[22] *Beloved* calls into question the taken for granted dimensions of mother love, ventures into the interior life of Margaret Garner and transgresses the boundaries of the commonplace in order to reveal the more complex constraints on that love that enslaved people – and enslaved mothers in particular – had to endure. In sum, though Weisenberger is interested in notions of agency under pressure, his focus on the facts of Margaret Garner's court case and trial and the delineation of the political and legal contradictions that define American life during slavery, can only take us so far. In some respects, his approach to the historical facts of the case, as discovered in court records, print media, and other public archives, performs a kind of historical rite, which maintains one status quo, while disrupting another. While such documentation fills in gaps left by previous historical accounts, by maintaining the historicist gaze on the past, it also overlooks the deeper, subjective, interior levels of experience of those who were the objects of exchange, and it overlooks the psychic resources on which they drew to survive such objectification and dehumanization. As Morrison has suggested, only fiction can direct readers to other forms of agency that explain how the enslaved survived their oppression and shaped an identity for themselves outside what those who enslaved them could imagine.[23]

To say that the subject of slavery in the United States has always been a contested terrain is almost to state the obvious, but when we consider that the use of the very word itself has been the subject of public discourse, we can begin to understand just how much of a challenge we face to discuss it even in the twenty-first century.[24] When we consider the recent currency of preferring the word 'enslavement' to the word 'slavery', or the need at least to interchange the two terms, we have a better notion of what has been and is still at stake. Moreover, to shift from viewing slavery merely as a 'peculiar institution' or condition to viewing it as a complex socio-political economic system that involved dehumanizing one so-called race of people and privileging the status of another, gives some idea of why it has been so difficult to discuss.[25] In one interview about the writing of her novel Toni Morrison states that she had always avoided the subject of slavery and the books written about it, not only because the books were so laboriously long, but also because of the emotional gravity of the subject matter, both of which made them seem cumbersome and inaccessible.[26] While her novel is relatively short in comparison to many scholarly texts and even compared to some of the famous novels on the subject of slavery and freedom, it has acquired a public reputation as a 'challenging read' in its own right.

The nature of the challenge that Morrison poses for her readers is threefold. First, as with many of her novels, *Beloved* begins *in medias res*, thus forcing the reader to enter the text with few of the familiar stylistic narrative guideposts. Second, the novel does not proceed in a linear chronological fashion, but develops the plot recursively, moving forward in time at one point, doubling back to the past, and dipping into the memories and subconscious desires of the protagonist and other characters at will in a way that seems wholly unpredictable in its relationship to the past and present. Thirdly, and perhaps most importantly for the focus of this essay, the challenge of reading and understanding Morrison's *Beloved* is complicated by its subject matter, which locates the reader simultaneously in America's racial history and the continuing significance of race in the present. Moreover, Morrison does not enter the subject from a purely fictional perspective. Instead, she turns to an actual slave mother, whose response to the vagaries of slavery precipitated the murder of her child and a court trial that exposed the nation and the institution to the inherent contradictions of enslaving human beings in the first place. Indeed, it is the scandal that surrounded Margaret Garner's life and trial that is the kernel around which Morrison weaves her fictional narrative. What remains fascinating is the degree to which Morrison's novel not only revisits this scandal, but also invites and incites public discourse on a topic that remains taboo for so many even in the twenty-first century.

## II

When *Beloved* was published in 1987, it was the fifth novel in a literary career that was already marked by a growing readership and numerous literary awards. Yet one group of scholars, artists, and civic leaders was so concerned that Morrison did not receive the National Book Award for *Beloved* that they submitted a signed statement of protest, which was published in the *New York Times*. In their statement, they also asserted that she deserved serious consideration for the Pulitzer. When the announcement was made in 1988 that she had indeed been awarded the Pulitzer Prize, she found herself at the centre of criticism that the literary prize had been politicized and that those who selected her had bowed to outside pressure. Moreover, in viewing her rendering of black enslavement as a way of locking African American people in 'cruel determinism', critic Stanley Crouch's review of the book entered an ongoing dialogue as to whether black people were powerless victims in an oppressive system or whether they routinely exercised agency in forms of resistance to domination.[27] Ironically, Crouch's reading of the novel is the very interpretation of history that the text intervenes in to provide a more complex reading of slavery and our responses to it. Crouch's reading of *Beloved* is so wedded to the protocols of race – that is, to binary notions of the right and wrong way to represent black pain – that he cannot discern the complex ways in which Morrison's novel defies them.

Despite the momentary cloud over the award, and despite the judges' reassurances that Morrison had earned it on the genuine merits of the book, the readership and popularity of the novel have grown exponentially since its publication.[28] Indeed the literary success of *Beloved* is a testament to Morrison's artistic ability to render the complexity of American history through a form of fiction that was more scandalous than the facts – exposing larger and more difficult truths about race, gender, and identity. By shifting the locus of meaning from the exterior dimensions of black life during slavery to the interior lives of the enslaved, Morrison created spaces for her readers to participate in her text. While it has become commonplace to refer to this shift as an aesthetic principle that governs her work, it also inspires a kind of discursive mediation between her narrative aesthetics and her cultural politics. In other words, she writes intentionally to de-familiarize readers and to inspire them to consider dimensions of the self and other that they might otherwise overlook or diminish. Moreover, the effect of her narrative aesthetics and cultural politics is not only that they disrupt readers' received notions about the past, but also that they direct readers to the present in ways that dispel the possibility of a domestic tranquillity at peace with the past. In the novel, this linkage between past and present has been insufficiently examined, creating a silence that frames another kind of unspeakable thing unspoken. It could be argued that Morrison attempts to tell the truth about the present by signifying on it with a fictional version of the past. As one critic suggests, this narrative strategy operates as a form of artistic distancing that comments on the present through the past, in a way that is less threatening to potentially resistant readers.[29] Ironically, however, because she achieves this distancing by focusing on 'unspeakable thoughts, unspoken',[30] she creates an intimacy between the text and the reader that remains unsettling and that forces the reader to confront the history of slavery in America in its hitherto excluded dimensions.

*Beloved* is part of a trilogy that Marc Conner says is a 'meditation on love'.[31] While indeed the first in a trilogy about love, it importantly explores the excesses of love and how those excesses manifest themselves in individuals and in the community. In effect, Morrison's text shapes our public discourse about the nature of love. The text enters into a contemporary historical moment traversed by late twentieth-century debates over a mother's rights over her body, gender conflicts of the 1980s and identity politics in general, to interrogate what love under the duress of another historical moment looked like. As Valerie Sweeney Prince suggests, Morrison 'explicitly take[s] issue with the logic that reduces the African American woman to her womb[s] . . . that black female subjectivity be understood as distinct from the black womb'.[32] Put another way, the novel explores the complex psychic realities of experiencing one's body as both the site of reproduction and production at the same time.

As a novel about the excesses of mother love, it points to the constraints on that love for women who did not have control over their own bodies, let alone the children they gave birth to. In the words of the novel, 'What she [Baby Suggs] called the nastiness of life was the shock she received upon learning that nobody stopped playing checkers just because the pieces included her children' (23). Moreover, the novel comments on love that would empower a mother to treasure her children enough to save them from enslavement by killing them, even if to do so would create public scandal and community shame. Yet the novel does not romanticize mothering.[33] Instead it portrays motherhood through Sethe's thoughts as 'needing to be good enough, alert enough, strong enough' (132). As a free woman who is living out the psychic consequences of the infanticide she committed while enslaved, Sethe sums up her feelings by thinking 'motherlove was a killer' (132). As the fictional version of Margaret Garner, Sethe occupies a kind of pariah status among mothers both in and outside her community. Indeed, the women in her community regard her as haughty, arrogant and disrespectful of community mores. A measure of their disapproval is in their sense that she had 'a profile that shocked them with its clarity. Was her head a bit too high? Her back a little too straight? Probably' (152). The community even went so far as to engage in 'longing for Sethe to come on difficult times. Her outrageous claims, her self-sufficiency seemed to demand it' (171). Despite his high regard for Sethe, Paul D also responds to her act with disapproval as well, saying that her 'love is too thick' (164) and condemning her by saying 'you got two feet, Sethe, not four' (165). Thus, while Sethe's act may have been one of excessive mother love, it made her the object of communal scandal, public scorn, and family shame, not only in the eyes of her mother-in-law, Baby Suggs, but also in the eyes of her daughter, Denver, who wondered whether her own life was at risk at the hands of a mother who could take the life of her own child. Despite the closeness Denver and Sethe develop after Baby Suggs's death, and after her two brothers,

Howard and Buglar, flee their ghost-haunted house at 124, the relationship between Denver and Sethe is a mother-daughter relationship partly haunted by loss. As the text states: 'Denver hated the stories her mother told that did not concern herself... The rest was a gleaming, powerful world made more so by Denver's absence from it' (62). So through this portrayal of presence and absence, life and loss, Morrison represents how the emotional toll of slavery on mothers and families distorts the bonds of love one might otherwise expect in the domestic sphere. Through this representation of mother love, Morrison does not pathologize the enslaved community, but instead humanizes it in ways that reveal the effects of oppression and what Tricia Rose calls the 'histories that have seeped into places many of us find it difficult and painful to go'.[34]

By shifting the locus of the story of enslavement away from the gaze of the white other, to both an interrogation of and a meditation on the routine and courageous ways in which enslaved persons exercised agency, Morrison creates a space for her reader to consider the psychic and emotional cost of slavery, not only on mother love, but also on other dimensions of identity. For example, through the ruminations of Baby Suggs, the reader learns of an enslaved woman's anxiety about her identity as a friend, mother, wife, sister, and daughter. Baby Suggs's ruminations about the very core of her identity suggest the ways in which enslavement challenged fundamental identity formation and notions of domestic tranquillity within enslaved families. Her sermons about how to heal and love even in the face of adverse circumstances are represented as an antidote to the brutality of everyday life on the plantation. In this sense Baby Suggs can be seen as a central character in the novel. As Sethe's mother-in-law, she is a kind of mentor, instructing her on being a wife and mother under the duress of slavery. As an elder, who has endured her own trials and tribulations in her attempts to mother her own children, Baby Suggs has been a central figure in her family and community's spiritual survival. She is, therefore, emotionally unprepared for her daughter-in-law's decision to kill her children in response to seeing the slave catcher. Her lack of understanding partly explains why she withdraws into such a depression, for Sethe's act of infanticide is represented as one that Baby Suggs and other women of Baby Suggs's generation would never have made. Baby Suggs's depression is described in this way:

> to belong to a community of other free Negroes – to love and be loved by them, to counsel and be counseled, protect and be protected, fed and be fed – and then to have that community step back and hold itself at a distance – well, it could wear out even a Baby Suggs, holy. (177)

Baby Suggs's thoughts reflect the generational difference in how members of the enslaved community responded to the 1850 Fugitive Slave Law, which demanded that slave catchers return enslaved people to their owner. It is difficult to read Baby Suggs's lament in the foregoing passage without noticing that it invokes a similar lament from more recent times, in which post-Civil Rights upward mobility created prosperity for some, along with a lack of reciprocity and a loss of a shared community for others. Indeed, as various critics have noted, the entire novel is a narrative of grief and mourning, for the life before enslavement and for the life after enslavement that has yet to materialize fully in the lives of the disenfranchised.[35] Or as Baby Suggs says: 'Not a house in the country ain't packed to its rafters with some dead Negro's grief' (5). *Beloved* has inspired resistance in many quarters supposedly on the grounds that it is stylistically difficult and emotionally demanding. This can certainly be seen on one level as a form of resistance to a history of such profound loss, a resistance that makes many Americans who are not African American uncomfortable.

Before Halle purchases her freedom from her slave master, Mr Garner, and prior to the onset of the depression that eventually takes her life, Baby Suggs has a moment of reflection that reveals the ways in which enslavement distorted notions of self-love. In that moment of reflection, the text shifts from exterior space, that is, the physical location of the Sweet Home plantation, a plantation that 'wasn't sweet and it sure wasn't home' (14), but was itself a kind of distortion of domestic tranquillity, to the interior space of Baby Suggs's own mind. Realizing she 'never had the map to discover what she was like' (140), she privately has fundamental questions about what kind of person, girl, woman, mother, wife and friend she could possibly be. Through this set of interior interrogations, Morrison reveals the ways in which the conditions of enslavement foreclosed black female subjectivity and ways of knowing oneself that might otherwise be readily available. Unlike more familiar historical, factual representations of slavery, Morrison's fiction thus offers an intimate portrait of the psyche of one of the strongest members of the community to suggest the vulnerability of those who were not as strong. As Tricia Rose says, *Beloved* 'explores the painful connection between the brutality of American slavery with its hatred of black flesh, and the urgent need for black self-love as a survival strategy and form of resistance'.[36] Nowhere is this survival strategy more explicitly articulated than it is in Baby Suggs's sermon in the Clearing. In her sermon, the reader bears witness to her ability to resist self-absorption with her own predicament by using her voice and the spoken Word to empower her people to love themselves despite their circumstances. Moreover, in introducing her sermon, the text even signifies on biblical imperatives the enslaved would have heard from their masters. Instead of preaching to them 'to clean up their lives or to go and sin no more' (88), Baby Suggs uses her sermon as a counternarrative to the narratives of condemnation she knows they had heard from their slave masters' religion. Indeed, the self-love that she teaches and the ethic of love that undergirds her sermon, not only constitute a 'form of resistance', but they also serve as an antidote to the physical and spiritual brutality of enslavement:

> 'Here,' she said, 'in this here place, we flesh; flesh that weeps, laughs; flesh that dances on bare feet in grass. Love it. Love it hard. Yonder they do not love your flesh. They despise it. They don't love it... *You* got to love it, *you!*' (88)

Contrary to Crouch's criticism that the novel compounds 'determinism', this passage suggests that Morrison's fictional representation of slavery constitutes instead a powerful portrayal of how black people survived a system that could have utterly destroyed them. The love that Baby Suggs preaches into the hearing of what Martin Luther King Jr would have referred to as the 'beloved community', is actually a radical, healing form of empathic love that inspires self-love as a balm for pain and self-loathing.

The sermon that Baby Suggs delivers in the Clearing also invokes the ways in which the black church was and has been a site of resistance that operates outside the boundaries of other political and social constraints on black life and culture in America. Unlike W.E.B. Du Bois's *The Souls of Black Folk* (1903), which needed to remind the nation that those who had been regarded merely as black bodies for free unpaid labour indeed had souls or a spiritual nature that had not been understood or duly acknowledged, Morrison's fictional representation of the black preacher as an 'unchurched' holy woman signifies on the self-loathing of the black body that slavery produced and introduces a counternarrative of self-love that is not selfish, but communal in its place.[37] By naming the site of this communal resistance 'the Clearing', Morrison locates agency and the desire for healing from oppression as a space outside of and between the domestic spaces that benevolent white powers (signified by Mr Garner, who treated his male slaves like men) and malevolent white power structures (signified by Schoolteacher, who treated the enslaved of both genders as if they were subhuman) could police. Likewise, as an open space outside the slave master's control, the Clearing represents 'a place where you could love anything you chose – not to need permission for desire... *that* was freedom' (162). Thus, the Clearing was also a site of desire and a political space of community. As Sethe's nostalgic longing reveals, it represents a safe sacred space for the enslaved to lay their burdens down and reconstruct their humanness. In the privacy of the Clearing, they could discuss difficult issues among themselves and experience a sense of 'being part of a neighborhood' (173). The Clearing operates in this novel, then, not only as a communal site of claiming and reaffirming one's subjectivity, but also as a space for interrogation of a world that had attempted to circumscribe the very terms of existence. Ironically, the Clearing is an intraracial, subversive space of domestic tranquillity that the enslaved created by themselves for themselves.

## III

At the same time that the novel documents in fiction the communal spaces where resistance to enslavement offered spiritual and psychic healing, it also documents the lived realities that produced such spaces, even after Emancipation. In other words, although the novel focuses on 'unspeakable thoughts unspoken' (199) or the interior spaces of black enslaved communities, Morrison incorporates intertextual snippets of history into the narrative to shape the uncomfortable counternarratives that black people experienced and that white people, over time, hoped to suppress. While white people's public accounts of slavery may have represented it in legal jargon that justified it and made it seem more benign, black people experienced dimensions of slavery that violently contradicted all benign narratives of the institution. For example, at one point, Morrison uses Stamp Paid's ruminations to incorporate elements of American racial history that illustrate the severity of black oppression during the late nineteenth century. In language that seems purposefully raw and graphic, Stamp Paid, a former Sweet Home man and an Underground Railroad worker, thinks, as he travels to 124 after Baby Suggs's death:

> Eighteen seventy-four and whitefolks were still on the loose. Whole towns wiped clean of Negroes; eighty-seven lynchings in one year alone in Kentucky; four colored schools burned to the ground; grown men whipped like children; children whipped like adults; black women raped by the crew . . . The stench stank. (181)

These historical snippets of black life as lived are included, not to return to a narrative pattern of victimization that we associate with nineteenth-century slave narratives and abolitionist literature, but to historicize the struggle for freedom and the contexts out of which black people survived in spite of slavery.[38] Thus, the text comments intermittently on the racial terror that dominated black life and that made the ongoing struggle so imperative. To the tension between these two concerns the text adds the less tangible longings and desires that partly form what Raymond Williams refers to as 'structures of feeling'.

It could be argued that Schoolteacher is one example of racial terror that Morrison inscribes into the text, both to comment on the dehumanization that slave masters wielded and on the consequences of such dehumanization. In a scene that haunts her memory long after its occurrence, Sethe explains that Schoolteacher is overheard saying: 'No, no. That's not the way. I told you to put her human characteristics on the left; her animal ones on the right. And don't forget to line them up' (193). This practice of quantifying black humanity by objectifying it is one manifestation of the dehumanization to which Schoolteacher subjected the enslaved. The beating that Sixo gets for being 'clever' is another manifestation. When he interprets stealing, killing, butchering and eating a shoat as 'improving [Schoolteacher's]... property', Schoolteacher beats Sixo just 'to show him that definitions belonged to the definers – not the defined' (190). The memory of overhearing how she was dehumanized undermines the literacy Schoolteacher provided for his slaves – he 'made his pupils sit and learn books for a spell every afternoon... He'd talk and they'd write. Or he would read and they would write down what he said' (193) – and partly accounts for Sethe's 'serious work of beating back the past' (73). On one hand, she remembers the value of gaining access to literacy. On the other hand, literacy gave her new access to how Schoolteachers and others dehumanized members of her community. It could be argued that the novel excavates and circulates for contemporary readers the multi-layered dimensions of the past that the enslaved routinely struggled to suppress just to maintain their sanity. Within the representation of Schoolteacher and white people, in general, is Morrison's representation of the white presence in the minds of the enslaved through the thoughts of Stamp Paid. He thinks:

> Whitepeople believed that whatever the manners, under every dark skin was a jungle... But it wasn't the jungle blacks brought with them to this place from the Other (livable) place. It was the jungle whitefolks planted in them. And it grew. It spread. In, through and after life, it spread, until it invaded the whites who had made it... Made them... worse than even they wanted to be, so scared were they of the jungle they had made. (199)

This passage not only contains Morrison's critique of the white presence during the enslavement of black people, but it deconstructs long-standing representations of Africans, Africa, and the influence of black-white interactions. The list embedded in these thoughts represents Morrison's analysis of black disillusionment, not only in the post-Emancipation period, but also in subsequent periods such as those of the Jim Crow south and the Civil Rights movement. Moreover, in shifting the references to the slave master who replaced Mr Garner from lower case 's', to name his profession prior to arriving at Sweet Home, to capital 'S', to name him and to signify on misuse and abuse of his profession, the text of *Beloved* comments on the linguistic behaviour of black folk who name people by their character and their deeds. In fact, the enslaved never reference him by any other name than Schoolteacher. Given that the novel was published at a time of a great deal of attention to inner-city schools and the state of education for

America's black and poor, it is not difficult to read the critique of American education inscribed in this name.[39] Again, though the weight of such a scandalous critique is inscribed and embedded in the past inside a work of fiction, it nevertheless circulates in culture to critique the 'unspeakable things unspoken' regarding the state of American literacy and education. In other words, although the 1980s were a period of much progress for many African Americans, the nuanced characterization of white racial attitudes in the novel was similar to what many African American communities were contending with at the time *Beloved* was published.

In at least two further senses, moreover, it is useful to argue that the text is not so much about the white presence as it is about the black response to their own longings, desires and sense of subjectivity. One such manifestation of these desires is in the intersubjective loving moment between Sethe, Denver and Beloved, the ghost. What Stamp Paid hears as 'undecipherable', is a moment in which the three women engage in a series of interior monologues, not as anyone's object, but as three speaking subjects, who communicate through their thoughts. Sethe, Denver, and then Beloved think about the relationship between themselves: 'Beloved/You are my sister/You are my daughter/ . . . You are mine . . . You are my face; I am you/Why did you leave me. You are mine/You are mine/You are mine' (217). When Beloved initially comes on the scene, she inspires this kind of intersubjective love, recognition, and understanding that they are interconnected as past, present, and future, and that the stories of their lives from the middle passage to post-Emancipation are inextricably linked. It is this same interconnectedness that Beloved exploits. She takes advantage of Sethe's trauma from Sweet Home, the guilt and shame of infanticide, and the weight of guilt and loss, to disrupt the modicum of domestic tranquillity the women had worked so hard to obtain inside the walls of their haunted home. As the novel says: 'the future was a matter of keeping the past at bay' (42). When the past returns as both memory and revenge rolled into one, it takes the form of the daughter Sethe killed. The disruption drives Paul D out and begins to consume Sethe, until Denver leaves the comfort of home and goes to the very community that had looked down on her mother and their household. Denver brings a community of women to 124 who are capable of saving Sethe by exorcizing the ghost by means of a spiritual power invoked through song. She remembers the sounds of the Clearing as a space

> where the voices of women searched for the right combination, the key, the code, the sound that broke the back of words. Building voice upon voice until they found it, and when they did it was a wave of sound wide enough to sound deep water . . . It broke over Sethe and she trembled like the baptized in its wash. (261)

It is Denver, who represents the hope of the present generation, who saves Sethe from being totally consumed by the guilt, shame, and grief of the past.

Ultimately, however, perhaps the most scandalous suggestion in this work of fiction is that enslaved peoples not only had the desire for freedom, but that they experienced other desires, namely the desire for love. By inscribing this dimension of black subjectivity, Morrison calls into question the normalized protocols of race in black fiction that effectively limit its representations to critiques of racism, slavery, sexism and other forms of oppression. With an agenda for her fiction of realizing another mode of representation, shaped by romantic desire and untainted sexual love, Morrison employs the love affair of Paul D and Sethe to do new kinds of cultural work. The love between them is first discussed in terms of Sethe's reluctance:

> There were two rooms and she took him into one of them, hoping he wouldn't mind the fact that she was not prepared; that though she could remember desire, she had forgotten how it worked; the clutch and helplessness that resided in the hands . . . Her deprivation had been not having any dreams of her own at all. (19)

In fact, she later wonders: 'Would it be all right to go ahead and feel? Go ahead and *count on something?*' (38). In language that invokes the emotional reluctance and fear of trauma victims, Sethe gradually allows Paul D, one of the Sweet Home men, to come back into her heart. Morrison includes a portrait of how Sweet Home and Schoolteacher affect him in the intervening years after enslavement. He says: ' "I wasn't allowed to be and stay what I was . . . Schoolteacher change me. I was something else"' (72). But when Sethe begins lovingly rubbing his knee, he temporarily interrupts his sharing of his story, thinking that '[s]aying more might push them both to a place they couldn't get back from. He would keep the rest where it belonged: in that tobacco tin buried in his chest where a red heart used to be' (73).

At the end of the novel, after Beloved has been exorcized out of the house, Paul D returns and realizes there 'are too many things to feel about this woman' (272). He realizes 'She is a friend of my mind. She gather me . . . The pieces I am, she gather them and give them back to me in all the right order. It's good, you know, when you got a woman who is a friend of your mind' (273). Upon his return, he realizes 'Only this woman Sethe could have left him his manhood like that. He wants to put his story next to hers' (273). Most of all, he makes way for their relationship as an intersubjective love, when he reminds Sethe that she can be the subject of her own story, and her own life. As Morrison says:

> We are the subjects of our own narrative, witnesses to and participants in our own experience, and in no way coincidentally, in the experience of those with whom we have come in contact. We are not, in fact, 'other.' We are choices. And to reach imaginative literature by and about us is

to choose to examine centers of the self and to have the opportunity to compare these centers with the 'raceless' one with which we are, all of us, most familiar.[40]

Morrison concludes *Beloved* on a note of expectation that Sethe and Paul D will both remember that their individual and collective stories are not stories 'to pass on' (275), and that they can have a new beginning, having confronted the very dimensions of the past they had previously avoided and been afraid to face. Though Morrison is aware that slavery is a topic many would prefer not to discuss or remember, the novel suggests that remembering and coming to terms with the past is the only way to come into a new sense of oneself and one's subjectivity.

In its closing words *Beloved* speaks back to a late twentieth-century audience of readers, some of whom are African American, who seemed to believe that '[r]emembering seemed unwise' (274) and counters this belief with the necessity of not forgetting how they not only survived the disruption of America's domestic tranquillity, but did so at a great cost. That cost means they must remember there is another side of their story that must be told. Inside that other story is a second liberation from slavery that will help them endure the next century. Paul D's reminder to Sethe that she is her own 'best thing' (273) suggests that the reward for disturbing domestic tranquillity, of telling a different story of black people and their ongoing struggle for freedom, is the hope for a new, more enduring love of oneself and one's community, that no strategies of containment can police or deny. By shifting from the known horrors of enslavement to the unknown and unrecognized interior life of the enslaved, Morrison has permanently altered how we think about this period of American history we thought we knew. She transgresses the borders of how we have both remembered and told this story and she has the nerve to suggest another story that must be put alongside it, if the nation is ever to heal and be made whole. *Beloved* entered the culture wars of race, gender, class and identity at a moment when such discourses profoundly shaped the public sphere. With its new perspective, Morrison challenges her readers to remember the greatest scandal of the nation's democracy and to recognize that acknowledging the trauma it caused for both the enslavers and the enslaved is a necessary beginning – discovering a new way to heal and to love in spite of our history, if not because of it.

## Notes

The epigraphs at the beginning of the chapter are from Michel Foucault, *Archaeology of Knowledge and the Discourse on Language* (New York: Pantheon Books, 1972), 7; Homi Bhabha, *The Location of Culture* (London and New York: Routledge, 1994), 7; Toni Morrison, 'Unspeakable Things Unspoken: the Afro-American Presence in American Literature', *Michigan Quarterly Review*, 28 (1989), 1–34, 3.

1. Toni Morrison, 'The Site of Memory', in William Zinsser, ed., *Inventing the Truth: the Art and Craft of Memoir* (Boston: Houghton Mifflin Company, 1987), 113.
2. See Ashraf H.A. Rushdy, 'Daughters Signifyin(g) History: the Example of Toni Morrison's *Beloved*', in William L. Andrews and Nellie Y. McKay, eds, *Toni Morrison's 'Beloved': a Casebook* (New York: Oxford University Press, 1999), 37–66.
3. See Toni Morrison, 'Unspeakable Things Unspoken: the Afro-American Presence in American Literature', *Michigan Quarterly Review*, 28 (1989), 1–34 and 'Rootedness: the Ancestor as Foundation', in Mari Evans, ed., *Black Women Writers (1950–1980)* (Garden City, NY: Anchor Press/Doubleday, 1987), 339–60.
4. For a discussion about the reluctance of scholars and critics to deal with Morrison's aesthetics, and to focus more often on her politics, see Marc C. Conner, 'Introduction: Aesthetics and the American Novel', in *The Aesthetics of Toni Morrison: Speaking the Unspeakable* (Mississippi University Press, 2000), ix–xxviii.
5. For a discussion of protocols of race, see Claudia Tate, 'Introduction', to *Psychoanalysis and Black Novels: Desire and the Protocols of Race* (New York: Oxford University Press, 1998), 3–21.
6. Attendance at the opera premiere was a highlight for participants at 'Toni Morrison Sites of Memory': The Fourth Biennial Conference of the Toni Morrison Society, 14–17 July 2005, which was held at the Hilton Cincinnati Netherland Hotel in Cincinnati, Ohio and at Northern Kentucky University in Highland Heights, Kentucky. The conference programme included a visit to the actual historical plantation site where Margaret Garner lived and to the Presbyterian church where she was a member.
7. See http://news.enquirer.com.
8. See http://news.enquirer.com.
9. The playbill for the opera contains excerpts from interviews both from Richard Danielpour and Morrison on their respective artistic intentions and motivations.
10. The city of Cincinnati made national news with incidents of racial violence as recently as 2004.
11. Morrison, 'Site of Memory', 100–11.
12. Morrison, 'Site of Memory', 112.
13. See Middleton A. Harris, *The Black Book* (New York: Random House, 1974). For an explanation about why Morrison's name does not appear on the cover of the book as its editor, see Marilyn Sanders Mobley, 'A Different Remembering: Memory, History and Meaning in Toni Morrison's *Beloved*', in Harold Bloom, ed., *Toni Morrison* (Philadelphia: Chelsea House, 2005), 67–77.
14. See Oprah Winfrey, *Journey to BELOVED* (New York: Hyperion, 1998).
15. See 'Site of Memory', 113.
16. See Rushdy, 43–4 for comments on how a Frederick Douglass speech was used as an example of how the Margaret Garner case symbolized the horrors of enslavement. Also see Frances E.W. Harper's *Iola Leroy, or Shadows Uplifted* (Boston: Beacon Press, 1892, 1987), which uses a reference to the case to illustrate the manifestation of an enslaved mother's discontent with slavery.
17. 'Toni Morrison, Profile of a Writer', produced and directed by Alan Benson, edited by Melvyn Bragg, 52 min., a London Weekend Television 'South Bank Show' co-production with RM Arts (1987), videocassette.
18. Steven Weisenberger, *Modern Medea: a Family Story of Slavery and Child-Murder from the Old South* (New York: Hill and Wang), 1998.

19. Thomas Satterwhite Noble, 'The Modern Medea', photographed by Matthew Brady and lithographed for reproduction in *Harper's Weekly Magazine*, 18 May 1867; Weisenberger, 8.

20. Weisenberger, 10–11.

21. Morrison, 'Rootedness', 340–1.

22. Weisenberger, 286.

23. Morrison, 'Site of Memory', 110–13.

24. It is unknown when the specific shift from the word slavery to enslavement occurred in public discourse as it regards the slave trade from Africa to America, but the shift represents the desire on the part of many to emphasize the dynamic power relations involved so as not to suggest that the institution was a static, given phenomenon.

25. This phrase has become the clichéd reference to slavery in much scholarship and public discourse.

26. 'Toni Morrison, Profile of a Writer'.

27. Stanley Crouch, 'Aunt Medea', *New Republic*, 19 October 1987, 38–43, and Rushdy, 64, for a review of the ongoing debate on how to interpret slave communities.

28. See William Grimes, *New York Times: Book Review*, 8 October 1993, Late Edition–Final: http://www.nytimes.com/books/98/01/11home/28957.html; and Paul Gray, 'Rooms of Their Own', *Time*, 18 October 1993: http://www.time.com/time/community/nobelprize.html.

29. Missy Dehn Kubitschek, *Toni Morrison: a Critical Companion* (Westport: Greenwood Press, 1998), 132.

30. Toni Morrison, *Beloved* (New York: Alfred A. Knopf, 1987), 199. Further references are to this edition and will be given as page numbers in the text.

31. Conner, 'From the Sublime to the Beautiful: the Aesthetic Progression of Toni Morrison', in *The Aesthetics of Toni Morrison*, 73.

32. Valerie Sweeney Prince, *Burnin' Down the House: Home in African American Literature* (New York: Columbia University Press, 2005), 5.

33. For a discussion of motherhood in Morrison's work, see Andrea O'Reilly, *Toni Morrison and Motherhood: a Politics of the Heart* (Albany: SUNY Press, 2004).

34. Tricia Rose, *Longing to Tell: Black Woman Talk about Sexuality and Intimacy* (New York: Picador, 2003), 390.

35. See Karla Holloway, 'Beloved: A Spiritual', and Rushdy.

36. Rose, 390.

37. See W.E.B. Du Bois, *The Souls of Black Folk* (New York: First Vintage Books/The Library of America, 1903, 1990).

38. See Marilyn Sanders Mobley, 'A Different Remembering: Memory, History and Meaning in Toni Morrison's *Beloved*' (cited above) for a reprint of my article addressing how Morrison's novel is a neo-slave narrative. Also see Angelyn Mitchell, *Freedom to Remember: Narrative, Slavery, and Gender in Contemporary Black Women's Fiction* (Rutgers: Rutgers University Press, 2002) for a discussion of neo-slave narratives as 'liberatory narratives', to change the focus from the legacy of slavery to the struggle for freedom. The neo-slave narratives include Margaret Walker's *Jubilee* (1966), Ernest Gaines's *The Autobiography of Miss Jane Pittman* (1971), Alex Haley's *Roots* (1976), Ishamael Reed's *Flight to Canada* (1976), Octavia Butler's *Kindred* (1979), David Bradley's *The Chaneysville Incident* (1981), Charles Johnson's *The Oxherding Tale* (1982) and Sherley Anne Williams's, *Dessa Rose* (1986) among others.

39. See US Department of Education, National Center for Education Statistics, *The Condition of Education 2001*, NCES 2001–072 (Washington, DC: US Government Printing Office, 2001) for historical data on racial disparities in American classrooms. Also see Carl A. Grant, ed., *Educating for Diversity: an Anthology of Multicultural Voices* (Boston: Allyn and Bacon, 1995).
40. Toni Morrison, 'Unspeakable Things Unspoken', 9.

# 9
# Helen Darville, *The Hand that Signed the Paper*: Who is 'Helen Demidenko'?[1]

*Sue Vice*

*The Hand that Signed the Paper* was published in Australia in 1994, a first novel by the twenty-four-year old Helen Darville.[2] It was received with a mixture of great acclaim, to the extent of being awarded three Australian literary prizes, and also, from the very first, much critical opprobrium. Darville published *The Hand* under the pseudonym 'Helen Demidenko', a name whose Ukrainian origin appeared to match the focus on that country's history in her book. 'Helen Demidenko' was no straightforward *nom de plume*, however, but part of an elaborate masquerade which extended far beyond the text itself. Helen Demidenko claimed that she was the first-generation offspring of a Ukrainian father and an Irish mother. Darville supported her masquerade by publishing articles about her alleged background and through her media pronouncements. Interestingly, it was the Ukrainian side of her invented genealogy, rather than the Irish, which attracted her. She developed an elaborate faux-Ukrainian persona by sporting long blonde hair, wearing peasant blouses, and relating stories about illiterate, working-class family members who doused her with vodka at her university graduation.[3] The fictive Helen Demidenko had a Ukrainian father who became a taxi driver in Queensland, and an Irish mother who had entered domestic service at the age of twelve. It was not until 1995 that the journalist David Bentley publicly outed Helen Demidenko as Helen Darville. She was in reality a middle-class brunette whose mother admitted in an interview with the *Australian* newpaper, ' "We are Poms, let's be honest about it".'[4]

Darville did not cling to her persona after Bentley's exposé and issued an apology in the Australian national press. Her book was reissued in 1995 with a correct attribution of authorship and a revised Author's Note, which emphasized the fact that historical research and not family legend lay behind *The Hand that Signed the Paper*. This contrasts, for instance, with the case of Binjamin Wilkomirski's testimony *Fragments: Memories of a Childhood*

*1939–1948*, about a childhood spent in wartime death-camps, which was shown beyond all doubt to be invented. Such was the writer's investment in his adopted past, or his degree of psychological instability, that *Fragments'* author has still to admit that he is really the non-Jewish Swiss musician Bruno Doessekker, born in 1941 rather than 1939.[5] Darville's masquerade, on the other hand, seems to have been a consciously adopted stance born of a tendency to self-romanticize, and of a wish to claim closer kinship to the events represented in her novel. As these events include the part played by the Ukrainian SS in the Holocaust, forging such a personal link with Holocaust perpetrators is surprising in itself. Ironically, in literary terms the adoption of a Ukrainian persona turned *The Hand* from Helen Darville's work of remarkable imaginative resource into Helen Demidenko's rather simpler project of recording family autobiography – resulting in a book which Demidenko herself called 'faction'.

The 'Demidenko scandal' of 1995 was a particularly overdetermined one, consisting of many facets whose relationship to each other is not always clear. These issues were not clarified by commentators' efforts to place this scandal within a broader genre, either that of Australian impostures – these include writing or paintings purportedly by working-class, immigrant or Aboriginal narrators who turned out to be nothing of the kind – or that of ersatz Holocaust testimony, such as Martin Gray's partly fictionalized *For Those I Have Loved*, Wilkomirski's *Fragments*, and another recent Australian example, Bernard Holstein's fabricated *Stolen Soul*.[6] In this chapter, I will explore the cultural and literary aspects of the Demidenko scandal and try to suggest how its very various constituent elements, ranging from charges of anti-Semitism and Holocaust denial to plagiarism and 'depthless prose', intersect with each other.

## Literary matters

*The Hand that Signed the Paper* takes as its subject-matter the Ukrainian famine of the 1930s, the Holocaust in Ukraine, and Australian war crimes trials of the 1990s.[7] The novel is narrated in a colloquial, affectless way which some critics likened to the style of American 'Dirty Realism',[8] although it represented horrifying acts of pre-war and wartime violence rather than the seamier side of contemporary American life. In even this relatively minor matter, before there was any reason to see the novel's distinctive style as part of a wider pattern of deception, critics' views were polarized about its appropriateness for subject-matter of this kind. For instance, while Serge Liberman writes of the novel's 'uncluttered prose', Robert Manne describes it, by contrast, as 'cold and vacuous'.[9] Such an extreme polarization of moral and aesthetic views, but based on identical evidence, was a constant feature of the scandal throughout its duration.

Added to this alleged discrepancy between form and content was the novel's focus on characters whose behaviour and views were, to say the least, unexpected. These include the novel's protagonist, Vitaly Kovalenko, a simple country boy born in Khmelnik, Ukraine, in 1921, whose family underwent depredations during the Soviet occupation of Ukraine, and who enlisted in the SS – by signing 'the paper' of the novel's title – when the Nazis invaded the Soviet Union in 1941. The reader learns of his career as a ghetto-clearer in Warsaw and then as a functionary at the death-camp Treblinka. So far, so controversial: Demidenko's was not the only work of fiction to focus on perpetrators rather than victims when representing the Holocaust. Martin Amis's 1991 novel *Time's Arrow* is about a Nazi doctor who worked at Auschwitz, while the short stories written by the Polish writer Tadeusz Borowski in the 1950s, in the collection *This Way for the Gas, Ladies and Gentlemen*, centre on his fictional alter-ego, Kapo Tadek, who helps to process Jews who arrive at Auschwitz.[10] Both these works of fiction also exhibit an unusual relationship between form and content, as the tone in each is characterized by sardonic or even aggressive irony. Like several other characters whose viewpoints the reader takes up, Demidenko's character Vitaly appears to volunteer for death-camp duty as a way of avenging himself on the 'Jewish Bolsheviks' whom he blames for the famine and the deaths of thousands of Ukrainians, including his own father, before the war. This is where 'Dirty Realism' threatens to turn from a generic label to a moral slur, as reviewers and critics asked whether this historically untenable narrative was endorsed by the novel's narrator.

However, as another striking stylistic feature of *The Hand* is its varied narration, it is even harder than usual to pin down this text's ideological orientation. The book is framed by the first-person narrative of Fiona Kova-lenko, niece of the reprobate Vitaly, in present-day Australia. Fiona orches-trates at least some of the novel's constituent first-person voices – including the stories of her aunt, Kateryna, and her uncle Vitaly's first wife Magda – which are transcriptions of taped interviews. This is a verisimilitudinous way of accounting for the book's viewpoints, akin to the more venerable one of having the narrator find papers in the attic, or receiving a manuscript in the post. There are yet other voices present in the text for which it is harder to account using conventional narrative categories. Pieces of fictive documentary evidence are cited, as if pasted into the text, including a letter home written by the unlovely 'Dr Judit', always identified in the text as the 'Jewish' wife of a Ukrainian commissar; and another from a 'vodka priest', who will not give absolution to the SS men working at Treblinka, to the local bishop. It is clear that Fiona cannot have had access to such utterances. One way of rationalizing these varieties of narrative is to assume that these letters are fictive within the novel's diegesis, and that we are to take them as reconstructions by Fiona herself. This might even be the explanation for the fourth variety of voice in the text, that of a seemingly non-diegetic third-person narrator. This narrator uses a rather stylized discourse, and is the source of the depthless prose which worried several commentators. The voice is intermittently omniscient, but also partial and personal. It could be read as Fiona's effort at writing at a remove, taking on the mantle, as it were, of a third- rather than first-person narrator for the duration of particular events. It is the persistence of Fiona's discourse within the narrator's that reveals her continued presence and explains the sometimes jarring changes of register, rather than the opposite explanation, that this is an instance of what Mikhail Bakhtin calls '*skaz*' – in which an impersonal narrator uses the idiom of informal utterance.[11] This is backed up by the fact that the reader learns that Fiona has also taped Vitaly's testimony, although these interviews are not transcribed in the first person but presented throughout in a third-person narration that relies heavily on free indirect discourse. It would be a logical assumption to make that Fiona must be the narrator of these third-person sections.

The difficulty of locating a source for much of *The Hand*'s narration led some critics to insist that not only the narrator, but the author, Demidenko herself, was putting forward the equation of Jews and Bolsheviks within the text. Because the novel's Ukrainian characters are shown to be avenging themselves on the Bolsheviks for the collectivization and famine of the 1930s, they are thus blaming the victims of the Holocaust for their own fate. This notion of authorial intrusion was furthered by the fact that Helen Demidenko made various published and televised pronouncements in which she claimed, for instance, that her father's family had been murdered by 'Jewish Bolsheviks' at Vinnitsa in the 1930s;[12] and that there was a clear 'ratio' between the numbers of Jewish commissars present in Ukraine during the famine, and numbers of Ukrainian volunteers for death-squads during the war.[13] It was clearly hard for critics to maintain belief in Roland Barthes's obituary for the author in the face of such remarks. I would argue, however, that the construction of 'Helen Demidenko' had the effect not simply of an ethnic and class-based performance, but was also a performance of the author-function itself, in an extreme and perhaps defamiliarizing way. Darville's unwitting parody of the figure of the author gives the lie to one of the explanations offered for this scandal, that post-structuralist and postmodern critical categories were to blame for the levelling out of all meaning and the dismissal of extra-textual reality.[14] Rather, it was humanist and modernist notions of authority and history that were enlisted and parodied, including the 'commodified authenticity', in Maria Takolander and David McCooey's phrase,[15] of authorial identity in the contemporary public arena.

## Critical concerns

Any account of the concerns voiced by critics and reviewers about *The Hand* reveals how hard it is – in this instance, and more generally – to separate extra-textual moral judgements from internal, literary ones. The critics themselves allowed moral estimates to stand for literary ones, and vice versa. Yet the case of *The Hand* supports the notion that there is no way of telling, from internal evidence alone, whether a testimony itself is authentic or fictional,[16] much less whether a novel is autobiographically based or not. Particular charges, of varying merit, were made by several different critics at various points during the Demidenko scandal and in its aftermath. These included accusations of Holocaust denial, of a particular kind;[17] didacticism;[18] 'moral weightlessness';[19] anachronism; representing genocidal characters who experience no remorse;[20] an unclear narrative voice; and 'historical howlers'[21] both unwitting and strategic, the latter including the conflation of Jews with Bolsheviks.

In his book *The Culture of Forgetting*, which puts forward the most sustained deconstruction of Darville's novel, the Australian writer Robert Manne analyses a scene from *The Hand*, where Vitaly meets his future wife Magda in the village of Treblinka, to highlight both the characters' indifference to what they do or witness, and the affectless means of representation:

> Nothing, however, explains little Magda. We are told that she was taken with Vitaly's pleasant face after spotting him murdering a Jew. In housewifely fashion she nags him about his nocturnal shooting expeditions – because of the mess they leave.[22]

In this passage, Manne emphasizes the fact that even within the novel no motivation is given for Magda's apparent anti-Semitism: as a Polish rather than Ukrainian character, she has not suffered ill-treatment at the hands of 'Jewish Bolsheviks'. The case of Magda, in Manne's view, shows that there is no explanation in *The Hand* for the characters' ability to live and love amid terrible atrocity other than the author's own indifference to the events she represents. Readers are dismayed, he argues, not by 'the words of *The Hand*'s characters but [by] the ambiguity of the authorial position in regard to them'. 'Ambiguity' here seems to mean an absence of moral sense, as Manne goes on to argue: 'With Helen Demidenko [sic] we sense . . . with regard to the evil done in the Holocaust, a pervasive and truly terrible indifference.'[23] If we turn to the offending passage from *The Hand* itself, we do indeed experience 'ambiguity', although of a more textual kind than Manne detects:

> He [Vitaly] looks a strong boy. [Magda] has seen him before, shooting a Jew in the street. She liked his face then. She likes it now. (107)

Manne reads this through a particular lens, as if, in the sentence 'She liked his face then', the word 'then' referred to the act of murder, rather than to the temporal moment, as the contrast with 'now' suggests. Rather than approving of Vitaly's anti-Semitic murder, Magda simply overlooks it – it reminds her of the time she saw him before. This is 'ambiguity' of the kind that also characterizes the following instance of free direct discourse about an old woman who sees the courtship of Vitaly and Magda: *'Shameless, kissing that Trawnicki boy in front of everyone like that'* (109). Once more, the old woman identifies Vitaly as 'that Trawnicki boy' not to condemn Magda for consorting with an SS trainee, as we might expect, but because she does not know his name. Both of these examples are ironically ambiguous, and at the expense of the character concerned, Magda and the old woman respectively. It is these characters who allow everyday choices – about romance, or social propriety – not only to stand alongside but to supersede the reality of the death-camp Treblinka and the SS training-camp Trawnicki. Both irony and affectless prose in *The Hand* stand in for moral comment on characters who have indeed, in Manne's phrase, 'lost their moral bearings'.[24] The same is true of the second instance Manne refers to in his comment quoted above. In this scene, where Magda 'confronts' Vitaly about his murderous behaviour, there is once more genuine ambiguity. However, this is not authorial ambiguity of the kind that Manne identifies, which would make it hard to know whether or not the author deplores this attitude to violence, but again of a more textual kind:

> 'You shot people in the trains last night. You woke everyone up, then kept doing it right in front of the whole town'.
> 'Did I?'
> 'Look at the mess there now. See. You did that'.
> 'I can't remember'.
> 'You should remember. I don't want you doing that at night. I want you in bed with me, like a proper husband'. (113)

As is characteristic of Darville's style, we do not gain access to the characters' inner lives here. The implication is that neither Magda nor Vitaly reflects upon the mass-murder very deeply. Magda's complaint is once more ambiguous: it may contain a subliminal moral element, but it seems that her concern is more for a trivial propriety. In my view, Darville's style, however disturbing to read, is appropriate to the novel's content. It is hard to imagine how this effort to represent the 'ambiguous' extremes of indifference and self-concern, placed alongside genocide at a death-camp, could be achieved without the priority given in *The Hand* to actions, description and dialogue over interiority or moral absolutes. In this way, despite – or because of – all its unevennesses, *The Hand* avoids the 'Manichaean certainties' of some other Holocaust fictions.[25] In an effort to make contemporary the events of the past, *The Hand* is narrated in the present tense, which itself, as the critic Adrian Mitchell points out, 'acts to limit reflection'[26] – on the part of the narrator, presumably. Mitchell sees this device as an emulation of the 'documentary realism' of faction, but it seems to me a strikingly literary device, akin to the French novel's 'classical narrative *figure*' of the 'narrative present, or historical present',[27] and to Dirty Realism's often present-tense immediacy. Once more, what appeared to be a moral aspect turns out to be a primarily textual one.

## Biography and fiction

Despite what I have argued above about the appropriateness of *The Hand*'s narrative structure and tone, the reader may still experience supplementary unease about its content. It is hard to explore this unease without recourse to author biography, or at least to the figure of Helen Demidenko as an embodiment of the *implied* author. In an article on the ethnic envy implicit in Darville's Demidenko persona, Jane Hyde argues that her Ukrainian-Irish masquerade was not adopted, as Darville explained, out of sympathy for her fictional Ukrainian characters. Rather, it was the other way round, that a 'fascination with anti-Semitic fascism'[28] inspired the novel. It does seem likely that Helen Darville was 'fascinated' in the way Hyde describes. While at school Darville wrote an article defending Ivan Demjanjuk, who was tried for war crimes committed at Treblinka but acquitted in 1993; and shortly after the furore over her book died down, she conducted an interview with the notorious Holocaust denier David Irving, which was published in the Australian *Style* magazine in February 2000. The question remains whether there are any textual traces of this fascination with fascism in *The Hand* itself, and whether we can attribute them to the novel's narrator rather than to its author.[29]

First, the narrator of *The Hand* is, as I have mentioned, hard to describe using conventional narratological categories. The novel is an often unexplained mixture of first-person and third-person narration. Several critics, including myself, have described the plethora of voices within the text as polyphonic, in Mikhail Bakhtin's sense of the term.[30] For Bakhtin, the polyphonic novel is one in which the characters' voices are themselves dialogic, or double-voiced, and where the narrator allows the characters autonomy by retaining 'no essential "surplus" of meaning' within the text.[31] I am no longer convinced that *The Hand* does exhibit genuine polyphony – rather, I believe that its apparent multi-voicedness conceals a fixed and undemocratic agenda.

As I have suggested, in *The Hand*, we could argue that Fiona is the narrator throughout the novel, even in the apparently omnisciently narrated sections. It is simply – but crucially – that her narratorial voice changes. In the framing narrative at the novel's opening and at its end, where Fiona is foregrounded as a character, her voice is that of a young, uncertain 'seeker', in John Docker's term, who does not know how to 'explain her shameful family history'.[32] Elsewhere in the novel Fiona's voice is impersonal and omniscient, and able to reconstruct life in Ukraine in the 1930s. It is the latter version of Fiona's voice which critics claimed was Darville's own. Of course, the presence in a novel of such a frame or diegetic narrator does not necessarily preclude polyphony. In Ford Madox Ford's 1915 novel *The Good Soldier*, for instance, the first-person narrator John Dowell's attempts to piece together events in the past and to justify himself retrospectively are relativized by his repetition of others' voices. This is an instance of a character unwittingly revealing the polyphonic construction of the novel in which he appears. In Philip Roth's 2000 novel *The Human Stain*, however, many of the utterances quoted by the first-person narrator Nathan Zuckerman are his own invention, making the characters' voices here, as in *The Hand*, 'merely objects of cognition' on the author's part, as Bakhtin puts it of Tolstoy's novels.[33] Although we might be tempted to amend Bakhtin's focus here and elsewhere on the author rather than narrator, *The Hand* has in common with *The Human Stain* a narrator who constitutes the author's alter ego so self-consciously that the gap between narrator and implied author is greatly reduced – again, I would argue, to the effect of diminishing the possibility of polyphony.[34]

The only parts of *The Hand* from which Fiona's voice is absent are the transcriptions of characters' utterances, and, as I have argued, at least some of these may also be Fiona's invention. It seems that Fiona's voice always orchestrates those of the other characters, thus robbing them of any 'free' expression, in Bakhtin's phrase. Bakhtin's example of a profoundly polyphonic novel is Dostoevsky's *Crime and Punishment*, in which the central character Raskolnikov enables polyphony through his guilt-ridden mental rehearsal of other characters' utterances. By contrast Fiona, or the narratorial principle of *The Hand*, either presents and reconstructs other characters' voices, or is entirely absent from their transcribed form. At times the subsuming quality of the narrator is betrayed within the text itself. I have already quoted the free direct discourse of the old woman who disapproved of Magda and Vitaly's behaviour: *'Shameless, kissing that Trawnicki boy in front of everyone like that'* (109). The blurring here between character and narrator acts to incorporate the former's voice within the latter, in the customary manner of free indirect discourse, but the old woman's words are mockingly repeated by the narrator later in the same episode, turning her doubly into an 'object of cognition' rather than a subject: 'Shameless, on the step, Magda and the Trawnicki boy are kissing' (109). The tone of triumph here not only answers back to the old woman but raises the suspicion that hers was a strategic, narratorial remark in any case. Indeed, the all-consuming nature of *The Hand*'s narrative voice explains other complaints levied against the novel, for instance that the characters' language is that of 1990s Australia rather than 1940s occupied Europe: even national and temporally specific languages are subsumed by the contemporary, English-speaking narrator.

It is this narrator who is responsible for the most conspicuous kind of 'fascination with anti-Semitic fascism' in *The Hand*, and that is the sexualizing and glamorizing of its perpetrators, through whom all the action is focalized. It is not just the perpetrators' appearance and romantic and sexual activities which are thus glamorized, but their murderous ones as well. In this sense, the narrator acts in a way similar to Magda, in the incident described above, in either overlooking acts of murder, or finding something about such behaviour appealing. Fiona does not admit to this – at the novel's outset, she says plainly, 'Vitaly did unspeakable things' (5) – but it is as if the personal attractiveness of the novel's perpetrators is metonymic of the hidden allure of fascism and murder. As a child, Fiona thought of her father as a pirate – 'Pirates were bad. They were also glamorous' (39) – and this view is not abandoned by the adult Fiona, but made a part of the narration rather than presented explicitly. Throughout the novel, German and Ukrainian SS alike are described in terms of their eyes and hair. The first time Fiona sees a photograph of the SS officer Wilhelm Hasse who married her aunt, she describes him as, 'an unknown man with white blond hair. The man had a handsome, wicked face' (6). To Vitaly, Hasse is positively iconic, possessing eyes that are like 'portals of light' (98) and 'silver' hair (101). Kateryna rejoices in 'strawberry-blond hair' (101), while Vitaly has hair so fair it is 'milky' and Magda sees it glinting in the sun on a death-camp watch-tower (113). The Ukrainian SS volunteer Voronikov has 'sloe green eyes' (68), while Vitaly's Volksdeutsche girlfriend Ulrike has 'vixen-green eyes' (92). These details are not simply evidence of an authorial preference for beautiful or stylized characters, but all point towards a fantasied and *racialized* conception of fictive detail. As an extension of this, the sexual relationships between the German SS and local women is a central focus of the narrative about the past. Indeed, these relationships – between Ukrainian Kateryna and German Hasse, Ukrainian Vitaly and Polish Magda – are a version of Fiona's fictive family tree. Her Ukrainian father and 'ginger-haired' (152) Irish mother – who not only rather implausibly speaks Gaelic, despite being a Protestant who 'believed in the flag and the Queen' (4), but can understand the Scottish Gaelic of yet another uncle – met in England and emigrated to Australia – as did Demidenko's. The novel's fantasy of unexpected cultural mixing, based on a wholly racialized awareness, as well as the allure of 'white-blond' hair, was transposed from Darville's novel to her own persona.

## The view from Ukraine

Many critics have pondered the reasons why 'ethnically unmarked'[35] Australians of Anglo-Saxon origin adopt other kinds of identity. These reasons naturally vary by circumstance, but they can perhaps be divided between the pragmatic and the psychological. In their introduction to the special issue of *Australian Literary Studies* on identity adoption, Maggie Nolan and Carrie Dawson comment on the notion that, for writers with either ideological or speculative motives, 'affirmative action policies might produce imposture'.[36] This does not seem to apply to Darville, even though the grounds on which she was fêted included the migrant and working-class aspects of her novel. Nolan and Dawson go on to argue that in contemporary Australia 'it is questions of cultural and racial difference, rather than sexual or gender difference, which preoccupy those who feel themselves to have "lost out" in the cultural changes of post-war Australia, who may also be those who are best able to articulate this sense of "loss"'.[37] It is true that the best known cases of imposture in Australia have been of this 'cultural and racial' kind. These include Nino Culotta's *They're a Weird Mob* (1957), apparently an autobiography by an Italian immigrant to Australia, actually by the Irish writer John O'Grady; B. Wongar's stories of Aboriginal life, *The Track to Bralgu* (1978), which were written by a Yugoslavian immigrant Stretan Bozic; the oeuvre of Ern Malley, a working-class poet invented by James McAuley and Harold Stewart as an attack on the modernist literary institutions of the 1940s; and a series of writers claiming an Aboriginal ancestry which turned out to be at least questionable – these include the writer and critic Mudrooroo and Roberta Sykes.[38] Nolan and Dawson suggest four categories for explaining such 'acts of imposture': identification, appropriation, creation and affiliation. Darville fits into the second category with elements of the first.

Readers might indeed see *The Hand* as the result of an unconscious wish for a special and unusual story of origins, in an Australia where possessing Anglo-Saxon ancestry is to be 'ethnically unmarked'. The critic John Docker notes that the news that Darville's parents were English was 'greeted with hilarity', as if being of such heritage in Australia 'was not to be ethnic at all, that it had no diasporic interest, no cachet, no pathos'.[39] We might wonder further, however, why the 'Pom' Helen Darville constructed an Irish-Ukrainian identity for herself, and focused her self-presentation on the Ukrainian aspects. In answer to this question, I will mention two responses to Darville's appropriation that put forward a Ukrainian approach. In an article entitled 'Demidenko/Darville: a Ukrainian-Australian point of view', Sonia Mycak identifies herself as 'an academic, a (second generation) Australian of Ukrainian descent, and a member of the Ukrainian-Australian community'.[40] She argues that the Demidenko saga would have been much more swiftly and less acrimoniously resolved if *The Hand* had been viewed in the context of contemporary Ukrainian-Australian writing. Naturally its author would have turned out to be unheard of – Mycak quotes Wolodymyr Motyka, former president of the Ukrainian Studies Foundation in Australia, who said of Demidenko, 'There was no resonance, nor trail within the community' of her name or her writing.[41] The notion of an ethnic, as much as a literary, Ukrainian community is called upon here. Furthermore, Mycak argues that *The Hand*'s 'theme and setting', of the Second World War, is not a 'preoccupation' in current Ukrainian-origin writing in Australia. The implication is that, had the novel been contextualized by its original critics in a specifically institutional manner, rather than taken on its own merits as if it existed in a 'cultural vacuum', they would have found it to be suspiciously untypical. However, Mycak's contention is also historically defensive, and she quotes members of the 'Ukrainian-Australian community' arguing that *The Hand* stereotypes and even libels their members by focusing on their wartime anti-Jewish activity. Mycak herself claims that aid to Jews during the war showed more evidence of 'courageousness' in Ukraine than elsewhere because 'unlike other countries occupied by the Nazis, in Ukraine assisting Jews was punishable by death'.[42] However, this was certainly also the case in Poland.

A second article, by C. Amanda Müller, which focuses on the Ukrainian content of *The Hand* also argues that the very features of the text which appeared to give it authenticity actually demonstrated its inauthenticity. The examples Müller gives include the 'factional' list of Russian and Ukrainian variant spellings which Darville provided in an Author's Note; and her apparently unwitting reliance in practice on Russian vocabulary and transliteration.[43] Again, this suggests that, had the judges and critics who first assessed the novel been more knowledgeable or more vigilant, they would have caught its imposture out sooner. Yet this is to confuse two different texts: Darville's novel, and her construction of Helen Demidenko. Müller sees the novel simply as serving to shore up Darville's persona: 'Helen Darville's use of non-English languages played an important role in bolstering the credibility of her identity as the Ukrainian "Helen Demidenko".'[44] But of course *The Hand* itself is not an imposture, except to the extent that all fiction is. Takolander and McCooey claim that 'literature itself is often about – perhaps fundamentally about – successfully faking it';[45] that is, the fictive nature of *The Hand* was not affected by its author's masquerade, except that, with hindsight, we can read it as an allegory of the construction of that masquerade.

Rather like Binjamin Wilkomirski's transformation of a troubled childhood into a Holocaust story, Darville's adoption of a Ukrainian ancestry served, in Susanna Egan's phrase, to 'insert' an individual life 'into public history'.[46] Although *The Hand* is not autobiography, Darville has effected this 'insertion' both by its narrator Fiona Kovalenko representing the implied – or even real – author of the novel, and by her extra-textual performance as Demidenko. In both scenarios, the world of 1930s' East and Central Europe has an anachronistically contemporary texture. Robert Manne pithily described the book's setting as 'Queensland with death camps'.[47] The characters' discourse is often rendered as colloquial Australian English – when the SS officer Wilhelm Hasse wants to show off his new girlfriend Kateryna we read, in free direct discourse: '*Look what I found in my breakfast cereal*' (61), and later he uses the term 'politically incorrect' (63). Once more, these 'anachronisms' are explained if we hold to the view that Fiona narrates the whole novel, and these are symbolic or 'modern translations', as Adrian Mitchell puts it, of the past into another language, akin to the subtitles on foreign films.[48]

These small anachronistic details are not of the same order as other shifts in temporality, which seem to reveal an authorial hand. The most striking of these is a wartime Nazi notice in a park, a detail which Darville has borrowed from Anatoly Kuznetsov's 'factional' novel *Babi Yar*, that reads, 'No Ukrainians and no dogs'.[49] This detail is transferred backwards in *The Hand* into pre-war Ukraine, where, it is implied, 'Jewish Bolsheviks' erected it (20). Another less obvious but perhaps more revealing example of anachronism takes the form of what John Docker calls the characters' 'daily racialized perception',[50] which could be seen as an extreme and deadly version of ethnic awareness in contemporary Australia. The buried historical referent here may be one that is closer to its Australian home. Darville's fascination with 'anti-Semitic fascism' may be the full explanation for her curious identification with her Ukrainian characters and their genocidal past. However, it is unusual for literary imposters not to take on an identity in which they are the wronged party – as does Wilkomirski, the ersatz Holocaust victim, and those who appropriated varying degrees of Aboriginal identity in the cases I have mentioned. We might wonder, therefore, whether Darville's novel and her imposture represent a return to a primal scene of racial mass murder which took place in her own country, perpetrated by the very 'Poms' she disavowed. This might become clearer if we see *The Hand* not as presenting excuses for genocide – can there be any? – but as an unwitting fictive refutation of Daniel Goldhagen's controversial thesis, which exclusively blamed German anti-Semitism for the Holocaust.[51] Instead, *The Hand* boldly reveals the complicity of local populations alongside the Nazis in the murder of the Jews of Europe.

## Conclusion

Over a decade after the 'Demidenko scandal' first erupted, there has been a clear shift in emphasis in the continuing debate about *The Hand that Signed the Paper*. Critics no longer focus on the politics of literary prize-giving in Australia in relation to *The Hand*, nor on whether the novel is anti-Semitic, nor even on the novel as an unusual instance of Holocaust representation. The latter is perhaps surprising, as Darville's novel raises in extreme form all the central issues of Holocaust fiction. These include reliance on anterior texts, whether these are testimonial or historical; questions about the relationship between author, narrator and protagonist in even a fictional text; and an ethical concern with the formal matters of style and structure. Instead, the issues raised by Helen Darville's novel and her imposture are to do with identity more broadly. They include the nature of the author-function in relation to fiction, and the ways in which ethnicity may be taken for personal identity. As *The Hand* has never been published outside Australia, it is not surprising that it continues to be read within an Australian context – but many of the ways in which it continues to be considered apply to any contemporary multicultural society.

## Notes

1. I am grateful to Cath Ellis, Pip Vice and Susan Watkins for their help in writing this chapter.
2. Helen Demidenko, *The Hand that Signed the Paper* (Sydney: Allen and Unwin 1994); reissued 1995 with correct attribution to Helen Darville. All page references are to the latter, and appear in the text.
3. See 'Writing after Winning', *Southerly*, 55 (Spring 1995), 155–60. An embryonic version of Darville's Demidenko persona preceded her novel, as she had enrolled in a course on Multiculturalism and Literature at the University of Queensland under the name 'Helen Demidenko-Darville' (John Jost, Gianna Totaro and Christine Tyshing, eds, *The Demidenko File* (Ringwood, Victoria: Penguin Books Australia 1996), 153).
4. Quoted in Jost et al., *The Demidenko File*, 108.
5. Binjamin Wilkomirski, *Fragments: Memories of a Childhood 1939–1945*, trans. Carol Brown Janeway (London: Picador, 1995). See Stefan Maechler, *The Wilkomirski Affair: a Study in Biographical Truth* (New York: Schocken 2001) for an account of the background to this imposture.
6. Martin Gray, with Max Gallo, *For Those I Loved*, trans. Anthony White (Boston: Little, Brown, 1972); Bernard Holstein, *Stolen Soul: a True Story of Courage and Survival* (Crawley, WA: University of Western Australia Press 2004).
7. In fact, as F.H. (Tim) Mares points out, there was only one such trial, which took place in Adelaide in 1993. The defendant, Ivan Polyukhovich, was acquitted; 'The Demidenko Affair: Who Writes, and Who Reads?', in D.G.B. von Lutz, ed., *Seeing and Saying: Self-Referentiality in British and American Literature* (Frankfurt: Peter Lang 1998), 179.
8. The term is Bill Buford's: see his introduction to 'Dirty Realism', *Granta* 8 (Harmondsworth: Penguin 1983). As well as its focus on blue-collar life and reaction against the contemporary political formation, 'Dirty Realism' was defined in terms of its economy of narration.
9. Serge Liberman, 'On Helen Demidenko's *The Hand that Signed the Paper*', *Southerly*, 55 (Spring 1995), 175–84; 176; Robert Manne, *The Culture of Forgetting: Helen Demidenko and the Holocaust* (Melbourne: Text Publishing 1996), 118.
10. Martin Amis, *Time's Arrow* (Harmondsworth: Penguin 1991); Tadeusz Borowski, *This Way for the Gas, Ladies and Gentlemen*, trans. Barbara Vedder (Harmondsworth: Penguin 1976).
11. Caryl Emerson defines 'skaz' as a mode of narration 'that imitates the oral speech of an individualized narrator'; Mikhail Bakhtin, *Problems of Dostoevsky's Poetics*, trans. and ed. Caryl Emerson (Minneapolis: University of Minnesota Press 1984), 8 n. b).
12. Demidenko, 'Writing after Winning', 159.
13. Cited in Manne, *The Culture of Forgetting*, p. 68.
14. See for instance Anne Waldron Neuman, 'The Ethics of Fiction's Reception', *Quadrant* (November 1995), 53–6; 53.
15. Maria Takolander and David McCooey, 'Fakes, Literary Identity and Public Culture', *Journal of the Association for the Study of Australian Literature*, 3 (2004), 57–66; 58.

16. See Robert Eaglestone's citation of the philosopher John Searle on this matter: there 'is no textual property . . . that will identify a stretch of discourse as a work of fiction', in *The Holocaust and the Postmodern* (Oxford: Oxford University Press 2004), 125.

17. Manne argues against *The Hand*'s representation of the Holocaust as an instance of ethnic hatred arising from particular circumstances, claiming rather that the Holocaust was inspired by a virulent version of ideological anti-Semitism (*The Culture of Forgetting*, 163).

18. Raymond Gaita, 'Literary and Public Honours', *Quadrant* (September 1995), 32–6; 34.

19. Manne, *The Culture of Forgetting*, 144.

20. Adrian Mitchell, 'After Demidenko: the Curling Papers', *Southerly*, 56, 4 (1996–97), 110–26; 112; Gaita, 'Literary and Public Honours', 32.

21. Manne, *The Culture of Forgetting*, 144.

22. Ibid., 123.

23. Ibid., 55, 57.

24. Ibid., 117.

25. See Bryan Cheyette, 'The Uncertain Certainty of *Schindler's List*', on the inappropriate 'Manichaean certainty of contemporary filmmakers and writers in relation to the Shoah', in Yosefa Loshitzky, ed., *Spielberg's Holocaust: Critical Perspectives on 'Schindler's List'* (Bloomington and Indianapolis: Indiana University Press 1997), 227.

26. Mitchell, 'After Demidenko', 121.

27. Philippe Lejeune, *On Autobiography*, trans. Kathleen Leary (Minneapolis: University of Minnesota Press, 1989), 58.

28. Jane Hyde, 'On Not Being Ethnic: Anglo-Australia and the Lesson of Helen Darville-Demidenko', *Quadrant* (November 1995), 49–52; 50.

29. In this way *The Hand* contrasts with Marina Lewycka's 2005 autobiographically-based novel *A Short History of Tractors in Ukrainian* (London: Viking). Like *The Hand*, *A Short History* is narrated by the daughter of a Ukrainian immigrant, who came to Britain rather than Australia. However, the narrator Nadezhda's father Nikolai is virulently anti-communist, not anti-Semitic; both he, as a character, and Nadezhda, as the narrator, ascribe the Ukrainian famine of the 1930s to Stalin (see pp. 65, 81), rather than to the 'Jewish Bolsheviks' of Darville's novel, and manifest only compassion for Jews killed at Babi Yar (206).

30. See the chapter on Darville in my *Holocaust Fiction* (London and New York: Routledge 2000); Adrian Mitchell, ' "Those Infernal Pictures": Reading Helen Darville, her Novel and her Critics', *Australian Literary Studies*, 18, 1 (1997), 72–9; 77; Peter Kirkpatrick, 'The Jackboot Doesn't Fit: Moral Authoritarianism and *The Hand that Signed the Paper*', *Southerly*, 55, 4 (1995–96), 155–65; 163; and John Docker, 'Debating Ethnicity and History: From Enzensberger to Darville/Demidenko', in Gerhard Fischer, ed., *Debating Enzensberger: Great Migration and Civil War* (Tübingen: Stauffenberg Verlag, 1996), 217. Interestingly, Docker sees some of the voices within the polyphonic debate as themselves 'monologic' (219).

31. Bakhtin, *Problems of Dostoevsky's Poetics*, 72.

32. Docker, 'Debating Ethnicity', 218.

33. Bakhtin, *Problems of Dostoevsky's Poetics*, 72.

34. Thanks to Rachel Falconer and Neil Roberts for discussing this matter with me.

35. Maggie Nolan and Carrie Dawson, Introduction, 'Who's Who? Mapping Hoaxes and Imposture in Australian Literature', special issue of *Australian Literary Studies*, 21, 3 (2004), v–xx; xv.

36. Ibid., ix.
37. Ibid., xi.
38. Ibid., xii.
39. Docker, 'Debating Ethnicity and History', 222.
40. Sonia Mycak, 'Demidenko/Darville: a Ukrainian-Australian Point of View', *Australian Literary Studies*, 21, 3 (2004), 111–33; 111.
41. Ibid., 121. This may be a view that benefits from hindsight, as Mares claims to have witnessed Demidenko, as she then was, 'escorted by members of the Ukrainian community' to the Study of Australian Literature Conference of July 1995, where she was presented with the Australian Literary Society's Gold Medal ('Who Writes, Who Reads?', 180).
42. Mycak, 'Demidenko/Darville', 122, 130, 117.
43. Müller's most convincing example is from another piece of writing by Demidenko, the published speech 'Writing after Winning' (see n. 3), which concludes with the cod-Russian 'Da Svidaniye' – a 'nonsense' phrase whose wide currency Müller traces back to the 1964 James Bond film *From Russia With Love* (C. Amanda Müller, 'So Called Fracts are Fraud: Language, Authenticity and Helen Demidenko', in Heather Merle Benbow and Guido Ernst, eds, *(Sub)Texts: New Perspectives on Literature and Culture* (Melbourne: University of Melbourne Press 2000), 50.
44. Ibid., 45.
45. Takolander and McCooey, 'Fakes, Literary Identity and Public Culture', 57.
46. Susanna Egan, 'The Company She Keeps: Demidenko and the Problems of Imposture in Autobiography', *Australian Literary Studies*, 21, 3 (2004), 14–27; 16.
47. Manne, *The Culture of Forgetting*, 84.
48. Mitchell, ' "Those Infernal Pictures" ', 76.
49. Anatoli Kuznetsov, *Babi Yar*, trans. Jacob Guralsky (London: Sphere Books, 1969), 253.
50. Docker, 'Debating Ethnicity and History', 220.
51. Daniel Jonah Goldhagen, *Hitler's Willing Executioners: Ordinary Germans and the Holocaust* (New York: Little, Brown, 1996).

# 10
# J.M. Coetzee's *Disgrace*: Reading Race/Reading Scandal

*Kai Easton*

In a contentious article in South Africa's *Sunday Times*, Colin Bower, a publisher in Cape Town, tried to argue that J.M. Coetzee is not as good a writer as everyone says he is: 'I have searched in vain for evidence of literary craftsmanship in Coetzee', he boldly wrote.[1] His timing could not have been worse: a week or so later, Coetzee was awarded the Nobel Prize for Literature. It was October 2003. Bower's article particularly highlights a local feature of Coetzee reception, for, mixed with great acclaim for the author and his work, there is also great displeasure. In the press, there is at least as much attention given to complaints about Coetzee's elusiveness and the inaccessibility of his prose as there is to the achievement of his novels. And despite Coetzee's quiet insistence on privacy, there are still those who persist in seeing the author as a public figure.

All of this has been magnified in the wake of the scandal and success of *Disgrace* (1999). Winning Coetzee an unprecedented second Booker Prize that year, the first of his novels to be set in the *new* South Africa is just as complex as his previous fiction and closer in its contemporaneousness to his 1990 novel *Age of Iron*, but with a difference: it provokes with a gesture to headline news – a Cape Town professor's scandalous affair with a student; a horrific attack on the professor – and the gang-rape of his lesbian daughter. Published five years into democracy, and nearly a decade after the dismantling of official censorship, *Disgrace* challenges readers with its many-layered plot, its choice of landscape, its preoccupation with Byron, the Romantics, animals, and ethics. So why would an author known for more obvious dislocations of time and place in his previous work, for his reluctance to enter into public debate, also choose to bring in the 'topical' and 'shocking'? Why, if the book is otherwise so intertextually rich, would he write to *invite* the possibility of a 'realist' reading focusing on the controversial material only?

This landmark text has only a very short history, but its influence in the public sphere has already been significant. 'Is *this* the right image of our nation?' asked the esteemed professor of literature and Director-General under Mandela, Jakes Gerwel, in an article for the Afrikaans weekly *Rapport*.[2] 'Feeding national paranoia?' was the headline of another article, questioning Coetzee's fictional portrayal of gender and race.[3] Similarly, the late Aggrey Klaaste, who said he found the novel 'gloomy' and 'unhappy', wrote in *The Sowetan*:

> It is the end of *Disgrace* that gives me serious problems. In sum the story of black men raping a white woman, who accepts this serious abuse as something like a badge of courage, is in my view quite offensive.
>
> At the *political* level it depicts a white male fear about black male sexual potency and the black males' inability to deal with power.[4]

Two days after Klaaste's critique of *Disgrace*, the ANC's submission was presented to the South African Human Rights Commission (SAHRC) hearings on racism and the media by then Public Enterprises Minister and ANC policy spokesperson Jeff Radebe. In the report, *Disgrace* was cited and Coetzee was accused of '*making the point*' that

> ... five years after liberation white South African society continues to believe in a particular stereotype of the African which defines the latter as immoral and amoral, a savage, violent, disrespectful of private property, incapable of refinement through education and driven by ... dark satanic impulses.[5]

The SAHRC had originally received specific complaints against two newspapers in 1998. It was their decision to investigate the prevalence of racism in the media more broadly. The hearings which, they made clear, 'should not be turned into a court process'[6] (here we have echoes of the Truth and Reconciliation Commission (TRC) – echoes too of David Lurie's hearing)[7] nevertheless had great implications for Coetzee's novel. Though the Commission claimed that 'it is not the purpose of the inquiry to find any individual journalist, publisher or *title* guilty of racism',[8] Coetzee's novel was certainly singled out.

As David Attwell has documented, the authorship of the report is complex, since there are two versions – one under the ANC banner and one somewhat distancing itself from its status as an ANC document. What seems likely, however, is that 'the guiding hand behind the report' was Thabo Mbeki.[9] While the incoherency of the submission (since it is an unedited transcription, with awkward phrasing and paraphrasing of the novel) means that charges of racism against Coetzee, or against his novel, are rather ambiguous,[10] what does not appear to have been asked in any of the coverage so far is why was *Disgrace*, a fiction, selected for an inquiry on racism and the *media*? How does the report – which confuses Coetzee with his character David Lurie, and other characters and events with real life – contribute to the reputation of this millennial novel, and how does the scandal in *Disgrace* become the scandal of *Disgrace*?

In the first section of this chapter, I want to consider how a book that cannot be officially 'censored' under the new Constitution, can still be censured through official channels. For if Coetzee's novel does not actually go to trial in the legal sense, one could argue that it is effectively 'put on trial' in the public sphere. In addition to some of the more prominent examples of the negative reception of *Disgrace* in the local press, however, we also need to think about how scandal circulates: just as often it is through gossip. My discussion thus includes several anecdotes, some first-hand, some offered to me by colleagues, friends, and new acquaintances upon learning about this project. In the second section of this chapter, I turn away from the present South African context of *Disgrace* to look at the case of a nineteenth-century novelist who, together with the poet Byron, is intertextually highlighted in the novel. Their real-life scandals from a previous century might seem marginal to the plot of *Disgrace*; however, I shall argue that their inclusion in this contemporary narrative is crucial to the way Coetzee cunningly configures the anticipated reception of his novel. The final section of the chapter returns to the ANC's citation of *Disgrace* in the context of South Africa's transitional politics, particularly as these relate to race and transformation in the university sphere. Although there is no mention in the novel of political specifics, for example, not a single reference to Mandela, Mbeki, or even the ANC, *Disgrace* has nevertheless had an unusually political response (both in the SAHRC hearings and even in Cabinet). The media have even casually referred to Coetzee's 'clash' with the ANC, but in terms that must be called conjecture – for Coetzee typically has withheld commentary both regarding the ANC's condemnation of his novel and regarding his own emigration to Australia (and yet these are conflated in the press). These issues are, of course, outside the text, but the text – as I will argue – pre-empts its own scandalous reading.

## Scandalous fictions/scandalous readings

That the local debate surrounding *Disgrace* is in tension with the novel's international image is perfectly encapsulated in two cartoons published in the national press shortly after Coetzee received the Nobel Prize. The first cartoon (see Figure 1)[11] mocks the discrepancy between the ANC's initial reaction to *Disgrace* ('then') and its praise for the author ('now') in 2003.[12] The second cartoon (see Figure 2)[13] uses a sporting event to tease the South Africans about losing J.M. Coetzee to the Australian side. As the cartoons illustrate, authors, when they receive international awards, are often considered 'national prizes' by their home country. Witness former President Nelson Mandela's praise for Coetzee as an 'intellectual hero', adding that 'he might have emigrated but we shall continue to claim him as

*Figure 1*   Coetzee Cartoon: Stidy, *Weekend Witness*, 4 October 2003

*Figure 2*   Coetzee Cartoon: Grogan, *The Sunday Independent*, 5 October 2003

our own'.[14] Smuts Ngonyama, spokesperson for the presidency under Mbeki, while defending the ANC's original denunciation of *Disgrace* (see box 1 of the first cartoon), refers to Coetzee – despite his move to another part of the southern hemisphere and the incongruity of referring to him in the language of liberation struggle discourse – as a 'son of [the] soil'.[15] Coetzee's emigration to Australia in 2002 – shortly after retiring from his professorship in English at the University of Cape Town – has caused much speculation in the press. If some journalists suggest it is because he was 'driven out' by the ANC, others think it precedes this – that *Disgrace* tells all – it's his 'vale-dictory', says the writer Rian Malan, in a BBC television profile on Coetzee.[16] What with the novel's bleak portrait of the nation in transformation – crime, rape, and the 'great rationalization' of higher education – it is no wonder, they say, that Coetzee packed for the quiet hills near Adelaide.

It is actually quite difficult to theorize 'scandal' as it applies to such a recent work as *Disgrace*; its very currency too precludes a long history of the novel's career. How do we assess the simultaneous celebration and denunci-ation, the delight and dismay, of a book that has surely become the central book, the most widely known, in the Coetzee canon?[17] How do we account for the fame of our award-winning author (the Booker Prize (1983, 1999), the Commonwealth Writer's Prize (2000), the Nobel Prize (2003)), as well as his general obscurity amongst the general public? While David Beresford reports in South Africa's *Mail & Guardian* in March 2000 that 'Unusually for up-market fiction here, Coetzee's Booker-winning novel has become a galloping bestseller',[18] another news item from October 2003 is headlined, 'SA delighted with Coetzee'.[19] What this reveals, however, is that South Africa's delight as a nation really means some 'academics' and 'publishers' in South Africa: an elite audience. It is certainly true that *Disgrace* has sold well and been promoted in the educational sphere: by course adoption at univer-sities, as a set text for Matric at South African Independent Schools[20] and, in a more unique case, by its adaptation to the stage (as in the production in Gauteng by high-school drama teacher Claire Mortimer). By and large, though, the reading public in South Africa is actually very small, most books are imported at high prices, and while Wilbur Smith may be something of a household name, J.M. Coetzee is not.[21]

To account for the way *Disgrace* has evolved into a kind of catchphrase or signifier in the South African imaginary,[22] we need to consider how much of the reception, influenced by remarkably continuous press coverage between 1999, when it was published, and 2003, when it won the Nobel Prize, resides in gossip and anecdote. A friend has told me how a group of white women who play bridge together in a rural area of the Eastern Cape expressed their outrage at *Disgrace*. My first assumption – before I knew what they were outraged about – was that, like many readers, at home and abroad, they reacted to the rape and to Lucy's choice to keep the baby; but this was not their main objection: what outraged them rather was land – Lucy's choice to give Petrus the farm.

It is not of minor importance that Coetzee sets Lucy's smallholding in Salem: it has been a contested space since, at least, the frontier wars between the British and the Xhosa.[23] It is one of the earliest villages settled by the

British after the emigration scheme to the Cape of Good Hope in 1819–20. Unlike Grahamstown, it has never expanded into any kind of metropolis or even town. The real Salem is indeed on the Grahamstown–Kenton road; it is noticeable for the white church on a slight rise overlooking the pristine cricket ground, one of the oldest in the country and still used. Its name was taken from the Bible: in Hebrew it means 'peace'. At a glance, on a brief visit or as one travels through it, it seems a very peaceful place now, which is perhaps why, when *Disgrace* was published, local residents were dismayed that Coetzee had chosen it for the site of Lucy's farm, the scene of the brutal attack and gang-rape, an episode which replicates, in fact, real stories of farm attacks and sexual violence in the news. A couple of years ago when I was lecturing at Rhodes University, I was introduced to a librarian from the area who, on discovering I worked on Coetzee, firmly told me that Coetzee had set *Disgrace* in the 'wrong place': 'Salem is a nice community', she said. That Coetzee has apparently never visited Salem (this is hearsay), or that he might have chosen 'Salem' for its biblical and literary allusions (the New England Salem of Nathaniel Hawthorne's *The Scarlet Letter* and Arthur Miller's *The Crucible* are both relevant to the themes of scandal, confession, and puritanical times we find in *Disgrace*), point to the very tensions – as I have argued elsewhere – between realism and romance that are played out in *Disgrace* itself.[24]

In addition to these select anecdotes, however, there is the more general gossip of ideas, the transference of readings of the novel in the form of reviews – both formal and informal. For indeed, the story of *Disgrace* has circulated so widely that many of its 'readers' have not actually 'read' it: rather the book and its author have been talked about to such a degree that what one has heard about *Disgrace* is apparently enough to enter into the public debate, as in the case of renowned South African playwright Athol Fugard. In interview, Fugard said the *idea* of it made him despondent:

> '. . . I'm sure the writing is excellent. . . but I could not think of anything that would depress me more than this book by Coetzee, *Disgrace*, where we've got to accept the rape of a white woman as a gesture to all of the evil that we did in the past.'[25]

This second- or third-hand interpretation throws into sharp relief one of the main storylines – out of all the plots offered by this complex novel – that dominates in readings of *Disgrace*: Lucy's choice to 'pay for history', to keep the baby fathered by one of her rapists and to give her land – and her hand – to her black neighbour Petrus.

While Lucy's decision is extreme in its moral pragmatism, 'realistically' impossible to comprehend, it is given to us as a fictional response to a situation that has been fictionally posed: behind it, of course, are real questions about ethical responsibility.[26] Fugard's borrowed critique, however, replicates a general interpretation of her excessive gesture as 'atonement',[27] but a reading of the actual text shows how this misreading is both expected and subverted. David Lurie explicitly poses the question to Lucy: 'Do you hope you can expiate the crimes of the past by suffering in the present?', to which Lucy replies: 'No. *You keep misreading me.* Guilt and salvation are abstractions. I don't act in terms of abstractions.'[28]

'Scandal' always involves a public reading, or misreading, of what is private: transgression in itself is not necessarily scandalous, but transgressions that are made public, that are in fact paraded to the public – in fiction or in real life – are indeed scandalous. They become subject to other codes of reading: moral, legal, political, religious. So what is actually scandalous about Coetzee's novel? Is its location – its geographical and temporal situation – the real issue (and if so, does that mean its scandalousness locally is what has sparked its scandalousness internationally?) Had it been set elsewhere, in another land far away, would the scandal in *Disgrace* – David Lurie's sexual harassment case at the university, the rape of his lesbian daughter on her smallholding – have the same power to shock and dismay? What is evoked by setting it in the *new* South Africa, in the Western *and* Eastern Cape, in terms of land, race, nation, and gender? What, in the end, causes some readers to 'take offence' and attack not only the text (a fiction), but also its author?[29]

## Style on trial

In a letter to the *Mail & Guardian* in October 2003, Mathew Blatchford of the University of Fort Hare writes:

> The tale is narratively framed by explicit racism, implicit sexism and homophobia. It gives a distorted image of contemporary South Africa, building on a similar representation in *Age of Iron* cheered by Afrophobes overseas.
>
> Since *Disgrace* panders to the self-image of the white South African liberal right, an industry has arisen around it. Some justify the book's misrepresentations. Others pretend it is not 'about' its repellent content, but Hegel, Kant, Byron, Death-in-Life, or anything long ago and far away.

And yet, *Disgrace* does at several points ask us to look at the 'long ago and far away', not just in its obvious references to scandal and Byron, to issues of land and history, 'to the long history of exploitation' evoked in Lurie's sexual conquest of a young student,[30] but also when we consider it as a successor – in its concerns with transgression and confession – to Coetzee's 1994 novel, *The Master of Petersburg*.

Published in the year of South Africa's first democratic elections, this twentieth-century reimagining of the genesis of Dostoevsky's *The Possessed* has not received nearly the attention one might have expected. Readers were baffled – as they were when he published *Foe* (1986) – both at his distancing from an obvious South African setting and at his choice to 'rewrite' the novel of another famous author from another century. In March 1994, Coetzee was one of four eminent speakers invited to a symposium in Tulsa, Oklahoma.[31] Prefacing his reading from *The Master of Petersburg* (which had not yet been released in the United States), Coetzee remarked that he was surprised to see that the conference programme contained no offerings on the fall of the Second Empire.[32] Five years later, in *Disgrace*, Coetzee makes two references to a famous character by a famous French novelist.

Emma Bovary appears briefly on pages 5–6 and 150. She is one, among many, of the nineteenth-century allusions in Coetzee's twentieth-century novel, but her presence as a fictional character is all the more intriguing for the absence of any mention of her author, Gustave Flaubert, or of the title of the book in which she plays the starring role. Let's consider what Flaubert – however peripheral he and his masterpiece may seem to be to Coetzee's contemporary South African novel – might offer an essay on *Disgrace* with a focus on 'scandal'. On the surface, all we have to do is remember that the story is about the adulterous affairs of the wife of a dull country doctor in nineteenth-century provincial France. Adultery, and the representation of adultery, particularly by a woman in the nineteenth century, is to be read as 'scandalous', shocking in the morality of the day, but also of course the subject of intrigue and gossip. Taking it to the next step, however, this fictional character is not only the subject of scandal, but the fiction in which these adulteries are carried out becomes, by association, scandalous. In other words, an author's imagined adultery between characters results – in Flaubert's case – in a real prosecution (the trial of 1857). The author who has created Emma Bovary (apparently out of thin air, but really, it would seem, from gossip – the story has its basis in at least two real-life scandals known to Flaubert) himself also becomes the subject of scandal because of the story he has written and released to the public.

The process of publishing his story is first of all gradual: *Madame Bovary* is serialized in the *Revue de Paris*, but as serialization proceeds there are increasingly letters from readers outraged by its 'immorality'. The editors of the journal, under the censorship of the Second Empire (Napoleon III), are forced to make some excisions: certain passages – the cab scene in particular – are cut. The result is that Flaubert is himself so incensed by these editorial changes that he disowns the work as it appears in the *Revue*. For the next instalment, he attaches a preface, declining responsibility for 'the lines which follow': 'The reader is asked to consider them as a series of *fragments*, not as a whole.'[33]

A crucial '*fragment*' of *Madame Bovary* makes its way into *Disgrace*. In Coetzee's second reference to Emma Bovary, he cites a passage that is ultimately critical to Flaubert's acquittal: ' "*I have a lover! I have a lover!*" '

sings Emma to herself.[34] Coetzee does not give us the rest of the original paragraph, but this is how it ends:

> So at last she was to know those joys of love, that fever of happiness of which she had despaired! She was entering upon a marvelous world where all would be passion, ecstasy, delirium.[35]

When this passage was read out at Flaubert's trial, the prosecuting attorney seized on it: not only does Flaubert represent adultery in his novel, he exclaimed, he glorifies it! But he was conflating Flaubert the author with his particular use of third-person narration.

> In this Flaubert's accuser fell victim to an error as the defense immediately pointed out. The incriminating sentences are not an objective determination of the narrator, which the reader can believe, but a subjective opinion of a person characterized by her feelings that are formed from *novels*. The scientific device consists in revealing the inner thoughts of this person without the signals of direct statement.[36]

Until the moment that the defence recognizes Flaubert's use of *style indirect libre* (a device that is only named later by a disciple of de Saussure), all those participating in the trial, as Dominick LaCapra points out, had given *Madame Bovary* an 'extremely restricted'[37] reading. Crucially, however, as LaCapra elaborates – and this has implications for *Disgrace*:

> this is not simply wrong, for it is *invited* by one level on which the novel itself operates or functions: the level of conventional expectations about how things make sense. What does not register at the trial is the manner in which the novel renders this first level of understanding and expectation highly questionable in its world and, at least by implication, in the larger social world in which the trial takes place.[38]

Like Emma Bovary, David Lurie's Romantic leanings have led him to act out the passions from his reading life. He calls himself a disciple of Wordsworth, but he identifies mostly with the great libertine Byron. As we learn in the opening section of *Disgrace*, his latest project is a chamber opera on Byron and his last great romance, the young Italian countess, Teresa Guiciolli. In his course on the Romantics at Cape Technical University (a morale-boosting elective in his area of expertise – his other teaching consists of teaching Communications 101 and 102), Lurie is in the middle of lecturing on Byron – no less to his '*inamorata*' Melanie, who has brought her boyfriend as a surprise visitor:

> 'We continue with Byron,' he says, plunging into his notes. 'As we saw last week, notoriety and scandal affected not only Byron's life but the way

in which his poems were received by the public. Byron the man found himself conflated with his own poetic creations – with Harold, Manfred, even Don Juan.'

Scandal. A pity that must be his theme, but he is in no state to improvise. He steals a glance at Melanie. (p. 31)

Since this is the very moment before Lurie is charged with sexual harassment, his last lecture before his transgressions are made public, the text's ironic self-reflexivity here is particularly sharp; more to the point, in its irony it anticipates its own misreading – the conflation of Coetzee with his fictional creation David Lurie. Coetzee clearly draws on Byron's scandalous reputation[39] for his character David Lurie, but there is also, significantly, a brief reference on page 34 to Byron's unfinished satire, *Don Juan*, which was so scandalously received by the public. Byron published *Don Juan* in progress, cantos at a time. As with Flaubert, there were cries of outrage for its 'shocking immorality',[40] so much so that Teresa prevailed upon Byron to stop the work. He only began work on it again, with her blessing, when Shelley praised it as a 'masterpiece' with the 'stamp of immortality'.[41] 'I obtained a permission from my Dictatress to continue,' he wrote, '*provided* it was to be more guarded and decorous and sentimental in the continuation than in the commencement ... The embargo was only taken off upon these stipulations.'[42]

In all three cases, Coetzee, Byron and Flaubert, a commitment to *style* leads to misreadings, to censure or censorship, in ways that each of the authors must have foreseen, even *desired*.[43] Coetzee's deliberate intertextuality with these literary predecessors is thus arguably inseparable from the 'realist' plot of *Disgrace*; indeed, it is a reminder that the political-literary 'reality' he is addressing at a fictional level is scandalously historical and far-reaching. In this regard we have at least two clues from his own book of essays on censorship, *Giving Offense*, published in 1996, when he was likely in the early stages of composing *Disgrace*. First, in his discussion of Soviet censorship, Coetzee points to the censuring/censoring of the writer by the state; here the requirement of repentance, of the writer 'recognising the error of his ways',[44] provides a template for the Committee hearing in *Disgrace*; secondly, Coetzee's interest in 'Emma Bovary' is revealed twice in this earlier text; notably, the emphasis again is not on Flaubert, the author, but on his scandalously suggestive prose regarding the adulterous crimes of his heroine:

The strings of Emma Bovary's corsets whistle like snakes as she disrobes; as long as that moment retains its scandalous power, something has been evoked, something is being transgressed.[45]

The trial of *Madame Bovary* under the censorship of the Second Empire cannot of course be equated with the censuring of *Disgrace* by the ANC in post-apartheid South Africa. Strong disapproval is not the same, as Coetzee warns in *Giving Offense*, as official sanctions.[46] However, the fact that the ruling party appropriated Coetzee's *Disgrace* for its own ends (a 'restricted' reading, as LaCapra puts it, revealing generic confusion) in a public forum such as the SAHRC hearings and in the inner sanctums of government (since the ending of the novel was even discussed in Cabinet),[47] might well constitute official censuring.

## The public sphere and Coetzee's *Disgrace*

How then can we define the 'public sphere' of *Disgrace*? How do we talk about 'scandal' and 'censure' in the context of a new democracy? Has the lifting of the bans pronounced by the Publications Control Board during apartheid – the 'undesirable' publications which Coetzee himself has written about in *Giving Offense* – created space for a democratic reading of *Disgrace*,[48] or has the banning and censorship of the past simply been replaced by something else? Briefly we should highlight a few of the more prominent democratic shifts. The new Constitution, for example, outlaws discrimination on the basis of sexual orientation, and this has backed up a number of recent land-mark court cases for gay and lesbian equality; women are being championed for senior posts in political office (indeed, Phumzile Mlambo-Ngcuka, the female minister who reformed South Africa's mines, has just been appointed South Africa's first female deputy president, after the popular Zulu leader Jacob Zuma was forced to step down following allegations of corruption). We have seen former rivals forming key political alliances; a rise in ethnic nationalism of the previously marginalized KhoiSan (and with this the return of the iconic Saartje Baartman), the marginalization of previously politically dominant Afrikaner nationalists.

Coetzee's only public commentary on transformation has been directed at his own realm – the university sphere – and since his first post-apartheid South African fiction opens here (no less than in the historical 'mother city' of Cape Town, the Cape Colony's original metropolis), we should consider the specific context out of which *Disgrace* emerged. Coetzee was writing *Disgrace* while he was still a professor in English at the University of Cape Town (UCT). The 'great rationalisation' that his character David Lurie experiences at 'Cape Technical University, formerly Cape Town University College', is indeed not that far removed from actuality.[49] As Mark Sanders documents, UCT:

in recent years, has undergone a massive rationalization of its own: the reduction of faculties from ten to six, the amalgamation of depart-ments, the institution of executive deans, the creation of new majors and programmes with a greater vocational emphasis.[50]

These 'facts' about the changes at Coetzee's home institution, combined with the rare occasion of the author's public remarks on higher education on a UCT platform with political scientist André du Toit, and his essay-fiction, 'The Humanities in Africa',[51] have led to readings of *Disgrace* as a critique of institutional politics post-1994: a time of streamlining, outcomes-based education, and the increasing marginalization of the humanities. As we read in Coetzee's response to du Toit:

> When people speak of the transformation of the university in South Africa they mean any or all of a variety of things. They mean making the student body and the academic staff more demographically representative. They mean making the university more socially accountable, which in practice today means making it responsive to the market. And they mean subjecting this historically European institution to an African critique with a view to turning it into a properly African institution.[52]

*Disgrace* was in progress during the Truth and Reconciliation Commission hearings, which were broadcast daily across the nation between 1996–98. An attempt to document a full account (within a selected timeframe) of human rights abuses both by the apartheid state, *and* by political opponents fighting a 'just war', the TRC's five-volume final report was submitted in October 1998; Coetzee's novel was published a year later. Significantly, however, as Jacqueline Rose notes, in the TRC report, 'Universities are named as one of the institutions of civil society into which the Commission did not reach.'[53] Rose then intriguingly suggests that Coetzee's novel can be read as a response to this omission in the TRC report, not only because in the novel the Committee hearing for the sexual harassment charges against David Lurie reflects some of the tensions of the TRC,[54] but also because of the autobiographical inferences to Coetzee and his place of work. As Rose writes:

> It cannot, I think, be wholly coincidental that J.M. Coetzee opens his much acclaimed and much critiqued novel *Disgrace* in the setting of a university, or that he chose, to the objections of many critics, to write this novel, at this particular moment in South Africa's slow emergence from the night of apartheid, about someone who could be taken for the author himself.[55]

A tendency to conflate the author with the focalizer of his narrative has also led to further revelations and anecdotes: one former university official has told me that the university hearing in *Disgrace* is 'wrong', that it resembles the real proceedings of such a hearing very little indeed! Several sources have offered the information that the sexual harassment case of David Lurie is based on a real case (or cases, or incidents: the persons named have varied) at the University of Cape Town. A group of white women who play tennis in Cape Town have recurring heated conversations about the book and its author to this day. In all these very local responses to Coetzee's novel, there is a temptation to read his fiction as 'real'.

Let's then return to the political context of the ANC's citation of *Disgrace*. Thabo Mbeki was deputy president when the final report of the TRC was submitted, but he effectively had been running the day-to-day affairs of the presidency since 1997. Mbeki became president of the ANC that year, but did not assume the office of presidency from Mandela until 1999, the year that *Disgrace* was published.[56] Nevertheless, he was bold and quick to judge. As we read in a recent political biography of Mbeki by South African journalist, William Gumede:

> On learning that the TRC, under Archbishop Desmond Tutu, had condemned the torture and execution of dissidents in ANC camps in Angola, Mbeki denounced the report without reading it.
>
> *'They are wrong'*, he said. *'Wrong and misguided'*.
>
> When the TRC refused to excise references to human rights violations in the camps, Mbeki went to court to prevent publication of the report. The Cape High Court turned down his application.[57]

On both sides, at the very moment of truth and transparency, there were attempts to suppress the historical record. At the eleventh hour, sections of the TRC report relating to former president F.W. de Klerk were censored, with the court's approval.

The question of accountability continues to provoke. Three taboo topics for Mbeki are rape, crime, and AIDS: all three are relevant to the ANC's citation of *Disgrace* to the SAHRC. Any criticism – even in the form of statistics – and Mbeki is quick to cry racism and rattle off a list of colonial stereotypes,[58] such as in this recent diatribe in response to verbal attacks by rape activist Charlene Smith and Democratic Alliance (DA) health spokesperson, Ryan Coetzee:

> 'I for my part will not keep quiet,' wrote Mbeki, 'while others whose minds have been corrupted by the disease of racism accuse us, the black people of South Africa, Africa, and the world, as being by virtue of our Africanness and skin colour – lazy, liars . . . sexually depraved, animalistic, savage, and racist.'[59]

## Conclusions

In its rhetoric the above statement by Mbeki is consistent with other statements he has made; its similarity to the ANC's citation of *Disgrace* is seemingly unmistakable. And yet, as mentioned earlier, we must negotiate

carefully its ambiguous authorship: clearly in terms of attribution and appropriation I risk having different criteria for Mbeki and the ANC than I do
for Coetzee – as authors, as public figures. I am also aware that there is a
distinct possibility that my own reading of *Disgrace* is 'restricted', even scandalous, to the many readers whose instinctive reaction to *Disgrace* is to take
offence.

It is typical of Coetzee to displace race, to offset the immediate expectation of the explicit presence of 'race' in novels from South Africa. If in
*Disgrace* the race of the rapists is barely referred to, why is it, David Attwell
asks, that they and, by apparent relation, Petrus, rather than the articulate academics on Lurie's Committee (headed by, as Attwell notes, the
Tutu-like figure, professor of religious studies, Manas Mathabane), are the
focus for many readers?[60] The journalist Zubeida Jaffer, for example, makes
reference to Coetzee's 'horror of blackness' in this novel.[61] Max du Preez,
a columnist for *The Star*, had only heard the storyline of *Disgrace* and
aligned himself with Fugard – until he actually read the book, and decided
that Coetzee's 'symbolism' does at least make one think. His analysis is
revealing:

> I think most readers will interpret *Disgrace* the way I did: the professor
> and his daughter are symbols of white South Africa and Petrus and the
> three rapists represent black attitudes.
>
>   If this is true, then the *message of Disgrace*, crudely put, is that black
> South Africans are revengeful of whites; that whites are not welcome in
> Africa unless they pay for it every day; that black and white attitudes and
> lifestyles are incompatible. In short: whites do not belong in Africa.[62]

South African literature has long been judged in the tradition of social
realism: this much can be seen in du Preez's reference to the novel's 'message'
and in the ANC's claim that in *Disgrace* Coetzee is making a particular 'point'.
Coetzee was only too aware of its cultural dominance and the framework
in which he was likely to be read. Why then would he effectively invite
it? The answer, I would argue, goes back to our discussion of Flaubert and
Byron, style and satire. It is in fact Coetzee at his most political, for what is
stylistically embedded in *Disgrace* is the interrogative: 'Can we read beyond
race?'

It would be simplistic to divide the reception at the level of the local
and global (local equals negative; global equals positive),[63] but there is
undoubtedly a sense in which the transgressions of *Disgrace* – particularly in
racialized and 'realist' readings of the novel – are most strongly articulated
on the local level. Gendered readings – strong dislike for Lurie, disbelief
over Lucy's choice – are not so restricted, but the attack on Lucy at the
farm, and the implications of her decisions to give Petrus her land are. Why
should this be so? What are the repercussions of such readings on ideas of
authorship and textuality?

At a time of transformation, it would seem that the transgression of *Disgrace* is its very staging of real events – violence in the new South Africa post-1994, post-TRC, combined with the mode of *realism* which Coetzee's novel deceptively seems to adopt.[64] Anecdotally, we recently had a lively discussion about *Disgrace* at a seminar on my own campus. The range of readings was fascinating, but the story of a young South African postgraduate student stands out: teaching in Malawi in 2000, he said, *Disgrace* was ubiquitous. It was such a talking point amongst his international colleagues that he himself had no desire to read the book. Two British women, however, took Coetzee's novel to heart: when they left Malawi, they flew home via Maputo, Mozambique instead of Johannesburg, in order to avoid the 'dangerous country' of South Africa at all costs.[65]

## Notes

An early version of this chapter was presented at the international conference, Contemporary Perspectives on J.M. Coetzee and Post-Apartheid South African Literature, Royal Holloway, University of London (April 2005) and, subsequently, as seminars at the University of KwaZulu-Natal (English Studies, May 2005 and the Centre for African Literary Studies, October 2005). I am grateful to the Andrew W. Mellon Foundation for research and travel funding. Thanks also to Stefan Helgesson, for his incisive comments on successive drafts; and to Lucy Graham, Liz Gunner, and Kate Highman.

1. Colin Bower, 'The Art and Artifice of JM Coetzee', *Sunday Times* (Lifestyle), 28 September 2003, 20.
2. Jakes Gerwel, 'Perspektief: Is *dit* die regte beeld van ons nasie?' ('Is *this* the right image of our nation?'), *Rapport*, 13 February 2000, 2.
3. Beverly Roos, 'Feeding National Paranoia?' *Saturday Argus* (The Good Weekend), 22 January 2000, 20.
4. Aggrey Klaaste, 'Odious Terre'Blanche is a Cartoonist's Dream', *Sowetan*, 3 April 2000, 9. Emphasis added.
5. Cited in David Attwell, 'Race in *Disgrace*', *Interventions: International Journal of Postcolonial Studies*, 4, 3 (2002), 334. South African Human Rights Commission (SAHRC), *Inquiry into Racism in the Media: Hearings Transcripts* XIV.3/3 (5 April 2000), 125.
6. SAHRC, *Inquiry into Racism in the Media. Opening Statement*, 1 March 2000: http://www.info.gov./speeches/2000/000302955a1003.htm.
7. J.M. Coetzee, *Disgrace* (London: Secker & Warburg, 1999), 48.
8. SAHRC, *Opening Statement*.
9. Attwell, 'Race in *Disgrace*', 332–3.
10. Ibid., 332, 334.
11. Stidy, *Weekend Witness*, 4 October 2003, 9. I am grateful to Jayne Glover and Thomas Jeffery at NELM for this cartoon.
12. Something which the Democratic Alliance did not fail to point out. Note that in the second box the words come straight out of Mbeki's statement of congratulations to Coetzee.

13. Grogan, *The Sunday Independent*, 5 October 2003, 8.
14. 'Presidents Salute Coetzee', *news24*, 3 October 2000: http://www.news24.com/News24/Entertainment/0,,2-1225_1425188,00.html.
15. 'DA Bickers with ANC over Coetzee's Novel Disgrace', *Saturday Weekend Argus*, 4 October 2003, 7.
16. See, for example, Rory Carroll, 'Nobel Prize for JM Coetzee – Secretive Author Who Made the Outsider His Art Form', *Guardian Unlimited*, 3 October 2003: http://books.guardian.co.uk/nobelprize/story/0,14969,1286602,00.html. Rian Malan in *Profile: JM Coetzee*, presented by Christopher Hope, as listed in 'BBC Looks South', *The Star* (Tonight), 19 April 2004, 10.
17. See also Derek Attridge, 'Editorial: J.M. Coetzee's *Disgrace*: Introduction', *Interventions: International Journal of Postcolonial Studies* (Special Topic: J.M. Coetzee's *Disgrace*, edited by Derek Attridge and Peter D. McDonald) 4, 3 (2002), 316.
18. David Beresford, 'What They're Reading in South Africa', *Guardian Unlimited*, 10 March 2000: http://books.guardian.co.uk/internationalwriting/story/0,6194,144968,00.html.
19. 'SA Delighted with Coetzee,' *news24*, 2 October 2003: http://www.news24.com/News24/Entertainment/Local/0,,2-1225-1242_1424764,00.html.
20. In 2002 and 2003, *Disgrace* was listed on the Independent Education Board's English set work list – the other option was D.H. Lawrence's *Sons and Lovers*. This choice was itself controversial, but in Grahamstown, where part of the novel is set, it was indeed taught at St Andrew's School and the Diocesan School for Girls, as well as at Kingswood. Teachers told me that students were receptive to its 'readability'. Further coverage on this debate can be found in David Attwell, 'Are Children Ready for Disgrace', *Sowetan*, 26 March 2004, 23. See also Shaun de Waal, 'Screening Coetzee', *Mail & Guardian*, 17–23 October 2003, 11, who refers to St Andrew's teacher Michael Crampton's article in the *The English Academy Review* (2003). 'What Crampton shows most lucidly', de Waal writes, 'is how. . . readers have used *Disgrace* and Lurie himself as a kind of screen on to which they can project their own issues – their place in the new South Africa, their position in relation to social change and new power structures.'
21. However, see David Simpson, 'Neither Rushdie nor Nobody: J.M. Coetzee on Censorship and Offense', *Pretexts: Literary and Cultural Studies*, 10, 1 (2001), 127.
22. This phrase comes rather distantly from Chris Dunton, 'Vicarious Reconstruction of an Uneasy Existence in the Interzone', review of *In Tangier We Killed the Blue Parrot*, by Barbara Adair, *The Sunday Independent*, 29 August 2004, 18. I am grateful to Cheryl Stobie and Jean Rossman for discussions of this quote.
23. See Gareth Cornwell's fascinating discussion of Salem land and land claims in '*Disgrace*land: History and the Humanities in Frontier Country', *English in Africa*, 30, 2 (2003), 43–68.
24. Kai Easton, 'Coetzee's *Disgrace*: Byron in Italy and the Eastern Cape *c.* 1820', Working Paper Series, no. 35, East London: Fort Hare Institute of Social and Economic Research, Fort Hare University.
25. Christopher Goodwin. 'White Man's Burden', *Sunday Times* (Lifestyle), 23 January 2000, 5.
26. See Coetzee in a rare television interview with BBC *Newsnight*'s Kirsty Wark (October 1999), a video clip of which appears in Hope, 2003. When Wark asks Coetzee to comment on Lucy's decision, he emphatically reminds her of the genre of *Disgrace*: 'We're talking about a *novel*, we're talking about a novel in which Lucy represents a somewhat extreme position but a not utterly uncommon one.

It's certainly not a representative position. It's a position that takes the moral responsibility of whites in South Africa very seriously indeed.'

27. Remember Klaaste's (2000, 9) comment, with its allusions to Hawthorne's Hester Prynne, about wearing her abuse as a 'badge of courage'.

28. See Michael Marais, 'Reading against Race: J.M. Coetzee's *Disgrace*, Justin Cartwright's *White Lightning* and Ivan Vladislavic's *The Restless Supermarket*', *JLS/TLW* 19, 3/4 (December 2003), 271–89. Marais's insightful discussion – very relevant to my argument here – is about the way in which ' "misreading" . . . lays bare the *hermeneutic* aspect of David Lurie's relationship with his daughter' (281). He elaborates furthermore that 'Lucy's use of the word "misreading" also aligns the reader *of* the novel with David Lurie, the reader *in* the novel' (282).

29. The late Phaswane Mpe defended the author in 'Hands off JM Coetzee', *ThisDay*, 15 October 2003, 15.

30. Coetzee, 53. This comment by a female colleague, Farodia Rassool, has racial implications, but this is typically left unexplained in Coetzee's novel. In 'Reading the Unspeakable: Rape in J.M. Coetzee's *Disgrace*', *Journal of Southern African Studies* 29, 2 (June 2003), 433–44, Lucy Graham argues that in *Disgrace*, 'Coetzee self-consciously performs a subversion of "black peril" narrative – by simultaneously scripting what Sol T. Plaatje referred to as "the white peril", the hidden sexual exploitation of black women by white men that has existed for centuries' (437). Graham has also reminded me of the marketability of this narrative, something which has implications for the celebrity and scandal of *Disgrace*.

31. Coetzee was joined by Ngugi wa Thiong'o, V.S. Naipaul, and Gayatri Spivak for the 9th Annual Comparative Literature Symposium: After Empire, University of Tulsa, 24–27 March 1994.

32. I was a delegate at the conference. The remarks are from my notes only.

33. Flaubert, cited in Francis Steegmuller, ed. and trans., *The Letters of Gustave Flaubert 1830–1857* (Cambridge, MA and London: The Belknap Press of Harvard University Press, 1979), 221–22. Emphasis added.

34. Coetzee, 1999, 150.

35. Paul de Man, cited in Dominick LaCapra, *Madame Bovary on Trial* (Ithaca & London: Cornell University Press, 1982), 58.

36. Hans Jauss, cited in LaCapra, 1982, 57. Emphasis added.

37. See LaCapra, 1982, 35: 'For both the prosecution and the defense, reading and evaluation are very much constitutive of a *process d'intention*, and it is assumed that the functioning of the text is essentially identical with the intention or "thought" of the author.'

38. Ibid., 31. Emphasis added. On Coetzee's use of Flaubert and *style indirect libre* see, however, Michael Holland, ' "*Plink-Plunk*": Unforgetting the Present in Coetzee's *Disgrace*', *Interventions: International Journal of Postcolonial Studies*, 4, 3 (2002), 400; and Graham Pechey, 'Coetzee's Purgatorial Africa: the Case of *Disgrace*', *Interventions: International Journal of Postcolonial Studies*, 4, 3 (2002), 337.

39. As Jane Taylor puts it in 'The Impossibility of Ethical Action', review of *Disgrace* by J.M. Coetzee, *The Mail & Guardian*, 23–29 July 1999, 25: 'Byron, identified in the English imagination as the great libertine of his age, was associated with the violation of taboos, incestuous liaisons and multiple affairs.'

40. Iris Origo, *The Last Attachment: the Story of Byron and Teresa Guiccioli as told in their unpublished letters and other family papers* (Chappaqua, NY: Books & Co./Helen Marx Books, 2000 [1949]), 257.

41. Fiona MacCarthy, *Byron: Life and Legend* (London: John Murray, 2002), 399.

42. Origo, 326.

43. It is important to note that none of his novels was ever banned by the censors, owing largely to the allusiveness of his fiction.
44. J.M. Coetzee, *Giving Offense: Essays on Censorship* (Chicago: University of Chicago Press, 1996), 126.
45. Ibid., 59. See also 91.
46. Coetzee, 1996, 18.
47. See David Attwell, 'Are Children Ready for *Disgrace*', *Sowetan*, 26 March 2004, 23. See also Rory Carroll, 'Nobel Prize for JM Coetzee – the Secretive Author Who Made the Outsider his Art Form', *Guardian Unlimited Books*: www.books.guardian.co.uk/nobelprize/story/0,14969,1286602,00.html.
48. de Waal, 'Screening Coetzee', 11.
49. Coetzee, 1999, 3.
50. Mark Sanders, 'Disgrace', *Interventions: International Journal of Postcolonial Studies*, 4, 3 (2002), 365–6.
51. His third version of this essay appears in *Elizabeth Costello: Eight Lessons* (London: Secker & Warburg, 2003).
52. J.M. Coetzee, 'Critic and Citizen: a Response', *Pretexts: Literary and Cultural Studies*, 9, 1 (2000), 110.
53. Jacqueline Rose, 'Apathy and Accountability: South Africa's Truth and Reconciliation Commission', *Raritan*, 21, 4 (2002), 191.
54. On the one hand, confession was required but atonement was not; on the other hand, this 'secular tribunal' – with Archbishop Tutu as chair – could not wholly avoid expressing its desire for contrition and forgiveness on the path to national healing.
55. Rose, 191.
56. After a controversial battle between Mbeki and Cyril Ramaphosa. (The other frontrunner was the leader of the South African Communist Party (SACP), Chris Hani, before his untimely death at the hands of a right-wing assassin in 1993.)
57. William Mervin Gumede, *Thabo Mbeki and the Battle for the Soul of the ANC* (Cape Town: Zebra Press, 2005), 64. Emphasis added.
58. See also Mandisa Mbali, 'Mbeki's Denialism and the Ghosts of Apartheid and Colonialism for Post-Apartheid AIDS Policy-Making', paper presented at the University of Natal, Durban, Public Health Journal Club, 3 May 2002: http://64.233.183.104/search?q=cache:dFvtIXPv8scJ:www.nu.ac.za/ccs/files/ mbeki .p . . . ; 'Mbeki Slammed in Race Row', *BBC News World Edition*, 5 October 2004: http://news.bbc.co.uk/2/hi/africa/3716004.stm.
59. Cited in the editorial, 'Mbeki's new race tirade', *Mail & Guardian Online*, 22 October 2004: http://archive.mg.co.za/nxt/gateway.dll/PrintEdition/MGP2004/31v00385/41v00433/51.
60. Attwell, 'Race in *Disgrace*', 2002.
61. In Hope, 2003.
62. Max du Preez, 'It's a disgrace, but the truth is . . . ', *The Star*, 27 January 2000, 18. Emphasis added.
63. The local–global divide is problematic for a number of reasons, not only because there are always exceptions to such a generalization, but also because these debates are certainly not limited to South Africa. Stefan Helgesson has reminded me of the trial of Michel Houellebecq's scandalous novel *Platform* which led a reluctant Salman Rushdie to comment publicly. See 'A Platform for Closed Minds', *Guardian*, 28 September 2002: http://books.guardian.co.uk/review/story/0,12084,799748,00.html.

64. On realism, see J.M. Coetzee, *Stranger Shores: Essays 1986–1999* (London: Vintage, 2002 [2001]), 22. Coetzee distinguishes between the 'realism' of Defoe (with his tendencies towards empiricism and forgery) and that of his nineteenth-century successors in the 'realist school'. In contrast to the 'fake autobiographies' of Defoe, for example, we again have Flaubert's masterpiece. As Coetzee writes: '*Madame Bovary* does not pretend to be the utterances or the handiwork of Emma Bovary, housewife of Tostes.' See also Coetzee's opening essay in *Elizabeth Costello*, 'What Is Realism?' (2003).

65. Just as I was finishing the final version of this chapter (September 2005), the evening television news featured J.M. Coetzee at an awards ceremony at the Union Buildings in Tshwane (formerly Pretoria). He received the elite Order of Mapungubwe (gold) by President Thabo Mbeki. Chancellor of National Orders, Frank Chikane, said the award was for 'his exceptional contribution in the field of literature and for putting South Africa on the world stage.' 'Orders for the extraordinary', *SouthAfrica.info*, 29 September 2005: www.southafrica.info/what_happening/news/features/nationalorders-2005b.htm.

# Afterword

*Jago Morrison and Susan Watkins*

In setting out to write *Scandalous Fictions* as an alternative account of fiction in the twentieth century, we were aware, at the outset, of the need to negotiate two competing literary-historical narratives. The first stresses the novel's association with the rise of modernity and characterizes it as the aesthetic embodiment of a new kind of civic, liberal voice, rising free from the habits of orthodoxy and patronage. The second, associated with feminist criticism, concerns itself with tracing the novel's emergence out of forms such as the letter and the diary, foregrounding its connection with interiority and domesticity. Neither history is satisfactory, not merely because each relies implicitly on a gendered binary opposition between public and private, but more broadly because both are unable to account for the novel's intrinsic capacity to 'straddle' public and private – or rather to make the flagrantly fictional and yet necessary nature of that opposition apparent to the reader.

This book set out instead to present the Janus faces of the novel and examine its continual, scandalous breaches of cultural protocol and propriety. We were concerned to capture a sense of the monumental ethical and public-historical responsibilities heaped on the novel in the twentieth century, and at the same time to offer a sharper focus on its tendencies to insubordination, licentiousness and irresponsibility. The novel's Colossus-like but precarious stance in the twentieth century had never, we felt, been 'put together entirely/Pieced, glued, and properly jointed'.[1]

One of the insights offered by the essays in this volume is that the novel's incursions and border crossings between the public and the private become especially scandalous in the twentieth century partly because this is a moment when the public/private opposition itself comes into particular crisis, a period when the link between personal privacy and public duty becomes especially troubled and fragmented. That this is not entirely unique to twentieth-century fiction is clear; one has only to think of eighteenth-century concerns over gothic fiction's disturbance of female morality to recognize that that for the novel, licence and public suspicion have often gone hand in hand. Not until the late nineteenth century, however, can the novel be considered a mass public form in the true sense. Not until the twentieth century, likewise, with such groundbreaking cases as James Joyce's

*Ulysses*, Richard Wright's *Native Son*, Chinua Achebe's *A Man of the People* and Salman Rushdie's *The Satanic Verses* do the aesthetic, ethical, legal and political circumscriptions of the novel form begin to be tested with such determination and creativity.

Despite continual fears of its licentious and seditious tendencies, from the 1930s onwards the novel's educative role becomes increasingly important. As we suggested in our introduction, however, the form's remarkable popular ascendancy in schools and universities over the last hundred years cannot be ascribed simply to matters of curriculum development. As the ubiquitous discussions of book clubs and (more recently) online readers' fora show, the novel has continually sought for new ways to connect with its readers, whilst those readers themselves have found ever new ways to mould genres, writers and texts to their own particular concerns. In this volume, with cases as diverse as Jack Kerouac's *On the Road*, D.H. Lawrence's *Lady Chatterley's Lover* and Helen Darville's *The Hand that Signed the Paper*, we have explored the different ways in which the novel has been consumed, transformed and sometimes violently tailored to contemporary anxieties or obsessions.

Since the early test cases against *Ulysses* and *The Well of Loneliness* in the 1920s, novelists have undoubtedly taken great freedoms in their use of the form, embracing a public conception of the novel as a licensed repository for experimentation, rejoicing in the seemingly inexorable decline in the power of censorship in Europe and North America. At the same time, as examples like *The Satanic Verses* and J.M. Coetzee's *Disgrace* amply illustrate, critical celebrations of the novel's aesthetic and political border crossings must always be tempered by a recognition of the continuing vulnerability of writers to persecution and misappropriation.

At the time of writing, at the beginning of the twenty-first century, it is possible to see that the novel's capacity to scandalize our sense of the public and private, engaging readers with a sense of the urgency and fragility of that distinction, will continue. Forty years after Barthes's proclamation of the 'death of the author', with postmodernism already long in the tooth, Michael Baigent and Richard Leigh's case against Random House and Dan Brown's *The Da Vinci Code* (which they unsuccessfully attempted to argue plagiarized their work) has a number of suggestive implications. Although the case certainly signals the continuing centrality of 'private ownership' as a governing doctrine in the circulation of texts and ideas, it also suggests various interesting ways in which the 'scandalous' fiction's public visibility is still intimately entwined with commercial success. Meanwhile, the situation of Turkish novelist Orhan Pamuk, who faced charges under Article 301 of the Turkish penal code after commenting on the deaths of Kurds and Armenians in a Swiss newspaper, reminds us that state suspicion of novelists and their productions remains fresh and real for many. Ideas about the acceptable boundaries of the cultural field, the 'ownership' of ideas and the putative purpose of fiction in a context of shifting notions of 'freedom of speech' are still hotly contested in these instances and others. In the twenty-first century, the novel's distinctive inward/outward gaze, a gaze that upsets our notions of privacy and publicity, seems far from exhausted or passé. Indeed, the capacity of the novel for both public irritation and private inspiration is likely to remain a defining part of the cultural, political and personal work that fiction does.

## Note

1. Sylvia Plath, *Collected Poems*, ed. Ted Hughes (London: Faber and Faber, 1981), 129.

# Index